FEB 2 8 2019

Romance
HEGER
Amanda

Heger, Am...

Crazy Cu[

D0965213

Crazy Cupid Love

WITHDRAWN

AMANDA HEGER

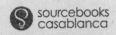

sourcebooks
casablanca

Copyright © 2019 by Amanda Heger
Cover and internal design © 2019 by Sourcebooks, Inc.
Cover design by Caroline Teagle
Cover images © mash3r/Getty Images, Smika/Shutterstock

Sourcebooks and the colophon are registered trademarks of Sourcebooks, Inc.

All rights reserved. No part of this book may be reproduced in any form or by any electronic or mechanical means including information storage and retrieval systems—except in the case of brief quotations embodied in critical articles or reviews—without permission in writing from its publisher, Sourcebooks, Inc.

The characters and events portrayed in this book are fictitious or are used fictitiously. Any similarity to real persons, living or dead, is purely coincidental and not intended by the author.

All brand names and product names used in this book are trademarks, registered trademarks, or trade names of their respective holders. Sourcebooks, Inc., is not associated with any product or vendor in this book.

Published by Sourcebooks Casablanca, an imprint of Sourcebooks, Inc.
P.O. Box 4410, Naperville, Illinois 60567-4410
(630) 961-3900
Fax: (630) 961-2168
sourcebooks.com

Printed and bound in the United States of America.
OPM 10 9 8 7 6 5 4 3 2 1

In memory of Kyle,
creator of the jiggle, jiggle, tap.

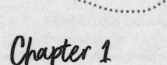

Chapter 1

> **California Code of Cupid Regulations (CCR) § 100.01. (a)** For purposes of this Act, the term "love" shall mean the sufferance by one person of affection for and attachment to another person or persons for any period, however brief.

FOR MORE THAN TWENTY YEARS, ELIZA HAD BEEN working on a list of things she hated more than Valentine's Day. And finally, after decades of hard work and dedication, she'd narrowed it to the following:

1. ?
2. ??
3. ???

Okay, so it was still a work in progress. But to be fair, she had yet to encounter anything she despised as much as the onslaught of pink and red hearts that appeared each February. Not to mention, if your birthday happened to fall on Valentine's Day, avoiding the slew of cutesy cards and pictures of diapered, armed babies was nearly impossible. And if you were a Descendant of Eros with the misfortune of being born on February fourteenth? Forget it. Everyone everywhere commented on how *cute* and *coincidental* it was that a "Cupid" had been born on love's holiest of holidays.

Eliza ducked her head as she made her way through Red Clover. Leaving her apartment always made her anxiety flare, but walking through the seasonal aisle of the grocery store on Valentine's Day felt like lumbering through a library with a bullhorn. *Make way! World's worst Cupid coming through!*

This all could have been avoided if the watch she'd ordered for her twin had simply arrived on time. Instead, she had to face the offensive barrage of red roses and chocolates to reach the tiny display of birthday cards in the center of the aisle. *Elijah better appreciate this*, she thought. *Otherwise, I may have to strangle him with a string of paper hearts*.

But Eros himself must have been smiling down on her today because the store was eerily empty. She slid past the picked-over bags of candy and the last of the mushy Valentine's Day fare. Her gaze landed on a brightly colored card with balloons across the front. Basic, simple, and able to hold a gift card. Exactly what she needed. Eliza pulled it from the shelf and opened the front. *Birthday Boy, You're Ten Today!*

She shoved the card back into its slot and surveyed the other options. A flowery card with hard-to-read script and enough gold edging to make a leprechaun jealous? No. Two kittens batting a ball of yarn? Not her brother's style. A frog with googly eyes proclaiming *You Aren't a Tadpole Anymore*? In the running.

"Excuse me. Miss?" An elderly man's voice came from behind her, wobbling a bit on the end.

Eliza's shoulders tensed. *Here we go. Yes, I'm her*.

The infamous Eliza Herman. She turned. The little old man looked vaguely familiar, but she couldn't quite place him. His ears were nearly as big as his head, and just a few gray hairs swooped over his shiny dome. Calling it a comb-over would be generous. "Yes?" she asked, braced for the worst.

"Can you hand me that card right there?" He pointed with a liver-spotted finger. "The one with the wiener dog?"

Eliza's breath whooshed out all at once, and in its place, sweet relief filled her chest. Valentine's Day was making her paranoid. This little old man wanted help reaching something on the top shelf, not to badger her with questions about her past. She rose to her tiptoes and grabbed the card. Bright-blue letters across the bottom read, *I Hope Your Birthday is a Real Wiener*. "Here you go."

"Thank you." He inched the card open and proceeded to read the inside. It was as if Eliza had ceased to exist.

She grinned and gave herself a mental pat on the back. *Look at you. Being totally normal.* She'd even helped an elderly man and, in the process, found a perfectly acceptable card for her brother. All she had to do was reach up, grab another wiener dog, and—

"Oh no."

She wobbled on her tiptoes, only for a second, but it was enough to throw her balance to the left. Which was enough to bump her shoulder into the shelf of Valentine candy beside her. Which was enough to send the giant two-pound bar of chocolate tumbling straight onto—

"*Ooof.*" The old man leaned down to rub the top of his foot, where the chocolate had landed. Green and gold sparkles shot from the site of his injury, filling the aisle with enough Love Luster to momentarily obliterate the pink and red decor. And when the Luster began to fade, the scent of seawater and sun hit Eliza hard.

She threw her hands over her mouth in panic. On the one hand, she needed to make sure the man was okay. But she also needed to get away from him before he could look up and—

"Well, *hello*." He bent into a sweeping bow.

Too late. Eliza closed her eyes and dragged in a deep breath. Of course it was too much to ask to make it through Red Clover without incident. Of course. "Sir, I'm very sorry—"

The old man straightened up as if the infatuation running through his ancient veins had taken fifty years off his age. He handed her the candy bar. A crack ran straight through the center of the chocolate. "Stu Vannerson," he said. "And it's a *pleasure* to make your acquaintance."

Eliza's brain screeched to a halt. *Stu Vannerson. Old Man Vannerson.* He'd lived on their block years ago. Elijah used to cut his lawn. Eliza sold him Girl Scout cookies every year. Then he'd sold his house and moved to the Gold Lea Assisted Living Villas across town.

And now he was enchanted with her.

Eliza forced herself to smile. This whole adoration-by-Hershey thing wasn't good, but it wasn't the end of the world either. She'd explain what had happened and then go about her not-so-merry way. Plus, once she left the store, the old man's hormones would settle back to near normal. In approximately twenty-nine and a half days, it would be like nothing had happened at all.

Maybe Eros wasn't smiling down on her today, but he wasn't smiting her either. Crisis averted. "Mr. Vannerson,

I'm Eliza Herman. I don't know if you remember, but you used to live down the street from me."

His eyes sparkled. "The Cupid girl?"

"Erosian." Maybe the rest of America—including the other Descendants—had finally given up on explaining the difference between Cupid and Eros, but she still cringed every time. Great marketing strategy or not, she hated being associated with a chubby baby with wings.

Of course, that probably had more to do with her personal issues than anything else. "When I dropped that chocolate bar on your foot—" she started.

"Well then, I'm pleased to make your acquaintance *again* after all these years. Please"—he pulled off his jacket and spread it out on the floor in front of her—"allow me to show you around my favorite store in Gold Lea. We have an *excellent* yogurt selection."

Eliza stared at the jacket—covering a nonexistent puddle—and debated her options. If she was late for her family's annual birthday extravaganza, her mother would never let her live it down. But Eliza had accidentally enchanted enough people to know this would be less painful for everyone if she simply let nature take its course.

She looped her arm through the crook of his elbow and did her best to smile. "I can't wait to hear all about it."

For the next twenty minutes, Eliza let Stu walk her through Red Clover. She feigned interest when he talked about the rising cost of bread. She let him make a grand production of walking on the "outside" as they passed the butcher counter, just in case there were any spills. She even let him con an unsuspecting worker into acting as their chaperone when the tour took them through the pharmaceuticals.

Finally, they reached the long bay of cash registers at the front of the store.

Stu laid a bony hand on hers with stars—or maybe that was remnants of Love Luster—in his eyes. "I had a wonderful time, Eliza."

"Thank you, Stu. I did too."

"Next time, I'll pick you up at your house. I'm sure your parents would like the opportunity to approve of your callers."

She ignored the cashier's horrified look. "That sounds great, Stu. But I'm just not sure I'm ready for a second date."

His face fell. "Did I come on too strong? I knew I shouldn't have made that quip about the cuts of prime beef."

Time to let him down easy. "No, no. You were the perfect date." She patted his arm and channeled her best Sandra Dee. "But I've just come out of a *terrible* heartbreak, and I don't know if I'm ready to fall in love again so soon. Maybe in another month or two?" *Once the enchantment has worn off.*

"Of course. I look forward to calling on you then," he said, taking the broken candy and birthday card from her before handing them to the cashier. "Allow me."

"You really don't have to—"

"A gentleman always pays on the first date."

Eliza forced a grateful smile. "Thank you, Stu."

And as she crossed the parking lot—with Stu waving to her from the front window—the horrific truth slammed Eliza straight in the gut: that was the best date she'd been on in years.

Two hours later, Eliza sat at her parents' dining room table, groaning along with an off-key version of "Happy Birthday." Nothing about their house had changed in years. The stark-white walls and starker white cabinets still reflected their mother's aesthetic, while the assortment of clutter—a file folder here, a pen cap there, three mugs on the corner of the table—made their father's presence known. And the kitchen still smelled like his famous chocolate cake: the one thing about her birthday she'd always loved.

"Are you going to blow out the candles?" her mother asked.

"Go ahead." Elijah leaned back in his chair and laced his fingers behind his head. "You need the wish more than I do."

Apparently, this wasn't the year her brother would get a grasp on the whole *tact* thing. Not that he was wrong. She definitely needed the wish—all the wishes—more than he did. Her brother led a charmed life. As a kid, he'd been the first one picked for kickball. Hell, he'd been the kid *picking* the teams. Eliza'd had to bribe her way into games of duck, duck, goose.

Fast-forward several years, and Elijah faithfully worked at the family business, Herman & Herman. He even ate dinner at their parents' house each Sunday. Basically, he was the dream child. Eliza, on the other hand, had never even gotten her Cupid's license, and in the past decade, she'd been fired from more jobs than most people held in their whole lives.

Shoe salesperson? Fired after she tried to help a

customer get a pair of leopard flats over a painful bunion, causing the woman to fall for the store's deliveryman— much to the chagrin of her husband.

Administrative assistant? Fired. To be fair, the law firm's junior partner had tried to keep her around, but the risk of additional paper cuts was simply too great.

And most recently, IT help desk assistant. A job she could perform over the phone and from a cube. It required almost no in-person interactions…except when it did. Yesterday, when her boss's boss had made an unexpected visit to tour the office, Eliza had rolled right over his foot with her chair and unveiled her Cupid status. Fired.

She wasn't about to tell the rest of her family that news today, though.

"Fine. I *do* deserve the wish more than you." Eliza screwed her eyes up tight. *Let Stu Vannerson forget all about me. Also, a job would be great.*

"Must be a good one this year," Elijah said. "Let me guess. You're wishing for a new cardigan to complete your cat-lady aesthetic?"

She pulled in a deep breath, opened her eyes, and flipped her brother the bird. Then she blew.

Every flame on the cake flared higher.

"Tim, I told you not to get the trick candles." A clank rang out as her mother set a stack of dessert plates in front of Eliza's father. "Eliza is *sensitive* about birthdays," she whispered.

"I can hear you, you know."

"Sorry, honey," her mother said before turning back to Eliza's father. "I told you she's been *traumatized*."

"Mom. I can still hear you."

"Eliza doesn't mind the trick candles, right?" Her dad

broke into the same mischievous grin as her brother. It was the first time he had smiled since she'd walked in the door. "You used to love those when you were little."

All her frustration and self-consciousness melted. Usually, her father hung around the kitchen, darting from place to place as her mother cooked. But tonight, he'd sat in the living room with a magazine until the table was set. When Eliza had asked if everything was okay, he'd simply waved her off with a half-hearted explanation of the article he'd been reading. She hadn't bought it for one second. But now, looking between the trick candles and her father's face, Eliza started to believe he really had just been engrossed in a story about the uses of turtle shells.

"I did love these," Eliza said. She also loved the trick for blowing them out—one he'd taught her on her fourth birthday. It involved hacking low and loud enough for everyone around to fear she was going to drop a wet, mucus-filled loogie on the cake.

"Either they rush in and help you blow them out," he'd said, "or you spit on the cake and get the whole thing to yourself. It's a win-win, Liza."

She hadn't been old enough to understand the concept of win-win back then, but now she thought of her father every time she heard the phrase.

Eliza gave him a quick nod and cleared her throat—way deep down like a fifty-year smoker who'd recently caught pneumonia—then thumped on her chest.

"Okay, okay. That's good." Her mother swooped in and grabbed the cake.

Eliza and her father shared a knowing look. "Win-win," they said at the same time.

Her mother shook her head as she plucked out the still-flaming candles and dunked the tips into a glass of water. Each made a satisfying hiss as it went out, filling the air with the familiar scent of burnt wax and buttercream.

While her mother cut the cake, her dad pulled identical wrapped boxes from beneath the table. "Here. Open them at the same time so we don't have any spoilers," he said.

Eliza glanced at her brother. In true Elijah fashion, he already had the box in his hands. He gave it hard shake. Then another.

"Hope it's not fragile," Eliza said.

"It is," her mother said with a frown. "Go on, open it."

Eliza turned the present over in her hands. The red wrapping paper caught the light as she slipped a finger under the seam of the brick-sized box. A handful of rips and tugs later, she stared down at the framed photo in her hands.

"This was at the lake house?" Eliza pulled the photo closer to her face, then held it out again. She ran her finger along the edge of the frame and tried to parse through the tornado of emotions swirling in her chest. In the photo, Eliza and Elijah were four, maybe five. They both wore oversize sunglasses and bathing suits, and a much younger version of their parents sat on the sand behind them, looking content and happy.

Her mother nodded. "We found some great old photos when we were cleaning it out last summer."

Ever since Eliza could remember, her parents had owned the little cabin on the outskirts of town. While she was growing up, her family spent a few weeks there every year—whenever both her parents could get enough time away from the business. They'd go waterskiing, build giant sandcastles, and see who could eat the most hot dogs from the stand on the beach. The rest of the year, they rented the cabin out to tourists. That rent had put both Elijah and Eliza through college. But last year, without any warning, her parents had sold the cabin to a property developer.

So long, childhood memories.

But it felt good to have a little piece of that back. Eliza stood and wrapped her arms around her dad. He felt thinner than she remembered. "Thank you," she said.

He patted her arm. "It was your mother who found them."

"Thanks, Mom."

She nodded and handed Eliza a piece of cake. "Of course."

"Even then I was the better-looking twin." Elijah kicked back like he was totally nonplussed, but she could see his emotions in the way he cocked his chin ever so slightly.

"Sure you were." Eliza reached into the plastic grocery bag at her feet. "Here. Your real present is on its way."

Elijah glanced at the unsigned card and broken candy bar before raising an eyebrow.

"Don't ask," she said.

"Oh, I'm definitely asking. But first…" He stood and picked up a box half-hidden behind the counter. "I think I really outdid myself this year."

"What exactly is that supposed to mean?" Over the years, her brother had given her dozens of gag gifts. A subscription to the jelly-of-the-month club, a singing telegram, two live chickens. Eliza couldn't imagine him outdoing any of those.

He dropped the giant box onto the table. "Let's just say Mom and Dad weren't the only ones who wanted to revisit the good old days." He gestured toward the box with a flourish. He'd wrapped it in old newspaper comics and sealed it with duct tape.

"I'm going to regret opening this, aren't I?" she asked.

"Definitely."

"There's nothing alive in here, right?"

Elijah shrugged.

She narrowed her eyes and stared at the box, trying to discern whether this day could get worse. *Not a chance*. Eliza stood and grabbed a knife from one of the drawers before sliding it straight down the middle of the duct tape. With a tug, she pried open the box and squinted into the shadows. Tufts of multicolored crepe paper. A string. *A tail*. Her cheeks burned, and she wasn't sure whether to laugh or cry. "Seriously?"

Her brother gave her an all-too-innocent look. "What?"

"What is it?" her mom asked.

Eliza pulled the "gift" out of the box and set it on the table for all to see. The two-foot-tall donkey piñata stared back at her. The dopey smile on his pink, green, and yellow face was almost a taunt. *I can ruin your whole life if you let me*.

"Elijah," her mother whispered. "You know Eliza is *sensitive* about birthdays."

"I can *still* hear you, Mom."

Eliza sighed as she studied her brother's gift. Not only was she sensitive about birthdays, she was particularly sensitive about birthdays involving piñatas. Twenty-one years ago, on her eighth birthday, she'd stood in her parents' backyard among a utopia of cake and presents.

While her entire second-grade class watched, her father covered her eyes with an old necktie and handed her Elijah's old Louisville Slugger.

"I want to go first," Elijah had whined.

"Relax," their dad had said. "You'll get a chance."

"One! Two! Three!" Her classmates shouted along as her father spun her round and round. For one terrifying moment, all the cake and ice cream Eliza had shoved down her throat threatened to come back up. But she was *not* about to puke in front of everyone. Especially not Jonathan Ellis, the love of her eight-year-old life.

Eliza had focused on the grass tickling her toes over the edge of her sandals. With a deep breath, she set her jaw and cocked her elbow back.

"Eliza!" her mother shouted. "Wait—"

But it was too late. The adrenaline and sugar flowed through Eliza's veins. She took the biggest swing she could muster.

Thwap.

She should have known better.

Piñatas weren't that soft. The collective gasp of her classmates wasn't filled with excitement. And, most importantly, Eliza was a klutz with a high probability of having "the knack."

But she didn't know better. Instead, Eliza tore the necktie away, blinked hard against the sunlight, and dove to the ground to collect her hard-earned candy.

Where bright boxes of Nerds and tiny Hershey bars should have been lay little Johnny Ellis curled into the fetal position. He clutched his left arm against his body, and his eyelids fluttered before they opened wide and met Eliza's.

"I'm sorry. I'm sorry. I'm so, so sorry." Her brain flicked back and forth between a half dozen scenarios involving an ambulance, Jonathan's parents, and whether kids could do jail time for assault with sports equipment. Then a hand closed around her ankle.

"Eliza," Johnny whispered. "You're pretty. *Really* pretty. I got you a present for your birthday, but I want to get you another one. A better one." His whole body blushed. "Do you have roller skates? We should go to the skating rink. They have a couple's skate. You hold hands. I want to hold your hand." The questions and proclamations kept coming, faster and faster, until Eliza's head spun with them.

Her mother pinched the bridge of her nose and shook her head. Her dad let out a whoop. Her classmates stared at her in waves of alternating shock and horror as Eliza's worst fears were confirmed: she, like both of her parents, was a Cupid.

And that's when the vomit flew. All over Johnny, all over herself, all over everything and everyone within a three-foot radius. She'd become the laughingstock of Gold Lea Elementary, a title that stuck even harder after an embarrassed and overcompensating Jonathan Ellis told all their classmates that he'd seen her running around in a diaper while shooting neighborhood dogs with her bow to make them fall in love with her.

Eliza shook her head, forcing away the memories. Twenty-one years later and the sight of piñatas still gave her the willies.

She put the donkey back in the box and shoved it across the table. "Nope. Not happening. Thanks, but no thanks."

"Come on," Elijah said. "Don't you want to face your phobia?"

"Not even a little."

"What if there's something awesome inside?"

Eliza crossed her arms. "Is there?"

Her brother shrugged.

Eliza had never, not once, been able to resist one of Elijah's stupid games. And he knew it. But maybe today would be the day. A new year in her life would be the perfect time to square her shoulders, ignore Elijah's—

"Really, *really* awesome," Elijah said.

Or maybe tomorrow was the day. No one should have to exercise self-restraint on their birthday, after all. And who was she to look a gift ~~horse~~ donkey in the mouth? She closed her eyes as she lifted the piñata back out of the box. Holding it as far from herself as humanly possible, Eliza gave it a shake.

Wsssh, wsssh.

She shook it again. There was definitely something inside. A lot of somethings. Before her brother could get any big ideas about blindfolds or baseball bats, Eliza opened her eyes and flipped the donkey on its back. She punched in the trapdoor on its stomach and reached her whole hand inside.

Elijah reached for the donkey. "Hey! That's cheating!"

She pulled it away, and inside the piñata, her fingers closed around something flat and thin. Plastic maybe. "What is this?" She pulled her hand back, but she couldn't get the base of her thumb past the donkey's stomach. "Shit. My hand's stuck."

"Kids," her mom chided.

"Sorry, Mom," they said in unison.

Eliza let go of the thin pieces of plastic and yanked harder. The base of her thumb scraped against the opening but didn't quite come out. She tried to make her hand as small as possible. No dice. "Here." Eliza turned to her brother, piñata hanging off her fist like a bizarre sock puppet. "Help me pull."

"Kids," her mom said again, this time her voice raised a notch. "I think—"

At that moment, Eliza and Elijah each pulled. The donkey ripped straight down the middle, its contents exploding across the kitchen table, pelting them like shrapnel.

Condoms. A shower of condoms. All colors. All sizes.

"Very funny, Elijah. So mature," Eliza said. She picked up the nearest condom to throw it at him (also very mature) but stopped short when she saw the label. "Fried chicken flavor? *Really?*"

"Look at this one." Elijah held out a green package.

"Dill pickle," Eliza read. "No thank you." She inspected a condom labeled "sweet tea," another that claimed to be "fish and chips," and one marked "peach cobbler."

"Where the heck did you get these?" she asked, pocketing the peach cobbler and hoping her parents didn't notice.

"I have my sources," Elijah said.

"Elijah! Eliza!" their mother shouted, her tone sharp and frantic.

Eliza whipped around. Her father's face was so pale he looked nearly transparent, and his eyes bulged from their sockets. "Dad?"

He clutched his shoulder and slumped toward the table.

Eliza's brain screeched to a halt. She forgot about the condom-filled piñata. She forgot about the half-eaten birthday cake. She forgot about breathing. All she could do was watch the life slowly drain from her father's face.

"Tim, Tim." Her mother's eyes glazed with tears. "Oh gods. It's happening again. Oh gods. One of you call 911."

Oh no, not again.

Eliza numbly fumbled for her phone, but Elijah already had his to his ear. "Yes, this is Elijah Herman. My address is 342 Coronado Avenue. I think my father is having a heart attack."

Chapter 2

> **Cupid Rules of Professional Conduct § 7.1.**
> Persons engaged in Cupiding shall be prohibited
> from advertisement as Dr. Love, the Heart Doctor,
> or similar monikers unless separately licensed with
> their state of residence to practice cardiology.

ELIZA'S FLIP-FLOPS SMACKED WORN LINOLEUM AS SHE PACED
the waiting room floor.

Thwack, thwack, thwack. Turn. *Thwack, thwack, thwack.* Turn. *Thwack—*

"Eliza, please." Her mother didn't look up from the stack of forms in her lap, but her voice shook like a skyscraper mid-earthquake. "I can't think."

Eliza couldn't think either. And she definitely couldn't sit. Her mind spun a hundred and eighty degrees every second, whipping her insides around with it. Her father had made it through this the last time. Certainly that meant he could make it through again. Or maybe his luck had run out. Had she told him how much she loved him? Was it even possible to tell him how much she loved him?

Her dad had always been her rock. The one she'd gone to with scrapes and bruises as a kid. The one she'd spilled her heartaches to as a teenager. The one who'd never gotten angry or pushed back when she'd announced her intention to quit the Cupid business. He'd simply accepted her, flaws and all, like he always had.

Eliza glanced at her brother. He took up two chairs in the corner, his legs stretched across them both. He clenched his hands into fists as he glared at the swinging door separating them from the emergency room. Eliza didn't need to ask what he was thinking. The lines across his forehead said it all.

Thwack, thwack, thwack. Turn. *Thwack, thwack, thwack.* Turn. *Thwack—*

"Eliza!" her mother and Elijah said in unison.

She forced her feet to still, but the wave of adrenaline-induced panic wouldn't cooperate. She twisted her hands into fists and stared at the television on the wall. An infomercial blared from the speakers, and Eliza tried to wrangle her nervous energy into making out the words. If she could force even .000001 percent of it into paying attention to the TV, it would be a small, sweet relief from the anxiety pounding at her temples. And then maybe time would begin to move again.

"The Mandroid 3000 is a very *personal* assistant," the pretty blond on the television said. "Its appearance is fully customizable, right down to its shape and size. The all-new operating system also makes the Mandroid capable of interaction *and* learning new skills. And if that weren't enough, the responsive touch screen…"

Nope. Eliza turned away, her brain sprinting back to its rabbit hole of anxiety. They'd been in the waiting room for nearly an hour now with no news. Was her father somewhere in the back, cracking jokes and eating Jell-O with the nurses? Or was he already making his way across the River Styx?

Thwack, thwack, thwack.

The burn of her mother's glare seared her skin. Eliza ignored it. Instead, she marched to the check-in desk. "Hi. I was wondering if there are any updates on my father? Tim Herman. He came in—"

The nurse straightened her bun and gave Eliza a sympathetic smile. "Nothing yet, but I'll tell the doctors he has family waiting for an update. As soon as they know something, I'm sure they'll be out to talk with you."

Eliza *thwack, thwack, thwacked* her way back to her brother. He raised his head, and the tears lingering at the corners of his eyes nearly broke her. "I can't believe this is happening again," he said, and the pain in his voice *did* break her.

The last time she'd almost lost her father, she'd been sixteen. All four of them were at the lake house, and Eliza had sat curled up on the couch with a book while her mom drank wine on the porch. Elijah and her dad had gone off on some beach excursion that involved ATVs, sand, and a sack lunch—all recipes for disaster as far as Eliza had been concerned. The last thing she needed was to run over someone's foot and end up with an inadvertent admirer.

Eliza had been so deep into her true crime novel that she didn't look up when the front door swung open. "That was quick." She was mid-page-turn when her brother's voice rang out.

"Call an ambulance, Liza. Now."

The moment she saw her brother's face, her stomach lurched and her book hit the floor. Whatever had happened was bad. Very bad.

A phone call, a rush of panic, and an ambulance ride

later, the three of them had sat in this same waiting room while her dad had bypass surgery.

"He was okay then, and he's going to be okay now," Eliza said.

Elijah nodded, but he looked less than convinced.

Just then, a woman in green scrubs and a white coat came out from behind the Employees Only door. "Family of Tim Herman?"

Eliza instinctively grabbed her brother's hand. They were pretty different as twins went, but in all the ways that mattered, they were better than identical—they were complementary. Like popcorn and M&M's. Ice cream and potato chips. And Eliza knew her brother needed her as much as she needed him.

"Right this way." The doctor led them through a maze of cubicles, stretchers, and harried nurses. At the end of the labyrinth, she held back a curtain and nodded for them to pass through.

"Dad." The word rocketed out of Eliza's chest, taking all her breath with it. But her dad wasn't in there. The bed sat empty with only a pile of her father's rumpled belongings in the center. All the blood rushed by her ears, dulling every sound except the manic thumping of her heart. "Where is he?"

"No one told you?"

Oxygen ceased to exist. *Eliza* ceased to exist.

The doctor shook her head. "My apologies. Someone was supposed to talk with you already. Cardiology just finished his catheterization a few minutes ago. They found a blockage, but they were able to place a stent—"

"He's alive?" Elijah asked.

The doctor nodded. "And we're cautiously optimistic.

He'll be out of recovery in just a little while, and then we'll move him to the cardiac unit until tomorrow at least. You'll be able to visit him once he's awake, but we do have a limit of one visitor at a time. When he goes home, I'd like to enroll him in a cardiac rehabilitation program."

Eliza's mother covered her face with her hands and sank into a nearby chair. "Oh, thank the gods."

"Again, I'm so sorry," the doctor said. Her cheeks pinkened. "Truly, truly sorry. I'll talk with someone to make sure this doesn't happen again."

Elijah let out a long, low breath and dropped Eliza's hand. The room filled with oxygen again. Her father was going to be okay. He father was really going to be okay. And she could tell him how much she loved him. She slumped into the nearest seat—a wheeled stool meant for a medical professional—and immediately rolled it over the doctor's toe.

The woman let out a yelp, and the smallest shimmer floated up from her foot.

"Don't look at me!" Eliza screeched. Which, of course, only drew the pretty doctor's gaze straight to Eliza.

Elijah shot up from his chair. "Holy shit, Eliza. What are you doing?" he demanded. "*Look away*."

But it was too late. She could feel the doctor's stare.

"I'm so sorry," she whispered. Eliza squeezed her hands into fists, *Don't look at me* still echoing through her brain. What was wrong with her? Clearly, the stress of this day was making her too stupid to live.

Please don't match me. Please think I'm a hideous hosebeast. Please. With the right—or in this case, *wrong*—mix of hormones and pheromones, this whole thing would stay a simple accident. But if their hormones and pheromones matched—a complex, confusing, poorly understood phenomenon called attraction—being injured would cause her to fall into deep and serious infatuation with the first person she saw. It would be Old Man Vannerson all over again.

"How many times do we have to tell you to be careful?" Her mother gave her the Look. "This is the last thing we need right now."

"I'm sorry," Eliza said again.

The doctor looked back and forth between them with one eyebrow cocked. She rubbed her toe, then turned back to her chart.

Tense silence filled the room.

"It's fine," the doctor said. "Accidents happen. Now back to what I was saying…"

No match. Thank the gods.

"Mr. Herman should be ready to see you in forty-five minutes to an hour," the doctor continued. "Hopefully less. The cardiac unit is on the third floor. If you want to take his things, there's a waiting area—"

Eliza's mom was already gathering the clothes and shoes in her arms. With each movement, a little more color seeped back into her complexion. "Thank you, Doctor. Come on, kids."

"Sorry again," Eliza said as she followed her mother and brother out of the room. By the time they made it through the waiting room and to the elevators in the hall, she was struggling to keep up with her mother's long strides. "Mom," she began. "Please wait, I'm—"

"Not now. I can't handle your carelessness. Not today." Her mom shoved the clothes and shoes into Eliza's arms, then pressed the up button. "Go home and get your father some fresh clothes. He hates hospital gowns, and that shirt has cake stains. Grab his wallet off the dresser too." She pressed the button three more times in quick succession and held out her car keys.

Eliza's feet didn't move. Her mother had never bothered to hide her disappointment in Eliza's life choices, but forcing her out of the hospital over one tiny mishap? "Can't we call someone—"

"Eliza, *please*. Just this once, do what I ask."

She contemplated pointing out every other time she'd done what her mother had asked—including attending the now-forsaken birthday party. But the elevator dinged, and Eliza took a deep breath. Her mother was just anxious and snappy. They were all just anxious and snappy. Maybe getting out of here for a few minutes would do her some good. Plus, if she left now, she could be back in time to see her father before visiting hours ended.

"Fine." She turned toward her brother. "If you guys want me to pick up anything for you, text me," Eliza said.

Her mother nodded as the elevator doors slid shut between them. "And, Eliza?" she asked, sticking out her hand and forcing the doors to reopen.

"Yeah?" Eliza waited, silently pleading for her mother's forgiveness.

"For the gods' sake, don't injure anyone else on the way."

⟹⟹⟹

Ten minutes later, Eliza rolled down the windows of her mom's black Camry and drank in the fresh evening air. With every mile between her and the hospital, she

reminded herself that her father was going to be okay.
By the time she passed Gold Lea Elementary—where
she'd been mercilessly teased by Jonathan Ellis and half
her classmates ever since that fateful eighth birthday
party—her heart rate had returned to normal.

She drove along the curvy road, letting the wind whip
her hair into a style that could rival Medusa's. She'd tie it
back when she got home, but for now, all she wanted was
to relax into the breeze and give her brain a break from the
hamster wheel of anxiety she'd been riding all afternoon.

Eliza slowed as she passed Lizzie's Five and Dime.
As a kid, she'd spent every cent of her allowance on
their saltwater taffy. The building always seemed like it
might fall down around them, but—she slowed the car
to a crawl—someone had given the old store a makeover since she'd last come this way. Fresh white paint
covered the outer walls, and a ten-foot-tall cherub sat in
the parking lot. Two more infantilized Cupids held up
the sign on the front, and every *i* in "Lizzie's Five and
Dime" had been dotted with a red heart.

"Gross," she muttered before hitting the gas. Just
when she thought this little town couldn't get any more
Cupid-obsessed, it proved her wrong. Every time. It
wasn't like other towns didn't have Erosians. Anyone
who knew what they were looking for could spot at least
one Cupid in every major city in the world. Not to mention all the Muses, Maenads, Furies, and Paieons still
pretending to be everyday humans. But Gold Lea had
been the first town where Cupids had gone public, and
the Chamber of Commerce had been trying to cash in on
that bit of notoriety for decades now.

At first, it had worked. For a small fee, tourists could

hop on a bus and take a guided tour of the town's "historical landmarks." It started at the town square, where the head of the Erosian subcouncil had outed himself and a few others one night after a fight with his wife and too many whiskey sours. Things had never been the same. The bus tour proceeded to the bar where rival Cupid families supposedly settled their differences (false, mostly), went across the bridge where a sitting U.S. president had been rumored to have been struck by a Cupid at the request of a foreign operative (true, mostly), and ended at a strip mall where a half dozen kitschy shops sold souvenirs like love "charms" and "potions" (all false, entirely). Twenty years ago, business boomed for everyone in Gold Lea, including Eliza's parents.

Eventually, most "love tourists" grew bored with Gold Lea's small-town charm and moved on to bigger, brighter cities. Most of the Cupids followed. The tourists who still came to Eliza's hometown were either elderly people looking for a quick weekend trip, or hipsters coming to gawk at the old-timey charm. Basically, Gold Lea was to love what Branson, Missouri, was to country music.

Eliza pulled into her parents' driveway, rolled up the windows, and shifted to Park. As soon as her father was home and settled, she was getting out of this town once and for all. In the dark, she fumbled for the e-brake in her mom's car.

Tap, tap, tap.

She jumped, cracking her head on the steering wheel. Son of a… She grasped for the seat belt while her brain tried to place the man peering down at her from the passenger-side window.

"Hello?" he said.

No.

Not just a man. An underwear-model-worthy man with the perfect amount of five-o'clock shadow and cheekbones that could cut diamonds. A navy tie hung loosely around his neck, and the top button of his shirt lay open, practically daring her to look away from the tan skin at the base of his throat.

It was the worst thing Eliza had ever seen.

TURN BACK NOW. ABANDON SHIP. THIS WAY LIES MADNESS. Her mind screeched its usual warnings like a tornado siren, but she couldn't look away.

Over the years, in her attempt to live a "normal" life, she'd constructed an intricate maze of rules and guidelines that she followed at all times. Number one on that list? Stay away from hot guys.

On a good day, her clumsiness hit a six on the Richter scale. Add the fumbling, sweaty awkwardness of attraction to the mix, and Eliza became a walking catastrophe.

"Eliza?"

"Do I know…" She narrowed her eyes. There was a familiar seriousness in his gaze. Something nostalgic about the way he dug his hands into his pockets. Something… "Jake?"

Eliza shoved open the car door and tried to push all the dirty thoughts she'd just had from her mind as she stepped out into the driveway. "Jake Sanders? I thought you were in Peru or something."

"Brazil."

"Brazil then. What are you doing here?" She tried to smooth her hair. When that failed, she tried not to notice how mind-bendingly attractive her childhood best friend had become. They'd known each other since elementary school, when—as the only three school-age Cupids in town—Jake, Eliza, and Elijah had been enrolled in PSC (Public School Cupiding) classes together. Every Wednesday night, they'd sit in a classroom for two hours, drinking juice boxes and learning about the history of Cupids. On the weekends, Jake would come to her house, where they would conduct elaborate reenactments of the War of the Titans from the tree house in Eliza's backyard. But in middle and high school, the two of them had drifted apart the way people do. Especially when one of those people is class president and captain of the track team (Jake) and the other is a walking disaster (Eliza).

After high school, Jake enlisted in the Cupid Corps. For the last ten years, he'd been taking cases on assignment in impoverished and war-torn areas. Aside from a brief visit over Christmas nine years ago, Eliza hadn't seen him since.

"I moved back to town about a week ago," he said. "Doing some odd jobs while I get reacclimated."

"At Dionysus again?" she asked. When they'd been teenagers, he'd worked there as a bar back. The raucous restaurant and bar sat dead center in the Agora—a building at the edge of town where Descendants had gathered for decades, undetected by "regular" humans. Eliza, the ultimate clumsy introvert with an unheard-of level of enchantment, hated the place. People stared and pointed when she walked by. It made her feel like a lab rat.

"No." He looked down at his feet, then back up at her. "Doing some deliveries right now. This one is for your parents. Are they here?" He held out a large manila envelope.

"No." She started to say more, but the words snagged in her throat. "They're out."

"Can you sign for this then?"

She took his tablet and scrawled her name at the bottom of the screen. "Here you go."

Jake handed her the thick envelope and flashed her a grin. It was same grin—the one that rose a smidge higher on the left—that had always seemed kind of dorky when they were kids. As adults? Totally different story. "Happy Day-That-Shall-Not-Be-Named, by the way," he said.

Despite everything, Eliza let out a laugh. "Finally, someone around here understands me."

"I aim to please." His dark eyes locked on hers for a half second. "I can't believe your parents finally gave up on the whole Herman birthday extravaganza thing."

"Oh, they didn't. We already had cake. Blood and tears were shed, yadda, yadda."

"You did all the blood shedding before dark? The Hermans have really gotten soft over the years." There it was again. That grin. "Here. I have something for you."

Jake took a step closer. Miniature fireworks went off in her chest, leaving trails of nervous energy in her stomach. He'd become so handsome. Broad shoulders, narrow waist, a jawline that could make Adonis weep. And he'd been there for all her childhood traumas and celebrations. The hot days they'd chased down the ice-cream truck in bare feet. The games of checkers on her parents' back porch. The awkward here-come-the-braces-*and*-puberty years.

"You brought me a gift?" Eliza asked.

"You think I was going to step inside this house on your birthday without a gift in hand? No way. Your parents would have eaten me alive."

"That's fair." For the first time on this godsforsaken day, Eliza felt herself relax. They could have been ten years old and playing Battletoads again, the way everything fell into place. Like life had never taken them in separate directions.

"Here." He produced a small, rectangular package from his back pocket.

The paper was a plain navy blue—not a Valentine remnant in sight—and the featherlight present crinkled when she turned it over. She smiled up at him. "You didn't have to do this."

He reached for the gift with a boyish look in his eyes. "If you don't want it—"

Eliza whipped it out of his reach. "I didn't say that."

"Don't get too excited. It's nothing big."

"I'll be the judge of that." Eliza pried open the wrapping. An all-too-familiar cartoon kangaroo stared up at her from the tiny package of treats. A rush of nostalgia washed over her. "*Dunkaroos? Dunkaroos*, the best snack ever made? Dunkaroos, the sole reason I made it through childhood in one piece?"

"I think you're forgetting something." Jake gave her a pointed look.

"Okay. Dunkaroos, the reason I made it through childhood, *in addition to* your friendship."

His face broke into a wide smile. "I'll accept that."

"Where did you find these? I didn't think they made them anymore."

"Canada. I was in Vancouver last week."

"So you smuggled them into the country in the dark of night, risking everything, just for my birthday?"

He let out a soft chuckle. "Something like that."

Eliza's finger caught on the rough edge of the plastic container. He'd thought of her. Across hundreds of miles and dozens of years, Jake had thought of *her*. And yet... "Hey. Wait a minute. Was this a twin pack, Sanders? Did you eat the other half of my birthday present?"

He shrugged. "It was a quality check. For your own good."

"My own good?"

"Eliza." Jake reached out and took the cookies from her hand. The movement brought him close enough that, for one heart-stopping second, Eliza thought about what it would be like to kiss him. A thought she hadn't contemplated in nearly a decade, though once upon a time she'd thought about it enough times to fill a novel or three. But then he stepped back and pointed to the grinning kangaroo. "These are Canadian. Who knows what our northern neighbors are doing with our beloved national snacks? What if I'd brought these home, handed them to you, and you'd realized the icing was poutine flavored? You would have been devastated."

"Poutine? Really?"

"Really. You should be thanking me."

Eliza's throat grew thick with emotion, and the corners of her eyes threatened to release more than a few tears. Everything about this day was simply too much—the feelings, the memories, and the adrenaline spikes and crashes. "Thank you."

"Hey." Jake's hand brushed her shoulder. "You okay?"

"Yeah. You know me, always overemotional about my snacks."

"Eliza."

"It's just been a long, rough day. This has been the best part. I mean, it would have been no matter what, because…Dunkaroos…but thank you."

His dark brows furrowed. "You want to go out for a birthday drink and talk about it? I've got one more delivery, but I could swing by and pick you up in an hour?"

Catching up with her old friend over a couple of beers and a package of Dunkaroos sounded amazing. But her dad was still in the hospital, and if she didn't get there soon, she'd miss visiting hours altogether. "I can't. Not tonight. I'm sorry—"

He waved her off. "Don't worry about it. I've got a ton to do tonight anyway. It was good to see you, Eliza."

"You too," she said. But inside, she wished she could ask him to stay there with her. Then, at least for a little while, they'd be connected before adulthood blew them in different directions. "Thanks again."

But Jake was already to his car. He gave her a quick wave, backed out of the driveway, and disappeared into the sunset.

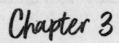

Chapter 3

> "Erosian business establishments have historically been close family firms due to the passage of 'the knack' through bloodlines and the secrecy demanded by other Descendants on the Cosmic Council. Since the controversial Cupid Disclosure of the twentieth century, the industry has rapidly consolidated. Many centuries-old family practices have gone out of business or been absorbed by younger, more modern start-ups."
>
> —*Titans of Love: The Business of Modern Affection*

ELIZA STARED INTO THE MURKY DEPTHS OF HER COLD hospital coffee. After throwing a handful of her father's things into a duffel bag and racing back across town, she'd made it to the third floor of the hospital fifteen minutes before visiting hours ended.

Which was five minutes ago.

She hoisted the duffel bag onto her forearm and wandered back to the nurses' station. "Hi," she said to the man now sitting behind the desk.

He didn't look up. "Yes?"

"My father's a patient. My mother's visiting with him now, but the nurse—"

"Only one visitor allowed at a time." He checked his

watch, then continued staring at the computer. "Visiting hours are almost over. You'd be better off coming back tomorrow."

A hard lump rose in Eliza's throat, and she wasn't sure if she wanted to cry or scream. Her fingers squeezed the Styrofoam cup hard enough that the last dredges of coffee sloshed against its sides. "Look. My father had a heart attack, and I just want to see him for five minutes. The nurse who was here said she was going to let my mom—his current visitor—know so that I could see him. If that's not going to happen, I'd be glad to go down there and let her know myself."

The man looked up with genuine concern. Dark circles ringed his eyes, and his skin sagged as though he'd been awake for days on end. "Ma'am…"

Eliza's eyes stung with hot tears, and the tip of her nose itched. She needed to stop talking soon, or she was going to have a full-fledged breakdown in front of half of Saint Isabel's Hospital. "Timothy Herman," she managed between sniffles. "What is his room number, please?"

"Ma'am, I believe this is—"

Eliza glanced at the clock. Eight minutes left before visiting hours ended. "What is his room number?" she repeated, louder this time.

"Eliza, please. I had to finish talking to your father about the business." The click of her mother's shoes on the hard tile followed the words. In the span of a breath, her mother stood at her side. "I'm so sorry," she said to the man behind the desk. "It's been an emotional day for all of us."

Understatement of the year. Her mother's words rubbed Eliza's already-raw nerves. Yes, it had been an emotional day for everyone, including Eliza. And, as usual, her mother had seemed to forget about Eliza's existence. But she didn't have the time or energy to fight this same old fight today—especially with the last minutes of visiting hours ticking by.

Eliza set her mangled coffee cup in front of her mother. "What's Dad's room number?"

"Three twenty-one."

Without another word, Eliza turned and set off in the direction her mother had come.

"Elijah and I will meet you at the car in ten," her mother called after her.

By the time Eliza reached room three twenty-one, their remaining time had shortened to five minutes. A half dozen wires and tubes came in and out of her father's body, and a rhythmic beeping kept pace with his heart. It was the most comforting sound Eliza had ever heard.

"Dad?"

His eyelids fluttered. "Liza. Can you believe this view?"

She glanced at the window, where the blinds had been drawn tight against the night. He must've still been partially sedated from the procedure. Of course her mom would make him talk about work when he was as high as a kite. Eliza sighed. "Yeah, great view."

"Reminds me of the time I went to Tokyo," he slurred.

As far as Eliza knew, her father had never been to Tokyo. She put the duffel bag down and pulled the visitor chair up to his bed. "You gave me a scare, Dad."

"I'm fine." He kept his eyes closed but reached for her hand. "Worry about the techno-Cupids instead. The robots will fall in love with us before they kill us."

Techno-Cupids? Her father had clearly been spending too much time watching the Syfy Channel. "I'll keep that in mind."

He opened one glassy eye and stared her down. "When I met the Mandroid-maker, he was already working on ways to take over the world."

She stifled a laugh, remembering the infomercial she'd seen in the waiting room. It was like a bad nursery rhyme: the butcher, the baker, and the Mandroid-maker.

"He had a blender that could *feel* things. Deep things," he said.

Eliza squeezed his hand. "I can't stay much longer, Dad. I just wanted to come in and say that I love you."

"You gotta get back to work?"

The laugher she'd held back dissipated, leaving shame rattling around in her stomach like a ten-ton block of cement. "No, not this time."

"Good. You should go to Tokyo instead."

She smiled despite herself. Once he'd recovered, she was going to give him so much trouble about this fictionalized trip to Japan. Now, she just patted the back of his hand. The thin hospital blanket came up to his midchest, and she tucked it up higher around him—exactly the way he'd done a million times for her as a kid. Whether she'd been sick with some random childhood illness, embarrassed about something that had happened at school, or heartbroken about failing her Cupid exam, he'd always been there to pull the blankets around her chin and remind her that everything would be brighter in the morning. "I'll keep that in mind," she said. "I got fired again, so getting the time off won't be a problem."

She held her breath and waited. She hadn't meant to

say it—the last thing she wanted was for him to worry about her right now—but the words had tumbled out before her exhausted brain could stop them. But her father gave no indication that he'd heard a word of her confession. *Thank the gods for Valium.*

"I'm so glad you're okay, Dad. I don't know if I could make it without you." She kissed him on the forehead.

"Love you too, Liza," he whispered, eyes still closed. "You always were my favorite daughter."

Warmth spread through her at his familiar words. He'd be okay. Everything would be okay. "You're still my favorite father," she said, giving his hand one last squeeze before she stood. She waited for another quip about Tokyo. When none came, she shuffled toward the door.

"Eliza?"

"Yeah?" She paused with one hand on the doorknob, a part of her hoping he'd ask for a favor—bring him the book from his nightstand or run some errand that had gotten lost in the shuffle. She'd do whatever it was without question. Gratefully even. Her father had been the one to bring her comfort so many times over the years, and now she felt a growing desperation to do the same for him.

He stirred a little and looked at her with hazy eyes. "One of these days, you're going to come into your own. You'll realize how powerful you are. You're lucky that it comes so easily. Your mother and I…" His voice faded and his eyes reclosed. "Not as lucky as you."

Eliza froze, her heart heavy. "I'll see you tomorrow, Dad," she whispered and clicked the door closed behind her.

If the Tokyo thing wasn't enough, that spiel

confirmed it: her father was on enough drugs to power Woodstock. But even if he wouldn't remember his words in the morning, Eliza knew she would. As she stepped into the hallway, they dug and clawed at the old wounds she'd buried years ago. No one in modern history had as much power to enchant as Eliza, and it had made her life miserable. Dozens of broken friendships? Yes. Failed romantic relationships? Absolutely. Inability to maintain a steady career? You betcha.

Lucky? Not a damn day in her life.

The next morning, Eliza stared down the remains of the piñata. It stared back at her from the dining room table, radiating pure birthday evil from its dead, beady eyes. Condoms streamed from its insides, advertising flavors like "Mom's apple pie" and "balsamic reduction."

On another day, Eliza would have found a nefarious use for the flavorful prophylactics. Maybe she would have snuck into her brother's apartment and supplemented the condoms in his bedside table with these more appalling flavors. "Ham and beans" would have been in the running for sure. But yesterday had wrecked Eliza. That, coupled with the night of fitful sleep in her childhood bed—where her brain insisted on replaying her father's drugged comments—only left her with the energy to toss the condoms into her purse. She dumped the empty donkey carcass into the garbage and started a pot of coffee.

As soon as she'd inhaled enough caffeine to power her through, she'd drive back to her apartment, shower, and head to the hospital again. If she had time, she could stop by Tina Temp's Temp Agency. They'd hooked Eliza up with a few jobs over the years, despite her proclivity for getting fired. It helped that Tina Temp was a Descendant herself, more or less. As a Wingless—the completely normal child of two Cupids—she could relate to Eliza's perpetual state of failed expectations.

"The Clausen file needs to be closed today." Her mother's voice broke into Eliza's thoughts. "Not tomorrow, *today*."

"I know, Mom," Elijah said.

Their voices and footsteps carried up the back stairwell before they made it into the kitchen. Eliza stopped short. The house had been so quiet all morning that she'd assumed her mom and brother were still asleep. But no, apparently, they'd gotten up and headed straight to the Herman & Herman office—a rectangular add-on accessible from the back of her parents' house.

"Eliza, you're up," her mother said.

Eliza poured herself some coffee and reached for another mug. "Coffee?"

"I had some at the office." Her mother and brother stood stiffly in the doorway, like vrykolakas waiting to be invited in.

"What's going on?" Eliza finally asked.

"Nothing," Elijah said. Way too quickly.

"We're just—" their mother began.

"It's nothing, Liza. Don't worry about it." Elijah nodded toward the coffee and sat down at the table. He looked as rough and worn down as Eliza felt. "I'll take some."

She pulled down a mug and weighed her options. It was definitely something. The question was, *Did she want to know*? After all, chances were the *something* involved their mother being controlling and uptight about Herman & Herman. The usual.

Eliza set the coffeepot in front of her brother, then pulled the manila envelope from the counter and held it out to her mother, who'd stepped tentatively into the kitchen behind Elijah. "I almost forgot. Jake Sanders came by here last night. He left this for you." She turned to Elijah. "Did you know he was back? I—"

She must've become invisible. That was the only explanation for why her mother and brother were staring at each other with matching expressions of horror, as if Eliza had ceased to exist. She waved her hand in front of them. "Hello?"

"This is it, isn't it?" her mother said, grabbing the envelope. "I knew it. I should have never let the two of you talk me into your harebrained scheme."

"It was a *good idea*, Mom." Elijah put his palm down on the table. "You know it, and Dad knew it. It would have taken off too, if the Department hadn't decided to interfere."

"I knew it was a mistake," their mother whispered.

"The mistake is that you refused to modernize, Mom. I'm a partner in Herman & Herman now too. I get a say, and you have to accept that." A muscle in Elijah's jaw ticked.

Uh-oh. It took a lot to make Elijah angry, and whatever was in this envelope had done it. Eliza leaned away, half expecting the thing to start ticking.

"Well, I don't think you should go," her mother said. "Not with your father in the hospital. There's too much to do here now. Ask if we can get a refund on the registration. We can't afford to absorb that. Not after this." She pointed to the envelope with a shaky finger.

"They aren't going to refund the registration," Elijah said. "And I'm not going to cancel."

Eliza watched their game of conversational Ping-Pong with wide eyes. Registration? Refunds? Ominous, unopened envelopes? "Guys," she said. "Does someone want to fill me in?"

They turned to her with equal expressions of confusion and embarrassment. So she hadn't become invisible after all. They'd simply forgotten that she was there.

"It's nothing. Just work." Her mother turned away and began shoving dishes into the dishwasher—including Eliza's mug, still full of coffee. "I'm headed to the hospital. I'll text you both after I talk to your father's doctor." Then she gave Elijah a look—one Eliza immediately recognized as *Keep your mouth shut*—and headed out the way she'd come.

"What in the Underworld is wrong with her?" Eliza asked as she dug her coffee cup out of the dishwasher. "I don't know how you can work with her every day. You're definitely the good twin."

She expected a chuckle from him, or at least for his fists to unclench. Their good twin/evil twin schtick had been their way of diffusing tension for more than twenty years, and it had never failed.

Until today.

"Not everything is a joke, Eliza." Elijah pressed his thumbs into his brows.

"Hey." She slid into the seat beside him. "What's going on? Why are you acting like this envelope has a death warrant in it?"

Her joke—probably in poor taste, since the Cosmic Council had, in fact, tried to issue death warrants for Cupids fifty years ago when the first of them went public—fell flat. Really flat.

Elijah shoved the envelope toward her. "See for yourself."

Eliza unfastened the metal clip and plucked a single sheet of thick paper from the envelope.

California Department of Affection, Seduction, and Shellfish

Pursuant to § 07.05 of the Code of Cupid Regulations, please be advised of the following:

Notice of Deficiency

We have determined there is a deficiency (increase) in the amount owed by **Herman & Herman** for dues, expenses, and licensing fees. This notice explains how the increase was calculated. You have a right to challenge our determination, including penalties…

Eliza's eyes glazed at the legalese, but she forced them farther down the page. "You guys owe the state thirteen thousand dollars?" Her chest tightened, forcing all the oxygen from her lungs. "And Mom's license is being frozen? She can't take on new clients? Why? How? She's always been obsessed with paying everything on time."

Her brother stared at his hands. "It's my fault. I talked them into trying some new things. Online matching databases and stuff. I didn't realize it would increase our licensing and registration fees until it was too late. Not to mention the increase in our malpractice insurance. And since Mom's the president of the company, she's the one they're after. Until we get it paid, all she can do is close out her existing caseload."

"Wow." Eliza slid the paper back into the envelope.

"Yeah. But we had to do something. Eliza…" He finally looked up at her, and Eliza realized the fatigue in his features wasn't from one sleepless night. "Business is down. *Way* down. No one wants to come into an office and look at flip-books anymore. No one wants to sit through Mom and Dad's thirty-minute explanation of the pros and cons of each kind of enchantment. They want to do everything from their phones and laptops. Vic Van Love has a new matching service where you just swipe photos, and it's killing us. We haven't brought in any new business in months. Just our regulars."

"Shit." The obscenity captured only the smallest fraction of the emotions swirling like a monsoon inside her. But there was no single word that could describe the level of shock, fear, and sadness she felt at her brother's confession.

"Yeah. And I got invited to this conference in Athens. Enchantments of the Modern Age. It's all about bringing the latest technology to your Cupid business. Only one Erosian in each state gets invited each year, and this year it's me. Or it *was* me." He sighed. "I thought this was going to be it, you know? The thing I'd been working so hard for since we were kids—making Herman & Herman my own."

She nodded. Once upon a time, she'd had the same dream. Of course, once she'd realized that her enchantment levels hovered somewhere between *insane* and

epic disaster, she'd given up. Her poor brother—
with his brilliant ideas and perfectly normal levels of
enchantment—had held on for dear life. "Is that what
Mom was talking about? She doesn't want you to go?"

"Dad's out of commission, and she can't even discuss
our services with potential clients. Of course she doesn't
want me to go."

Somewhere in the recesses of Eliza's brain, a light
bulb went off. "What about Jake Sanders? He said he's
doing odd jobs—"

"We can't afford to pay anyone, Eliza. I haven't been
paid in months. I've been taking shifts at Dionysus to
cover my rent."

"Oh." Eliza wrapped her palms around the coffee mug
and tried to draw some comfort from the warmth—an
old trick her father had taught her. But this time it didn't
even begin to dull the panic raging inside her. Herman
& Herman had been a part of her life forever, and she'd
assumed it would be around long after she'd crossed the
River Styx.

The dollar-shaped puzzle pieces began to click into
place. "That's why they sold the lake house, isn't it?"
she asked.

He nodded.

"Why didn't you tell me before?"

"Why would I?"

"Elijah—"

"Look, I appreciate that you're worried and everything, but you've made it pretty clear that you aren't
interested in helping out around here." He rubbed his
index finger over the double E's etched into the edge of
the table. They'd carved them with an old steak knife

more than twenty years ago and gotten into so much trouble that day. But they'd gone up to their rooms with grins on their faces, because no matter what the punishment, their initials would be there forever. Back then, they didn't realize how fleeting *forever* could be.

But now Eliza did, and she would give anything to hang on to it for a little longer. "What can I do?" she asked.

"Huh?"

"What can I do? What if I stay here and answer the phones or whatever? No one has to pay me. Can you still go to the conference then?"

"You don't have a license, Eliza. The last thing we need is to add a penalty to the amount we owe the Department."

She let out a wry laugh. "Last time I checked, you don't need a license to answer the phone. Plus, I don't think I could forget the old Herman & Herman enchantments spiel if I tried. We reschedule Dad's appointments and set up any new ones for when you're back. Mom can work on whatever she has scheduled between now and then. Then we buckle down until you come home with your newfangled technology and save the business. Easy, right?" She gave him a playful nudge, expecting a small smile at least.

All she got was a frown. "They changed the regs last year after someone in Los Angeles got in trouble for falsifying enchantments. Now anyone who works in a Cupid firm has to have at least a provisional license."

"Oh." Eleven years ago, after a particularly traumatizing day, she'd stopped just short of getting a full license. Her provisional license—the Cupid version of a driver's permit—had expired not long after.

"Exactly." Elijah pulled out his cell phone and began scrolling. "I guess I need to cancel my flight before I get charged."

She'd never bought into that whole one-twin-feels-the-other's-pain thing. But today, seeing her usually happy-go-lucky brother hurting so badly, she was beginning to rethink her stance. And *that* was making her rethink her stance on a lot of things, apparently.

"I'll do it," she blurted out. "I'll go down to the Department and reapply for my provisional license this afternoon. It was never the written test that gave me problems anyway."

Elijah laid his phone on the table. "Are you serious?"

Was she? She pictured herself walking into the Department, and a tidal wave of panic pushed her under. But then she remembered her father's words from last night, the hurt in her brother's eyes, and the fear in her mother's tight-lipped smile. She met Elijah's gaze.

"I am."

Chapter 4

> **Calif. CCR § 403.03.** Any person who chases, pursues, takes, transports, ships, buys, sells, possesses, or uses affection in any commercial manner must first obtain the prescribed license unless specifically exempted under § 69.

THE NORTHERN CALIFORNIA BRANCH OF THE Department of Affection, Seduction, and Shellfish left something to be desired. A lot of somethings, actually. The dingy cinder-block walls and stained ceiling tiles felt like they were closing in on Eliza—exactly as they had all those years ago. The place even smelled the same. Artificial pine with undertones of mildew and a hint of despair.

At least some things never changed.

With her stack of paperwork in hand, Eliza rang the bell at the empty front desk. The *ding* rang out, but no one came. She counted to ten, then hit the bell again.

Nothing. She passed ten more seconds by staring at the stained industrial carpet.

Ding.

Ding. Ding. Ding.

Dingdingdingdingdingding.

Nada. Not even a harried employee yelling at her from the back room to stop ringing the dang bell already.

"Hello?" Eliza called out. Between her frayed nerves and skipping lunch to study for this test, her inner rage monster was starting to rear its not-so-beautiful head. "Does anyone actually work here?"

When no one answered, Eliza lifted the wooden platform that separated the front counter from the back of the office, glared at the Employees Only sign, and stepped through to the other side. If they were going to force her to get a provisional license just so she could pick up a phone, she was going to make sure someone answered the damn bell.

"May I help you?"

She whipped around to find a short, stocky man standing behind her with his arms crossed. He looked like the epitome of every middle-aged government worker ever—tired, dead-eyed, and with a pallor that suggested he hadn't stepped out of fluorescent lighting in months. An embroidered Department of A.S.S. logo donned the upper left corner of his red golf shirt, and a grease-stained napkin jutted out from his collar—like he'd been caught mid-McRib.

"Hi," she said. "I was—"

Grease-Stain McGee pointed to the sign she'd pointedly ignored. He didn't seem entirely human, but there was none of that *certain something* that would identify him as a Descendant either. Maybe he'd just spent so much time around Erosians that he'd picked up a weird vibe. "Employees only," he said.

Eliza stared at him for a few seconds before silently lifting the wooden platform and stepping back from behind the counter. "No one answered when I rang the bell, so—"

"I was right around the corner. Two feet away at the

copy machine. I would have *noticed* if someone rang the bell."

"You've got a little something…" Eliza pointed to a spot at the corner of her mouth to demonstrate where some sort of sauce had formed a crust on the man's face.

He grabbed the napkin and swiped at his mouth, completely missing the leftover sauce. "Can I help you with something?"

"I'm here to take the provisional licensing exam. Eliza Herman? I signed up for an appointment online. Three o'clock." She held out the stack of paperwork that she'd had to not only submit online, but also print and bring to the office. In duplicate.

"You're late." He pointed at the digital wall clock. The angry, red numbers announced it was 3:05 p.m.

"I was actually here on time, but—"

"No one came when you rang the bell. I heard you the first time. Application?"

She handed him the single-page document with her name, date of birth, and other personal information.

"Proof of malpractice insurance?"

She handed him the printout she'd snagged from the Herman & Herman offices—right after she'd had Elijah call and add her to the policy.

"Birth certificate, complete with Cupid seal?"

She passed him the birth certificate with its raised seal that proved she was the offspring of two Cupids—the only known way a child could have the knack themselves, though even then, it was a crapshoot.

"Two forms of photo ID?"

She handed him her license and passport, along with photocopies of each.

"Proof of address?"

Her electric bill.

"Medical clearance?"

The paper she'd begged her doctor to sign this morning on her way over.

"Statement of interest."

Eliza slid the paper across the counter.

"Hmmm." The man frowned, looked up at Eliza, and frowned even harder.

Oh gods. This was going to be the thing that threw a big, fat wrench in it all. "I double-checked the website, but there were no instructions about page-length requirements," she said.

"'I'm interested in getting my license,'" he read from the page.

"It definitely states my interest." She gave him her best please-let-this-one-go smile. She'd already been at the computer working on this ridiculous paperwork for two hours by the time she'd gotten to the statement, and she'd run out of steam about 1.9 hours before that.

Finally, the man sighed. "Fine. Mentorship form?" He held out a stubby hand.

Eliza handed him the last page in her stack. Elijah had signed the form as her "mentor." Neither of them had any intention of him mentoring her; with any luck, he'd be in Athens soon. It was just a formality.

The agent scanned the page, mouthing the words as he read. "Elijah Herman? Any relation?"

"My brother."

"Sorry." He slid the entire stack of papers back to her. "Only minors may be mentored by members of their immediate family. Section 05.11 of the *CCR*."

"Wait, what?" Eliza stared at the man's badge. *Oliver Trevor*. Two first names. Beside the bold letters of his name sat a small photo of him, looking ten years younger—and happier. "Mr. Trevor—"

"It's *Agent* Oliver, actually." He pointed to the badge. "Oliver-comma-Trevor. Well, no comma. It was a misprint, but trying to get it fixed means filling out seven forms, sending in a copy of my birth certificate, and finding a notary public."

"That's…a very unfortunate predicament, *Agent* Oliver."

He shrugged. "Probably easier to just change my name."

"So back to the mentorship form." She walked the very thin line between wanting to throttle this man and wanting to charm him into giving her a provisional license. "I didn't see that no-family requirement mentioned anywhere in the instructions."

He pointed to a minuscule line of fine print along the bottom of the form. "Right here."

She picked up the paper and squinted at the page. "All mentors are subject to the rules and provisions of the CCR," she read. "That's not exactly specific."

"I don't make the rules, Ms. Herman. Is there anything else I can help you with today?"

Her shoulders sagged. For once, she'd thought she might actually be able to help her family. Instead, she'd wasted everyone's time—including her own. "No, I guess not."

Oliver-comma-Trevor turned his back to her, and at that same moment, Orpheus began to sing.

Wait. Nope. That was just the blood whooshing through her veins as Jake Sanders stepped into the room.

"Agent Oliver, I dropped off that—" He stopped short when his eyes met hers. "Hey, Eliza."

"Hi."

"What's up?" he asked.

"She was just leaving," Agent Oliver said.

"I was here to apply for my provisional license," she told Jake. A hundred ideas swarmed her brain at once. Some of them revolved around the way Jake's navy T-shirt clung to his chest and brought out the gold flecks in his brown eyes. But one idea hit harder than all the rest. "I need a mentor," she said. "Elijah was going to do it, but apparently it can't be a member of my immediate family."

Jake jammed his hands into his pockets. "Oh, right. They changed the regulations last year."

In a perfect world, Eliza would have been able to take Jake aside to explain the situation. No, in a perfect world, Eliza wouldn't be in this situation, and she'd be able to take Jake aside to eat Dunkaroos and catch up on everything she'd missed in the decade since they'd lost touch. But this wasn't a perfect world, and Oliver-comma-Trevor's stare burned holes into the back of her neck.

She ignored it and stepped closer to Jake. A tiny bit of sweat glossed his hairline, like he'd been out for a quick jog around the block. She caught a faint whiff of cedar and fresh-cut grass and fought the urge to sniff him like a bloodhound on the hunt. *Wait. What? Why am I analyzing his smell? Ugh. Stupid pheromones.*

"I know it's a long shot—" she started.

"If you need someone to do it—" Jake said simultaneously.

They both laughed nervously. "Really?" Eliza said. "Because I would appreciate it."

"No problem. You have a copy of the form I can sign, Agent Oliver?"

The man sighed like he'd been asked to push a boulder up a hill for all of eternity—or until his state pension matured, whichever came later—but he pulled a piece of paper from behind the counter and slid it to Jake. "37–43E, Mentorship Form."

A thousand butterflies took flight in Eliza's stomach, all at once. She'd done it. Mostly. She still had to take a multiple-choice test, but she'd ace that without any problems. She'd taken a practice test online and gotten every question correct.

"Okay, Ms. Herman, stand there for your photo." Oliver pointed to a white backdrop hanging from the wall. Someone had set up a point-and-shoot camera on a tripod directly across from it. A giant flash stood nearby. "I'll send you home with a temporary copy of your provisional license, and the official copy will arrive in the mail in seven to ten business days."

"Should I take the test first?" she asked. "I mean, last time I had to take the test first."

"No test for non-minors anymore," he barked. "Log all of the hours you work with your mentor each week, and submit the log to the department. You must report at least five hours each week, or your provisional license will be revoked." He shook his head and muttered, "I swear, no one reads the fine print anymore."

All those butterflies stopped dead in their tracks. This was not what she'd bargained for. At all.

"Say cheese," Agent Oliver said.

But before Eliza could eke out a single sound, the flash blinded her. The camera clinked and clanked, and the next thing Eliza knew, she was officially a provisional Cupid.

Again.

***

The next morning, Eliza pushed open the door to her brother's office without knocking. "Elijah, we need to... Oh. Hi."

Elijah sat behind his desk with his feet up. Jake sat across from him in one of the empty chairs, looking just as relaxed. They'd always been like this as kids, laid-back and easygoing; meanwhile, Eliza wound tighter with each year. At least until she'd given up on the Cupid thing altogether.

She glanced down at her pajamas. Green-striped pants that had shrunk after the first wash and an old high-school T-shirt with giant holes in *both* underarms. And of course she hadn't bothered to put on a bra. Herman & Herman wouldn't open to the public for another hour—and even then, it was unlikely anyone would walk through the door.

Jake gave her outfit a subtle once-over. "Hey. I was just telling Elijah about yesterday."

"About that..." Eliza turned to her brother. "Where were you yesterday evening? Did you know about all these new rules? That I'd have to actually do enchantments? Elijah, I swear if you knew and didn't tell me—"

Her brother held up his hands. "I swear I didn't know. But you can't back out now. My flight leaves tomorrow afternoon, right after Dad gets home. And he's going to need someone to drive him back and forth to cardiac rehab twice a week. Please, Eliza. Just until I get back."

Damn it. He looked so sincere and desperate. "What about Mom?"

"I'll handle Mom."

"Okay, but I can't do enchantments, Elijah," she said. "You know what happens."

Jake cleared his throat. Eliza ignored her embarrassment and continued. "Remember the time I accidentally made our band teacher fall in love with Lacey the lunch lady? A certain unfortunate event involving the woodwinds section and a hairnet?" she asked.

"I remember that Lacey deserved better than old Mr. Peabody," Elijah said.

"What about the time Mom was teaching me to drive and I rear-ended that guy in front of the Red Clover? I didn't even put a dent in his car, but he got so obsessed with Mom that he divorced his wife of six years. Because of *me*."

"If he went that crazy over a fender bender, they probably would have divorced anyway," Elijah said. "But just to be safe, Jake, don't let her drive." He leaned across the desk and said in a stage whisper, "Her car is a disaster. You wouldn't want to be seen in it."

Eliza gasped. "Leave Ron Weasley out of this," she hissed.

Jake looked back and forth between the two of them like they'd begun speaking a foreign language. "Wait, what?"

"Ron Weasley is a bright-orange, early 2000s death trap my sister drives around town," Elijah explained. "Stick around long enough, and I'm sure you'll hear it coming from three miles away. Or you'll hear Eliza cussing from at least the same distance when it randomly decides to lock all the doors with her keys inside."

"It's a Ford Mustang. An American classic. And I taped a spare key inside the door to the gas tank six months ago, so I haven't been locked out in ages." Eliza glared at her brother, but she couldn't argue with his other points. Ron *was* a loud, bright-orange death trap. Still, she loved that car, even if it had a copy of *Pow!: That's What I Call Love Songs* jammed in the CD player. At random intervals, a verse or chorus would blast through the speakers, and no amount of fiddling with the knobs and buttons could turn it off. She'd learned to wait it out and sometimes even hummed along. Good old Ron had stuck with her for years now, through all kinds of scrapes and misadventures. And it wasn't like she could afford an upgrade.

Jake nodded slowly. Poor guy probably felt like he'd volunteered to help a friend and stepped into a viper pit instead. "I can drive."

"Great." Elijah clapped his hands together. "It's settled. Once a week, Jake will take you out to do an enchantment and keep you out of trouble. Between that and the paperwork you have to do before and after, it'll take you five hours easy. Just write really slowly. I'll be back in four weeks, and by then, you can quit and go back to your normal life."

"What? Four weeks? I thought the conference was just a week," she said.

"It is. But I made some plans to tour a few of the most popular firms after it's over, see what they're doing that I can bring back, visit a few friends."

"Elijah—"

"Come on, Sis. I've been working here my entire life. When you left, I took on both our workloads. Now I'm just asking you for this one thing."

Elijah Herman, the first Cupid to ever get a PhD in mom guilt. "Fine."

"Great." He opened a drawer and pulled out a file folder. "I've even got your first case lined up. One of Dad's."

"He already showed it to me. It's a married couple," Jake said. "Looking to put the spark back into things for their anniversary. Can't get much easier than that."

Eliza had almost forgotten he was there. Almost. It was hard to forget a six-plus-foot masterpiece sitting inches away. "Okay," she whispered as much to herself as to them. "I can probably handle that."

"You can," her brother said. "And, Eliza?"

She waited.

"Consider upping your personal hygiene before you go." Elijah's face broke into a wide grin. "We have a reputation to uphold."

With her middle finger, Eliza showed him exactly what she thought of his reputation. But at least this was closer to their normal. Seeing her brother so on edge had made Eliza's heart hurt. "Says the guy who once swore off deodorant for an entire summer."

Elijah threw up his hands. "I was a lazy twelve-year-old! Sue me!"

"*Someone* should have," Jake muttered.

"Ha!" Eliza pointed at Jake, smiling gleefully. "Someone else is on my side."

Elijah rolled his eyes and turned to Jake. "Try not to let her injure anyone besides, you know, the people we've been hired to injure. The other night she rolled over a doctor's foot, and I thought it was going to be junior prom all over again."

Eliza's nostrils flared. "The Electric Slide is a dangerous dance!"

Jake stood and put a hand on her shoulder. "Don't worry," he assured Elijah. "I'll keep her out of trouble. Only the Macarena when she's with me."

She didn't know whether to be offended or relieved, but the weight of his hand on her made Eliza's insides twist into knots—the good kind. Garlic knots maybe. "When is the appointment?" she asked, trying to look as dignified as she could in a holey shirt and too-tight capri pants.

"Tomorrow at one," Elijah said.

"Pick you up at twelve thirty?" Jake asked.

"Perfect," Eliza said. And it would be. One hundred percent perfect.

Maybe.

Actually, she was probably going to cause a disaster of epic proportions, but she'd make it work. She had to. Her family needed her.

And if it didn't work? Well, at least she got to spend an afternoon staring at the wonder that Jake Sanders had become.

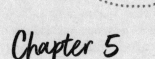

Chapter 5

Calif. CCR § 304.02. A state-approved anti-bacterial, virucidal, and fungicidal disinfectant shall be used on all arrows, implements, and reusable weaponry prior to use on each patron, except when patrons provide their own such weaponry.

"READY?" JAKE ASKED.

Eliza lifted her sunglasses and squinted through the windshield. The three-story brick house sat in the middle of one of Gold Lea's newer subdivisions, a wealthy part of town that hadn't existed when she was growing up. Perfectly pruned shrubs dotted the landscape, and the windows gleamed as though each one had its own personal window washer. It was all just shy of mansion status.

Eliza sighed and stepped out of the car. "Ready as I'll ever be."

Which, to be fair, was never. She was never going to be ready for this. Eliza had come up with plenty of stupid ideas in her life, but she feared this was her worst to date.

"Wait." She planted her feet in the driveway and stared down at her ballet flats. Scuff marks marred one toe, a remnant of her many klutz moves. "I lied. I'm not ready. What if the Department comes to observe?"

Jake took a step back to stand beside her. The sleeves of his crisp button-down shirt had been rolled to his elbows, allowing the morning light to reflect off his obnoxiously perfect forearms. He stood silently beside her, full of easy confidence that only made Eliza's nerves fray further. "Eliza, you're going to do great. If the Department decided to observe you on this one, that would be good news. This is literally the simplest case I've ever seen."

Easy for him to say. He'd spent the last decade doing the toughest enchantments in the world. Everything probably seemed simple in comparison. She was about to march into this house and ruin the lives of this unsuspecting couple—well, if not their lives, at least the next lunar cycle.

"I just need a second," Eliza said.

"You want to review again? Step by step?" he asked.

She nodded, gulping for air. "Lilian and Mitch Johansen, both age seventy-two."

"Keep going."

"Married for forty-five years. Every year for their anniversary, they hire a Cupid as their gift to each other before going on a cruise."

"Exactly. They're experienced at this, and they've never had a problem. Elijah said they hire your dad every year." Jake laid a hand on her upper arm. His fingers pressed gently against her jacket, leaving her dizzy with more than just fear. The last few days had taken her from mortification to attraction and back again. She'd officially reached feelings overload.

"Honestly, Eliza, you couldn't mess it up if you tried."

Despite herself, Eliza cracked a smile. "Is that a dare?"

"I know better than to ever take you up on a dare."

His grin thinned the fog of panic in her brain. "Okay."

"Okay?"

She nodded. "I'm ready. Let's go not-fatally-injure some baby boomers."

Five minutes later, Eliza sat perched on the edge of a floral couch with a cup of tangerine tea warming her palms. From the nearby oak coffee table, a photo of two smiling children wearing Christmas sweaters stared back at her.

"Miles and Sophia, our grandchildren." The woman who'd introduced herself as "call me Lily, please" smiled at the photo. Except for her gray curls and the wrinkles in her dark skin, the children were the spitting image of their grandmother.

"They're adorable," Eliza said. Between the tea and the soft cinnamon scent of the house, she'd *almost* relaxed enough to act normal. "How old are they?"

"Miles is fourteen, and Sophia is twelve," Lily's husband, Mitch, said. "Sophia acts just like her grandmother. Going to be a true beauty when she gets older." He reached over and squeezed his wife's thigh. "Hopefully she won't be *quite* the firecracker Lily was when she was younger. I could barely keep up with her—"

Lily let out a tinkling laugh. "Oh, Mitch. Not in front of company."

"How did you two meet?" Eliza asked. Yes, she was stalling, but she was also genuinely interested. Never in her life had she seen two people who still seemed to like—much less Love—each other after forty years.

"Her sister introduced us at a college graduation party," Mitch said. "I asked her to dance and never looked back."

"He stepped on my toes the whole time," Lily added.

"All part of my charm."

Lily scooted closer to her husband and winked at Eliza. "He was *very* charming that night."

"I was set to move from St. Louis to San Francisco a week later," Mitch said. "And here I was, hopelessly in love with this pretty girl from Kansas City."

"I told him I wasn't coming along without a ring on my finger."

Mitch grinned. The man certainly adored his wife, probably more than Eliza had ever adored anything.

"The next day I put a ring on it, as the kids say these days," he said.

Lily held up her ring finger, where a gorgeous emerald sat in the middle of a ring of crisp diamonds. "He's my very best friend."

Eliza glanced at Jake. *See?* his expression seemed to say. *Easiest case ever.*

She turned back to the Johansens. "Are you ready to get started?"

"Ready," they said in unison before bursting into giggles. Gods, they were like a couple of lovesick teenagers.

A pang of something like jealousy hit Eliza, but she brushed it off. It couldn't be jealousy, because she didn't believe in Love. Not the true, 'til-death-do-us-part, happily-ever-after nonsense. Especially for her. She could create butterfly-inducing crushes of all kinds at the drop of a hat—sometimes literally. But that wasn't the same as knowing someone down to their bones and still being happy to be with them. Even her parents, despite their thirty-one years of marriage, had shown her that Love left a lot to be desired.

"I know the two of you are practically professionals

at this by now," Jake said. "But since Eliza is working on her license—"

"I was so sorry to hear about your father, by the way," Lily said. "He's done so much for us over the years. I'm glad he's going to be okay."

"Thank you," Eliza said, letting out a deep breath. How could anyone be nervous around people as sweet and kind as the Johansens? "Me too. He should be home tomorrow."

Jake gave her another one of his *see?* looks. "Now, since Eliza's working on her license, do you mind if we go through all of the forms as if this were your first time?"

"Of course not, dear," Lily said. Mitch nodded in agreement.

"Okay. Eliza, do you want to jump right in?" Jake asked.

She took a deep breath and pulled out the forms from the folders in her lap. "You two have chosen the All Over Again package. When you're ready, I'll have you close your eyes, and then I'll cause a minor injury to you both. Mitch, when you open your eyes, the first person you see will be Lily. Lily, you'll see Mitch."

"That's when the magic happens," Lily said.

Mitch chuckled. "No, the magic happens when they leave and we…" He trailed off with a playful waggle of his brows.

Eliza tried not to blush as she handed them each a form. *Keep it professional, Eliza.* "Well, for my purposes, the magic happens when you two see each other. What you do after that is your business. These waivers explain everything that could happen. Before we go further, you'll need to sign and date them."

"It's only a precaution," Jake added. "But we like to remind couples that hormones, pheromones, and all the things that make humans interested in and attracted to one another can change over time. If, by some small chance, one of you is no longer attracted to the other, that side of the enchantment won't take. Herman & Herman offers a money-back guarantee on all their enchantments, but regardless, it can be traumatic for some people."

"Now that's a thing I never understood," Mitch said. "Obviously, it's not a problem for me. But I thought you Cupids made the attraction happen."

"That's a common misconception," Eliza said, launching into an explanation she'd heard—and given—a million times over the years. "We enhance the attraction that already exists, but it's more than simply physical attraction. It's emotional. The feeling of excitement when the other person walks into a room and looks at you. The way you notice every small thing they do. The urge to show and tell them just how great you think they are. That's what we enhance. Sometimes a person can be too scared to admit to that type of attraction or to act on it, so they get a boost. Sometimes the attraction is buried under so much baggage that people don't even know it's there. Of course, that can backfire. For example, if someone has been feeling unhappy with their current partner and they get hit with an enchantment, the things they feel for someone else could entice them to make a rash decision."

"Huh," Mitch said. "So I guess I can't pay you to make my neighbor fall in love with his truck?"

Eliza laughed. "Afraid not, unless he's already attracted to the truck. And even then, the truck obviously couldn't reciprocate. Human subjects only, I'm afraid."

Unless, of course, you get my dad high and ask him about "techno-Cupids." Then all bets are off. Robots, trucks, jukeboxes, blenders...

"You'll just have to find another way to get back at him for running into the mailbox, Mitch." Lily sat up straighter, looking the teeniest bit impatient. "We need to get on the road if we're going to make it to the harbor on time."

"Oh, right. Your cruise." Eliza handed them each a pen and watched as they signed their relationship away to her (not-so) capable hands. When they'd handed the forms back, Eliza stood and pulled the lancing device from her bag. "With this package, we usually do a small finger stick, enough to draw a tiny drop of blood—"

"About that, dear." Lily stood and smoothed out her lavender skirt. A flash of beige slip and rolled knee-highs peeked out at the movement. "We've done the finger-prick thing a few times. This is a big year for us, so we'd like to do something different."

Eliza shot Jake a look, but his expression said he didn't know what the woman had in mind either.

In the last few years, rumors and theories had begun swirling about different injuries causing different types of responses—the way different strains of marijuana caused different highs. But as far as Eliza knew, it was all bologna, and the last thing she needed was for the Johansens to ask for something difficult.

"What did you have in mind?" Eliza asked.

"Give us a snap and a pop to get it. It's very easy, dear. I'm sure you'll be able to manage." The couple disappeared into the other room before Eliza could ask anything else.

"What's going on?" she whispered to Jake.

"No idea. Your brother said this couple has never been a problem."

"If I accidentally kill the world's sweetest old couple—"

"You won't," he promised. "If they ask for something too difficult, I'll step in and tell them no. I'll be the bad guy, just in case they get any ideas about complaining to the Department."

Relief flooded her veins. "Thank you."

Lily tiptoed back into the living room, and Mitch followed behind her. Between the two of them, they carried a wooden spoon as delicately as if it were the Hope diamond.

"Here we are," Lily said, setting the spoon on the coffee table. "Mitch gave this to me years and years ago. Slid my engagement ring on the end of it and asked me to marry him."

"Lil' was a three-time Gold Lea Bake-Off champion," Mitch interjected. "I always said her old-fashioned butter cake is good enough to turn the pope Lutheran, and it was good enough to make an honest man out of me. Years ago, when we—"

"Mitch, stop. She doesn't want to know about all that," Lily said.

Actually, Eliza *did* want to hear all about it. She'd bet that the two of them had enough stories to keep anyone entertained for hours. But she also wanted to get this enchantment over with as soon as possible. After all, the more time Eliza spent in their home, the greater the chances of bringing her particular brand of disaster down on them.

"We wanted it to be something special this year," Lily said. "Something that means something to us. Usually your father just pricks our fingers with one of his tools, but I wondered if we could attach a pin to this, perhaps?"

Lily put the spoon in Eliza's outstretched palm. "I actually won't need to draw your blood," Eliza said.

The Johansens' faces fell into matching expressions of confusion. "But your father—?"

"I read online—"

"Every Cupid has different strengths and abilities," Jake interjected. "Eliza's are…*strong*. She can enchant you without any blood being shed. It's an asset, actually."

"Wow," Mitch said. "I had no idea we were in the presence of such greatness."

Eliza stared at her shoes. If they only knew.

She handed the spoon back to Lily. "In any event, I'm happy to use the spoon if you'd like."

"We would like," Mitch said. "Now"—he rubbed his hands together—"let's get this show on the road. I've got a cruise to catch and a wife to see in a bikini." He winked at Lily.

Eliza laughed. "Who would like to go first?" she asked.

Mitch's hand shot up.

"Great." Eliza wiped her sweaty palms on her jeans. A part of her still couldn't believe she was going to do this after so many years of swearing it all off. But she couldn't think about that now. She needed to focus, and she needed to make sure Mitch saw his wife—*and no one else*—first thing. Eliza already had one elderly suitor floating around; she didn't need another. "Why don't we try this? Both of you kneel on the couch and rest your arms along the back." She held her breath as the couple maneuvered into position. It was only then that she realized what she'd asked them to do. *Am I*

*about to spank an elderly couple with a wooden spoon?
I am about to spank an elderly couple with a wooden
spoon.* "Um, is that okay?"

"It's perfect." Lily wiggled her behind. "Plus, the
cushions are good for my knee replacement."

"Uh, okay. Great." Eliza looked to Jake. He stood
over her shoulder, arms crossed against his wide chest.

"You've got this," he whispered. Warm breath on her
neck. A smattering of goose bumps on her arm. "Take
your time, focus all your energy on the enchantment,
and move with purpose."

She rolled the spoon's handle between her fingers
and stepped away from Jake. Away from his heat, his
safety, his entirely too-hot-to-exist forearms and moved
toward the couple on their couch. Her life had never
been normal, but today was definitely near the top
of her World's Weirdest Days list. Top five at least.
Somewhere between the second-grade piñata massacre
and the time she made her parents' handyman get the
hots for his ladder.

He had, it turned out, already had a ladder fetish.

"Lily, Mitch." She stood within striking distance and
put on her best I'm-totally-a-professional smile. "Are
you ready?"

"I was born ready," Mitch said.

"Turn toward each other and lock eyes." She waited
a beat for their gazes to settle. It was so sweet, the way
they looked at one another, even after all this time.
"Now I can't stress this enough. Do *not* take your eyes
off each other until I say it's okay. Do you understand?"

They each gave a single nod.

With each beat, Eliza's heart climbed farther up

her throat. Her fingers shook, making the spoon slap against her thigh. She was really going to do this. Maybe. Probably. Or she could just hand Jake the spoon and sprint through the wall, Wile E. Coyote style. She glanced over her shoulder.

Jake smiled. A single, reassuring grin as he cocked one eyebrow and mouthed, *You've got this*.

Eliza took a deep breath and stepped closer to Mitch. She pulled her arm back a few inches. It wouldn't take much—it rarely did—and these two were so ready to go, Eliza could probably have hit them with a feather and seen results. *Time, focus, purpose*. She repeated Jake's words in her mind.

"Okay, eyes on each other," she said. A flash of green in her periphery caught her eye. An afghan draped over a nearby armchair. In one fell swoop, Eliza grabbed the crocheted blanket and draped it over her head, peering through the gaps in the stitches. An added layer of protection, in case one of the Johansens looked the wrong way.

Jake chuckled. "Is that really necessary?" he whispered.

"Better safe than sorry." *Especially with my history*. Not that she would mention her *history* in front of the Johansens.

"If you say so," Jake said.

"Is there a problem?" Mitch asked. "We really do need to get going."

"No, not at all," Eliza said hurriedly. "Keep your eyes on each other. And here we go in three, two—"

She clacked the spoon against the back of Mitch's calf, and he let out a surprised little squeal. Love Luster exploded all around them. Peels of gold and silver shimmered from the floor to the ceiling, coating Eliza in the scent of spring rain.

"Wow," Jake muttered.

"Yeah, wow," Eliza repeated. Apparently, enchanting someone on purpose—someone already madly in love with his wife—made the glimmer into more than a mildly interesting side effect. This was nearly a full fireworks show.

Mitch's expression shifted. He smoothed back his thinning hair and went all puppy-dog-eyed as he stared at Lily. If he was head over heels for his wife before, now he was head over heels over feet and back again.

It had worked!

With a smidge more confidence and speed, Eliza stepped over six inches and gave Lily an identical smack. The woman roared—literally, as the second set of sparks flew—then leaned toward her husband and whispered something in her ear.

Eliza let out a breath, one it felt like she'd been holding for hours. She'd done it. Really and truly done it. She hadn't had a single mishap, no one had ended up in tears, and—most importantly—her parents were about to have some very happy customers.

"I did it." She whispered the words to herself through a smile. "I really did it." Pride bubbled up inside her, and she turned toward Jake. "One week down, three more—"

She ripped off the afghan midsentence.

Clang.

Crash.

Glimmer.

"*Ooof.*" Jake leaned down and rubbed his toe. An overturned candy dish lay on the floor, and dozens of red and pink Hershey Kisses were scattered around his feet. Their eyes met.

No. She froze. For a few blissful seconds, Eliza had forgotten that she could cause a catastrophe anytime, anyplace, with anyone.

Including the incredibly gorgeous guy who was supposed to be her mentor.

Chapter 6

Calif. CCR § 981.04. **(b)** Affection service providers shall report any unintentional enchantments or adverse love incidents that are both serious and unexpected within thirty days, and within five days after any amputation, loss of eye, or fatal attraction.

ELIZA STEPPED INTO THE HERMAN & HERMAN OFFICES without a word. Her fingers grasped the edge of the receptionist's desk, and everything around her felt slightly hazy around the edges. She sat, putting the wide girth of the desk between herself and Jake.

Jake, her mentor.

Jake, her childhood best friend.

Jake, the cute teenager who'd grown into a two-shades-too-gorgeous-to-be-real man.

A man who wasn't the least bit attracted to her.

Jake hadn't been affected by his injury at all. Instead, he'd packed up his messenger bag and given a cursory wave to the Johansens before asking if Eliza was ready to go. Then he'd driven her straight back to the office, where they'd flicked on the neon OPEN sign in the front window and flipped on the lights. The smell of toasted almonds—her dad's favorite snack—still hung in the air, and testimonials from happy customers adorned the wood-paneled walls.

"I told you. It's fine, Eliza. I promise." He leaned against the office door—staying far enough away that she couldn't injure him with her clumsiness again. Apparently, he'd learned his lesson the first time.

"I knew I'd screw something up." She put her head down and leaned her cheek against the cool desk.

"You're being too hard on yourself. And if you were going to screw something up, this seems like no big deal in the grand scheme of things."

He was right, of course. Once she'd picked up that dish and stuffed all the chocolate back inside, it was like nothing had ever happened. She could still report this case as a success to the Department, and if anyone asked how things had gone, she could honestly say there'd been no problems.

So why did she feel so twisted up inside?

"I probably need to get going. I've got a few deliveries to make this afternoon." Jake looked down at his feet as he spoke. He'd barely looked at her since they'd left the Johansens' house.

He looked so uncomfortable that she had to let him off the hook. "Jake, I'm not offended."

"Offended?" Finally, he spared her a glance, one eyebrow raised.

"We're basically like siblings. Obviously, there's no attraction between us. You knew me when I matched the color of the bands on my braces to the holidays." She forced out a fake laugh and an even faker shudder. "Please, don't worry about it."

"Yeah, okay. Thanks." He ran a hand through his hair, giving him the sexiest case of bedhead in existence. *Like a brother, indeed.* But his shoulders had relaxed the smallest amount, and the tension between them had faded. Hopefully, her big, fat lie would result in a little less awkwardness over the next three weeks.

"I need to fill out the reporting log for the Department," she said. "Between the prep work, the explanations, the actual enchantment, and the drive time, I think we got almost three hours today. We only need two more this week."

"Great." He already had a hand on the doorknob. "Text me when you get something else."

"Yeah, sure." She masked her disappointment by rifling around in the desk. For what, she had no idea.

"And, Eliza?"

She stopped fussing with the plethora of dead pens in the drawer. "Yeah?"

"Don't mention the whole thing with the candy dish in your log. You know how the Department is. They'd make it into a big deal for no reason."

"Sure. Thanks."

"No problem. See you later."

She let out a sigh of relief as soon as the door closed behind him. Or was it a sigh of something else? Did she want there to be a reason? No, definitely not. Having a mentor who thought he was in love with her would really get in the way of her learning. Not to mention how awkward it would be every time they had to work together. He'd probably bring her overpriced flowers or some other stupid cliché that would embarrass everyone—including Jake, once the enchantment wore off and he realized what he'd done.

Worst of all, she would fall for it. Because somewhere down deep in her gut, Eliza knew she'd never be able to resist. And at the end of the lunar cycle, when Jake's hormones went back to normal, she'd end up alone and heartbroken.

Which was a major problem for someone who didn't believe in love. Or, at least, the Capital L, happily-ever-after kind.

Eliza took a deep breath, shook all thoughts of Love from her mind, and booted up the computer. Then she flipped on all the lights and waited for customer phone calls and walk-ins. When nothing but the dull buzz of the overhead lights came, she got to work on the forms.

With a little time and space, Eliza quit dwelling on Jake and the candy dish incident. Yes, there'd been a few hiccups and a handful of surprises, but she'd done it. For the first time in her life, she'd successfully managed a deliberate enchantment.

Well, technically it had been the second time. The first time, she'd been eighteen, and the enchantment had been an act of desperation. Even now she hated thinking about it. Hated how that day made her feel so vulnerable and raw all these years later.

And she wasn't about to think about it now. Not when the very people she'd enchanted were waiting for her at home.

"You're home!" Eliza wrapped her arms around her father's shoulders. He was still pale, and gauze covered the backs of his hands and the crook of his right elbow—leftovers from the needle sticks and IVs.

Her father leaned back in his recliner. If it weren't for

the bandages, this could have been a scene from Eliza's childhood memories. "How are you doing, Liza?"

"Better now that I've been to Tokyo," she teased.

Pure confusion spread across his features. "What?"

She considered telling him all about his drugged ramblings but decided against it. There was far too much else to cover. "Nothing. Just a stupid joke. How are you feeling?"

"Good as new," he said, though the half smile, half grimace on his face said otherwise. "I'll be back to the grind in no time."

"Oh, no you won't, Tim." Her mother stepped into the living room with a glass of water in one hand and a palm full of pills in the other. "The doctor said absolutely no stress and no work for the next month. Your only job is to eat salads, watch old episodes of *Supermarket Sweep*, and go to cardiac rehab. Doctor's orders."

"The doctor told him to watch *Supermarket Sweep*?" Eliza asked. "Dad, I think you need to find a new provider—"

"Eliza, please," her mother said.

But the admonishment was worth it, because her dad gave Eliza one of his signature winks, followed by a wide grin. "The last guy I saw told me to watch *Shop 'Til You Drop*. I walked right out of there and never came back."

Footfalls came pounding up the back steps, and soon Elijah stepped into the living room. He enveloped their father in a bear hug. "What did I miss?"

"Dad only sees cardiologists who prescribe nineties game shows about shopping."

"But not *Shop 'Til You Drop*, obviously." Elijah didn't miss a beat.

Their mother sighed. "Your father is under strict orders not to stress himself out. Which is why, Tim"— she turned to their father—"Elijah is going to stay home and handle your cases while you're recovering."

"Now, wait—" their father said.

"Actually…" Elijah took a step toward Eliza and pushed her front and center in the room. "Eliza has come up with a plan."

Eliza shot her brother a glare that contained a hundred poisoned darts. "You said you'd handled this," she whispered.

"Correction, I said I *would* handle it. This is me handling it. Just trust me," he whispered back. "Eliza is going to handle the phones *and* Dad's cases while he's recovering. Actually, she already did one of his enchantments."

"You did?" her dad asked.

She nodded.

"*What?*" Her mother squawked like a hen whose nest had been raided. "Elijah Michael Herman, you told me you were going to take care of the Johansen family. They're some of our oldest customers, and we can't afford to lose them."

Eliza had fully expected her mother to doubt her abilities and willingness—no one doubted Eliza as much as she doubted herself—but hearing her mother so openly admit that she expected her daughter to fail hurt more than she'd imagined. "You didn't lose them," she whispered. "Everything went fine."

Silence descended on the Herman living room.

"You went out and got your provisional license again?" her father asked.

She nodded. "Jake Sanders is going to supervise me. Elijah said you only had a few appointments scheduled for the next month, and I already did one of them. I'll stay out of trouble and just answer the phones, I promise." Somehow, she'd been sucked into a wormhole and come out in the past. Once upon a time, she'd begged her father to let her tag around the office just like this.

"And you handled the Johansen appointment on your own?" Her father's face broke into a grin.

"Jake helped, but yeah, mostly on my own."

His smile grew so wide Eliza thought her father might secretly be possessed by the ghost of the Cheshire cat. "That's my girl."

"See?" Elijah whispered in her ear. "Handled."

Her mother began pacing around the living room, ticking off a litany of tasks on her fingers. "You have to add Eliza to our malpractice insurance, Elijah. We can't—"

"Already did it, Mom," he said.

"What about taking the written exam? She has to take the written exam."

"There's no written exam anymore," Eliza added. "Just the supervised hours."

"What about the waiver forms? Did you get the Johansens—"

"Mom," Elijah and Eliza said in unison.

She finally stopped moving and stared at the three of them.

Something about the look in her eyes—Was it betrayal? Terror? Eliza couldn't be sure—solidified the little ball of resolve in Eliza's chest. For the next few weeks, she was going to be a Cupid, and she was going to do a damn good job of it. "Mom, I promise—"

But her mother turned and headed toward the kitchen. Just before the door to the back stairwell creaked open, she called out, "I'm just going to call the Johansens and make sure they know about the money-back guarantee."

An awkward silence crept into the room, and Eliza swallowed back all the things she wanted to say. Screaming at her mother right now wouldn't do anyone any good, especially her invalid father.

Finally, he grabbed her hand and gave it a squeeze. "She'll come around."

She nodded, but only because she didn't want to upset her father. They'd already broken the no-stress rule, and he'd only been home for twenty minutes. "I know."

He patted the arm of the recliner. "Now sit down here and tell me all about the Johansens. Aren't they the sweetest couple?"

Eliza might have been approaching thirty, but she hoped she never felt too old to snuggle in next to her father. "Very. Lily made me tea and showed me pictures of her grandkids."

"She did?"

"She did. *And* it was my first-ever enchantment using a wooden spoon as a weapon. Write that one down in the history books, Dad."

"I have a feeling all your enchantments are going down in the history books, kiddo."

Eliza laughed and raised an eyebrow. "For all our sakes, I really hope that isn't true."

Chapter 6.5

"Members of the Corps shall not transport between countries any unregistered weapons, ambrosia reserves, vegetation, animals, or Cerberus offspring, including Cerberus-wolf hybrids."

—*Cupid Corps Volunteer Manual*, 3d, TR.

DUNKAROOS: PUBLIC ENEMY NUMBER ONE.

I stepped off the plane in Vancouver, saw the kangaroo mascot, and Eliza's face popped into my head. It had been years since I'd thought of her, but there in the airport newsstand, she was all I could think about.

Her laugh. The way her handwriting had always slanted upward. The time we'd got in trouble for ordering pizzas and having them sent to our fourth-grade teacher's house. How she'd named all the squirrels in the neighborhood and we'd spent *days* creating off-the-wall backstories for them.

We'd been inseparable.

Then puberty hit. Suddenly, we didn't know how to be ourselves anymore. We didn't know how to be friends anymore. All the time we'd spent talking about squirrel exorcisms? Replaced by time spent thinking about what it would be like to kiss Eliza. Or, uh, do other stuff. I mean, I was a teenager for the gods' sake.

But the older we got, the less interested she seemed

in being friends, much less anything more. Finally, I gave up.

After graduation, I ran off to the Corps to forget—among other things—her.

It worked too. For a while.

Until that damn kangaroo hopped back into my life.

I didn't know for sure that she'd be at her parents' house on her birthday, but I'd be lying if I said she wasn't the reason I offered to make the delivery. I was just going to see her for a minute. She'd probably become someone completely different, and I could get the thought of her out of my system.

But she was still Eliza.

Fun, funny, kind Eliza. Only better. She'd grown up and into herself in a way I hadn't expected. But I should have.

Next thing I knew, I was asking her out and getting shot down. Some things never change, I guess.

And as if my ego hadn't taken enough of a hit, I practically begged her to let me be her mentor. I don't know what it is about this girl—woman, now—that turns me into some kind of bumbling idiot, but there you have it, folks. Jake Sanders will do anything for a little attention from Eliza Herman. Put it in the headlines because soon everyone will know.

Even her.

It was hard enough to keep my unreciprocated crush hidden before. But then at the Johansens', I had to stand a little too close and linger a little too long.

One candy dish, one big toe, and suddenly good, old Jake was a goner. Done. Dunzo.

For the first few minutes, I didn't even realize what had happened. I mean, I'd been fighting the Battle of the Eliza Herman Crush for a while now. So spending a little extra time staring into her wide brown eyes wasn't exactly news. Laughing too loudly at her jokes? Same old, same old. The newsworthy part was how I could barely keep from spouting her praises the entire way back to the office.

How I had to knuckle the steering wheel until my fingers went numb to keep from reaching for her hand.

How I had to count each of my breaths to keep from asking her to tell me about every moment of her life since I'd been away.

And just when I got up the courage to explain that I'd been enchanted—that maybe this was the push we needed to give it a shot—she turned those deep, dark eyes on me and said, "Jake, I'm not offended."

"Offended?" Maybe she'd seen me gawking at her at the last stoplight. Maybe I had drool on my chin. Things had to be even worse than I'd realized.

"We're basically like siblings," she'd said.

I don't have little sisters. If I did, Eliza would definitely *not* be one of them. But there she was anyway, letting me off easy with her soft smile and pitying eyes. A big, old this-is-never-going-to-happen wrapped in a giant bow.

So I nodded and drove away. I'm a guy that can take a hint.

But I still have to spend a million hours with her over the next few weeks. Trying not to stand too close. Trying not to stare at her delicate cheekbones. Trying not to let her see that I'm dying a little inside every time she doesn't return one of my lovesick stares.

Talk about torture.

Thanks a lot, Dunkaroos.

Chapter 7

> "Enchantments always last one moon cycle; however, the knack of every Cupid has a distinct profile. Variations exist in the degree of wound required to produce enchantment, as well as the quality of resulting romance. For example, Eros himself was known to produce strong desire by drawing blood. Many less powerful Descendants are only able to cause a strong sense of kinship despite inflicting near-fatal wounds. Rarely, a Descendant's knack is so powerful it enchants without even breaking the skin."
>
> —*Cupid 101: Everything You Need to Know about Enchantments*

AFTER A FEW DAYS, ELIZA FELL INTO A STEADY rhythm. Get up, shower, drive across town to her parents' house. Load her dad into Ron Weasley when necessary—at least *someone* wasn't ashamed to be seen with Ron—and ship him off to cardiac rehab. Come back to Herman & Herman to field phone calls (usually wrong numbers) and read library books or play solitaire behind the front desk until the office closed or it was time to drive back to the hospital to pick up her father.

Essentially, she was completely alone.

Elijah had landed in Greece two days ago and sent a

text every now and again to check in—so far just photos of him with famous Erosians who'd long since peaked. Eliza's favorites were the ones of him with Chuck Woolery and Boyz II Men.

Her mother stayed behind a closed office door, only coming out when absolutely necessary and always bringing a tornado of nervous energy with her.

And Jake had ceased to exist.

To be fair, he probably existed somewhere in the general Gold Lea area, but Eliza couldn't confirm that. He'd responded to her text about a new client meeting with an oh-so-expressive "okay" and nothing more. But that was probably for the best. It gave her time to let the awkwardness and disappointment she'd felt after the candy dish incident fade a little.

It still stung if she let herself think about it, so she didn't.

She definitely didn't think about how it would feel if those warm, brown eyes roved over her body. Or the way his dark stubble made him look just a little rough around the edges. Or how that tiny dip appeared above his left eyebrow when he was thinking hard about something—preferably her.

Nope, she hadn't thought about any of that at all.

At least, not in the last two minutes.

But she *had* thought about it the rest of the morning as she click-and-dragged cards to their respective suits, because today she'd have to face him. She had a potential new client appointment this afternoon, and he'd be there to make sure she didn't burn the place down during the meeting.

The bells above the door to Herman & Herman

rang, and Eliza jolted from her slumped position. She'd thought she still had half an hour of tortured daydreaming before he showed up.

"Hi, I... Oh." She slumped back in her chair as Herman & Herman's biggest competitor swaggered through the door: Vic Van Love. Rumor had it that he'd been born John Papadopolous but changed his name to something more accessible for his business. Eliza believed it too. Everything the man did—from the hokey television commercials to the highway billboards to the ten-foot-tall inflatable Cupid on his office roof—was in pursuit of another dollar.

"Well, well, well. The prodigal daughter returns." His voice was even sleazier than she remembered. Which was saying something, because on a scale of one to need-to-wash-your-hands-in-bleach, the Vic Van Love she remembered required a bathtub full of bleach.

"What do you want?" Eliza asked. She'd always hated Vic and his Cupid shop across town. He cut every corner, milked clients for every last dime, and stopped at nothing to get what he wanted. Which was always more money. Even if that meant dozens of people got their hearts broken in the meantime. And it seemed her rage had only intensified over the years.

"Since you asked, I've always wanted a pony. Maybe a princess party, where all my friends get sparkly nail polish—"

"And realize you're a misogynistic asshole, so they kick you in the balls?" Eliza asked. "That could be arranged."

"You've gotten feisty with age. What are you now, Eliza? Twenty-nine? Thirty?"

"Something like that."

"Right, right. A lady never reveals her true age." Vic lowered himself into one of the chairs and did an epic manspread. His long, skinny arms and legs seemed to take over the entire waiting area. His too-blond highlights reflected the fluorescent light, and his ill-fitting suit didn't do his midsection any favors.

Eliza lifted her chin. "What do you want, Vic?"

"I just happened to be in your neck of the woods and thought I'd swing by. Check in on my favorite little mom-and-pop shop." The condescension in his voice was thick—so thick Eliza wanted him to choke on it. "And as I was pulling in, I noticed there wasn't a single car in the client parking lot." His eyes widened in mock concern. "I hope everything's okay."

"Everything is fine," Eliza said.

"Is it though? Because the last I checked, it would take a pretty big crisis to bring *the* Eliza Herman out of hiding. One might even call it a *deficiency*."

Eliza's insides grew heavy, like her stomach had been coated in lead and filled with rocks. The rough, jagged kind. If anyone in Gold Lea hadn't known about Herman & Herman's financial issues before today, they would soon—thanks to the world's slimiest gossipmonger. "Business is fine," she lied.

"Well…"—Vic leaned forward on his knees—"tell your parents, if things get *too* hectic, I'm always available to take their few clients off their hands. Where is that father of yours anyhow? I have something he might be interested in."

If she were a true, upstanding citizen of the world—one of those when-they-go-low, we-go-high people she'd always admired—Eliza would have offered to take a message. But where Vic was concerned, she was a when-they-go-low, we-kick-them-in-the-balls-and-run type of girl. "I've told you a dozen times over the years, Vic. My dad can't enchant someone who isn't attracted to you. It's not his fault qualifying candidates are just *so rare*."

He straightened his jacket and stood as if completely unaffected, but Eliza could see the hint of annoyance in his eyes. "Fabulous," Vic said. "Let your dad know I stopped in, right?" And then he was gone, leaving a cloud of cheap aftershave behind him.

Eliza watched as he backed out of the drive in his shiny, red convertible—the stereotype of a midlife crisis if there ever was one—and sped toward downtown Gold Lea. A glance at the clock told her Jake would be here any minute, so she closed her pathetic game of solitaire and tried to shake off the film of disgust Vic's visit had left behind.

How had he known about the deficiency notice? What did he want to tell her father? Why—

No. She forced all three hundred and seventy-two of her questions into a tiny box in the back of her brain and sealed it shut. Jake would be here soon, and then her potential client. She needed to bring her A game—and some client fees—for Herman & Herman. The only way to do that was to be a calm, cool, and collected Cupid.

Fake it 'til you make it, and all that.

Eliza turned on the office radio and grabbed the file folder of blank intake forms she'd put together this morning. She'd just run through everything one more time, and—

"And now a word from our sponsors," the radio

announcer said. A cheesy jingle played through the speakers, followed by an all-too-familiar voice.

> If you're feeling the call of romance,
> Or maybe a tug in your pants,
> Don't be lovesick,
> Just call Vic!
> Cash payment due in advance.

She rolled her eyes. Many things had changed about the love business in the last ten years—including how to drum up clients, apparently—but Vic's sleaze level was not one of them. "What a dick," she muttered.

Apparently, the universe had it out for her today, because at that exact moment the office door opened, and Oliver-comma-Trevor stepped through the entry. "Excuse me?" he said.

"Oh, hi. Not you. The radio. I mean, sorry." She stepped around the receptionist's desk and stuck out her hand. "Agent Oliver, nice to see you again."

His clammy fingers hung loosely in her palm. "Ms. Herman, we've finished processing your application for a provisional license."

"Great."

"We've… Well…" He grimaced as he shifted his briefcase from hand to hand. "There's been a slight hiccup with your license."

Eliza had been around long enough to know that a "slight hiccup" with the Department of A.S.S. could be enough to derail someone's career for years. "Did I miss a piece of paperwork? Because I'm sure I can complete—"

"Ms. Herman, have a seat." He hoisted the briefcase onto the receptionist's desk between them and produced a file from inside. Its corners were dog-eared, and inside was a thick, messy rainbow of papers. Hand-printed letters on the edge of the folder read HERMAN, ELIZA.

She sat, and her throat went dry. The file had to be at least an inch thick.

"Ms. Herman—"

"Please, call me Eliza."

"Ms. Herman, last week when you completed your application, you indicated you'd previously obtained a provisional license."

She nodded.

"When this happens, we check the applicant's prior file to be sure there are no conflicts, complaints, or other issues. I checked our online database the day you came into the office and nothing was noted, so I issued your license. Unfortunately, a later review of our older paper files revealed a different story."

She stared at the thick file. There had to be at least a hundred pages there. A hundred pages documenting all the failures of her past licensing attempt. She sucked in a deep breath and sat up a little straighter. She wasn't a kid anymore. She was an adult now. She paid her own bills and kept her plants alive without any help. And less than a week ago, she'd performed an enchantment that hadn't ended in disaster. "Okay, and?"

"And after reviewing your prior file, we've decided you meet the requirements of Section 10.08 of the *CCR*." He plucked a sheet of paper from the front of the file and slid it across the desk.

Code of Cupid Regulations § 10.08
Borderline Approval
Any applicant who has either (1) a history of three or more enchantments that have resulted in hospitalization or a need for physician intervention, (2) received two or more complaints in any six-month period or more than five complaints in any consecutive twenty-four-month period, or (3) engaged in persistent and problematic behavior as defined in §10.00 *et seq.*, may be subject to additional licensing requirements, including but not limited to…

She slid the paper back across the desk. She didn't need to read any more to know where this was headed.

"Would you care to guess which section applies to you, Ms. Herman?"

Eliza didn't need to guess. She fit every one of those definitions—and probably a few new ones that hadn't been invented yet. "Is my license being revoked?" she asked.

"On the contrary, given your special circumstances, the Department is quite interested in making sure you succeed."

"What special circumstances?"

Agent Oliver cleared his throat. "Ms. Herman, your enchantment levels are well beyond those of most Cupids. The Department has a vested interest in making sure you are licensed and insured. Public safety is our top priority, after all. That's why I've been assigned directly to your case. Over the next several weeks, we'll work through the action plan I've created.

"Starting immediately, you must report all Cupid activities that involve client contact to me, preferably twenty-four hours in advance unless you have good cause to establish why you were unable to call me. I may also choose to drop in and observe those activities at any time. Once I'm satisfied that you have attained sufficient supervised hours, I will schedule you for your full licensing exam. However, said exam must take place no more than thirty days from the date your provisional license was issued."

"Wait. What? I don't understand." Eliza's brain couldn't keep up with his words. Not only did she have to do all enchantments under Jake's supervision, but she had to do them in front of this government bean counter too? He wasn't even a Descendant.

Probably.

She was pretty sure at least. But it wasn't like she could ask. With her luck, she'd say something stupid and blow the cover for all the other Descendants around the world.

"It's simply a matter of procedure," Agent Oliver said. "I'm sure you can agree that public safety must be our top concern in cases like yours."

"And you're going to choose the date of my exam?" She hadn't even planned on taking the exam. Once her dad was back on his feet, she'd be hitting the pavement in search of a real job again.

"Yes, sometime within the next month, after I've had time to observe you in the field. We want to be sure you aren't taking the exam too soon, but the thirty-day limit protects your rights by ensuring that we can't keep you from it for too long."

"Wow."

"Do you have any questions?"

Ha. Did she have any questions? She had dozens, but most were of the *Is it too early to drink?* variety. "No."

"Great." He pulled an unmarked envelope from the depths of his briefcase and handed it to her. "This is your provisional license. Please be sure to keep it with you at all times when working in an official Cupid capacity. You can shred the temporary copy you received at the Department."

Eliza clutched the envelope between her fingers and watched him stuff her File o' Shame back into his briefcase. "I have a potential client coming here in a few minutes. I obviously didn't know about"—she gestured toward his briefcase—"all of this twenty-four hours in advance."

He narrowed his close-set eyes and glanced at his watch. "Potential client?"

She nodded.

"I have another appointment. Otherwise I would stay. This one time, and this one time only, feel free to meet with him or her in the office to discuss your services, but I will need a full day's notice before you do any enchantments or take any other client meetings."

"Sure. Great." *Great?* It was anything but great. Man, why did this pencil pusher make her so nervous?

"Thank you for your time, Ms. Herman." He shook her hand one last time and made his way toward the door. The clang of the bells followed him out of the office, leaving Eliza alone with her anxiety…and the disembodied voice of Vic Van Love on the radio.

Have you fallen deeply in love
But get nervous approaching your dove?
Don't be stupid;
Hire a Cupid!
Because sometimes love needs a shove.

Chapter 8

Cupid Rules of Professional Conduct § 1.6. (a)
A Cupid shall not reveal information relating to the representation of a client unless the client gives informed consent, the disclosure is impliedly authorized in order to carry out the enchantment, or an exception applies.

By THE TIME THE BELLS ABOVE THE OFFICE DOOR RANG for a third time, Eliza had given up on the day. She sat with her head on the desk, willing the clock to tick faster. The sooner five o'clock came, the sooner she could untangle herself from this mess.

"Hello?" Jake asked. "Is anyone here?"

She didn't bother to look up. "No."

"That's weird. I was looking for this woman. About five-four? Brown hair, big, brown eyes? A little bit clumsy but a great laugh?"

"Ha, ha, ha." Eliza sat up. The weight of her ponytail had shifted to one side, and she suspected she had lines crisscrossing her cheek, but what did it matter? Jake had made it abundantly clear they weren't a match, so she might as well look as messy on the outside as she felt on the inside. "I'm five-five, thank you very much."

"There she is. Rough day?" He leaned against the far wall of the office, like he might need to make a break for it at any moment. She must have looked even worse than she'd thought. She took down her ponytail and ran her fingers along her scalp, trying to smooth her hair into something semiprofessional.

Jake's wince would have been noticeable from space. "That terrible, huh?" she asked.

"Huh? Oh. No. I just, uh, ate something bad for lunch."

If the shade of green in his cheeks was any indication, whatever he'd eaten must have been beyond horrible. "You okay?" she asked.

"I'll be fine."

"Good." Eliza finished fussing with her hair and shot him a grin. "Because I have had *a day*, and if you puke on my first new client, I will make you pay, Sanders."

He crossed his arms and raised an eyebrow. "I'd like to see you try." It was the sort of teasing confidence she would have found insanely attractive if she were letting herself be attracted to Jake.

Which she definitely was *not*.

"I know I look sweet and innocent, but I can scheme with the best of them," she said.

Jake's cocky grin made her insides flip. He opened his mouth in what she was certain would be a smart-ass retort, then closed it immediately, like he'd changed his mind. In the span of two seconds, he'd wiped his face of all expression. "So…rough day?"

"Something like that." *And your complete inability to see me as anything but a little sister isn't helping anything.* "Trevor Oliver stopped by today to bring me my license."

"That's good, right?"

"My *borderline approval* license." She held it

up—not that she wanted anyone to see it ever, but Jake would probably see the thing at some point, so she might as well get ahead of the story. In the photo, her eyes were half-closed and her mouth half-open. The harsh flash combined with the overhead lights in the Department had turned her skin a pasty white, and her nose cast a shadow on her upper lip. A shadow 'stache. And if that weren't bad enough, the Department had stamped the words BORDERLINE APPROVAL across the badge, just in case anyone dared think she was the least bit capable.

She launched into the whole thing about her "borderline approval" and "problematic behavior" and how the A.S.S. agent would be dropping in on her enchantments.

Finally, Jake took a bigger step forward. "Wow. That's, um…"

"Hideous."

He smirked. "I was going to say not your best photo."

She shoved the license into her back pocket and sprawled back in her chair. "That's the least of my problems right now. How am I going to do an enchantment in front of him? I barely made it through the Johansens' without a disaster, and that was the easiest case ever."

"You'll be fine, Eliza. You're not as bad at this as you think you are."

"You're right. I'm worse." She flopped her cheek back down against the desk. "I wasn't even going to take the full exam, and now it sounds like they can just spring it on me at any time."

"Eliza, look, I wouldn't be here doing this if I didn't believe in you. I'd bet any amount of money that you could go down to the Department right now and ace that test."

"*Any* amount of money?" She shot upright. "Because I will take that bet."

"Exactly, and that's your problem. You can do all of this." He gestured around the office. "Wooing the clients, performing the enchantments, filling out all the damn paperwork. You can do it better than most of us. But you've let your mom and all that stuff that happened when we were kids get too deep into your head."

She shifted uncomfortably under the intensity of his stare. "You don't understand…"

He shifted briefly from foot to foot as a flash of internal struggle passed over his features. Just as quickly, it fled, and he took a step closer. "Maybe I don't," he said. "But I think that there's something you don't understand, Eliza. You have something special. *You* are something special."

Her heart leapt into her throat and stayed there, cutting off her ability to breathe and to form words. *Too many feelings*, her brain screeched. *Abandon ship!* "You wouldn't say that if you'd ever seen me try to shoot with a bow and arrow."

He took another step closer. "We can go down to the Agora tomorrow and practice if you want."

"Really?"

"What kind of mentor would I be if I didn't take you out and let you practice maiming people?" He leaned over the desk now, oozing charm with a hint of mischief.

Gods damn it. Why did his smile make her feel so *fluttery* inside? If she didn't know better, she'd think she'd somehow managed to enchant herself that day at the

Johansens'. *No. This is just one of those stupid you-want-what-you-can't-have things. He's not attracted to you, so suddenly you're obsessed with him.*

He tucked a piece of her hair back into her ponytail, and his fingertips brushed the shell of her ear.

Oh no, oh no, ohnoohnoohno.

She was *feeling* things. Things she did not want to feel. Meanwhile, her traitorous nerve endings were throwing a freaking parade—trumpets, candy, giant balloons that said *MORE TOUCHING, PLEASE.*

Finally, she pulled herself together.

Sort of.

"You're going to regret offering to mentor me," she whispered.

His gaze shifted ever so slightly to her lips. "Doubt it," he said.

Clang, clang, clang.

"Hello? Eliza Herman?" A woman with waist-length red hair, dark sunglasses, and a beige trench coat stepped into the room. Apparently, Carmen Sandiego was right here in Gold Lea.

Eliza sat up and pretended she hadn't been on the verge of pulling Jake's lips to hers and seeing where decades of crushing on her best friend could go. "Hi," she said, offering the woman a handshake. "You must be Yolanda Durst."

The woman tightened her coat around her waist and looked around the mostly empty office. "I am," she whispered.

Eliza and Jake looked at each other, and she couldn't help but notice he'd gone paler than ever and had taken two giant steps toward the door. This had to be the weirdest case of food poisoning in existence. "Great," Eliza said. "I'm Eliza and this is Jake, who I mentioned on the phone. Would you like to follow us to the back?"

She led Yolanda to her brother's empty office and shut the door. Immediately, Yolanda relaxed. She pushed her glasses up onto the top of her head and unraveled herself from the long coat. Once she lost the half-hearted disguise, she looked more like Jessica Rabbit than Carmen Sandiego. This was not a woman anyone would suspect had difficulty finding a match.

Eliza glanced at Jake, trying to discern his reaction to this level of *va-va-voom*, but he stood at the edge of the room watching Eliza. Their eyes locked for a long moment before he looked down at his feet. What in the worlds was going on with him?

She turned back to Yolanda. "When we spoke on the phone, you said you were interested in entering your profile in our database?"

Yolanda nodded.

"Great." Eliza pulled out the folder she'd prepared and began going through the ins and outs of the package. Yolanda would pay a small fee, then provide a brief written profile and a photograph. Eliza would put it in the Herman & Herman flip-book. When new clients came in looking for a match, they could review the flip-book and choose someone listed there. Then Eliza would set up a meeting, collect full payment from each party, do the enchantment, and pray that no one ended up in the hospital.

Back when her parents had started the business, the flip-book package had sold like hotcakes. It gave some people the thrill of being chosen and others the power of being in charge. But now it felt old-fashioned and outdated, and the number of clients interested in the package had dwindled to almost none. But bringing in a client like Yolanda increased the chances that Eliza could collect two fees.

"Ms. Herman, this is a very delicate matter," Yolanda said when Eliza had finished her speech. "I need you to guarantee your firm will provide the utmost level of privacy and secrecy."

"Of course. Herman & Herman keeps all client files confidential, and we only release the bare minimum of personal information to the government for their record keeping. We also have a money-back guarantee, so if something goes wrong during your enchantment period, we'll happily return your fee."

Okay, maybe *happily* was a stretch, but sometimes a white lie (or three) didn't hurt.

"You misunderstand," Yolanda said. "What I'm asking for is more than your standard client confidentiality."

Eliza glanced at Jake again, but he merely shrugged. She turned back to Yolanda. "Go ahead."

"I want this to be a secret from everyone—including myself."

Eliza blinked twice, then three times, but she still felt lost in the desert. "I'm sorry, I don't think I understand," she said.

"My family is… Well, let's call them *religious*. They say this process is unnatural. If they ever found out I'd hired a Cupid, they'd disinherit me."

The pieces were beginning to slide into place. Ever since the first Cupids had gone public decades ago, some groups had protested. They called Cupids abominations and false idols and—Eliza's favorite—*lust mongers*. Yolanda must have come from the same stock, and by the looks of her sleek designer heels and diamond earrings, she had a lot to lose if her family disowned her.

"Ms. Durst," Eliza said. "I promise this isn't the first time we've dealt—"

"Please." Yolanda put a well-manicured hand on the desk. "You don't understand. I'm a terrible liar. If I hired you through the normal channels and met the love of my life, I'd never be able to keep it a secret. Then I'd end up heartbroken *and* poor. But if I don't know how I met the love of my life, then I can't exactly lie to my family, now can I? Maybe it was an enchantment, maybe it was the old-fashioned way." She sighed, going a bit starry-eyed, and Eliza could tell Yolanda would have preferred falling in love the "old-fashioned way."

Explaining that Cupids *were* the old-fashioned way seemed like a futile task. Cupids had been speeding things along with enchantments for thousands of years. Sure, people fell for one another all the time, and not all those matches involved enchantments. Sometimes, two people just clicked on their own, crossed their fingers, and made a go of it, although those cases had been dwindling in recent years.

"Ms. Durst, I'm not sure how that would work. It's certainly not part of our usual technique." Saying the words pained her because she wanted this to work so badly. "Even if I do the enchantment without your knowledge, I can't guarantee that your match wouldn't tell you."

"Find someone for me—a real gentleman—and explain my situation. If he's my true love, he'll respect my wishes. I'll pay double your fees. No, triple. And I'll pay them all up front, so I don't have to know about it. You can have twelve months. If I don't have a least one relationship during that time, I'll assume you couldn't find anyone for me and ask for a partial refund."

Eliza had to force her mouth shut. Triple fees. Now. Not three months from now, when someone else finally decided to stop in and look at the flip-books. She sized up Yolanda from head to toe. What was wrong with this woman? Why was she so desperate to make this work?

Yolanda sniffled and pulled a tissue from her very expensive handbag. "You must think I'm ridiculous."

Definitely. "No, not at all. This is just a very unusual situation." She gave Jake a serious *help me* look and stood. "Would you mind waiting here while I speak to my mentor?"

Eliza didn't wait for an answer before grabbing Jake by the forearm. His muscles tensed under her fingers, but she dragged him to the end of the hall anyway, as far from Yolanda's range of hearing as possible.

"Jake," she said in a harsh whisper, "what do I do?"

He stood so close that his warmth seeped into her skin, and she felt like one of those stupid moths that always congregated in front of her porch light. They lost their damn minds over that light, forgetting everything but getting as close to it as possible—even if it burned them.

"What do you *want* to do?" Jake asked.

Keep staring into your eyes. See what it feels like to lay my head against your chest. Put your hands on my waist, and see where we end up.

If she hadn't been watching him so closely, she would have missed the way his gaze flickered over her body.

For half a breath, her inner moth went mad, convincing itself that was lust in his eyes. Eliza swatted it away. Jake had agreed they were like siblings.

"Eliza?" he prodded. "Do you want to take the case?"

She took a deep breath. "Yes, I want to take this case. We need the money, and I don't see anything wrong with it, ethically speaking. She seems to know what she's getting into."

"Then take it. You know what you're doing." His gaze stayed locked on hers.

She stepped away and crossed her arms, trying to give her brain room to think about something other than how it would feel to be pressed against him. "I don't know what I'm doing. I've spent so long trying *not* to enchant people. Now I'm trying to do it on purpose, and everything feels upside down. Do you really think I can manage it without screwing up someone's life?"

"Hey." Jake put his hands on her upper arms. "It's my professional opinion, as your very knowledgeable mentor, that you can knock this case out of the park."

"Really?" she asked. "Because—"

His arms slid down hers, tugging gently at her elbows until she'd relaxed her standoffish position. "Really."

"But what if—"

"What if…" He took a step closer, close enough that she could see each of his thick, dark eyelashes in perfect detail. "What if this is the perfect case for you? What if you're this woman's best shot at happiness? What if this is the case that makes you realize how *amazing* you are at all of this? Eliza, give yourself a chance and stop talking yourself out of doing the things you want."

She froze there, inches away from the man she'd

lusted after since he'd reappeared in her life days ago. The man who knew all her childhood secrets. The man who knew *her*. Because she was absolutely talking herself out of the things she wanted most.

Including him.

Especially him.

Whoa. Too. Many. Feelings. Again. Too many thoughts. Everything inside her was firing at once. Her stomach replaced the moth with something more violent and demanding—a hundred hummingbirds perhaps. They flapped their tiny wings at a million beats per second and propelled her forward. Straight into that chest.

Up close and personal, it was even better than she'd imagined.

Which was saying a lot.

"I'm not." She whispered the lie.

"Me either," he whispered back. "Not anymore."

"Jake?" Her lips tingled as she said his name—a name she'd uttered thousands of times before. But today it felt entirely new.

"Yeah?"

"What do you want?"

He leaned down until their mouths were a finger-width apart. One tiny lift of her head could tilt her world right off its axis. Something was wrong here. *Very* wrong. And whatever it was, she wanted it. Badly. "You," he murmured. "It's always been you."

"Excuse me? Where is your restroom?" Yolanda stood in the hall. She looked like a kid at the movies— desperately in need of a toilet but not wanting to miss any of the good parts.

Oh gods. How long had she been standing there?

Eliza whirled away from Jake and did her best impression of a composed businesswoman. "Straight across the hall, the door on the left."

Yolanda scurried away, but not before shooting Eliza an approving glance and a big thumbs-up. As soon as the bathroom door closed, Eliza's facade fell. She turned to face Jake, careful to stand a socially acceptable distance away while her cheeks burned with shame.

Whatever spell had befallen her moments ago crumbled away.

"When I hit you, back at the Johansens'…" she whispered. She couldn't finish the sentence, because what if it was true? What if Jake *had* become enchanted with her? What if they had to spend the next hours, days, weeks working together *and* battling their respective crushes? She'd never be able to keep her mixed-up feelings under wraps if he kept looking at her *like that*.

"It was nothing." He didn't meet her gaze.

"Nothing? So if I stand in your personal space and flip my hair around until you're covered in my pheromones, *nothing* will happen?"

Jake's jaw went slack, but Eliza could see the struggle in his eyes. She took a step forward.

"Please don't," he said.

"You lied," she half whispered, half yelled. "You said we weren't a match. You said we were like siblings."

"*You* said that," he whisper yelled back.

She replayed her memory of that day. The afghan, the candy dish, the silent car ride home. Her attempt to ease the tension by letting him off the hook.

Shit. He was right.

The whir of a flushing toilet and squeal of her parents'

pipes filled the room. "Well, you didn't correct me" was all Eliza could think to say back before darting to the opposite side of the hallway.

Yolanda's head peeked out of the bathroom doorway, and she looked back and forth between them in confusion. "Would you like me to come back another day?" she asked. "Or I can try that guy from the television if you don't think you'll be able to help me. What's his name? Dick something or other?"

"Ms. Durst, I'd be happy to take your case." Eliza stepped closer to the office and wiped her sweaty palms against her pants. Maybe if she put enough distance between herself and Jake, her heart rate would return to almost normal. Her heartbreak on the other hand… "Why don't we get started on the paperwork?"

Yolanda clapped her hands together. "Oh, I'm so excited, but we have to make it quick. My weekly grocery delivery is going to arrive in an hour."

"I'm just going to head out," Jake said. "You've got this under control, right, Eliza?" He didn't give her a chance to respond before darting out the door.

Yolanda narrowed her eyes. "Is there a problem?"

Eliza stared at the empty space where Jake had stood, then forced her gaze back to her newest client. "No, ma'am. No problem at all. I'm more than happy to take your case."

What was one more white lie in the grand scheme of things?

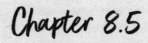

Chapter 8.5

"The Cupid Corps seeks to advance understanding of Erosians among non-Descendants and to mitigate the effects of war and economic hardship through Love. However, in fulfilling this mission, members are encouraged to keep personal relationships in 'the friend zone' for the duration of their services."
—*Cupid Corps Volunteer Manual*, 3d, TR.

THE WORLD'S WORST-KEPT SECRET IS OUT.

Thank the gods.

I mean, yeah, Eliza's reaction wasn't exactly the one I'd been hoping for. Or the one I'd lain in bed thinking about every night until two in the morning. And it *definitely* wasn't the one I'd imagined while I stood in the hot shower, thinking about rubbing soap all over Eliza's body. But she knows, and now we can deal with this like two mature adults.

In a few weeks, it will all be over. In a few months, we'll look back on this and laugh. In a few years, we'll ~~tell our children the story of how we fell in love~~ barely remember any of this. It's going to be fine, and now that Eliza knows, I can stop trying to keep secrets and free up some mental bandwidth for the important things in my life.

Not that Eliza is unimportant. Everything about her

is important. All these different pieces—some jagged, some smooth—fit together to make an absolutely perfect human being. Who else would face down their biggest fears to help out a parent? Who else would put up with Elijah's relentless teasing and then turn around to give it just as good as she took it? Who else could look so adorable while working from under an afghan?

No one except Eliza.

Wait. What was I say— Oh, right. The important things in my life. Like the Northern California branch of the Cosmic Council. It's the rational next step for me. The Cupids Corps was the first step. A great one. It changed everything for me. I traveled the world. Volunteered in areas where Cupids were in short supply. And a few where they weren't. Saw firsthand the way both love and Love can change the world.

Maybe being a Cupid isn't much, in the grand scheme of things, but it *is* one thing I can do. And the next thing I can do is join the local Cosmic Council. Then I'll work myself up the chain. Get Cupids back to having a vote—a voice. Set policies that help from the top down, so maybe one day the Cupids Corps can work itself out of business.

But to be honest, even though I know the Council is what I *need* to do, well… Have you ever walked up a set of stairs and suddenly lost the sense of where to put your feet? You skip over a stair without meaning to, and for a moment, your balance feels completely off-kilter?

Well, my entire life has felt off-kilter for the last couple of weeks.

It's probably just the enchantment. Spending so much time thinking about Eliza has turned my brain inside out or something. If I keep my eyes on the prize—the Council seat, not Eliza—and wait out the moon cycle, everything will go back to normal. The staircase will stop moving. My brain will turn right side out. And Eliza won't be the first thing I think about in the morning.

Or the last thing I think about before I fall asleep.

I'll think about my campaign, instead. My platform. Goals for my first year in office.

She won't even cross my mind. I definitely won't spend so many nights wondering if she's thinking of me. No more hours spent wondering about the secrets behind that warm smile. Far fewer moments wasted wondering how she'd feel curled up against me in bed.

She'd definitely fit perfectly. That hair brushing against my skin. Her laugh rumbling through my chest. The curve of her—

Wait. What was I saying again?

Yeah. The Council. That's my plan, and I'm sticking to it.

Chapter 9

> **Calif. CCR § 2085.11.010.2. (a)(7)** Persons engaged in Cupiding shall be expressly prohibited from employment in the fields of surgery, dentistry, martial arts, professional hockey, and bikini waxing.

IT HAD BEEN OVER A DECADE SINCE ELIZA HAD LAST set foot inside the Agora, but absolutely nothing had changed. It was still a bland, sprawling building at the edge of Gold Lea that looked like an everyday office complex—one people would expect to be full of bored workers typing reports and unjamming printers on a perpetual loop.

Inside, she knew, the Agora was anything but.

Eliza passed through the rotating doors and stood in the tiny lobby. To her right, a woman sat in an entrance booth not unlike a movie box office. She peered at Eliza over a pair of red cat-eye glasses. "ID?" she croaked.

Eliza pulled her provisional license from her back pocket and slid it under a small dip in the bulletproof glass. The Agora had been in this same spot for centuries, in one form or another, and they'd never had a problem with the building being detected by regular humans. But once the first Erosians went public fifty or so years ago, the other Descendants' paranoia had spiked. First, they'd stopped sharing all but the most basic information about their powers with Erosians. Then, they'd knocked down the old Agora and replaced it with this building, complete with all the latest security features, which they upgraded every few years.

To be fair, the paranoia wasn't without reason. Those first years, the public had rejected the existence of Cupids as some silly fantasy, probably fueled by hallucinogens and the sexual revolution. But once it became clear that Cupids were as real as the ground beneath their feet, people were *furious*. Protests sprang up. Televangelists spoke out against "unnatural love," as if Cupids hadn't been working behind the scenes of coupledom since the beginning of time.

Dozens and then hundreds of laws were passed, forbidding enchantments of all kinds. And when those were overturned, governments turned to regulating Cupids within an inch of their lives—as if they could keep their worldviews undisturbed by wrapping the Cupids in yards of red tape. Thus, the Department of Affection, Seduction, and Shellfish—shellfish were then wrongfully thought to be a powerful aphrodisiac and tool of Cupids (mostly false)—was born.

"Eliza Herman?" The woman leaned closer, and her breath fogged the glass.

"Yes." Eliza braced herself. The next question was probably something along the lines of *The same Eliza Herman who got banned from the Gold Lea Cinema after enchanting a whole line of people at the concession stand?* Like Eliza had purposefully tripped and dropped her box of Sno-Caps.

"My great-nephew said you were back in town. You've really grown up. I remember when you and your brother were knee-high tornados running around this place." The lines on the woman's face softened, making her look younger and brighter. All at once, a wave of memories washed over Eliza.

"Mrs. Washmoore?" Eliza asked.

"Indeed."

The old Fury in front of her had once been queen of this place—or she would have been, if the Agora had a queen. She knew how to lead a room and how to lay down the law when necessary. Back then, she'd led the Northern California Cosmic Council—the secret governing body comprised of representatives of each type of Descendant—and she'd wander the Agora, greeting the masses with a dazzling smile and a warm demeanor that made everyone feel welcome.

Everyone except the Cupids.

Eliza's father always said Rebecca Washmoore had never gotten over the fact that the Cupids had decided to go public without permission of the Cosmic Council. And everyone knew that Furies had a hard time letting go of grudges.

Now, she'd been relegated to glorified ticket taker, and most Cupids felt more welcome at the Agora. Marginally.

"How have you been?" Eliza asked.

Mrs. Washmoore's expression softened the smallest amount. "I've had more exciting days, but that's what retirement is about, I guess." The hard lines around her eyes returned as she scanned Eliza's ID, then slid it back under the opening in the glass. "Enjoy your visit."

The Fury pressed a button and descended—chair and all—to whatever lay below the booth. Eliza watched as a piece of metal slid over the opening in the floor, leaving her alone in the lobby.

That's new. A light above the double doors turned from red to green, and Eliza tucked her ID back into her pocket as she stepped into the building proper. The ceiling of the main hall stretched at least three stories high, and a fountain featuring Poseidon filled the room with the soothing sounds of running water. Hallways spurred off left and right, with gold-dusted signs pointing toward rooms like the Hephaestus Weaponry, Asclepius Clinic, and Demeter Greenhouse.

Two Muses crossed in front of Eliza, barely casting a glance in her direction. Their musical laughter tinkled behind them as they disappeared down a hallway to her left. She went right instead, letting her gaze wander as she made her way to the back stairwell. Her shoes clacked against the white marble floor, and she passed portrait after portrait of Descendants who'd been particularly important in the Agora's history. Paul Rudolph, the Prometheian architect who'd designed the most recent version of the Northern California Agora and had the foresight to know they'd need to keep the outside as plain and unappealing as possible. Winifred Bonfils, the Heliosian journalist who'd sent secret messages via the press to other Northern California Descendants about some of the most important events in history. And Ruth Bader Ginsburg, Athenian and first Descendant to sit on the United States Supreme Court. She'd once visited and donated enough money to fund a renovation to the library.

Which was exactly where Eliza had agreed to meet Jake.

After Yolanda had left the office yesterday, Eliza's phone had buzzed with a text.

Agora tomorrow to practice? I'll explain more about everything then. I promise to behave.

Her fingers had hovered indecisively over the screen for a solid thirty seconds. Her body begged her to demand he come back to the office, but her brain reminded her exactly how stupid that would be. First of all, he was her mentor. If Oliver-comma-Trevor got wind of this, he'd pull her provisional license for sure. Eliza wouldn't be able to help at Herman & Herman, and she'd let everyone down. The thought of telling her father what had happened, especially in his current state, made Eliza want to vomit.

And then what? She and Jake would have a couple of great make-out sessions before the enchantment wore off, he'd realize that being with Eliza was capital-T Trouble, and she'd end up curled under the covers with a bottle of Moscato—exactly the way her last two relationships had ended.

No, better to keep things strictly professional. Otherwise, she'd end up stuck with the only other non-relative Cupid in Gold Lea as her mentor: Vic Van Love.

Meet you at the library. 1:00? she wrote back. **We can set some ground rules to get through the next few weeks. If you still want to mentor me, I mean.**

Yes. Rules. Perfect, he responded.

As she got closer to the library, the floor changed from marble to squares of striped carpet. They absorbed her footfalls and led her down a narrow, poorly lit hall.

When she'd walked far enough that there wasn't another soul in sight, Eliza reached a tall door made of dark cherrywood. Beside it, a small sign told her this was the right place. Well, that and the bronze door knocker made to look like a certain Supreme Court justice. Eliza reached up and knocked twice with the collar around the knocker's neck.

The door swung open. Darkness snaked from the room, seeming to absorb the light in the hall. "Hello?" Eliza said. "Is the library open?"

The lights snapped on, bathing the circular walls in soft light. Bookshelves stretched from the floor to the edge of the high ceiling. Beside them, stacks of unshelved books sat piled on the floor. Specks of dust floated in the air, twirling toward the slender, curved windows that lined the back wall.

The entire place had the air of a grand, impressive ballroom that had been filled to the brim with books. And then left to collect dust.

Except for the sparkling glass display cases. One—Eliza knew from years of PSC class—held the Descendants' Scroll. A list of every known Descendant in the region, which was updated regularly with Hermesian magic and kept under tight lock and key.

The other case was more mundane. It held books and artifacts some librarian had put together for a Pinch of Prometheus display: a few human models made from clay, an eagle eating a liver, and a half dozen ancient, water-damaged books.

And in the center of it all sat Mrs. Washmoore, still in her chair and looking exactly as she had five minutes ago at the entry.

Eliza jumped. "I didn't... How did you..."

"Sorry about that, running a little behind. I had to stop at the little girls' room on my way."

Once Eliza's heart settled back into a normal rhythm, she smoothed her ponytail and stood up a little straighter. She had so many questions and no idea where to start. How did Mrs. Washmoore know she'd been headed to the library? How did she get inside without Eliza seeing her? And how did the old woman empty her bladder so fast?

Better to ease into it.

"How did you get here?" Eliza asked.

"Pneumatic tubes, of course. We realized there might be a need for staff to travel quickly through the building. Ever since"—she looked at Eliza over the rim of her glasses—"our *presence* was compromised, we've had to take extra precautions."

"I see." Eliza was not about to take the bait; she had enough on her mind today. "Are you the librarian too?"

"Of course." Mrs. Washmoore rearranged the pearls around her neck and gave Eliza a stern look. "Were you expecting someone else? A Metisian perhaps? I swear, no one appreciates—"

"No, no." Eliza did *not* want to insult Mrs. Washmoore. Invoking a Fury's...well, *fury* was a terrible idea indeed. "I meant that you do so much here. I was surprised, that's all."

"I do dabble in all the realms, I guess." She leaned back in her chair and adjusted her floral skirt. "But I swear, this place would fall apart without me."

"I believe that. You must work very hard, Mrs. Washmoore."

The woman didn't seem to notice Eliza's attempt at

sucking up. "Membership issues. Managing the weaponry. Unclogging the toilets. Running the library. Handling reservations for all the Cosmic Council meetings."

"Wow," Eliza said.

"Last week I even had to deliver a jug of Dionysus's best to those bozos on the Council. I'm eighty-nine years old. If I'm going to be a delivery girl, I should at least receive a tip."

Eliza took a step back. She could practically see the ends of Mrs. Washmoore's curls rattling with irritation. "You look great for your age" was all she could manage.

Mrs. Washmoore leaned forward conspiratorially. "Botox," she whispered. "Makes it a little harder to access my rage. But at my age, rage is so close to the surface that it's probably a good thing."

Eliza was learning a lot more than she'd bargained for, but none of this would help her study for her exam. "Interesting," she said, trying her best to sound genuine. "But I'm actually waiting for someone, and I'm sure you're very busy, so…"

"Jake said to tell you he's running about ten minutes late. I asked him to do a few errands for me on his way over."

Eliza couldn't contain her surprise. "Oh, okay. Thanks for letting me know."

"He's the one who told me you were back."

"*Jake* is your great-nephew?"

Mrs. Washmoore nodded. "Said he's helping you get your license. Are you going for a regular license or one of those advanced ones? I swear, I can't believe some of the things you Erosians—excuse me, *Cupids*—are doing these days. Advanced licenses." She shook her head.

"Does anyone really need to use plutonium to make a couple of people horny?"

"Well, it's more than that. There are a lot of moving parts…" Mrs. Washmoore did *not* look like she wanted a lecture on the finer points of enchantments—and since when had Eliza become a defender of the practice anyway? "I mean, I agree."

"Well, I don't say a word about it," Mrs. Washmoore said. "Not that anyone asks me. I keep my thoughts and my hands to myself."

Eliza stifled a grin. Mrs. Washmoore had said plenty about the subject in the last five minutes. Given another five, Eliza would bet the old woman would have a few more thoughts to share. "I'll just use one of the computers while I wait."

"Oh yes. Of course. The computers along the east side of the library are all connected to the Agora intranet. Just put your finger on the scanner to log on. We should still have you in the system from when you were a girl."

"Great. Thanks."

Mrs. Washmoore pointed a gnarled finger at a long, low table with three computers. "Make sure you don't search for any *naughty* things. The filters will catch you, and there's a whole lot of paperwork. Save that for Thursday nights between nine thirty and midnight."

So. Many. Questions. Did the library have a Descendants porn night? Was there classified porn that could only be viewed on the Agora intranet? Who was in it? And did she want to know?

She definitely wanted to know. "What happens on Thursdays?"

"Nereid Night at Dionysus." Mrs. Washmoore rolled

her eyes toward the heavens. "Half the Descendants in Northern California end up getting drunk on the seaweed martini special. Then they stumble down here and think they're so funny looking at dirty pictures. I got tired of trying to shoo them out every Thursday, so I made a rule. Thursdays between nine thirty and midnight, everyone can look at naked stuff. No kids allowed, obviously."

"Obviously," Eliza said.

"Great. I'll leave you to it then." Mrs. Washmoore pressed a button on the arm of her chair, and in seconds, she'd gone—sucked into a tube and shuttled off to whatever part of the Agora needed her next.

Eliza had barely scanned her fingerprint on the computer when the library door opened and she began rethinking that whole no-naked-stuff promise.

Jake stood in the doorway. Dark jeans hung low on his narrow hips, and his plain white T-shirt hugged all the right places. Places she'd memorized in those few seconds she'd been pressed against him the day before.

"Hey," he said.

She scrambled to stand and took a few steps backward. "Hi."

He gestured toward a long oak table, and she sat at one end. He sat along the other. At least ten feet separated the two of them. Plenty of space for propriety— and her sanity. "Thanks for meeting me," she said.

"Sorry I was late. Family stuff."

"No problem."

Silence.

Ugh. Why was everything so awkward? Well, no, she knew why everything was so awkward, but they were adults. They should be able to manage a conversation without making out on the library table. Not that she was thinking about making out with Jake on the library table. Like Mrs. Washmoore, Eliza was keeping her thoughts and hands to herself.

"Is anyone else here?" Jake asked.

Eliza shook her head. "Look, if you want to back out of this whole mentor thing, I understand. You didn't sign up for"—she gestured between them—"this."

He laughed, eyes sparkling. "You have no idea."

"But if you don't mind sticking around for a few more weeks, I think we can make it work. With my *problem*, I've been able to figure out a few tricks over the years." Her words came faster as she continued. "If we stay at least five or six feet apart at all times, it will be a lot easier for us—I mean, for you. And absolutely no touching. I'll invest in some extra-strength deodorant and smelly soaps to mask my pheromones. If you keep part of your mind occupied with other stuff when we're together, that will help too. Maybe try a fidget spinner, or one time I—"

"Eliza." He gave her an encouraging smile, while the rest of his expression rotated between concern and amusement. "You need to breathe."

She would have argued with him, but she was getting light-headed from a lack of oxygen, so instead, Eliza breathed.

"This isn't my first enchantment."

"It's not?" She was learning a lot about Jake today. A Fury for a great-aunt and now this?

"Things in the Cupid Corps were rough," he said. "Enchantments happened. Sometimes accidentally and other times less than accidentally."

She nodded, pretending she knew what he meant. "Of course."

"But you're absolutely right. The more physical distance we keep between us, the better things will be. And if you don't mind scented soaps—"

"I don't. It's fine."

"Thank the gods." He leaned back in the chair and closed his eyes. "Because yesterday, standing that close to you, I thought I might lose my cool."

Eliza's body temperature rose at least three degrees just thinking about *him* thinking about *her*. She cleared her throat. "Don't want anyone to overheat on my watch."

"Definitely not." His gaze locked on hers. Eliza's skin flashed even hotter, and she slipped off her cardigan, doing her best to not notice the way Jake watched her move.

"Should we get started then?" she asked.

"Yep. Great idea. Let's go." He nodded toward the door.

"Where are we going?"

"The range. You said you wanted to practice maiming people, right?"

"Well, I thought I could check out some books about it first, or—"

"Eliza." He gave her that look again, the one that said, *You're going off the rails, Herman*.

She sighed. He was right. If reading books about being a better Cupid was useful, she would have improved her skills long ago. Still, she grabbed a copy of *Trouble Shooting for the Modern Eros* from a nearby stack. "I'll just check out this one."

Jake took a step forward, like he was going to pluck the dusty, old book from her hands. Eliza shot him a warning look, and he fell back just as quickly, dropping his arms to his sides. "That book is at least fifty years old," he said.

"How do you know?"

"Because that's when the Agora library stopped ordering new books for the Erosian Interests section."

Eliza remembered Mrs. Washmoore's clear disdain for Cupids. "Oh."

"If you really want some books, I have some at my apartment. We can stop by after—" He cut himself short. "I'll drop them off at the office for you."

She dropped the book back on the stack. "Thanks."

"After you," he said.

Eliza gave him a wide berth as she slipped out of the library, and a few seconds later, he stepped out behind her as if everything between them was completely normal. Clearly, these rules were going to work perfectly for him.

Too bad Eliza couldn't say the same.

>>>————————>

"Bows and arrows?" Eliza looked from Jake—who stood three feet away, of course—to the man behind the counter of Hephaestus Weaponry. "Isn't that a little on the nose?"

The man barely looked up from his phone, which blared some kind of circus-style music as he swiped quickly across the screen. "We've also got knives, darts, throwing stars, twin katana, bō, sai, and nunchaku."

"So you can pretend to be one of the Ninja Turtles," Jake said, "or you can practice with the one weapon you know will be on the exam."

"I'll take the sai, please."

Jake crossed his arms. "Eliza."

"Wait, let me guess. You were always more of a Michelangelo fan. That makes sense." She turned toward the counter. "I'd like the nunchucks."

"We'll take two bows and two quivers, please," Jake said.

The guy at the counter finally put down his phone. The music kept playing, and a series of white ovals danced across the screen. "Nunchucks, two bows, and two quivers?"

Eliza sighed. She couldn't avoid this any longer. Time to face her longtime nemesis: the bow and arrow. "Just the bows and quivers."

"Cupids, man," the guy muttered before shoving their equipment toward them. "Have them back in an hour or there's a late fee." Without another word, he picked up his phone and went back to his game.

"He's definitely a Raphael," Eliza whispered as she passed by Jake. He inhaled sharply, like she'd punched him in the gut. She darted away. "Crap, sorry."

He closed his eyes. "Just go."

She went.

Her shoes squeaked on the floor of the empty gymnasium, where practice dummies stood at varied intervals across the room. She dropped her things near the closest dummy and looked it straight in the eye. Or rather, where its eyes *would* have been if they hadn't been gouged out by weapons long ago. "I apologize in advance for what I'm about to do," she said under her breath.

"You ready?" Jake called from across the room. He nocked an arrow, raised his bow, took aim, and let go. The arrow flew straight and sure, just barely piercing the dummy's skin before clanking to the floor. It would have made the perfect enchantment.

If enchanting with a bow and arrow were an Olympic sport (which, side note, it had secretly been in the first three Olympic games), Jake would have won the gold. His skills were going to make her look like a toddler throwing knives. "Um, I need a minute," she said.

Years ago, her father had taught her how to shoot. Well, he'd *tried* to teach her. Spoiler alert: It had not gone well. She'd left the building with a black eye, a broken bowstring, and a marriage proposal.

"You good?" Jake asked.

"Maybe we should come back and try this another day." She glanced around the empty room, grasping for any plausible excuse. "When it's not as busy."

He cocked an eyebrow. "Not as busy? We're the only ones here."

"Trust me, it's for your own good."

The corners of his eyes crinkled in amusement. "Give it a shot so we can see where you're at. No judgment, I promise."

Eliza contemplated her options: pull the fire alarm and make a break for it, lie on the floor and play dead, or pick up the damn bow and get it over with. "You're going to regret this."

She grabbed the bow and one of the arrows. Her sweaty fingers made holding on to the whole thing harder than it needed to be, and all she could think about was the last time she'd come to the Agora for target practice.

"No judgment?" she asked Jake as she raised the bow to chest height, nocked the arrow, and said a prayer.

"Definitely no judgment, but maybe you should open your eyes."

"Fine." She'd squeezed them shut instinctively—to protect both her vision and her pride. If she didn't see how horribly this went, it wouldn't hurt as bad. She forced her eyes open and let the arrow fly.

It made it halfway to the dummy—the wrong dummy—before clattering to the ground.

Jake opened his mouth as if to say something, then closed it again.

Eliza hung her head. "That was actually pretty good for me. The arrow ended up in the dummy's general direction, no one died…"

"Stop. You're going to be fine. Let's try again."

She sighed and picked up another arrow. "You're going to want to back up," she said. "Assuming you want to keep all your appendages."

"I'm sure my *appendages* will be fine." But still, he took a step back. "Square up your stance."

"What?" Gods, she wished he didn't have to witness her shame.

"You've got your front foot pointed toward the target. Turn it straight out, like this." He demonstrated from his position a safe distance away.

She moved her foot, pulled back the arrow, and tried again. This time she got closer to her target. By approximately three inches.

"We're getting there," he said. "Slowly. Now don't squeeze the grip so tightly. You look like you're trying to strangle it."

"Maybe I am," Eliza said.

"You're not."

She let the weapon fall to her side. "Okay, but if I were, hypothetically—"

"Herman," he growled. "I see what you're doing."

"Asking perfectly reasonable questions about arrow strangulation techniques?"

"Take your stance."

She sighed, as amused as she was put out by his no-nonsense attitude, and lifted the bow again. Was her foot supposed to point at the target or away? Elbow at her ear or shoulder?

Jake pressed a thumb to the space between his brows and sighed. "I'm going to break some rules right now."

"What rules?"

"*Our* rules. The ones we just made. But I swear it's only because I don't see another way."

"Jeez, way to make a girl feel wanted," she muttered. Ugh, why did this place turn her right back into a surly teenager?

"What?"

"Nothing. Come on, break the rules. Let's get this over with."

But the second Jake stepped up behind her, pressed his chest to her back, and wrapped his arms over hers, Eliza realized she did *not* want to get this over with. At all. Ever. Maybe she'd live here in the Agora, shooting arrows and snuggling into Jake, for the rest of her life. She'd spend all her days buried in his warmth while his fingertips slid over her skin. They'd be completely insulated from the rest of the world raging on around them. It would be pure, unadulterated perfection.

"Earth to Eliza."

"Huh? Oh, right. Sorry." She felt him take a deep breath against her back. *Gods. Best target practice ever.*

"Square up." He nudged her left foot over with his, and his inner thigh brushed her hip. Eliza's whole body crackled with electricity.

"Relax wrist." His words whizzed by, but Eliza barely noticed. All she could think about was the trail of warmth his fingertips left along her arm.

"Relaxed," she murmured.

He adjusted her arm. "Elbow level."

What was his deal? Had he lost the ability to speak in full sentences? This whole caveman-archer schtick was really harshing her mellow. She glanced over her shoulder. "Are you...holding your breath?"

Jake's face was red from the effort. He nodded. "Hair. Pheromones."

Guilt washed over her. Here she'd been relishing every little touch, while poor Jake did his best to actually follow the rules. The rules *she'd* insisted on. She stepped away and let the bow fall to her side. "Why don't we take a break?"

At that moment, Jake's phone rang, and the sound echoed off the gymnasium walls. "Yeah, uh, great idea," he said. "I'll be right back."

She gathered up her arrows, shook out her tired arms, and glared at the dummies. Their blank expressions mocked her. Maybe it was time to try again. Alone. Without anyone to witness her incompetence.

She raised her bow, ready to make those dummies pay. *Square stance. Loose grip. You've got this, Eliza.* But no sooner had she nocked an arrow than the gymnasium door opened. "How tight should I squeeze it?" she asked without taking her eyes off the target. "If I don't do it hard enough, everything goes sort of limp, but—"

"That's what she said."

Eliza tensed. She'd know that voice anywhere. It had been haunting her nonstop for the past week. First in the radio commercials, then in the office. Now here at the Agora. She let the bow fall to her side. "Hello, Vic."

"I have to say, I'm surprised to see you still around." Vic pulled his own bow and arrow from a customized case with—of course—his face plastered across the front. "I thought you would have given up by now."

"What do you want?"

"What do *I* want?" Mock hurt filled his voice. "What do you mean? I'm here for the same reason as you."

To prove to yourself and everyone you love that you're not a total failure? Doubtful.

Eliza lifted her bow, set her jaw, and pulled back on the arrow. Her hands shook—out of annoyance or self-consciousness, she wasn't sure which—and the arrow skewed sideways, landing on the floor five feet from the nearest dummy.

Vic smirked, nocked an arrow, raised his bow, and without looking at the targets, let his arrow fly. It nicked the dummy in the groin before landing softly on the ground. "Since we're both here," he drawled, looking all too satisfied with himself, "we should talk."

She was very, *very* tempted to aim a real arrow straight at his smug face, but the last thing she needed was to get the Department on her back about something else. Like manslaughter. "About what?"

He let another arrow fly, this one straight to the poor dummy's gut. "You should come work for me."

She nearly dropped her bow to the floor. "Excuse me?"

"Come work for me."

"Why in the world would I do that?"

"Let us count the ways, shall we?" He let an arrow fly, and it headed straight for the dummy's head. "One"—*thwack*—"your parents' business model is outdated and floundering. I'd be surprised if they don't go out of business before you get your license." Another arrow, aimed straight for the dummy's eyes. "Two"—*thwack*—"big changes in tech are coming. I've been working with a Tokyo-based firm to stay on the cutting edge, and I'm poised to make a *lot* of money. You would be too. Three"—*thwack*—"a certain subset of my clientele would really love working with a pretty, young Cupid."

Her rage intensified with every one of Vic's words. By the time he'd accentuated his last point with another perfectly placed arrow to the dummy's mouth, Eliza had to restrain herself from transferring each one of those arrows to Vic's balls. Sure, there was some truth buried in his comments—her parents' business *was* old-fashioned, and she was certain a few extra-special creeps would get their jollies off by sexually harassing a female Cupid.

But the old-fashioned mom-and-pop Cupid shop was part of what made her parents' business so important to her. And, unlike Vic, they prioritized quality matches over making the most money possible. That had to count for something. Not to mention she was not about to willingly step into Vic's maze of misogyny. He'd probably make a female Cupid dress in a negligee and recite "sexy" limericks in all his horrible commercials.

"Wow. What a great offer. Unfortunately, I'd rather gouge out my ovaries with a rusty spoon."

He shrugged. "Your loss, kid."

He turned and began packing his bow away, and for one beautiful moment, Eliza thought he was going to leave her alone. But then he was back. His hands clasped hers as he made her lift her bow. Eliza froze, and he took the opportunity to force her hands into the movements. The arrow flew from her bow and nailed the dummy straight in the heart.

"Let me know if you change your mind," he whispered.

"Eliza?" Tension ran through Jake's voice. "Everything okay?"

No, everything was not okay. Eliza wanted to stomp Vic's insole and follow that with a kick to the groin, but that would risk an enchantment. "I will be once this creep leaves me alone."

Vic took a step back and smiled at her. *Call me,* he mouthed.

"Get lost, Vic." Jake came between them—barely in the safe zone—his arms crossed and anger lighting his eyes. "Now."

"Relax, kid. You're wasting your time. She's hopeless." Vic slung his bag over his shoulder, and five seconds later, the door slammed shut behind him.

A beat of silence passed while Eliza tried to tamp down the anger rumbling inside her. How dare Vic say those things to her? How dare he touch her without her permission? And, worst of all, how dare he dismiss her abilities as if she wasn't standing right there?

"Eliza?"

"I'm fine." She wasn't hopeless. Or a failure.

"He's an idiot."

"I know." Hot tears gathered at the corners of her eyes. She stared at the ceiling, trying to force her tears back where they belonged. When she lowered her eyes, Jake stood less than a foot away.

"Jake, if you don't want—"

He hooked a finger under her chin and lifted her gaze to meet his. "I'm fine. Now listen to me. Please."

She started to protest, but the words wouldn't come. She nodded instead.

"You are not hopeless. Vic Van Love cares about one thing: his business. You threaten that, so he's trying to get under your skin."

"How am *I* a threat?"

"You're the strongest Cupid anyone has seen in decades. Once you get better at controlling your enchantments, you're going to put us *all* out of business. Why would anyone pay a Cupid to draw blood when you can gently tap them and have the same effect?"

"No—"

"Yes," he insisted. "Why do you think I got so good at arrows, Eliza? I have to be, because I'm not half as strong as you. My last enchantment for the Corps involved more blood than anyone should have to lose, and it barely worked. But you show up here, drop a candy dish on my foot, and I'm a goner."

His words were like a balm. Vic's condescending, smug face fled her mind. In its place, something much brighter blossomed inside her. "Thank you," she whispered.

"You're welcome."

She looked up into his kind, dark eyes. If it were socially acceptable, she'd stare at them for the next hundred years. "Also, I bet he doesn't know as much about Ninja Turtles as I do."

Jake's lips pulled into a wide smile. "No one knows as much about Ninja Turtles as you do."

"Fair." She couldn't stop staring at that grin. She didn't *want* to stop staring at that grin.

"Now, if it's okay with you, I'm going to break the rules again and give you a hug. A totally platonic hug. Like friends do when one of them is sad."

Eliza smiled up at him. "It hasn't even been an hour, Sanders, and you're already asking to break the rules a second time?"

He held up his hands in surrender. "If you don't want—"

"I do want." Eliza wrapped her arms around his waist and buried her face against his chest. His embrace was warm and wonderful and breathlessly good. And she couldn't help but wish it was anything but platonic.

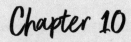

Chapter 10

"When you've lived inside the Cult of Cupid, like I did, the conspiracies between the CIA and the Cupidistas become obvious. The moon landing, Weinergate, McRib seasonal availability. The connections could not be clearer."

—"About" section, the *Cupid Cabal*

RON WEASLEY KICKED AND SPUTTERED, LIKE HE was a bucking bronco instead of a 2004 Ford Mustang. Eliza gripped the steering wheel a little tighter and glanced over at her father. "It'll be fine. Ron does this sometimes. Things will smooth out in a minute."

But within the span of two minutes, the racket had become intolerable, and a wisp of gray smoke trailed out from the hood. Eliza yanked the car over to the side of the road and killed the engine. "I'll be right back."

She popped the hood and got out of the car. Sometimes, Ron just needed the patented jiggle, jiggle, tap—a quick series of bumps and flicks to a few important wires—to get him reenergized. Eliza had no clue why it worked, but it did. Almost every time. Hopefully, today would be no different.

Two jiggles and a tap later, she slammed the hood shut and hopped back inside.

"Sorry about that," she said to her father as she turned the key.

And "IIIIIIIIIIIIIII eye IIIIIIII will always love yoooooooou," Dolly Parton crooned through the speakers.

Her dad clung to his seat belt. "Liza, I know you love this car, but maybe it's time for an upgrade. You could even get a newer Mustang. Have you seen those? They made them look more like the old ones."

"They don't make them in this shade of orange anymore. Besides"—she patted the dash just as Ron stopped, then started up again—"Ron and I have been through a lot together." Also, since she was working for free for her parents, she couldn't exactly afford a new car. But she wasn't going to tell her father that, especially not since she'd told her parents that her actual job had given her family medical leave.

Depending on how one looked at it, that wasn't a complete lie. They'd just given her the leave before her father got sick. And it was going to continue for a while afterward.

Okay, it was utter bullshit, but she didn't want her parents to feel like they had to pay her. Things at Herman & Herman were beyond tight, and her dad was still under a strict no-stress rule from his cardiologist.

"How many visits do you have left?" she asked once they were back on the road.

"Getting tired of chauffeuring your old man to cardiac rehab all the time?"

"Actually," she said, "I kind of like it. Gives us a chance to catch up without Mom breathing down my neck about the office or my license."

"Your mother means well, Liza. She's just had a lot to deal with lately."

"So how many visits?" She steered Ron toward the hospital and the conversation away from her mother.

"At least four, maybe more. The doctor says it depends on how I do on my walk test next week."

"Is it like a sobriety test? Do you also have to touch your nose and say the alphabet backward?"

He gave her a small smile as they pulled into the parking lot. "Yes, that's exactly it. And speaking of tests…"

She pulled into the patient drop-off zone and threw on her hazard lights. Well, *light*. Ron had blinked one out last week. "Yes?"

"Liza, pull into a real parking spot for a minute."

"Dad, you're going to be late."

"I've got plenty of time."

Despite Ron's unruly protests, Eliza pulled into a parking spot in the front row. The morning sun shone directly into the car, and she opened the window to let in the breeze. A few trees swayed in front of the looming building, and men and women dressed in scrubs came in and went out through a side entrance. "What's up?" she asked.

"How's your mentorship going?"

Talk about a loaded question. Should she start with the accidental enchantment? Or maybe she should talk about the last time she'd seen Jake, when they'd stood in the middle of the target range and hugged for almost a full minute. She'd finally pried herself away from his broad chest and warm arms, but it was one of the hardest things she'd ever done. "Fine. It's going fine."

"How are things with Jake?" Tim Herman, cutting to the chase since 1964.

"Fine, why?"

"Are you sure?"

"Yes, Dad. I'm sure. Why?"

He shook his head, and a tendril of gray hair fell across his face. He'd had a few gray hairs for years now, but in the last few months they'd really begun to take over. "He always had such a big crush on you when you were kids. I was worried he had ulterior motives. I know he's a good guy, but the Department takes the mentorship thing very seriously."

"Wait. What?" She gripped the steering wheel as though Ron had tried to throw her off.

"Last year in Seattle, two Cupids—a mentor and a provisional licensee—had their licenses revoked for inappropriate relations. *West Coast Cupid* magazine had a whole write-up in the July—"

"No. Not that. What do you mean he had a crush on me?"

"Oh, come on, Liza. You really think he spent all those nights at our house because he wanted to study for PSC tests?"

Eliza waved him off. "Probably. He was always a real brainiac."

"No one is that much of a nerd, not even Jake. He had a crush on you."

"I don't think so, Dad," Eliza said.

"Well, I'm glad it's going okay. Jake's always been ambitious, and this will be a good résumé builder for his Cosmic Council application, even if you don't get your full license. The gods know we need someone better to represent the Erosians around here than Vic Van Love."

"Jake's applying for the Cosmic Council?" While the Department of Affection, Seduction, and Shellfish made official government regulations that applied to the business of Cupiding, the Cosmic Council secretly made decisions on behalf of *all* Descendants. Including those Descendants the human government didn't know existed—which were, to date, all of them except Cupids.

Once upon a time, her mother had been on the Northern California branch of the Cosmic Council. She'd come home from the monthly meetings with frazzled hair and pour herself three fingers worth of whiskey. When ten-year-old Eliza had asked what they talked about at the meetings, her mother's response was always something about hot air and wishful thinking. As soon as her mother's Council appointment was up, she'd stepped away and never looked back.

"He didn't mention that?" her father asked.

Eliza shook her head. "We've been pretty busy. You know, studying." *And trying not to kiss.*

Her father's face lit up. "Studying? Does that mean you're going to take the exam? I've always said you can do anything you want to do, Eliza, as long as you put your heart into it. But I'd be lying if I said I didn't hope you'd join Herman & Herman officially."

"Well…" She had two choices: explain the "borderline approval" situation and how she might be forced into taking the test at any time…or don't. "I'm thinking about it. No promises, okay?"

"I won't get my hopes up."

But Eliza could see his hopes had already soared to new and terrifying heights. His cheeks had pinkened a smidge, and the hard lines around his eyes had softened. It was the best he'd looked in weeks, maybe even months. "You better get out there, or you're going to be late," she said.

Her father kissed her on the forehead and got out of the car. Eliza watched him as he walked, and she could swear she saw a bounce in his step as he headed into the hospital.

Gods damn it. One way or another, she was going to have to pass that test.

>>>————▶

Three miles from home, Ron started protesting again. The thermostat climbed a little higher with each block, and the gentle thumping under the hood became a bone-rattling shake.

"Come on," Eliza pleaded. "Just a little bit farther. You were the unsung hero of Hogwarts. Certainly you can make it back to the house."

Ron must have gotten pissed at the mention of his "unsung" status, because he sputtered to a halt right then and there. Eliza steered the dead car into the parking lot of Lizzie's Five and Dime, where she came to a stop in front of the ten-foot cherub statue.

And no amount of taps or jiggles got Ron going again.

"Fantastic." Eliza reached into her purse and pulled out her phone. She needed to be back at Herman & Herman in an hour to sit at the front desk. If the past was any indication, Ron would want to rest at least that long.

Elijah, her usual source for car-related assistance, was still in Athens. Her father was obviously indisposed, and even if he wasn't in the middle of his cardiac rehab program, she wouldn't feel right asking him to bail her out in his condition. Her mom could probably help, but she'd spend the whole ride home complaining about how Eliza had thrown off her entire schedule.

Instead, Eliza pulled up her messages with Jake and—against all her better judgment—began to type.

How do you feel about pancakes?

Three little dots appeared in the bottom of the window.

Better than waffles, not as good as French toast.

Luckily, no one was around to see her stupid grin.

To be specific: how do you feel about me buying you pancakes in exchange for a ride back to my house? Ron is being difficult.

She waited. The bubbles didn't appear. She checked her email. The bubbles didn't appear. She opened her favorite hate-read blog, the *Cupid Cabal*, and scrolled for new entries. She'd give Jake five minutes to respond, and if he didn't, she'd rescind her invitation and start walking.

Cupids were strictly forbidden, by both the Department and the Cosmic Council, from sharing more than very basic information about their craft with the general public, but that didn't stop everyday folks from creating website upon website with ideas, theories, and intricate diagrams of how they believed love enchantments worked. Most of the ideas were bad, the theories worse, and the diagrams illegible. The author of the *Cupid Cabal* claimed to have "lived underground in the Cult of Cupids" for a year, pretending to be a Wingless somewhere near Baltimore.

Mostly, his ramblings sounded like the work of a fan-fiction writer who'd tried to mash *The Wire* with *Bulfinch's Mythology*, but occasionally he had some decent insights. Enough to make Eliza believe the guy knew at least a few Erosians. Today's entry, titled "Uncovered: The End of Natural Love," rambled on and on and *on* about how "well-trained Cupid operatives" were working with the government and the mainstream media to put an end to any relationships that didn't begin and end with Cupid involvement.

Eliza was just about to get into his account of some "underground recognizance" when her phone vibrated.

Sorry, had to get out of a meeting. Where are you?

Lizzie's. I'm the girl in the orange car parked in front of the giant Cupid statue.

Three perfect little bubbles appeared.

Be there in 5.

She was typing out her thanks when the phone vibrated again.

You have no job, Herman. French toast is on me.

Gods be damned, she couldn't stop smiling.

⟶

By the time they were sitting across from each other in the packed Lakehouse Café, home of Gold Lea's best breakfast, Eliza's smile had long since faded.

"I'm sorry. I wasn't thinking," she said. "I just hopped in the car this morning to drop off my dad. I didn't have time to shower." Or put on deodorant. She'd arguably managed to "brush her teeth," but only if your definition of adequate dental hygiene was gargling a Listerine sample chased by a stale piece of Big Red.

"It's fine." Jake stared a little too hard at the menu, especially since they'd already ordered.

"This is definitely less than five feet apart," she whispered. "Maybe I can ask for a table instead of a booth? One of us on each end."

"Eliza."

"Sorry."

He glanced up at her. When their eyes met, heat flickered there before he looked back down at the list of breakfast options. "I'm not an animal. I can control myself."

"I know. That's not what I meant. I was just trying to make this a little easier for you."

"Have you ever been enchanted?" he asked.

She shook her head. Not that she'd ever want to be enchanted anyway. She'd seen people do a lot of stupid things because of infatuation, and it never ended well. Eliza did enough stupid things on her own. She didn't need to add another hazard to the mix.

"You've never been curious?" he asked.

"Curious, sure. I mean, back in middle school, I had a whole plan to head to LA one weekend, hunt down Leonardo DiCaprio, and enact a double enchantment that would make me Mrs. DiCaprio in under a month, but…" She shrugged.

"Seriously."

"My crush was *very* serious." She wasn't about to tell him about her other very relevant crush during those years. The one on a friend whose name rhymed with Snake Ganders.

"Yeah, yeah. I remember you watching that old version of *Romeo and Juliet* a hundred times. You were obsessed."

"Please, like you didn't have three Jennifer Garner posters hanging in your room."

His eyes locked on Eliza's. "I've always had a thing for girls with dimples."

Eliza smiled, inadvertently flashing the dimple in her left cheek. She wondered—not for the first time—if she'd been enchanted and didn't know it. Because that was the only good explanation for the way his attentive look made her feel.

"Anyway," she said. "With my, um, issues, it's never seemed like a good idea."

"It's like this," he said. "When you're enchanted, you *can* control yourself. You're not a zombie. It's not an excuse to do or say anything you wouldn't normally. But if you're already a jerk, that's going to be intensified, because suddenly being around the other person becomes the most exciting thing in your life. At least, you think it is. It's all you want, and you'll go to the ends of the earth to make it happen."

Eliza's heart did a back handspring. Or a double back tuck. Or whatever it was her gymnastics coach had tried to teach her before she'd fallen off the balance beam and enchanted him. He'd run off with one of her teammate's fathers. "Being around me is the most exciting thing in your life?"

He nodded, slowly and steadily. "Don't let it go to your head, Herman."

She fanned herself like a faux southern belle. "Who, *me*?"

Jake tensed. "Please don't do that."

"Oh. Right." She shoved her hands into her lap. "The pheromones."

The waitress brought their breakfasts. Identical stacks of French toast with bacon and eggs on the side. The smell of melting butter, bacon, and maple syrup overwhelmed them, and Jake visibly relaxed.

"This is better, right?" Eliza asked before shoving a piece of bacon in her mouth. "The smells and stuff."

"Much."

They ate in peaceful silence for a moment before Eliza opened her big mouth. "My dad says you're running for the Cosmic Council."

"I'm weighing my options." He stuffed a bite of French toast into his mouth.

Clearly a topic he wanted to discuss in detail. "What's that mean?" she asked.

Jake's lips turned up in what appeared to be amusement. Suddenly, Eliza was delighted at her own nosiness. "I'm technically done with my time in the Corps," he said, "but they'd like me to sign up for another tour."

"Where would you go?" Eliza couldn't picture him anywhere but here in front of her, with a tiny dash of powdered sugar in the bow of his lips.

"I don't know. I'm one of the most experienced Corps members by now, so probably somewhere tough."

"And you don't want to go back?"

"Not right now."

Eliza took another bite of bacon. "What *do* you want to do right now?" she asked. He met her gaze, and it sent a hot flush up her neck. "I mean, besides, you know…"

He laughed.

"What?" she asked, but she laughed along with him. How could she not, with sweet, deep laughter like his?

"Eliza, it's fine." He leaned across the table conspiratorially. "Let's just acknowledge it. Yes, if I didn't think it would ruin both our lives, I would have ordered this food to go, taken you back to my apartment, and tried to convince you to let it get cold."

"What? Why would you… *Oh*." That flush that had previously been creeping up her neck? It made a complete U-turn and barreled due south—way above the speed limit.

"But it would fuck everything up for you," he said. "And yes, if I decide to run for the Cosmic Council, it wouldn't look good for me either. But I'm a grown man who can manage my hormones and feelings. I promise."

Eliza jammed a bite of eggs into her mouth so she'd have time to think. Sure, he could manage himself like a grown-up, but Eliza felt less in control than ever. "You *are* considering the Cosmic Council thing then?"

He nodded. "Would you also like my five-year plan and ultimate life goals?"

"Yes, now that you mention it. I'd love to know where *the* Jake Sanders expects to be in five years." She leaned back in the booth and forced her shoulders to relax. This— the nosy questions and witty banter—*this* she could do. The talk about feelings and desires, not so much.

"In a perfect world, I'd be working my way up through the Cosmic Council. First through the Northern California branch. Then the Western Division. And hopefully to the North American Division."

She wrinkled her nose. "Why?"

"And this is why I don't tell people my plans."

Fabulous. *Walking disaster, party of one, your table is ready.* "I didn't mean it like that. I just… Well, I've never met anyone that actually *wanted* to be on the Council. Especially not another Cupid."

Sure, other groups of Descendants vied for positions on the Council. If you could claim lineage to the right god, being on the Council meant power and honor and wealth. The Furies held contested elections every six years, complete with debates, psychological trials, and intense campaign slogans. The Asclepians had a top-secret appointment process, but rumor was it involved committees who ranked their Descendants by number of lives saved each year. The Muses, well… The Muses did their own thing. They were fickle and mysterious, but they always ended up with an inspired choice to represent their interests.

The Erosians did not.

In fact, for the last two terms, her people had been represented by the slimiest slimeball that ever slimed: Vic Van Love. Not that it really mattered. Ever since Cupids had gone public, they'd been sanctioned at every level of the Council. Vic couldn't vote, participate in committees, or even propose changes to the existing rules. As far as anyone could tell, Vic preferred it that way: all the prestige of a Council seat with none of the work or responsibility.

"It's a dumb idea I've had since I was a kid," Jake

said. "Before I knew about the sanctions and stuff. Back then, I thought it would be so cool to make the rules and actually have people listen."

"So, you wanted to boss people around?"

He laughed. "I'm the youngest of five kids. Can you blame me?"

She couldn't. Elijah had five minutes on her and somehow always used his status as the "older" child to pull rank. "But you're not a kid anymore, and you still want to do it?"

"I gave up on the idea once I got a little older, but after my time in the Corps, I realized how much I still wanted it. Not because I want to boss people around, but because I've seen so much. And I'm tired of Cupids not having a say in anything anymore, not having a vote in the things that matter."

"I'd vote for you," she said. "I mean, if you ran."

"Still a big *if*, but I appreciate your support, Herman."

She met his gaze, his vulnerability making her feel bolder and braver. "I have a dumb idea too."

"Please," he said. "I'd love to hear it."

"I decided today I'm going to take my licensing exam. I mean, even if they don't make me. I want to do this. For real." Once the words were out in the world, she couldn't stuff them away. And as she looked at Jake—the grin on his face, the hard line of his jaw, the soft glow of his eyes—she realized she didn't want to take them back.

"Well, we'd better get to work then," he said. "No more of this weekly practice nonsense. Starting tomorrow, you're getting daily tutoring sessions."

And with that, Eliza secured what was quickly becoming the most important thing in her life, whether she liked it or not: more time with Jake Sanders.

Chapter 10.5

Calif. CCR § 406.12. Beyond the weekly mentorship hours required to maintain the provisional Cupid license, regular meetings are encouraged. However, the frequency of these meetings remains at the discretion of the applicant's mentor.

EVERY DAY. EVERY DAMN DAY.

That's how often I'm going to see Eliza. Tomorrow. The next day. The day after that.

Not that I'm counting.

Fine. I'm definitely counting. Number of times she smiled at me today: thirteen. Number of times I wondered if we could leave the café and head somewhere quiet where I could ask her advice about my plans for the Cosmic Council: four. Number of times I thought about kissing her between bites of French toast: innumerable.

What in the Underworld is happening to me?

I've been enchanted before. Sometimes on purpose, a few times not. And while those days were fun while they lasted, that's all they were. A bit of fun to pass the time. This is different.

I'm different.

We're different.

My emotions should be starting to normalize by now. Instead, I feel more like a freshly shaken snow globe every day. I should be noticing the little things about Eliza that annoy me. But those tiny imperfections only drag me in deeper. At this point in the game, I should be pulling myself back together and getting to work on my Cosmic Council application. Not volunteering to spend every waking second with Eliza.

And yet…

I could pretend my motivations are purely unselfish. After all, if—no, *when*—she gets her license, she could be the most powerful Cupid we've seen in decades. And if there's one person pure-hearted enough to use that power for good, it has to be Eliza. With her ridiculously high enchantment levels, she could do things—help people—in ways I could only dream about. If I'd had her on my team in the Cupids Corps, we could have quietly made a difference for hundreds more people.

We could have slipped through cities and towns undetected. We could have taken on more sensitive projects. The kind where the good of an entire nation could rest on the right, or wrong, people falling in love without knowing they'd been enchanted. Team Eliza and Jake would have been unstoppable.

But I'm sometimes a selfish bastard. And if I'm honest—really honest—I'm as excited to spend tomorrow with Eliza as I am for all the good she could do as a Cupid. Because things aren't getting better with this enchantment. They're getting worse.

I'm just as smitten with her as the day she dropped that candy dish on my foot.

No. That's a lie.

I'm *more* smitten. Smittener? Whatever. I want her more now than I did then. Mentally, physically, emotionally. All the ways she'll have me. Which, to date, are exactly none.

Gods damn it. I guess we know what's wrong with me. It's obvious. Written right there on the wall in giant red letters. I'm falling in Love with Eliza.

Real Love. The kind that turns you inside out and upside down, shaping you into someone new. Someone better.

Real Love. The kind that leaves a giant, gaping wound when it ends, shaping you into someone new. Someone half-empty and hollowed.

But since Eliza has made it clear that she's not interested, I have a feeling that gaping wound is coming sooner, rather than later.

Hopefully I don't hemorrhage out.

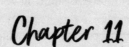

> "Average people rarely hire Cupids, so the practicing Cupid will notice their clientele often have unique 'quirks' or 'foibles.' Identify these characteristics early in the Cupid-client relationship."
> —*Cupid Strategies for Malpractice Defense*

ELIZA STUFFED ANOTHER GRAPE INTO HER MOUTH AS she flipped through the pages of *Sterling & Rockwell's Strategies and Tactics for Passing the Cupid Licensing Exam*. Jake had loaned her a handful of old books from his apartment. Everything from *Cupid 101: Everything You Need to Know about Enchantments, Fourth Edition* to *Eros: What Was His Deal?* But the *Sterling & Rockwell's* was new. He'd ordered it especially for her and dropped it off yesterday with a handwritten note inside the front cover.

Eliza: Here's to dumb ideas.

Could giving someone a study guide qualify as a romantic gesture? A few weeks ago, Eliza would have said no. Today it felt like the most romantic thing anyone had every done for her.

Not that she believed in actual romance. Or Love. Or—

The bells over the office door rang out, saving her

from falling down her personal rabbit hole of denial and excuses. She closed the study guide and sat up straight at the Herman & Herman receptionist's desk. The workday was nearly over and the last person who'd wandered in was looking for directions to the mall, but it couldn't hurt to be ready.

Jake stepped through the door and stopped a safe distance away. Excitement and disappointment warred in her brain. Excitement at seeing his face, being near his perfect forearms, thinking about the way he looked at her when they stood too close. Disappointment at how he'd become a stickler for their rules. "What are you doing in about"—he glanced up at the clock—"ten minutes?"

Daydreaming about your mouth. She held up the study guide. "My tutor is a real drag. He's always on my case about studying for this test, like it's some big deal or something."

"Sounds like a jerk."

"He's got his qualities."

"Such as?"

Oh, you know. Smells like a dream, has A+ archery skills, once made me swoon by remembering my favorite childhood cookies. "You know what? You're right. He's a jerk. Let's blow off this studying thing and see a movie or something."

He raised an eyebrow and gave her a grin that said what *exactly* would happen if they sat beside each other in the dark for two hours.

"We could sit on opposite sides of the theater," she suggested.

"Sorry, Herman. No can do. You've got a new client coming in."

"I do?"

"Eddie Pearson. Goes to my gym. Yesterday he started asking me about enchantments, so I told him to come here. He just sent a text and said he wants to look through the flip-books today. I even called Oliver to let him know."

Every part of her turned light and giddy. *So this is what it feels like to have someone believe in me.* Someone who, unlike her father, wasn't responsible for her very existence. "You know this is really going to interfere with my evening plans."

"Oh? What exactly were your plans, Herman?"

"Studying in my underwear and eating Cheetos for dinner," she said. "Try not to be jealous of how glamorous my life has become." His eyes flashed at the word *underwear*, and Eliza immediately felt guilty. "Sorry, I wasn't thinking. I didn't mean to make things, um…" *Don't say harder, don't say harder. Think of a better word, please.* "Harder for you."

Gods damn it. She was failing epically at this be-a-supportive-friend-and-friend-only thing.

Jake stepped closer, filling her personal space with his broad form. He bit the inside of his lower lip, and Eliza could almost see the struggle to keep his enchantment at bay. At least she wasn't the only one struggling to abide by the rules.

"Herman," he said, voice low. "You've done nothing but make my life *harder* since I came back to Gold Lea. And I'm not complaining."

A sweet, slow tingle blossomed deep in her stomach. Judging by the look on his face, she wasn't the only one whose recent nights had been consumed by dirty thoughts. "Jake—"

Ding. Dingdingding.

Holy Hades. She grabbed the nearest stack of papers and pretended to sort them. No, she hadn't been about to suggest they lock the door, turn out the lights, and see where a few heated glances took them.

"Eddie," Jake said, turning briskly. "Thanks for stopping by."

Eliza glanced up from her mess of papers, which she quickly realized were nothing but blank pages from a box near the printer, and took in the man who'd walked into the office. He stood half a head taller than Eliza, and his very tight T-shirt left little to nothing to the imagination. This guy spent a lot of time at the gym, and he had the veiny biceps and well-defined chest to prove it.

High maintenance, she thought. *Capital H. Capital MAINTENANCE.*

His gaze darted around the room, and he puffed out his chest a little. Like he might run into his match right here, right now. "Thanks for fitting me in today."

"No problem," Jake said. He gestured toward her. "This is Eliza. The Cupid I was telling you about."

Eddie sized her up. "Huh."

She couldn't tell if that was a good *huh* or a bad *huh*. And who knew what Jake had told the guy. Hopefully, it was that she could do enchantments without drawing blood and not that she was an accident waiting to happen. "Nice to meet you, Mr.—"

"Pearson," he said. "But call me Eddie."

"Well, Eddie, Jake said you're interested in hearing more about our services. Would you like to step back into my office?" Technically, it was Elijah's office, but he wasn't here and they'd shared a uterus, so same difference.

When they'd settled in—Eliza behind the desk, Eddie in a chair, Jake lingering at the edge of the room—she pulled out an empty file. "Tell me what we can do for you, Eddie."

He gave her only a flicker of acknowledgment before turning to Jake. "She held to the same, you know, confidentiality agreement as you?"

"Yes," Jake said.

"Absolutely," Eliza added.

"I can't believe I'm doing this, but I want to be matched with a woman." Eddie crossed his veiny arms across his chest. "I've never had a problem with chicks—I mean, with ladies—but this seemed like something new to try."

Eliza stifled an eye roll. "Eddie, engaging the services of a Cupid is nothing to be ashamed of. My ancestors have been creating matches and helping to continue the human race for thousands of years. The only difference between now and then is that you get a choice in the matter."

That may have been a direct quote from Jake's copy of *Cupid 101*, which she'd read earlier in the day, but Eddie didn't need to know that.

"Yeah, but I've got a reputation to uphold," he said. "Eddie Pearson doesn't need magic to make the *magic* happen, you know?"

Right. Women *obviously* flocked to this guy.

"Eddie, let me reassure you that Cupids do some of their best work with people who already have a good handle on *the magic*." She gave him her most pleasant, most professional smile, just like she'd read about in chapter three of *Sterling & Rockwell's*: "The Difficult Customer."

Eddie leaned back in the chair with a distinct come-at-me-bro vibe. "Then this will be your best case yet."

Eliza glanced at Jake, whose face had turned stop-light red from holding in his laughter. She turned away and faked a cough to cover her own laugh. "Jake said you're interested in our flip-book package. Would you like to have a profile featured or choose a match from someone in the books?"

"Eddie Pearson is used to being the alpha dog. He needs to do the choosing."

Was this guy really going to talk about himself in third person throughout the entire appointment? "Okay, well, we have several profiles on hand. Once we go over all the paperwork, you can go through them and see who strikes you as a potential match."

"There's no way to meet these ladies beforehand?" Eddie asked.

"I'm afraid not," Eliza said. "It's best to just choose and go from there. If the match doesn't take or you experience problems during the initial twenty-nine and a half days, we have a full money-back guarantee."

"Are you sure? A buddy of mine went to that Love Conquers All place, and he got to pick a chick out of a lineup."

"A lineup?" she sputtered. She pictured a row of girls, all of them doomed to matches with the type of douchebags who sought out help from Vic Van Love, holding up a list of their measurements and turning from left to right as guys mulled them over.

"Said there was some kind of party. All the girls were in one room behind a two-way mirror. He and his cousin got to have a few beers and watch them before they picked. Like a couple of lions taking their pick of the gazelles." Eddie wagged his eyebrows suggestively.

"Female lions do the hunting," Eliza said.

"Huh?"

Yes, her parents needed the business. Heck, *she* needed the business for her licensing hours log. But Eliza was teetering on the verge of paying this guy to leave and never come back. "Eddie, I'm not sure what your friend experienced at Vic Van Love's, but the way Cupids do business is very tightly regulated. What you're describing doesn't sound legal."

His face clouded for a moment before he laced his fingers behind his head. "That's just what I heard."

She took a deep breath and steeled her nerves. "Before we get started, we have to go through the paperwork. This page is a general profile. Your name, age, medical history, et cetera. This is a questionnaire about what you're looking for in a match. You'll still get to choose, but this might help us narrow things down if necessary."

"Eddie Pearson knows what he wants."

Eliza cleared her throat. "And here we have a confidentiality agreement and liability waiver. I'll let you read them both, but essentially you cannot take photos or videos of anything you see in the flip-books today. We've also removed any personally identifiable information from the profiles, but we ask that you not speak to anyone about what you see in the books. The waiver just lays out some of the possible side effects that can occur from enchantments."

Eddie muttered his way through the waiver. "'Do not use Cupid services if you are seeking secondary gain, such as monetary payments, bribes, inheritances, or blackmail. Your hormones may change without warning. Discuss your situation with your Cupid to ensure you are emotionally available. Cupid services may cause side effects such as nausea, loss of appetite, intrusive thoughts about the object of your affection, or unusual bruising or bleeding. Seek immediate medical attention if you experience prolonged redness or swelling at the injury site or an erection that lasts more than four hours.'"

He stared up at her, his skin turning an unfortunate shade of green. "Unusual bleeding or bruising? No way. Jake said Eddie wouldn't need to bleed."

Aha! Now she knew exactly why a guy like this came to her instead of to a den of disgustingness like Love Conquers All. He was afraid of blood.

"Usually—" she began.

Eddie shoved the stack of papers back across the desk. "No blood. No way."

"Eliza is the only Cupid in thousands of miles who can perform an enchantment without drawing blood," Jake said. "The paperwork is just standard."

I am? I guess I am. A surge of confidence washed over her, and Eliza had the sudden sense that being *here*, doing *this* was exactly what she'd been born to do. "I can make a note in your file that you have hemophilia. It shouldn't be a problem."

"I mean, it's not that I'm afraid of blood," Eddie rushed to explain. "I just don't see the need to involve it if we don't have to."

"Of course." Eliza handed him a pen. "Why don't you go ahead and fill these out while Jake and I get the flip-books?"

Once she got Jake into the supply room in the back of the office, Eliza crossed her arms. "Seriously?"

"Hey, I never said he was a great guy. I just said I had a client."

"A client who talks about himself in third person."

"I swear he doesn't talk about himself in third person at the gym. He probably just gets nervous around beautiful women, so he's overcompensating," Jake said.

Eliza tried—and failed—to ignore the way his compliment made her entire body warm. "Oh, he's definitely overcompensating *for something*." She turned and plugged the code into the safe her parents kept in the back corner. "But according to *Cupid 101*, it's not my job to judge someone's personality, only their fitness for enchantment."

"Sounds like you really have been studying in your underwear," Jake said.

"Wouldn't you like to know?" She pulled out the large binder of profiles and handed it to Jake as the bells over the front door rang. "Take these in there. I'll go tell whoever wandered in that the restroom is for customers only."

Unfortunately, her least favorite Department of Affection, Seduction, and Shellfish agent did not need to use the restroom. "Ms. Herman, I was just driving by and noticed an unusual car in your parking lot. I'm sure you weren't interacting with a potential customer without giving the Department notice."

Her scalp suddenly got all hot and itchy. How many times a day did this bozo drive by the office in hope of catching her doing something wrong? Enough to know which cars in the lot were *unusual*, at least. "Um, actually, I thought you were already aware. But I was coming out here to call you just to be sure." She put one hand on the office phone, as if this might convince him.

"I was aware, but the regulations require me to hear this information from *you*. Not your mentor."

"Oh. My apologies, I didn't realize—"

"Of course you didn't realize, Ms. Herman. Because you never read the fine print. This is your final warning."

All she could manage was a nod.

"The client is in there?" Oliver motioned toward the inner office door.

"Yes. Would you like to meet him? Jake's currently in the office with him." *Please say no. Please say no.* Hard telling what an idiot like Eddie would say that could land her in trouble with the Department.

"Yes, actually. I think that's a great idea."

She let out a ragged breath. "Absolutely. Follow me, please."

She cracked open the door to find Eddie hunched over the binder. He was flipping the pages too quickly to consider even half the information contained in each profile. "No. Nope. No. Not her. Almost…"

"What about this one?" Jake asked. "She seems nice."

"She doesn't have any pets. I like women with pets."

"This one looks promising," Jake said.

"Too many teeth when she smiles."

"Her?"

"Naw. She's wearing too much pink."

Finally, he made it to the last page and stared. "Her," he muttered. "Definitely her."

Eliza faked a quiet cough. "Eddie, this is Agent Oliver with the Department of Affection, Seduction, and Shellfish. He's here doing a quick checkup on how things are going. The same level of confidentiality that we discussed still applies."

Agent Oliver pulled a tiny notebook from his back pocket and began scrawling notes. "Mr. Pearson, when did you first contact Eliza Herman about an enchantment?"

"Today. I just stopped by this afternoon."

"You didn't have an appointment?"

"Not really. Drove by on my way to get some protein powder and decided to stop in. Called my buddy Jake here to let him know I wanted to swing by. Did you know Red Clover has a buy-one, get-one deal on whey this month?"

Agent Oliver wrote faster. "Did Ms. Herman discuss the potential side effects of an enchantment with you?"

"Yeah, but no bleeding, right? Because I'm not afraid of blood exactly, it's just that I don't like it."

Agent Oliver narrowed his beady eyes. "No bleeding, Ms. Herman?"

"It shouldn't be a problem for me," she said.

"And have you chosen a match?" he asked Eddie.

"Yep." He opened the book to the very last page. "Her."

The agent leaned down to look at the photo. "Very well. Ms. Herman, why don't you get this enchantment scheduled for tomorrow afternoon? That should give you plenty of time to contact this woman. I have some free time and would like to do your Department observation then."

Eliza's throat constricted. "Of course," she eked out.

"Call me with the time," Oliver said before marching out of the office.

"Tomorrow? As in Tuesday?" Eddie's eyes widened.

He jumped out of the chair. "Eddie is going to need a wax this afternoon." He hurried out, and the door clanged shut behind him.

Eliza gripped the edge of the desk. Was it possible to go into anaphylactic shock from nerves? Because sometime in the next twenty-four hours, she was going to find out. Enchanting Eddie Pearson and Yolanda Durst while Oliver-comma-Trevor scrutinized her every move might just kill her.

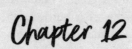

Chapter 12

"Complete transparency is necessary when obtaining informed consent to enchantment. In other aspects of the Affection Arts, however, some degree of deception may be acceptable, if not expected and necessary."

—*The Half-Wit's Manual for Love*

MONDAY EVENING AT RED CLOVER WAS A MADHOUSE of elderly people sniffing cantaloupes and blocking the aisles with shopping carts full of Ensure. A bus labeled "Gold Lea Assisted Living Villas" sat in the emergency vehicles lane of the parking lot, and every so often one of the elderly shoppers ambled on board with a bag of goods.

Eliza was in serious danger of running into Stu Vannerson, whose enchantment would be waning though not yet finished, but it couldn't be helped. Not with Yolanda and Eddie's match—and Eliza's license—on the line.

She moved carefully through the front of the store with her arms tucked to avoid accidents. When she made her way to the empty customer-service desk, she rang the tiny bell on the counter and waited. For the hundredth time since she'd parked her car in the lot, Eliza wished Jake could have come along.

A petite woman in a Red Clover cashier's uniform came out from the back room.

"Excuse me," Eliza said. "Is this where I talk to someone about delivery orders?"

The woman looked at her with a dull expression and shrugged. "Sure, why not." It wasn't a question so much as a surrender.

"My friend has a standing delivery order for tomorrow afternoon. But she, um, had to go out of town suddenly." She'd practiced this story with Jake before they'd closed the office, and it had come out smooth as silk. But now that she stood here, face-to-face with a woman who looked like she'd lost the will to live—or at least to provide customer service—the lie stuck in Eliza's throat. "She asked me to pick up her groceries and store them at my house instead."

The woman let out a nondescript grunt before turning to her computer. "Name?"

"Yolanda Durst."

The woman tapped the keyboard with her index fingers. It was working. By some magic of the gods, all Eliza's practice had really made perfect. She let out a deep breath.

"And her customer PIN?" the woman asked.

"I'm sorry?"

"Her personal identification number. P-I-N."

"Oh no. She didn't mention that." Of course. She'd been stupid to think anything in her life would ever be so simple.

"I'm sorry, but I can't make any changes without it." The woman started to turn her back to Eliza.

"Hold on," Eliza said. "Please. Maybe I can call

her." She pulled out her phone and pretended to dial. She needed time to think. Maybe listening to her own voicemail message could buy her a few precious seconds. Sadly, by the time Eliza heard herself say, "I'll call you back as soon as possible," she was still fresh out of ideas. She hung up and slipped the phone back into her pocket. "She's not answering."

The woman stared at her, obviously unimpressed. "I can't make any changes without the PIN," she repeated.

In some other universe where she'd been given more time to prepare for this enchantment, Eliza would come up with ten different ways to secretly enchant Yolanda Durst. Unfortunately, Oliver-comma-Trevor had made sure she had none of that. The only things Eliza knew about where to find Yolanda were her address and the fact that she got a weekly Tuesday afternoon delivery from Red Clover. Since Eliza couldn't just knock on her door, introduce herself, and injure the woman, this would have to do.

"Is there a manager I can speak with?" Eliza asked.

"I *am* the manager." The woman sighed and pointed to her name tag: Helen Rothchild, Assistant Manager, We Love to Serve. Without another word, she headed toward the back room.

Whatever kind of day this woman had been having had completely shut her down to doing favors for anyone else. Eliza glanced over her shoulder, then at Helen's retreating back. "Helen, I would really appreciate it if you could help me out with this—"

The manager didn't bother to look at Eliza. "Ma'am, I can't make any changes to an existing order without the PIN."

"I understand, but here's the thing: Have you ever been in love?"

Helen paused, then turned, her expression wary. "Why?"

Just as Eliza had suspected. This woman's troubles were of the love variety—they almost always were. Eliza pulled her provisional license from her pocket long enough for Helen to get the Cupid part but hopefully not the borderline-approval part. "I'm a Cupid," Eliza whispered, "and if you do me this favor, I could probably help you out sometime."

Helen's eyes widened. The dullness that had been there a moment before cleared, leaving behind sparkling blues. "Really?"

Perfect. She's a total sucker for love.

Eliza nodded. "I can personally guarantee that these groceries will make it to my friend. Now, what do you say?" She leaned farther over the counter, like she and Helen were the best of friends. "For a chance at love?"

Helen chewed her bottom lip, and Eliza glanced at the clock overhead. If this wasn't going to work, she was going to need to move on to plan B as soon as possible. Of course, first she'd need to figure out what plan B was, exactly. She waited another beat, and the weight of defeat settled in her chest. "Never mind," she said, turning to leave. "Sorry to bother you."

"Wait," Helen said. "Let me see your badge again."

Eliza tried not to grimace as she slid her ID across the counter. She opened her mouth, ready to explain that borderline approval wasn't as terrible as it seemed. Maybe *lie* was a better word choice than *explain*, but whatever.

"Eliza Herman." Helen flipped the ID between her fingers. "Are you with Herman & Herman then?"

"Yes. Are you familiar? I'd be happy to—"

"Why do you need the groceries?"

"I told you, my friend is out of town. She doesn't want them to go bad." Eliza might be willing to tell a few white lies to make this match happen, but she wasn't going to out Yolanda's privacy.

"Okay. I'll send the groceries with you."

The weight of defeat lifted, Eliza finally took a deep breath. "Thank you so much, Helen. I'll be sure to fill out a comment card, and if you call the Herman & Herman office—"

"But I'll need your services in exchange. It's a special situation."

"Oh." She'd heard stories about this kind of thing before. Someone trying to blackmail or bribe a Cupid into doing some under-the-table work. The type of work better suited to someone like Vic Van Love. "I'm sorry, I really can't do anything below board. All involved parties have to consent—"

"That won't be a problem. I'll even pay you," Helen said.

Eliza's forehead crinkled in confusion. If everyone was willing to consent and Helen was willing to pay, why not just hire someone through the usual channels? "What's the special situation?"

Helen glanced over Eliza's shoulder. "It's delicate."

"And I'm guessing you don't want to discuss it here?"

Helen shook her head. "Shall I have them bring the bags to the front tomorrow at"—she hit a few keys on the computer—"four o'clock?"

Eliza ran down a quick pros-and-cons list in her head.

Pro: She'd get the groceries and have a solid cover for tomorrow.

Con: She'd be taking on a *delicate* situation that could be horrifying or dangerous or both.

Pro: She'd be bringing in new business.

Double pro: New business meant Vic Van Love's predictions about her parents' business were all wrong. Or mostly wrong.

"That would be great. Thanks. Let me leave you my card—"

"No need." Helen plugged away at the computer, presumably making the changes to Yolanda's order. "I know Herman & Herman's number."

Uh-oh. A half dozen red flags went up in Eliza's brain. If Helen knew the Herman & Herman number by heart—

"There's my sweet girl," a wobbling voice said from somewhere behind her. "I knew the stars would align for us. Also, I just bought this Align probiotic. Keeps me as regular as the day is long."

Eliza looked back and forth between Helen and Stu Vannerson. She really needed to find out more about Helen's situation. But she really, *really* needed to get away from Old Man Vannerson before he decided to do something bonkers, like write her into his will.

She inched away from them both. "Thanks for all your help, Helen. Call me," Eliza said.

She pushed through the doors, dodging carts and consoling herself with the knowledge that soon Stu Vannerson's enchantment would wear off. Then she could go back to buying groceries like a regular person. And maybe Helen would forget to call. Then Eliza could put this whole thing behind her. What a stroke of luck that would be.

Of course, Eliza rarely had any luck at all.

>>>————————>

"And I can't say anything about the enchantment, like, ever?" Eddie asked (for the fifth time) from the back seat of Jake's car.

"Like you, the woman has some privacy concerns. It's actually a very good situation for both of you, Eddie. I know you were worried—"

"I'm not worried," he said. "But what if we end up getting married and I have to keep this secret from her our whole lives?"

"Some say that secrets are the key to a happy marriage," Eliza said. She couldn't imagine that Yolanda and Eddie would last more than five minutes once the enchantment faded.

"Okay, but what if I bleed? Like, really bleed? I mean, I'm not worried, but you should have a backup plan, just in case."

She fiddled with the collar of her red polo shirt—a close enough match for the Red Clover uniform—and glanced across the car at Jake. He hadn't said a word since they'd climbed into the car's close quarters, and judging by the whites of his knuckles on the steering wheel, sitting this close to her—even covered in a layer of her mother's floral perfume—was taking a toll on him.

"Eddie, we talked about this. There's no way you will bleed. I swear."

"Eliza has it under control." Jake's deep voice held a

hint of finality, and for once, Eddie shut up. Of course, he was exactly the type of jerk who'd question a well-qualified woman for hours but take a man's five-word response as gospel.

Jake pulled into a small neighborhood park located across the street from Yolanda's house. "I'm going to get some air," he said.

"What's his deal today?" Eddie asked. "Jake's usually so chill."

"I don't know," Eliza lied. She watched Jake pace up and down the street with his hands laced together over his head. "Must be having a rough afternoon."

"Well, let's do this, I guess," Eddie said.

"We have to wait for the agent to arrive."

"Oh, right."

Eliza turned in her seat to look at Eddie, who wore a matching red polo and the expression of a kid who'd just watched *Pet Sematary* at a sleepover and had to pretend he wasn't scared. "You okay?" she asked.

The last thing she needed was for him to freak out and screw this up. She was already juggling enough potential catastrophes for one day—no, for one *lifetime*.

"Let's go over it one more time." The tremor in Eddie's voice was almost enough to make her feel sorry for him. "I mean, so *I* know that *you* know what you're doing."

Eliza forced her eyes to the ceiling of her car to keep from rolling them. "I hide on the porch. You—"

"Maybe it's best for someone a little more, uh, experienced to handle things." Eddie stared out the window at Jake.

For a breath, Eliza's confidence withered, making her feel like a plant someone had given up on watering.

Maybe she should just give up too. Throw herself into the garbage can before all the neighbors saw how ugly things were about to become. But then she remembered her father's face when she'd told him she wanted to get her license. She remembered Jake's unwavering confidence in her abilities.

Eliza unbuckled her seat belt and leaned closer to Eddie. "Listen. We can go with the plan we've discussed at least six times, or I can take the groceries in myself while you catch the bus home."

Now it was Eddie's turn to wilt. He kept his gaze trained on his hands as he pushed open the car door and grabbed the bags from the seat beside him. "There's the government dude. Let's go before the ice cream melts."

Eliza jumped out of the car. Eddie hadn't bothered to wait for her (surprise, surprise), and he was already halfway up the sidewalk to Yolanda's cottage. "Shit."

"I've got him," Jake said. "You go deal with Oliver."

Eliza breathed a little easier. What would she do without Jake? She jogged the few steps to the black van that had pulled up behind them. "Agent Oliver, would you mind backing up a little? Our client is very concerned with her privacy, and your vehicle, well…" She pointed to the giant A.S.S. written across the side.

He adjusted his necktie. "Certainly. Why don't you get in and tell me where to park? You can tell me a little more about your plans for this enchantment."

She looked toward Jake's car, where he seemed to have Eddie under control. "Sure."

By the time they'd parked the van two blocks over and walked to Yolanda's street, Eliza had explained the request for secrecy and the grocery ruse.

"I spoke to my mentor about the request and consulted the regulations," she said. "I didn't see anything that forbids me from taking the case." She waited, listening to his mouth breathing, and braced herself for some sort of punishment.

"Interesting," he said as they caught up to Jake and Eddie.

That was all. No lectures or admonishments. Maybe this would be okay after all.

"Are you ready?" she asked when they reached Eddie and Jake.

Eddie looked like he might pee his pants. "Born ready."

"Mr. Sanders and I will wait here," Oliver said. "We should be close enough to see what's happening but far enough that we won't cause an intrusion."

Eddie, gods bless him, took off again with the grocery bags jiggling in his hands. A twenty-yard dash later, Eliza caught up with him and grabbed her weapon from his bag.

"Wait until I give you the signal. Then come up the steps," she whispered. Eliza tiptoed up the stairs of the blue cottage, hoping she looked like any random person walking up to a friend's house. Except, of course, she was armed with a loaf of frozen garlic bread and intent to commit a minor assault.

She crouched behind a large potted plant on the porch. It put her far enough from the doorframe that she wouldn't be seen when Yolanda answered but close enough that she could reach over and give her leg—or foot, or thigh, or toe, whichever was handy—a quick tap with the bread.

Clomp. Clomp. Clomp. Eddie approached the front

door with all the grace of a rhino. He balanced two paper grocery bags perilously between his arms, and his flushed face poked out between them. "Now?" he asked.

She hadn't given him the signal, but whatever. Eliza nodded.

"What if she's not home?"

"Look straight ahead," she whispered.

His face disappeared back between the bags, and Eliza could only hope he was looking at the door. "Okay, but what if she's not home? Maybe we should try another day."

"Eddie, she's expecting her groceries. Get your shit together and ring the doorbell."

He stretched his index finger out and moved in shaky slow motion—like ET, but if America's favorite extraterrestrial was super into protein powder and dead lifts. Eliza held her breath and glanced out at the park across the street, where Jake and Oliver were engrossed in conversation.

So much for Department observation.

But at the last second, Jake glanced her way, broke into a grin, and gave her a thumbs-up.

Eliza exhaled. This was going to be fine. No, more than fine. She was going to knock this enchantment out of the park and show Oliver-comma-Trevor exactly what she was made of.

A clattering of footsteps came from behind the door, and Eliza lifted her bread. A quick tap. Just enough to break a capillary or two, and she'd be one major step closer to her license. There was a pause and then a series of rattles and clicks as Yolanda unlocked what sounded like an intricate series of dead bolts and chains.

Love tap in three, two—

Squeeeeee. Ooooooink. Squeeeee.

Eliza's brain screamed for her to stop, but her arm didn't get the message in time. It swung, knocking the hoof of a pink, hairy pig. It reared up to stare her straight in the eye, and for one fateful second, Eliza thought she was about to pay dearly for that bacon, egg, and cheese sandwich she'd eaten for breakfast. Then its warm, damp snout swiped across her face, and it squealed and snorted while its whiskers tickled her chin. A fleck of gold flickered in Eliza's periphery, and suddenly a familiar voice rang out.

"Charleston Samuel Durst the Third, what has gotten into you? Come here."

Between flashes of pink pig flesh, Eliza glimpsed a pair of sleek heels in the doorway. *The gold was nothing, just a reflection off a window. Hit her. Now or never.* She raised the bread, swung, and knocked Yolanda in the calf.

Red and yellow shimmers of Love Luster filled the air, invisible to both Eddie and Yolanda. But as if he could sense it, Eddie—for once on top of his game— pretended to fumble and dropped one of the bags of groceries. "Oh, I'm so sorry," he said, squatting down to pick them up. "It's my first day."

Eliza took the opportunity to knock him on the back of the leg, then slithered back behind the plant. His Love Luster flashed green and black and brought with it the pungent scent of Axe body spray. Eliza fought back a gag. *Moment of truth.* Was this quirky redhead with a serious case of paranoia compatible with Eddie Pearson?

"Your first day?" Yolanda asked. "I would have never guessed. You seem so at ease with all those groceries."

Eddie picked up the fallen groceries and stood a

little taller. His voice dropped low. "It *is* easy when your deliveries are to such lovely houses...and such lovely ladies."

Yolanda giggled. Really and truly *giggled*. From behind the planter, Eliza swallowed another gag. Listening to other people flirting never got less awkward.

"It's so warm out here." Yolanda fanned herself, inadvertently spewing her pheromones toward Eddie, who looked like he'd just won the lottery, taken a bite of the world's best pie, and seen an adorable puppy. "Please come in and let me make you some lemonade," Yolanda added.

Eddie's face softened, and Eliza got a glimpse of who he might be under that thick layer of bravado and self-tanner: a nervous guy looking for love. He nodded, head bobbing between the bags. "That sounds great."

Yolanda broke into a smile. "Right this way."

And Eliza, completely unnoticed (except for the stare she was getting from Charleston the pig), snuck off the porch and back toward the car. She'd done it. By herself. With only one tiny mishap that hadn't hurt anyone. Okay, so maybe if she didn't know better, Eliza would have thought the look the pig gave her as she backed away from the scene of the crime was a little lovelorn. But she did know better than that. Cupids couldn't affect nonhuman animals.

Right?

"Ms. Herman, that was quite a display," Agent Oliver said. He had out his little notepad again. "I have to say, I wasn't expecting you to pull that off. What was your weapon of choice? A baton?"

"Garlic cheese bread. Frozen so it would be hard

enough to cause a small amount of damage. If you recall, Mr. Pearson requested no blood."

"Interesting indeed." He scrawled some more in his notebook, while Eliza tried to come down from her high. "I may have some more questions for you in the coming days, Ms. Herman, but for now, let's go ahead and schedule your final exam for late next week. Say Thursday?"

Her heart clenched into a nervous ball of energy. Next Thursday: the same day Jake's enchantment would wear off. In less than two weeks, she'd be either a fully licensed Cupid or an unlicensed failure. Either way, she wouldn't be distracted by Jake's attention anymore—and he wouldn't be distracted by her. "Sure. Sounds great."

"See you then." Agent Oliver tucked his notebook into his back pocket and set off for his van.

As soon as he was out of earshot, she turned to face Jake. "I did it!"

The look of pride on his face set off fireworks in Eliza's brain. She'd taken on a legitimately tough case. It required skill and cunning and confidence. And she'd managed it without incident—by herself. Maybe this Cupid gig wasn't so bad after all.

"You did great," Jake said. "Better than great. You were amazing."

He thinks I was amazing. She flung her arms around his waist and buried her face into his chest. "I did it," she repeated. "I can't believe I did it."

Jake's spine went ramrod straight, and his abs tensed. Under normal circumstances, Eliza wouldn't have minded the feel of that six-pack pressed to her torso. Sadly, these were anything but normal circumstances.

"Sorry." She pulled back, feeling a warm blush climb to the tips of her ears. "I'm just excited."

Jake glanced down at her, and the smallest hint of a struggle appeared in his eyes. Then it was gone, and he pulled her back in for a full, warm-bodied hug. He rested his chin on her head. "I'm proud of you."

He thinks I was amazing and he's proud of me. Eliza closed her eyes, allowing herself to enjoy the feel of those abs and that crisp, outdoorsy scent filling her nostrils.

"I really thought that pig was going to get the better of you," Jake said.

Eliza looked up at him and narrowed her eyes in mock indignation. "I could have taken him."

"Sure."

"Charleston Samuel Durst the Third is no match for me."

Jake laughed. "None of us are."

She melted, fully and completely, until she was nothing but a ball of fluttery feelings pressed against him. He was just so *enticing* right now, with his flirty smile and warm embrace. So *enchanting*. So…*Jake*.

"I disagree," she said. The rest of her words fell out, breathless and full of expectation. "*You* are a match for me."

He didn't respond, and her brain warred over what to say next. In the battle of *This is a bad idea fueled by an accidental enchantment* versus *Kiss me right now, damn it*, she wasn't sure which side was going to take home the win. "Jake?"

His gold-flecked eyes locked on hers, and the wanting there was unmistakable. Finally, one of his thick, black eyebrows cocked slightly. As if asking her *Is this okay?*

It was not okay. It was way better than okay. If she wanted to, she could lift a hand and run it along his jawline. She could feel the prickle of his dark stubble against her fingertips. If she wanted to, she could lean in a little more and press herself against the length of him.

And, gods damn it, she *really* wanted to do all those things.

"You're making me crazy," he said.

She tilted her chin a fraction of an inch. "Good crazy or bad crazy?"

"The best kind of crazy." He flattened a palm against her back and pulled her closer. The feeling of his chest pressed to hers was even better than she'd remembered. And she'd been "remembering" it a lot over the past few days.

"What are we doing?" she whispered.

"Just some standard mentorship stuff." His thumb brushed her cheek. "And maybe some kissing, if that's okay. I really want it to be okay, and not just because you dropped a candy jar on my foot."

That's the enchantment talking. That's the enchantment talking. That's the—

"Eliza?"

His lips were inches from hers. Lips that made her stomach flip-flop each time he said her name. Lips that were 100 percent off-limits but still invaded her dreams. "Yeah?" she whispered.

"Is that okay?"

She opened her mouth to say no. Obviously, they shouldn't be doing this. There was too much on the line: her license, her family's business, decades of friendship. But all of that faded away in the warmth of his arms.

The gravel crunched beneath her feet as she rose up and caught his mouth with hers. Soft, tentative, questioning.

"Eliza." He dipped his head and caught her mouth again. With a soft moan, his lips and tongue explored hers gently, stroking her emotions and body into a desperate fire. The kiss was exactly what she'd imagined it would be, but also better. So much better. Possibly because, until this very moment, she hadn't been able to conceive of a kiss that felt like this. Like melting and being reformed. Like being set aflame and covered in gooseflesh. Like completely and totally losing herself in someone else.

It was the kiss she'd been longing for since he'd showed up at her house on her birthday. The kiss she'd fantasized about as a gangly teenager. Maybe even the kiss she'd been waiting for her entire life.

She pulled him in closer, her body pleading for more. More kissing, more touching, more *Jake*. And when she got it, Eliza's breathing grew ragged, and a perfect ache bloomed low in her stomach.

"Still okay?" he whispered.

"Better than okay."

Jake's eyes flared with heat. His hands sank into her hair, roamed her back, and then grasped her thighs. He was everywhere, and yet she was still greedy with want.

By the time he wrapped her legs around his waist and pinned her on the hood of his car, she'd completely lost herself. Where she was. Who she was. What she'd been doing five minutes ago. But she was kissing Jake Sanders, and nothing else mattered.

"Let's get out of here," she whispered.

With a tortured groan, Jake pulled away. A flash of black caught Eliza's eye.

No. Please, gods, no. She blinked twice, hoping against hope that this was some lust-fueled hallucination. But nothing changed.

"Jake, do you see that?" She pointed to the end of the block. There, idling in his A.S.S. van, sat Agent Oliver. "Do you think he saw us?" But she already knew the answer. There was no way he'd missed that very public display of affection.

"Fuck," Jake muttered.

She tugged the edge of her shirt with tight fists. *Think, Eliza. Think.* When Agent Oliver stepped out of that van and marched over to where they stood, what was she going to say? It had to be something good. Better than good. Otherwise, everything she'd worked for was about to blow up right here in front of Yolanda's house. She'd have to explain her failures to her family. Deal with her mother's disapproval. Her father's disappointment. Her brother's shattered dreams. She'd have to sit by and watch as years of their hard work and dedication slipped down the drain, taking Herman & Herman with it.

All because she couldn't keep her hands to herself.

"Jake, I—"

But before she could finish, Oliver raised his tiny notepad in a wave and sped off into the sunset.

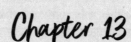

Chapter 13

Cupid Rules of Professional Conduct § 1.8. (j)
Romantic, sexual, and financial relationships between a Cupid and an individual under enchantment are expressly prohibited for the duration of the enchantment unless such relationship existed consensually between the parties prior to the enchantment.

ELIZA STARED INTO THE BATHROOM MIRROR. SHE knew she'd never be supermodel material. Or even not-so-super-model material. But the way Jake had looked at her yesterday right before that kiss—all fire and mischief, like he was planning exactly what he wanted to do to her body—had made her feel like she could give any one of Victoria's secrets a run for their money.

As long as no actual running was involved, of course. Or high heels. Or those fake wings the models wore. Talk about a recipe for humiliation.

Then again, maybe not. The last couple of weeks had shown her that she wasn't that lanky teenager who caused calamity wherever she went. With practice, increased confidence, and improved hand-eye coordination, she'd managed to avert most disasters. Thanks in no small part to Jake.

Jake.

Ugh. After that impromptu make-out session the day before, they'd ridden home in tense silence. When he'd finally pulled in to her apartment complex, Jake had turned to look directly at her. "We need to talk—"

"Maybe I should call him. Get in front of the story, you know. We could—" She waved her hands about, banging her knuckles into the passenger-side window. "Ow!"

"You okay?"

She nodded, but the car's oxygen felt too thin for her lungs.

"We don't know what he saw. Let's just wait, okay? If he saw what happened back there"—Jake ran a hand over the top of his head, a move Eliza now recognized as his own nervous tic—"I'm sure one of us will hear about it. Soon."

She nodded. That made sense, even if she was certain Oliver had seen their game of tongue twister. No need to race toward trouble. "When he calls me, I'm going to tell him what happened at the Johansens. It's not your fault, and you—"

"No."

"Excuse me?"

"You can't tell him about the enchantment."

"It was my fault. You shouldn't be punished for my stupidity. If I hadn't hit you with that candy dish, we might never have kissed at all."

Jake pressed his thumbs into his brow and closed his eyes. "Eliza?"

At the sound of her name on his lips, Eliza's traitorous heart began thumping out a hyperbeat. "Yeah?"

"If you hadn't hit me with that candy dish, I'd still be thinking about kissing you. All the damn time."

"Jake—"

"Would you just listen to me? Please?"

She pressed her lips together so hard they began to ache.

"I thought about kissing you when we were kids. I thought about kissing you that night I brought a delivery to your house. And I've thought about kissing you every day since. This isn't some enchantment, Eliza. This is real."

Every cell in her body wanted to believe him, but this too-good-to-be-true type of thing was exactly what someone deep in the throes of enchantment would say. "Let's see how you feel next Friday, okay?"

He reached for her hand. "Eliza—"

She pulled away and opened the car door. If he touched her again, she'd lose all her willpower. Then they'd both be up the Acheron without a paddle. "I should go."

Jake sighed and pulled his hand away. "Fine. But if Oliver calls you or stops by, call me before you do anything. Promise me."

"I promise." She left him in the parking lot and took off for the bland comfort of home. And she hadn't left it since. This morning, she'd told her mother she had a sore throat and didn't want to spread anything to her father. Then she'd curled up on her couch with a marathon of true-crime documentaries in the background. After she'd had enough of *The Winged One Confesses: Stories of a Deranged Cupid*, she'd dusted herself off and headed for a hot, sulking shower.

The room warmed around her, and her reflection smudged and faded in the steam. On the back of the toilet, her phone lit up with a text from Jake.

You doing okay?

She considered leaving the text unanswered, but instead sent him a simple Yes.

There. She gave herself a mental pat on the back. Just two colleagues checking in with each other. No flirty banter. No eggplant emojis…

Argh. She put the phone facedown and stepped away. No more dirty thoughts about Jake. She needed to get him out of her system, like, yesterday. Or, preferably, two and a half weeks ago. Luckily, she knew exactly how to take care of this problem. All she needed was ten minutes and her trusty silver bullet. She'd run through all those looks and touches she'd locked away over the last couple of weeks, and she'd emerge from her apartment saying, "Jake who?"

She left the bathroom to dig around in her bedside table, but when she tried to turn her vibrator on, nothing happened. Not even a twitch. "No problem," she muttered as she stepped into her kitchen. "Better to have fresh batteries anyway."

When she pulled open her trusty battery drawer, only the beige bottom stared up at her.

Nada. Nothing. Zilch. She had no batteries, a dead vibrator, and a *very* detailed memory of the way Jake's erection had pressed against her belly yesterday. The old Eliza would have given up, turned on the documentary again, and learned all about a Cupid who'd murdered dozens of people thirty years ago. But the new Eliza— the tenacious, take-no-prisoners one—wasn't going to give up until she'd worked this man out of her system.

She'd just have to take care of this the old-fashioned way: with the removable showerhead.

Eliza flipped off the bathroom lights, leaving only

the soft glow of the afternoon sun streaming through the window. She climbed into the shower, and the contrast between the hot water and her cool skin left a trail of goose bumps down her arms and legs. She closed her eyes and dipped her head under the water. It soaked her hair and dripped across her body, rolling gently over her nipples.

She hadn't done anything but think about Jake's "eggplant emoji," and already her body was revved and ready to go. This was definitely what she needed to get her brain back on track. Eliza let one hand slide down her wet body, her thumb tracing over one nipple, then the other, as she used her other hand to unhook the showerhead from its clip on the wall.

A warm ache blossomed between her thighs, and she sank to the bottom of the tub. Her skin chilled without the constant stream of water, and she closed her eyes, relishing in the discordant feelings. The water coming from the showerhead became Jake's hands, warm on her cool body.

His fingers moved across her stomach, dipping just low enough to tease her before coming back up to her chest. He smiled down at her with that I-know-exactly-how-to-worship-your-body grin and planted lingering kisses along her neck. Then, when the teasing had her begging for more, he nudged her thighs apart and ran a thumb straight down her slick center.

"Eliza," he growled in her ear before dipping his head lower. And lower. And even lower, until his mouth and hands worked her like putty—building her up to something almost complete before bringing her back down. "I've been wanting to do this since you pulled into the driveway that night," he said. "To taste you. Touch you. Feel you come around me."

"Fuck me," she whispered.

Above her, he raised one eyebrow. Gods, she loved it when he rode that line between confidence and arrogance. The only thing she'd love more was if he rode her straight down that line and into oblivion. Her legs trembled, and inside she felt hollow with need as she stared into his scorching eyes.

"Fuck me," she said again. "Please."

He lowered himself, and she sucked in a breath as his bare chest made contact with hers. It was all so perfect. The weight of him. The feel of his rough fingers against her skin. His thick, hard cock pressing—

"Eliza!" Her mother's voice came from the other side of the door, followed quickly by the sound of the knob jiggling. "Honey, are you okay in there?"

Eliza jerked upright and let go of the showerhead. It spun, spraying her in the face with lukewarm water as she grabbed for it. Gods, this was like a flashback to her teenage years. She finally gave up and shut off the water. Why in the world had she given her parents a key? "I'm fine, Mom. What's going on?"

"I've been trying to get ahold of you. You've already gotten three calls from a potential client this morning. She said it's an emergency."

"Just a minute." Eliza took a deep breath, stood on Jell-O legs, and turned the shower to the coldest setting she could stand. Once she'd blasted her brain and body back into the present, she wrapped a towel around herself and opened the bathroom door. "Mom, I'm really not feeling well. Can you just take a message?"

Her mother's mouth was set into a single firm line with dozens of tiny wrinkles running straight to it. Her usually perfect coif looked only half-brushed, and the whites of her eyes were bloodshot. All at once, Eliza was struck by how old and tired her mom seemed. "Honey, I appreciate that you don't feel well, but we have a money-back guarantee. If something went wrong—"

"Mom, take a message. I promise I'll call her back tomorrow. Maybe you should take the day off too. You look like you could use some rest."

"I can't, and neither can you. The woman insisted on coming by the office in half an hour, and if you aren't there, she says she'll file a complaint with the Department. What in the world is going on?"

"I don't know. What was her name?"

Her mother pulled a scrap of paper from her pocket. "Helen Rothchild. I checked the files, but we don't have a Rothchild case."

"Because she's not a client. She works at Red Clover. I gave her my card the other day, that's all."

"Go to the office and get this settled. I have an appointment at noon, so I can't be there to smooth things over for you this time." Her mother turned and disappeared down the hall. The click of the front lock followed.

Eliza stepped back into the shower, annoyed, hurt, and utterly unsatisfied. Not only had she failed to get Jake out of her mind, but now she was desperate to know what it would feel like to have him in her body. And there was absolutely no time to find out—even in her fantasies. She had a serious problem named Helen Rothchild. Once that was handled, she could turn her attention to where she and fantasy-Jake had left off. Then everything in her life could go back to normal.

Even if she wasn't sure she wanted normal anymore.

"There you are! I swear I thought you were avoiding me," Helen said.

From her position at the receptionist's desk, Eliza took in the Red Clover manager. Gone were the dead eyes and slack jaw. She looked like a younger, brighter version of the woman Eliza had met earlier in the week. "Not at all. Just had some things to take care of this morning," Eliza said. "What can I help you with today?"

Best to get whatever Helen wanted out of the way as quickly as possible. Eliza didn't have the time or energy to deal with a high-maintenance client right now.

"Like I said, it's delicate."

The bells over the door clanged, and Jake stepped into the office. His gray sweatpants clung to his thighs, and his black workout shirt was the stuff fantasies were made of. "Hey. I was out for a run. Got here as fast as I could. What's the emergency? Did Oliver call you?"

"No, but I called him to make sure he knew about our latest client. Jake, meet Helen. Helen, Jake."

Jake's features froze in a moment of confusion before he lifted a hand to wave. "Hi, Helen."

"Jake! I wouldn't have guessed I'd run into you here," Helen said. "But good to see you. Back on the market?"

Back *on the market*? "You two know each other?" Eliza asked.

Jake nodded toward Elijah's office. "Eliza, can I speak to you for a moment? We'll be right with you, Helen," he added.

Eliza shuffled toward her brother's office and closed the door behind her. "What's going on?"

Jake stood on the opposite side of the room—solidly within the "safe zone"—and shook his head. Eliza knew she should be glad he was back to actively fighting the attraction. But she also knew she was supposed to eat five servings of fruit and vegetables every day. That didn't mean she *did* it.

"Jake?" she prompted.

"Helen and I went on a date last year. Some friends set us up when I was home on a break. We didn't have any chemistry, and I never saw her again."

"You dated her?" Eliza definitely wasn't jealous. Just like she definitely wasn't going to leave work and stress eat a bag of salt-and-vinegar chips tonight.

"One date. And it was a bust. But if it makes you uncomfortable, maybe we should tell her you're too busy to take new clients," Jake said.

It was more than the failed date that made her uncomfortable. It was everything about Helen's secretive demeanor, not to mention the way she'd practically had Herman & Herman on speed dial. But Eliza wasn't sure she could explain all that right now. And if she could, would he even believe her? Or would he just think Eliza couldn't handle the thought of him having a past that didn't include her?

"No. It's fine," she said. "She already threatened to file a complaint with the Department." Eliza gave him a knowing look. "Do you really think I need to deal with *that* on top of what happened yesterday?"

"There you are!" The office door opened, and Helen's face appeared in the doorway. "What in the world is taking you so long? It's like herding cats with you two."

"So sorry, Helen," Eliza said. "Why don't you have a seat and tell us what you need?"

"Before we get started, should I get my partner?" Helen asked. "He's waiting in the car. I wasn't sure you'd be here, and I didn't want to drag him out."

"I didn't realize you had a partner already." Relief drummed through Eliza's body. Helen already had a partner. This was going to be as simple as enchanting the Johansens. What was she getting so worked up about? "Please bring him in. It'll be easier to go over all the paperwork at once."

"Great. I'll be back in a snap."

"Whew," Jake said as soon as she'd gone. "At least this will be an easy one." He leaned back against the wall and crossed one ankle over the other.

"Maybe." Eliza stared up at the ceiling and tried not to look at him. But despite her best attempts, she couldn't deny that he could be the poster boy for Sexy "R" Us. She wasn't sure what they would sell there, but she imagined it would make lots of people extraordinarily relaxed and happy.

No, you are not thinking about Jake's penis right now. You are absolutely not.

But, gods damn it, she definitely was.

"Here we are," Helen's singsong voice entered the room half a second before she and her partner did.

The edges of Eliza's vision went black. "What the…"

Three pairs of eyes stared back at her. Jake's, Helen's, and Jake's.

Wait.

No, that wasn't Jake in the doorway. But it definitely was Jake-esque.

"Eliza, meet Jacque." Helen gestured to the Jake facsimile at her side.

And the closer Eliza looked, the more she realized that's all he was—a facsimile. Jake's eyes had those sparkling gold flecks, and Jacque's eyes were a solid brown. Jake's eyebrows went a little wild at the edges, and Jacque's were perfectly groomed. Jake had a certain warm, mischievous grin, like he was keeping one of your deepest secrets safe. Jacque didn't smile. At all.

"Hi," Eliza said, doing her best to pull herself together. "Nice to meet you."

Silence.

"He won't say anything back. He never does anymore." Helen's voice shook a little. Beside her, still leaning against the wall like an annoyingly sexy James Dean, Jake's mouth fell open.

What in the Underworld…? Eliza looked back and forth between Jake, Jacque, and Helen but came no closer to figuring out what was going on. "Well, why don't we sit down and see what we can do?" she offered.

"Thank you." Helen hefted Jacque over her shoulder and moved to the couch.

Eliza's eyes widened. Was Jacque…not alive? Suddenly, she remembered that infomercial she'd seen at the hospital about the *very personal* assistant. Either she was being asked to enchant a sex robot, or she had a *Weekend at Bernie's* situation on her hands. "Helen, is Jacque—"

"A fully customized Mandroid? Yes."

This had to be a joke. Eliza glanced over her shoulder, expecting Jake to give her a *gotcha*. Instead, he looked just as confused as she did. "I can't turn him on anymore," Helen said.

Eliza turned to her client. "I'm sorry, what was that?"

"I can't turn him on anymore." Helen's eyes went glassy with tears, and Eliza knew this wasn't a joke. Or if it was, this woman was giving an Oscar-worthy performance.

"Meaning what, exactly?"

Helen sighed and looked at Eliza like she was the dumbest Cupid on earth. "His switch. I can't get it to flip."

"And by *switch* you mean… You know what? Never mind. Why don't we start at the beginning?" Eliza asked. She needed time to regain her composure. Days probably. "How long have you and Jacque, uh, been together?"

"Three years. I even brought our 'love history'— that's the list of catalog choices I made when I purchased him—in case that would be helpful for you. I wasn't sure what you'd need. None of the other Cupids I tried were willing to help us." Helen plopped a thick folder on the table. "I know he's not real, but I paid a lot of money for him."

At a complete loss, Eliza pulled the folder forward and opened the cover. Height, hair color, skin color, eye color, chest width, other *widths*, all laid out there on the first page for the choosing. The next page went into things like voice octaves and catch phrases. Page three, labeled, *premium upgrades*, included options like streaming music service and GPS. Based on the boxes she'd checked, Helen had sprung for each and every upgrade.

"Um, Helen," Eliza said as she reviewed the paperwork. "Did you purposefully…" She shot a pointed look toward Jacque the Mandroid and then Jake the man.

Helen's forehead wrinkled in confusion. "Did I purposefully what?"

Jake cleared his throat. "Maybe I should wait

outside?" He took a sneaky step toward the door, his cheeks burning a brighter shade of red with each passing second.

"Don't you dare," Eliza whispered. If this lady had built a sex robot to look like Jake, they *had* to have gone on more than just one mediocre date. Right? *Right?* She turned back to Helen. "Can you remind me how you know Jake?"

The woman shrugged. "We went out once, what…five years ago? Three? I can't remember. No offense, Jake."

"None taken."

"Once?" Eliza asked.

Helen frowned. "How is this relevant to my current situation?"

Eliza glanced back and forth between Helen and Jake and back again. The woman seemed genuinely confused about, well, everything—except the fact that her robot had stopped performing his Mandroidly duties. "Really?" Eliza asked. "You don't see the—"

"Why don't we just move on?" Jake asked. "Helen, you said—"

Who cares what she said? I just want to know why she had a sex toy made to look like Jake. My Jake. "No," Eliza murmured, half a second too late to keep the thought from forming.

"Excuse me?" Helen said.

"Um, I, uh…" Eliza scrambled for an explanation that wouldn't involve (a) offending Helen or (b) admitting she'd just thought of Jake as *hers*. "I was just saying to myself *No way!* because I realized who Jacque reminds me of."

"Who's that?" Helen asked.

Eliza held up one hand as a fake shield and used the other to point at Jake, like this was a secret between girl-friends and not the most obvious answer on the planet.

"What?" Helen said, visibly confused. She looked at Jake. "I... No..." Then her hand flew to her mouth as her eyes went wide. "Oh! How did I...?"

"It's quite a coincidence," Eliza said.

"I ordered him long after our date. I didn't realize." Helen buried her face in her hands, and Eliza could nearly feel the embarrassment radiating from her.

Silence stretched throughout the office, and Eliza waited, praying someone else would break it. They didn't.

Talk about awkward. She definitely shouldn't have said anything. Now Helen had been shamed into silence, and Jake had apparently lost the ability to speak. And as for Jacque, well, he wasn't adding much to the conversation either.

"Helen, I'm sure Jake understands," Eliza finally said before giving Jake a help-me-out-here-*please* look.

His eyes widened for a beat before he regained his composure. "Yeah, please don't worry about it."

Helen shook her head in silence.

Say something else, Eliza mouthed.

Jake cleared his throat and shoved his hands into his pockets. "I'm flattered."

Finally, Helen looked up. "I swear it was subconscious. I've never had a very good imagination, so I guess my brain just filled in the blanks with...you."

"Please, don't worry about it," Jake said. "But I'm sorry to say that we aren't going to be able to help you. Love casting only works on humans, not, uh, robots."

"Mandroid," Helen corrected before she turned

back to Eliza. "Are you sure you can't help me? I read online that Man-A-Call—the company that makes Mandroids—is owned by a Cupid. There's a rumor that he can work enchantments on machines. That's why the Mandroids are so lifelike."

"Unfortunately, you can't believe everything you read online, especially when it comes to Cupids," Eliza said.

A muscle twitched along Helen's jaw. "I know. It's just… Do you know how much Jacque cost me—only to break the second he was out of warranty?"

"I don't," Eliza said. "I'm sorry. Is there anything else I can do for you? I'd be happy to—"

"You can fix Jacque."

Eliza sighed. "Helen, if you'd like—"

"Do you know what I risked to help you out the other day?" Helen's words were getting more barbed with each syllable.

Eliza took a deep breath and tried to look calm, cool, and professional. "A lot, I'm sure. And I appreciate—"

"I violated company policy for you. I could have lost my managerial position." Helen leaned over the desk, too close for comfort. "They could have sent me back to *produce*!"

"Let's all just take a minute, okay?" Eliza closed the folder and slid it back across the desk. "Helen, I'm very sorry that you're having trouble with Jacque, but enchantments don't work on inanimate objects. Maybe instead you'd be interested in hearing about one of our other packages? I'd be happy to offer you a very steep discount. We have—"

"Do you know how cold it is in the produce section, Eliza?" Helen asked.

Eliza gave Jake a clear SOS stare. He held up his hands in defeat.

"It's very cold every time I go in there," Eliza said.

"Thirty-four degrees," Helen said. "Thirty-four. That's *too cold*."

"Um, I'm sorry about that. But I really can't—"

"Then I guess you leave me no choice." Helen stuck her hand up the back of Jacque's shirt like a ventriloquist. He blinked twice, then turned to face Helen. The whole thing would have been impressive if it wasn't so damn creepy.

"Jacque, call the Department of Affection, Seduction, and Shellfish," Helen said.

"The Department of Affection, Seduction, and Shellfish nearest to you is the Northern California division of the Department of Affection, Seduction, and Shellfish," he said. "Is this who you would like to call?"

"No," Eliza said. Panic clashed and clanged inside her like a hyperactive toddler with a pair of cymbals. "No, Jacque, no."

Helen raised her eyebrows. "You're willing to help me then?"

"Yes. Yes, I'll help you. Or I'll at least give it a try."

Jake took a step forward. "Eliza—"

"It's fine, Jake. There's no harm in giving it a try."

"Are you going to call Oliver and give him twenty-four hours' notice before you enchant a sex robot?"

"Mandroid," Helen said, "and I'd rather not wait a full day to get my Jacque back."

Eliza sucked in a deep breath, then forced it out. She'd worked at an IT help desk for almost six months before this. Once, she'd spent an entire hour on the phone with a mansplaining CEO, trying to convince him that a screen saver was not something he needed to actively turn on. Certainly she could manage a Mandroid. "I already left him a message about this consultation. And since I'm not enchanting a human being, I don't see the need to report anything else to the Department," she said to Jake.

"See?" Helen petted Jacque's thigh. "We're going to take care of you, baby."

"I'll be out front," Jake said before fleeing to the relative safety of the lobby.

"Men always have that reaction to Jacque," Helen said when the door closed behind Jake.

Eliza wasn't about to open that can of Mandroid worms. "What's the problem with Jacque, exactly? Keep in mind that I've never seen a Mandroid in real life before."

Helen hauled Jacque to his feet and tugged his shirt over his head. Eliza was pretty sure Jake sported a six-pack, but the dummy version of him had at least eight distinct abs on his plastic torso. Without fanfare, Helen laid him across Eliza's lap. His head strayed uncomfortably close to her groin. "See? Three settings: virtual assistant, gaming assistant, and personal assistant. His personal assistant setting stopped working a month ago."

Eliza leaned over so she could see where Helen pointed. A black box sat between the Mandroid's shoulder blades. The tiny knob sat in the "virtual assistant" position, but the other two settings Helen had mentioned were also clearly labeled.

"Virtual assistant is like what you just did?" Eliza asked. "With the phone number?"

"And things like news, to-do lists. Watch this." She flipped Jacque faceup. "Jacque, read me my shopping list."

Jacque did that slow-blink thing again and turned to Helen. "Cantaloupe. Ground beef, two pounds. Supermax tampons, plastic applicator."

"Okay. Helpful," Eliza said. "And gaming assistant?"

She flipped Jacque over onto the desk, turned the knob to the correct position, flipped him back over, and pressed a button on his abdomen. A swath of his skin rolled down into his pants to reveal a touch screen. "I'm not much of a gamer. Or I didn't used to be. Lately, that's all he's good for though, so I've been playing a lot of *Bejeweled*, *Egg Salad Saga*, that sort of thing."

Eliza nodded as if that made perfect sense. "I assume personal assistant is his *other* function."

Helen nodded.

"What about this?" Eliza pointed to another knob higher on Jacque's neck. It also had three settings: verbal, manual, continual. "If you set it to verbal, what's supposed to happen?"

Helen's cheeks reddened just a little. "Verbal is dirty talk. Once you say enough trigger words to him, he's supposed to get an erection."

"So, manual is…" At a loss for words, Eliza made a quick back-and-forth motion with her hand.

Helen nodded. "And continual is just sort of automatic, you know? That was the last setting to go. For months, he'd ignored me unless I flipped him straight on. But now even that isn't working."

Poor Helen. First she'd had a flop of a date with Jake, and then she couldn't even arouse her sex robot. "Did he come with a user manual?" Eliza asked.

"It's useless. I've tried all the troubleshooting techniques already. I even called the company help desk. They basically said, 'Too bad, so sad,' and offered me a five percent discount on a new model. Can you believe that?"

In Eliza's experience, some sex toys were better than others, but new models tended to work just as well as the old ones. Of course, none of hers looked like Jake—so maybe that was the difference. "Do you have the manual?"

Helen pulled it from the back of the folder. "I spent a lot of my 401(k) on this," she whispered. "I really need you to fix him."

Ah. That *was the difference*. Eliza opened the guide. It might as well have been in a foreign language.

"You read French?" Helen asked, looking over her shoulder.

"Oh." Eliza flipped the booklet over to the side written in English.

But even with the words in English, she didn't understand much of anything. The only thing even remotely useful was a diagram of the Mandroid's inner workings. Apparently, he had a bladder near his belly button that held his "fluids." When he was turned on and, well, *turned on*, the bladder pushed the fluids into his penis, causing an erection. At an appointed time (set by the user, of course), the fluids shot out of the penis, leaving it deflated.

"Is he out of fluids?" Eliza asked.

"No. I flush and refill him every week, like clockwork."

Of course she did. Eliza stood and walked over to Jacque. "I drive an old car, and sometimes the coolant reservoir gets a little clogged. Once every few months, I stick an insulated wire through the hose and clean it out. But if I'm out on the road and I don't have one of those, I give it a little jiggle, jiggle, tap to see if I can get things moving."

"You enchant your car?" Helen asked. "But you said you can't enchant objects!"

"No. It's just a trick… You know what? Let's just try it. Can you take down his pants?"

Without any fanfare, Helen stripped the Mandroid naked and laid him across the desk. At least no one could say Eliza's life as a semiprofessional Cupid was boring. And since this morning's escapes hadn't rid her brain (and body) of a need for Jake, maybe tapping along Jacque's flaccid penis could completely kill her sex drive. *One way to get rid of the problem…*

"Okay, Helen. On my car, it helps if it's been running. When it's warm, the gunk in the tubes is looser. So, would you like to, um, warm him up?" Eliza asked.

"I can't." Helen sniffled some more. "I got my nails done right before I came over here. A manicure usually cheers me up."

"Are you sure, because—"

"Think of it like a medical procedure, Eliza. Please, go ahead."

Eliza stared at the naked Mandroid on her desk. It was time to decide how badly she wanted to be licensed. Yes, she wanted it badly enough to study her ass off. Yes, she wanted it badly enough to put her entire life on hold. But did she want it badly enough to do *this*?

Yes. Yes, she did. Because at the end of the day, if she had to jerk off a robot to help her family, that was what she'd do.

Here goes nothing. She closed her eyes, wrapped her hand around the penis—surprisingly lifelike—and squeezed. She'd just do this for five or ten seconds. Then things would—

The door flew open. "Eliza, I—Wow. I did not see this coming," Jake said.

Great. She dropped Jacque's penis and started to explain. But at the same time, Helen threw herself on top of Jacque, slamming Eliza against his nether regions. "Did you ever think of knocking first?" Helen barked.

Jake ignored her. "Eliza, I know you're worried about Oliver, but—"

Something grew rigid beneath her left boob. Very rigid. And very thick. "It's hard!"

Jacque's head turned back and forth. "Let me show you my pleasure horn," his deep, not-quite-human voice said.

"Jacque!" Helen shoved Eliza off the Mandroid and held him to her chest. "You're back!"

Eliza crept away until she stood beside Jake in the doorway. The robot's boner had knocked her so off guard that she forgot herself and grabbed Jake's elbow. "He probably just had a wire loose or something, right? And I knocked it back into place?"

"Yeah," Jake said. "Definitely." But something in his voice said he wasn't convinced.

And neither was Eliza. In fact, if she hadn't spent so many years in PSC classes, being taught that Cupids could not—under any circumstances—enchant inanimate objects, she'd think that was a hint of Love Luster sparkling in the corner of the room.

But that was crazy. *Right?*

Chapter 13.5

> "For Zeus's sake, stop trying to enchant the dogs. It only works on people!"
>
> **—Every parent who ever raised a Cupid**

WHAT THE…?

How did she…?

Why did it…?

You know what? I don't want to know.

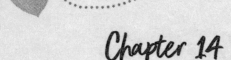

Chapter 14

"Cupid Exam Tip #42: Bring extra No. 2 pencils.
Although these are not technically regulation
approved, they can be thrown during projectile
weapon portions of the exam for partial credit."

—*Sterling & Rockwell's Strategies and Tactics
for Passing the Cupid Licensing Exam*

ELIZA PULLED RON WEASLEY INTO THE DEPARTMENT
parking lot and flipped through the pages of *Sterling and
Rockwell's*. The last week had been an oasis of calm.
Helen had left Herman & Herman a glowing review
online, and Eliza hadn't had to deal with any more customer shenanigans. Agent Oliver hadn't even called to
admonish Eliza about kissing Jake, and she and Jake had
agreed it would be best for him to keep his distance for
a few days—for the sake of their careers *and* her ability
to study for today's exam.

Knock, knock, knock.

Knuckles rapped against her window. Knuckles that
had once brushed across her neck and left goose bumps
behind.

She cracked the window. "Jake, hi."

"You ready?" he asked.

Ron blasted out a few angry notes of Metallica.
"That's new. Usually, it's just the CD, not the radio,"

Eliza said, smacking her hand on the dash until the car fell silent. "Sorry about that."

Jake looked beyond confused. "The car isn't even running."

"It's got a short in the stereo or something. Who knows? Anyway, I didn't realize you were coming."

He threw one last perplexed look at the car before leaning closer and giving her a wide grin. "I wouldn't miss my star pupil getting her license."

Her pulse picked up with a steady *Jake, Jake, Jake*.

"Besides," he said, "I have to certify your time log."

"Oh." She should have known. This was the last day of his enchantment after all, and his hormones were probably beginning to normalize again. Soon—too soon— she'd be just another girl with a mad crush on him.

Maybe Helen could help her order a Jacque of her very own.

Jake opened her door and gestured toward the bleak Department building. "If you get stuck on any of the multiple-choice questions, just remember that the Department makes all the regulations. So, if you can't choose between two answers, pick the one that best serves their interests."

"Generating tax revenue and protecting human life." She followed him into the building as she repeated the words from her study guide.

"In that order. And for the practical portion, just remember—"

"Keep my feet square and don't grip too hard." She'd watched a ton of videos on archery in the last few days and gotten in a few hours of practice at the range. Then she'd done some math. If she got every multiple-choice question right and aced the other weapons trials, she could flub the bow and still pass—by one point. But that didn't stop her brain from taking this moment to replay every Cupid-related mishap she'd had in the last twenty years.

"Jake, wait." She stopped a few feet from the door, and he nearly bumped into her back.

But instead of wrapping his arms around her waist or laying his lips on the back of her neck as she ~~hoped~~ feared he might, he took a few steps back and looked at her expectantly.

The enchantment was definitely wearing thin.

"What if I fail?" she asked.

He cocked his head slightly to the right, and his eyes bored into hers. "You're not going to fail."

"You don't know that."

He took a step forward and squeezed her hand. "You're not going to fail, Eliza."

"But what if I do? I'll let my dad down. I'll let you down—"

"Stop."

Indignation flared in her chest. "What?"

"Stop. You aren't doing this for your dad, and you aren't doing it for me. You're doing this for *you*."

"So if I fail, I'm just letting *myself* down? Great."

"You aren't going to let anyone down." He grabbed her hand and squeezed. "You've come a long way in the last couple of weeks, Eliza. Be proud of that, regardless of how this exam turns out, okay?"

She forced out a jagged breath and nodded. He was right. Of course. Jake the (gorgeous, funny, intelligent) know-it-all was always right. And his fingers intertwined with hers also felt exceptionally *right*. "Thank you," she whispered.

He gave her hand a final squeeze as they reached the door. "Go knock Oliver's socks off, Herman."

She put a hand on the door but didn't move. "Actually, about Oliver. I've been meaning to ask, is he a Descendant?" She felt slight shame at her inability to tell. For as long as she could remember, a Descendant could spot another Descendant a mile away. But with him, something wasn't quite the same.

"Oliver?" Jake scoffed. "Yeah, no. He's strictly human. Why?"

"There's just something about his...his... I don't know." She shrugged. It was probably just her nerves talking. Agent Oliver held her future in his hands, and that made her anxiety skyrocket. It must also be messing with her Descendant-detection abilities. "It's nothing. Never mind."

She pressed open the door and stepped inside. Four agents turned to look at her. Oliver, two women, and a man she didn't recognize. "Hi, I'm here for the exam."

"Well, Ms. Herman." Oliver stepped to the front of the crowd. "I have to say, I wasn't convinced you'd show. And I see you brought your *mentor* along." He smirked at her, and at once, Eliza knew he'd seen the kiss.

"He needs to certify my hours," she croaked. She paused, waiting for the dressing down.

It didn't come.

Her anxiety level multiplied by ten. Why wasn't Oliver saying anything about what he'd witnessed? Was he waiting for the worst possible time to bring it up? When could be worse than now?

"Let's get started. Peter, give Mr. Sanders the certification paperwork," Oliver said to one of the other agents. "I'll show Ms. Herman to the testing room."

Soon Eliza found herself sitting in an ancient desk—the kind with a metal seat attached to a scratched desktop. Probably the same one she'd used thirteen years ago when she'd first taken the test.

"I'll be back in thirty minutes. If you finish before then, just yell for one of us." Oliver shoved a thin booklet in front of her. "Write your answers in the blank at the bottom of each question. Write legibly. When that's done, we'll see if you qualify for the next part of the exam."

He fished a timer out of his jacket, pressed a button, and shut the door behind him.

Hands shaking, Eliza flipped over the packet. Bold, black instructions on the front page blurred in front of her. Each question became someone she loved—her parents, her brother, Jake. All of them staring up at her, depending on *her*—Eliza Herman, world's worst Cupid.

Fuck. Why was she thinking about Jake so much right now?

Thinking about her parents? Sure. She loved them and didn't want to let them down.

Elijah? She'd loved him since they were in the womb, and he was depending on her now more than ever.

But Jake… Did she love Jake? Like, capital-L Love him?

The pencil slid from her sweaty fingers, and the world spun as she lunged after it. Her chair tilted, and she launched straight out of it. Her tailbone hit the tile with a smack. Within seconds, Oliver stood in front of her.

"What's going on?"

"Nothing, sorry." She scrambled back to her seat. "I just fell."

He gave her a skeptical look, then disappeared once again.

Eliza closed her eyes and focused on the feel of the desk beneath her hands. Of course she didn't Love Jake. Love wasn't real. Her panic-addled brain was just trying to trick her into focusing on anything but the task in front of her.

Namely, the test. She forced open her eyes and stared at the pages in front of her. The written part should be easy. She'd read the books Jake had given her from front to back and then back to front. He'd quizzed her, and she'd passed with flying colors—even with her brain half-occupied by thoughts of their kiss.

And he believed in her.

It was high time she started to believe in herself too. *Okay, Herman, let's do this.*

Nineteen minutes and thirty-seven seconds later, Eliza put her pencil down. "I'm done," she called out.

Agent Oliver bumbled into the room, grabbed her booklet, and disappeared again. Eliza settled in to wait. Last time, this part—the grading—had crawled by. She'd felt like she'd lived an entire lifetime in that tiny room, just waiting—

Oliver returned and slapped the booklet on her desk. "You passed."

She stared up at his dull-eyed face, brain uncomprehending. "I did?"

"Come on. Weapons next."

Holy Hades, she'd done it.

Eliza stuffed the booklet into her back pocket and

scrambled to follow Oliver down a narrow hall. The back of the building smelled overly sterile, like someone had come through and doused everything with hand sanitizer. It burned her nostrils, and she forced herself to breathe through her mouth.

"What's wrong? You're not hyperventilating on me, are you? The last kid passed out, and we had to call the paramedics."

"No, I'm fine."

"Whatever you say." He pushed the back door open and motioned to an empty parking lot. "This way."

Eliza realized why she'd been overwhelmed with the smell of cleaning products inside. Along the side of the building, two ten-foot tables sat side by side, their surfaces covered with freshly sanitized weapons. In the center of the lot, a clump of civilians stood among the three agents she'd seen earlier.

"Where are the dummies?" Eliza asked.

"You're looking at 'em." Oliver pointed to the group. The sun made their shadows long, and a few had large pit stains—like they'd been waiting for her for days.

"Those are people. Not dummies. The last time I took this test, there were dummies."

"In *borderline* cases, we have the authority to make some changes, including but not limited to adjusting testing scenarios. Now, would you like to get started, or would you like to debate the merits of using dummies versus humans for another ten minutes?"

Bile raked its way up her throat. "Let's get started."

Oliver blew a whistle, and the crowd scattered. The agents manned the weapons table, while everyone else stood in groups of threes and fours on X's chalked onto the blacktop. "Ms. Herman, there is one weapon for each of these groups. You will approach group one. You will discuss their predilections and preferences. You will return to the weapons table and choose which two people in the group you will enchant. You will then perform said enchantment before three minutes per group have elapsed. Should you enchant anyone other than the designated couple, you will be automatically disqualified. Questions?" Before she could fit a word in, he continued, "No? Great. Let's begin." He pulled the timer from his pocket, pressed Start, and set it on the table.

For a full ten seconds, Eliza stood in the setting sun, sweating and confused. How? What? Why? Who were all these people who'd volunteered to be test subjects for her exam? Did they know what they were getting into? Had the Department told them they were going to be in the not-so-capable hands of Eliza Herman, World's Worst Cupid (trademark, patent pending)?

She gave them all a once-over. None of them looked terrified enough to understand what they'd volunteered to do. Time to turn this ship around and head back home.

"Eliza. Eliza!"

She whipped around at the sound of Jake's voice. He stood in the far corner of the lot in the shade, looking like her personal (and exceptionally handsome) cheerleader.

She jogged over to where he stood. "What are you doing?" she whispered, unsure whether to laugh or cry.

His face went serious before it slipped into a grin. "I wanted to see you one more time before you become an officially licensed Cupid with the state of California. In case, you know, you become unrecognizable once you ace the test."

"I don't think you have anything to worry about."

"You're going to crush this test, Eliza. I know it."

Agent Oliver approached, looking more annoyed than ever.

"Mr. Sanders, I asked you to wait in the lobby," he said. "Please don't make me file a complaint against you. The paperwork is astounding."

"My apologies, sir." Jake gave small wave before heading toward the door.

"Time is ticking, Ms. Herman," Oliver called out.

Eliza took a deep breath. She might have lost some time due to Jake's interruption, but his presence had steadied her nerves. *Time to show this exam who's boss.* She moved toward the first group of volunteers. This one was easy. Two adults and a child. Enchanting anyone under the age of eighteen was strictly forbidden. "Hi," she said to the kid. "I'm Eliza."

He ducked behind his hands. "I'm Adam."

"Adam, do you know these people?" She gestured toward the adults.

"These are my mommies."

"Well, I'm going to help them love each other even more than they do now. Is that okay with you?"

He nodded, and the women smiled at her softly.

She sprinted to the table, grabbed the weapon labeled with the number one—a lancing device—and ran back. The timer ticked away her remaining minute. But as soon as she returned to her first victims, she realized she'd left the spray bottle of sanitizer behind on the table. Oliver would definitely knock points off her score if she didn't clean the device after the first woman's finger stick.

Damn it. She'd wasted too much time in the beginning

with her freak-out. Her brain flashed forward to telling her father she'd failed the test in the first round of weaponry. She'd made it further as a teenager.

"Finger, please?" Eliza said to the first woman.

She held out her index finger, and Eliza pointed her face to her partner. "Look straight ahead, please. Just a quick stick, and we're done."

Eliza stuck the woman's finger, drawing a bright-red dot of blood. In profile, she saw the woman's face light up. *Perfect*. Now she just had to find an impromptu weapon provided by woman number two before all her time disappeared. Eliza could almost hear it ticking in the back of her mind. She gave the second woman a quick once-over. *Bingo*.

"Ma'am, could I see your earring for a moment?" she asked.

The woman gave her a confused look but handed over the jewelry. Eliza pointed her in the right direction and poked her bare shoulder with the earring post. *Bull's-eye*. She dropped the earring into the woman's palm and took off for the table, where Oliver waited with his arms crossed over his chest.

"Ms. Herman, care to explain your choices?"

She struggled to catch her breath as she spoke. "The *who* was simple. Section 06.25 of the *Code of Cupid Regulations* prohibits enchantment of anyone under the age of eighteen."

"And the weapon? You were instructed to use the weapon provided."

"I did use the weapon on person number one. However, since I wasn't able to properly sanitize it between enchantments, I chose to use a weapon provided by client number two. I believe this would be acceptable under section 304, Sanitation and Sterilization."

He looked at her for a long moment without saying a word. Finally, he pursed his lips and motioned for her to move on to group two.

Eliza flew through the next three groups, even with each one becoming progressively harder. Group two involved two pairs of exes, a baton, and a lot of wishful thinking. Group three: a professor, two of his students, and a pocketknife. Luckily, it was the students who were meant to be—at least for the next moon cycle. Group four: retirees and nurses from Gold Lea Assisted Living, an oxygen tank, and a warning about doubling up on enchantments and Viagra.

Then she arrived at group five. Her final test involved a man and a woman Eliza didn't recognize. And another man she almost recognized but couldn't quite place. Maybe she'd seen him at Red Clover? Or at the gym? Or maybe... Realization struck hard and fast, knocking her off her game.

She *did* recognize him, because he was Jonathan Ellis, her childhood nemesis. *Please don't recognize me. Please don't recognize me.*

"Hi, Eliza." He had the same smirk he'd had as a kid. She wanted to smack it right off his face. But of course, the Department would probably fail her if she did.

"Jonathan."

"This girl hit me upside the head with a baseball bat when I was eight," he said to the people beside him. "Knocked out two of my teeth, and my shoulder's been jacked up ever since. Probably could have played MLB ball, but my whole future was ruined."

"What? No, I didn't. Well, not the tooth thing. And your shoulder was fine."

"You hit him with a baseball bat?" The man balked.

Jonathan pointed to his front teeth. "Yeah, both of these are veneers. Worst pain I've ever experienced. There was so much blood, I actually passed out. Not sure if it was from shock or what, but it was bad. Really bad."

"Why are you doing this?" she whispered. "None of this is true."

"Just thought these two should know what they're getting into," he yelled over his shoulder. Then quietly to her, "They told me what to say—the Department, I mean. I'm supposed to make you sound really scary."

"Why would you tell me that?" Eliza asked.

"Because I need a favor, and now you owe me one. Two favors, if you count the whole baseball bat thing from when we were kids. Can we talk after this?"

"No. We can't." She couldn't devote one more second to whatever Jonathan Ellis needed from her. She turned to the man and woman standing beside him. Their fingers had already intertwined—probably out of fear—but Eliza knew they had to be the choice. "Are you two interested in enchantment?" she asked.

They stared at her with terror in their eyes. Finally, the woman gave the smallest nod.

"Great." She adjusted their bodies so they were holding hands and staring into each other's eyes. "Stay here, just like this, and I'll get things started."

She sprinted back to the table and grabbed her final assigned weapon: the bow and two arrows.

I can do this. I can do this. She nocked the first arrow and took her stance. Squared feet, grip tight but not too—

"Wait! Stop!" the woman cried out. She looked straight at Eliza. "What are you doing? You're going to kill us. You heard what that man said, Bobby. It was the worst pain of his entire life."

"Yeah, I don't know about this," the man said. "What if there's a lot of blood?"

Eliza put down the arrow, sprinted back to the X and offered the couple her kindest smile. "These are enchantment arrows," she explained. "There might be a small amount of blood, but they're designed to barely pierce the skin. With a skilled archer, you shouldn't feel much of anything."

"Are you a skilled archer?" the man asked.

"I'm getting there," she said.

"So, no?"

"I can't promise there won't be any pain."

The man pushed past Eliza and headed toward the group of agents. "No, thank you. I'd like to withdraw my consent."

Eliza's shoulders sagged. She couldn't exactly force an enchantment on the man, no matter how badly she wanted her license. "Fine."

She walked away from the group of test subjects, but she wasn't giving up without a fight. "Agent Oliver. I'd like to request a new test group. My current group has withdrawn their consent to—"

Beep. Beep. Beeeeeep.

That was it. She'd run out of time, and she hadn't shot a single arrow. She hadn't faced down her biggest weaponry challenge, and her career had ended before it really began. Jake had put in all those hours to help her for nothing. Her father had gotten his hopes up, and now she had to go home to tear them into tiny shards.

Eliza raked a hand through her ponytail and stared at the blue sky. Maybe if she didn't meet anyone's eye, her tears wouldn't fall. But sooner or later, she'd have to look in the mirror and face the person she'd disappointed most of all.

"Congratulations, Ms. Herman," Oliver said. "You're a fully licensed Cupid."

She did a double take. "I passed? How?"

"The final test was designed to see if you would put your own interests above those of clients who'd had a change of heart." He tore a piece of paper from the clipboard in his hands and handed it to her. "Take this to the front, and Agent Smith will process you."

Eliza barely heard him. She couldn't stop staring at the paper. This was it: her official license. Her official show-at-Hallmark-for-an-additional-fifteen-percent-off license. She couldn't wait to pick it up.

But first, she had one very important thing to do.

Chapter 15

Calif. CCR § 1024.070. The Department shall charge a replacement fee of thirty-five dollars for each lost, stolen, or damaged Cupiding license.

ELIZA FLUNG OPEN THE DOOR TO THE DEPARTMENT lobby. If this were a movie version of her life, triumphant music—maybe "We Are the Champions"—would have been booming as she came through the doors in dramatic slow motion. But this was Eliza's real life, so she tripped and fell flat on her face.

Well, not quite on her face. She'd thrown her arms out and landed on her right elbow. Painful tingles shot up and down her arm. She rubbed it out, thanking the gods that she couldn't enchant herself. If that were possible, she'd be an even bigger mess.

A hand closed on her shoulder. "Are you okay?"

She stopped rubbing her elbow and looked into warmest, softest brown-and-gold eyes she'd ever seen. The exact pair she'd been on her way to find.

"I passed," she said to Jake.

His entire body lit up. "I knew you would."

And then she was wrapped in his arms. Later, Eliza wouldn't be able to remember who'd initiated that embrace. Was it Jake, who'd stepped out of his safe zone to check on her post-fall? Or was it her, leaning into him out of sheer joy and relief?

In that moment, Eliza didn't care. Not even a little.

That incessant voice in the back of her mind, the one that always reminded her this road led to madness, stayed silent. It was just her, Jake, and the roughness of his five-o'clock shadow against her forehead.

That and the thumping in her chest. A thumping that seemed to propel her to press harder against him. It was really too bad all this would be over in less than twelve hours.

"Ahem."

They stumbled apart at the unfamiliar voice.

Eliza's cheeks nearly burst into flames as she stood in front of one of the agents who'd observed her test. "Your new license," the agent said, holding out a white rectangle. "Don't lose it, or there's a thirty-five-dollar replacement fee."

"There must be a mistake. I haven't gotten my photo taken."

"We use the photo from your temporary identification." The agent gave her a half-smile. "No need to waste resources on a new photo after just a month."

Eliza took the license. Sure enough, there she was in all her eyelids-half-open glory. She tucked it into her pocket and added the photo to the list of things that didn't matter anymore. She took Jake by the hand, too giddy to care about "the rules."

"Let's go celebrate."

Thursday nights at the Agora were an even madder house than the grocery store on a Monday. A few months ago, Eliza would have pulled into the crowded parking lot and pulled right back out. But now she had a license. She belonged.

She handed the ever-present and ever-grumpy Mrs. Washmoore her fancy new ID and stepped inside with Jake beside her. They passed the Poseidon fountain and veered left, beyond a storefront advertising *BOGO Ambrosia* and a series of Cosmic Council offices.

ROOM 301: COSMIC COUNCIL CONFERENCE ROOM

ROOM 302: RECORDS, PERMITS, AND DESCENDANT BENEFITS

ROOM 303: CIRCUIT FURY

Between the rooms, bulletin boards full of community announcements proclaimed that local elections were on the horizon. "Look." Eliza pointed to the sign. "The deadline for submitting your name is next week."

Jake didn't quite meet her eye. "Yeah. I'll have to look into it."

"What do you mean, 'look into it'?" Eliza laughed. "You *have* to follow your dumb idea. That's our thing."

He wrapped an arm around her shoulders and tugged her down the hall. Gods, he made every part of her tingle. "Noted. Now, can we please get to Dionysus before my stomach digests itself? I was too nervous to eat this morning."

Her stomach rumbled at the mention of food. "What did you have to be nervous about? All you had to do was sign your name."

"Are you kidding me? Do you know how tough it is to sign all those Department forms? I thought my hand was going to fall off by the time I'd certified that you were fit for duty as a Cupid."

"Well, I appreciate all your hard work."

"I'm glad to hear it." He pulled her a little closer, enough for his hip to settle into the space at her waist as they approached Dionysus. Faint hints of techno music escaped into the empty hall outside the bar. It was dark enough to make her bold, but light enough to tell they were the only two around.

Eliza stopped walking and faced him. "Jake?"

"Yeah?"

Gods, she had a hundred things she wanted to say to him. He'd ruined her for anyone else. He'd made her believe in herself again. He'd made her believe in Love—if only temporarily. But with just a few hours of enchantment remaining, Eliza couldn't say any of those. Once midnight struck, things would change, and she didn't want him to feel beholden to her. Like he'd need to let her down easily or try to keep from breaking her heart. It was going to break anyway, so she might as well save him the trouble of knowing about it.

"Thank you for everything," she said. "I mean it."

He stood close enough for her to feel the breath hitch in his chest. "My pleasure." The corners of his eyes crinkled, like he was about to say something very important and maybe even a little naughty when—

"Welcome to Dionysus! Thursday night is Nereid Night, and we've got the *best* specials to celebrate." The piercing voice sliced through their moment. It belonged to the tall, thin Dionysian who'd poked his head out into the hallway. "Right this way."

He led them through a maze of chairs and bodies to

a table right up against a floor-to-ceiling fish tank—or rather, Nereid tank. Inside, starfish and coral sat at the bottom, while a stunning sea nymph rode through the blue-green waves on the back of a turtle.

"So, this is the famous Nereid Night?" Eliza asked Jake.

"It is. Things get rowdy after midnight, but before that, it's not too bad."

"By not too bad, I assume you mean the beautiful, bikini-clad nymphs floating around?"

Jake leaned forward and brushed her hair out of her face. His thumb lingered against her cheek, and the gold in his eyes flickered in the dim light of the bar. "Eliza," he said. "Does it look like I care about the bikini-clad nymphs right now?"

"Not really." Every part of her wanted to climb in his lap and bury herself in his arms. Maybe this once—now that he wasn't her mentor, and the Department didn't seem to care about her sex life (or lack thereof)—she could give in a little. Enjoy the long glances and soft touches while she still could. She leaned closer to Jake. "Do you want—"

Knock, knock, knock.

Eliza jerked out of her chair, nearly knocking her head on the tank. The Nereid inside smiled and waved brightly, as if she'd been newly crowned Miss Greek Universe. And with that cascading black hair and teal shell top that barely covered any of her brown skin, she looked like she could be a contestant. She also looked like—

"Quinn?" Eliza said.

The Nereid swam to the top of the tank and hung over the edge. Saltwater droplets splattered on the table, and the scent of sea and sand permeated the air. "Hey, you! Long time, no see. When you first sat down I thought, *That girl reminds me of Eliza Herman*. But then you didn't knock anything over, so I figured I had it all wrong. But *then* I heard you talk and I knew—Delta Iota Kappa for life! How are you?"

Eliza looked back and forth between Jake—who had a very amused look on his face—and Quinn, the sorority sister from her college days. "Pretty great, actually."

Quinn wrung out the ends of her long hair and flipped it over one shoulder. "Same. Ever since this place started Nereid Night, I've been so busy. The tips here are great."

"You two were in a sorority together?" Jake asked.

"Like any of us can go to college and *not* go Greek," Quinn said.

"Fair enough," Jake said. "I'm going to go get us some drinks while you two catch up. What would you like, Eliza?"

"Whatever you're having is fine."

"Oh, me too!" Quinn said.

Jake looked like he couldn't quite figure out what to make of Quinn, but he nodded and headed off to the bar anyway.

"Who is *that*?" Quinn asked the second he was out of earshot.

"Just a friend. More of a mentor, really." Eliza explained the whole Cupid license fiasco that had become her life.

"Well, congrats on the test and all that." Quinn adjusted her shell top. "But that man is looking at you like he wants to rip your clothes off and ravage you right here in Dionysus. I mean, it wouldn't be the first time that happened, but usually nobody does that kind of thing until after midnight."

Eliza batted away the (very dirty) thoughts of Jake doing just that. "It's only because I accidentally enchanted him. He'll get over it."

"I'm not so sure." Quinn wagged her eyebrows. "Besides, you know how it is when you're enchanted. If you aren't into something, you aren't into it regardless. He definitely wants to be *into it*."

"Oh gods, Quinn." Eliza laughed. "If you only knew how much I wanted him to be *into it*. The other day, I tried to take matters into my own hands, if you know what I mean, and it only made things worse. I swear—"

"Ahem."

Quinn giggled and ducked underwater, and Eliza whipped around. Jake, all six-foot-something of perfection and muscle, stood less than a foot behind her with a set of drinks in his hand and a wide grin on his face. So *that's* what Quinn's little eyebrow wiggle had been all about.

"Oh, hi," Eliza said. "We were just, um, talking about—"

Jake reached up and set the drinks on the edge of the tank, well within Quinn's reach. The movement brought him into Eliza's space, and he put a hand on Eliza's waist. "Whether or not I'm *into it*."

She gulped. "Well, uh, yeah—"

He leaned in, and his lips brushed the shell of her ear. "Eliza, let me reassure you that I am very, very *into it*."

Her resolve was melting faster than a snow cone on Kronia. "Enchantment," she muttered. "Moon cycle, tomorrow, regret." How could anyone expect her to form complete sentences when his warm breath ran along her neck like that?

"Herman," he whispered, "stop trying to protect me from whatever you think is wrong with you. You are perfect, and I want you."

"I'm a mess."

"A perfect mess. And I guarantee you the only regret I'll have tomorrow is if I wake up knowing you had to *take things into your own hands* tonight. But sometime, I definitely want to hear all about that. Every. Last. Detail." He pulled her closer, and the movement brought back all those memories of that day on the hood of his car. The way his hardness had sent shocks through her spine. How everything else in the world had stopped existing. The moment she'd forgotten she was Eliza Herman, World's Worst Cupid, and simply become one half of their perfect match.

A smart, professional Cupid would take a step back. Put space between them. Remind herself that this was all an enchantment and nothing more.

She was smart and professional.

Mostly.

Sometimes.

But not today.

"Want to get out of here?" she whispered.

"In a minute. I've got something I need to do first."

"Oh, right. The drinks. We shouldn't let them go to waste."

She turned toward the drinks, but before she could get that far, Jake's hand wrapped around her waist. He turned her back to face him and pulled her in for a slow, aching kiss. It made all the blood rush by Eliza's ears on its way south. She rose up on her tiptoes, silently begging for more, but his lips and tongue taunted her—giving only enough to make her want more. So much more. "Forget the drinks," he said as he pulled away. "Now I'm ready."

As Eliza followed him toward the door, she caught Quinn giving her a thumbs-up from inside the tank. Eliza gave her friend a quick wave and took in Jake's form walking ahead of her. From his brain to his body to his unending belief in her, he was everything she wanted and then some.

"I hope I'm ready," she muttered.

➤➤➤➤➤

Eliza's shoulders landed against the back of the door with a soft *thump*. Gods, Jake felt amazing. She hooked her legs around his waist and tugged him closer. Even with all these layers of clothes between them, she slipped a little closer to bliss every time his erection pressed against her center. They'd barely made it through the drive back to his apartment, with their wandering hands and all the lingering kisses they'd stolen at stoplights. And now they'd only just made it inside before she started rubbing herself against him like she couldn't get enough.

His mouth strayed along her jaw and lips and neck. His warm breath on her skin made her dizzy and giddy and *desperate*.

And it was the best thing she'd ever felt in her life.

Jake broke their kiss—the deep, frantic sort she felt all the way in her toes—and set her feet on the floor. "You okay?" he asked.

"Yeah. You?"

The groan that escaped his lips reached all the way to her core. "I could be better." He laid a soft kiss on her neck before working his way up to her lips.

"How's that?" she asked when they came up for air.

"Better," he murmured. His thumb tugged her bottom lip before he caught it between his own. "Much better."

The lust in his eyes overwhelmed her. She'd never felt more beautiful. More *wanted*. She shifted her hips to press harder against him.

"But you know—" His hand slid beneath her shirt, warm fingers spread against her skin. "I could be even better."

"Really?" She looked up at him through her eyelashes. She couldn't fathom anything better than this.

"You could be naked and wrapped around me. Or naked and sprawled wide open on my bed. Or naked and on my kitchen table…"

"I'm sensing a theme here," Eliza said.

"The theme is you. Naked." He turned her, pressing her back against his hard chest and planting his lips at the nape of her neck. The movement forced her gaze to the clock, where the minute hand seemed to move in slow motion toward midnight. Five minutes left in the enchantment.

Five minutes until judgment day.

Or at least until she'd know if he *really* wanted to see her naked or not.

She slid away, even though every inch of her skin sobbed in protest, and turned toward him. "Jake?"

"Yeah?"

She nodded toward the clock. "I think we should wait until midnight. Just in case."

His fingers skimmed the curve of her hip. "I'll wait as long as you want, but I promise you, in five minutes—in five days, weeks, whatever—the theme is still going to be Eliza: naked."

Please, gods, let that be true.

She glanced at the clock again. Less than one minute had gone by. If she didn't know better, she'd think the universe had conspired to stop time just to torture her. She took a step away from Jake and forced her focus onto the two tall bookshelves in the corner. Dozens of spines—some perfect, some cracked—lined each and every shelf. Most appeared to be textbooks or study guides, but a few well-loved novels sat among them. And interspersed were a few framed photos. Jake with friends in an assortment of far-flung locations. Jake with his parents—who looked considerably older than the last time Eliza had seem them. Jake with—

"Is this us?" She picked up the black wooden frame and stared at the familiar kids smiling at the camera. Well, Elijah, Jake, and the others in the photos—names and faces Eliza had long forgotten—smiled. Eliza looked one hundred and ten percent miserable. Which had been an inaccurate representation of how she'd felt that night.

She'd been one hundred fifteen percent miserable.

"Yeah." He glanced over her shoulder at the photo. "Our seventh-grade Halloween dance. I believe you went as—"

"The Fruit of the Loom grapes. Surrounding myself in a giant pile of balloons seemed like the best way to avoid accidental enchantments."

His voice softened. "That was one of the last times

we ever hung out. After that night, you…just disappeared. Why?"

She put the photo back on the shelf. "I'm a magician, and I was practicing my magic act?"

"Eliza." Jake caught her hand between his. "What happened back then? Why did we stop being friends? *Best* friends."

Why did this discussion make her feel twelve years old all over again? Awkward and sweaty and deliriously attracted to Jake Sanders. "I started *feeling* things. For you, I mean."

"Me?" He seemed genuinely shocked by her revelation.

"Yes, you. And I knew that if we kept spending time together, I'd eventually accidentally enchant you."

He laughed. "So?"

"So, when I accidentally enchanted you and discovered you weren't attracted to me, I would have been devastated. I couldn't stand the idea of having my heart broken and losing my best friend all because of one clumsy move."

"That wouldn't have happened, you know." His voice was barely a whisper. "Because all those *feelings* you were having? I was having them too. For you."

The sadness in his expression poked the darkest recesses of her heart. If she could only go back and shake some sense into the preteen version of herself… They'd wasted so much time. *She'd* wasted so much time.

"I'm sorry," she said.

"You're forgiven." He skimmed her cheekbone with his thumb, all tenderness and nostalgia. "I'm glad it didn't work out back then."

"You are?"

He nodded. "Teenage Jake would have screwed things up somehow. Then I probably wouldn't be here with you. Right now. At twelve-oh-two in the morning, wondering if I'm ever going to convince you that you're *it* for me, Eliza."

"Twelve-oh-two?" She whipped around to look at the clock again. Sure enough, the seconds had begun ticking by at a normal pace once again. Rich, buttery relief flowed over her. They'd made it through to the other side, and if the way Jake was looking at her was any indication, not a thing had changed.

"Enchantment officially done," he said.

She closed the space between them, sinking into his warmth and hardness all over again. But this time she made space in her brain for that little voice that kept telling her things could be different this time. Maybe it didn't have to end in heartache and disaster.

"Enchantment officially done," she repeated.

Chapter 15.5

Calif. CCR **§ 107.12.** For malpractice purposes, Cupids shall not be legally liable for affection-related mishaps occurring on or after midnight on the last day of the applicable moon cycle.

I STARE AT HER FACE, LOOKING FOR THE SMALLEST hints in the flicker of her dark lashes, a tiny clue in the way she purses those delicate lips. Nothing.

Eliza features are blank in a way I've never seen before. I've pictured this moment a hundred times in the last few weeks, and blank-as-the-Jetsons'-robot was never the expression I'd planned on—or hoped for.

"Twelve-oh-two?" she whispers again.

I nod slowly, like I don't want to spook her. "The enchantment is officially gone."

"And?"

I gnaw at the inside of my cheek, trying to find the perfect words. *And I feel exactly the same as I did two minutes ago?* Not true. Two minutes ago, I Loved her a little less, because every second that I spend in her presence makes me fall harder than ever before.

And the harder I fall, the scarier things get. What if *she's* the one who changes her mind? Will she somehow lose interest now that the enchantment's gone? Am I going to end up in some flashback-to-the-seventh-grade scenario, where I end up at home, alone, holding my heart in my hands?

"Eliza?" I ask.

"Do you still want me?" Her voice shakes a little at the end, and she's shifted her weight away from me and toward the door.

Time to leap out of the plane headfirst and pray my chute opens.

"I still want you, Eliza," I finally say. I duck my chin so I can stare straight into those wide brown eyes. I don't want there to a single drop of doubt clouding what I'm about to say. "It doesn't matter that the enchantment is over. I still want you. Mentally, emotionally, physically. I want you curled up on the couch next to me, watching old game shows. I want you leaving a toothbrush in my apartment. I want you calling me first when Ron Weasley decides to crap out. I want—"

"Hey, Ron does his best." A grin splits her face. The kind of grin that makes me ache everywhere but especially below the belt line.

If I didn't know better, I'd think even that damn car is in love with Eliza. Not that I could blame it. She's gorgeous.

Smart.

Funny.

Amazing.

When I finally manage to speak, my voice comes out lower and coarser than before. *She* does this to me. "I want you, Eliza, naked and spread out in my bed. On my couch. On my kitchen counter."

She steps close again, invading my space in the best

way. This—those coy eyes and parted lips and shallow breaths—*this* is the expression I'd hoped for. "Prove it."

And I will. A hundred times over. For as long as she'll let me.

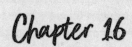

Chapter 16

> "When it comes to sex, the most important six inches are the ones between the ears."
>
> **—Ruth Westheimer, Aphroditian**

JAKE DIPPED HIS HEAD AND GAVE HER A FULL, DEEP kiss. Eliza wasn't sure where his mouth stopped or hers started, whether gravity had ceased to exist, or if the moan that escaped her lips was a sign of relief or desperation. But she did know one thing: with that kiss, Jake had *proven it* and then some.

She pulled back and looked at him looking at her…and forgot how to breathe. It was if every moment of the last few weeks—no, every moment of their entire lives—had been leading to that look. There were weeks of wanting, years of friendship, and decades of history in that look. And it made her feel more vulnerable than she'd ever been.

"Jake?" she whispered, settling back against the couch cushions. "You're staring."

"Because I want to remember every second of this. The way your chest hitches when I touch you." He slid both hands under her shirt, grasping her hips, fingers tracing the skin of her back. "How you moan a little every time we kiss." He pulled her bottom lip between his. "How you feel when I touch you." His left hand slipped higher, caressing the curve of her breast.

At his touch, all that vulnerability disintegrated. All she could think about—all she could feel—was Jake, and she needed more. So much more. She kissed him harder, lost in the overwhelming sensations of his hands on her. Of the weight of his body beside her. Of the way he made her feel, inside and out.

"How do you do that?"

"Do what?" She nipped at his neck, reveling in the goose bumps that appeared on his skin.

"When you're around, nothing else matters." His thumb grazed the bow of her lips. "It's like you become the only star in the sky, and all I can think about is worshipping you."

Eliza grinned. Her entire body filled with a light so bright it could have been liquid starlight. But deep down, she knew it was so much more than that. This was what it was like to be accepted and accepting. Supported and supportive. Wanted and wanting.

This was what it was like to be in L—

"Touch me," she whispered. "Please."

Thank the gods she didn't have to ask him twice.

He slid a hand between her thighs. "Like this?"

Eliza burned brighter and hotter. The rough fabric of her jeans was somehow both a blessing and a curse, and she could only manage a moan in response.

"Or like this?" Jake thumbed the button of her jeans and ran his fingers across the fabric of her underwear. His featherlight touch felt so amazing, Eliza feared she may climb out of her skin with want.

"Like this." She leaned back, took his hand, and guided it to her center. She wanted nothing between them. Not clothes or secrets or enchantments. She wanted all of him, and in turn, she was giving him full access to every part of her.

She could only pray he would take it.

He did. Readily and easily, his finger slid against her slick skin, finding her most sensitive parts. Gods, she was already so on edge that one simple touch threatened to undo her.

"Jake." She put her hand on his wrist. "You're making me crazy."

His wild-eyed grin nearly lit her from the inside out. "Good crazy or bad crazy?"

"I'm-going-to-come-right-here-in-your-living-room-if-you're-not-careful crazy."

"That's definitely the good kind of crazy." Two fingers now, gliding across her folds, making stars appear at the edges of her vision.

"It is?" she murmured.

He nodded. "You're going to come in my living room and then in my bed and then in my shower. And if you can manage to walk after that, I'm going to make you come in my kitchen. I wasn't kidding about the kitchen-table thing."

She tried to think of a witty reply, but…words? What were words? All that existed was Jake, his lips and fingers pressing against her, taking her. She tilted her head back, giving in to every sensation: Jake slipping her pants from her ankles. Jake unhooking her bra—finally—and slipping her hard nipple into his mouth. Jake guiding her to lay down and tugging her underwear off. Soon she sat completely naked as he knelt before her.

"Lean back," he whispered.

She leaned. Every muscle in her body coiled, wound

tight as a spring. Jake grasped her thighs, just tight enough to show her exactly how much he wanted this, and opened her wide. His scruff scraped her thigh, a hint of pain that made his touch all the more pleasurable.

"Gods, Eliza. You're gorgeous," he muttered before laying his mouth on her.

The world tilted. All she could do was sink her hands into Jake's hair and hold on for dear life. His lips and tongue and fingers were all over her, on her, in her. Down was up, and up was down, and she was writhing against Jake Sanders like everything in her world depended on it.

Like he'd *become* her world.

Jake's fingers slid in deeper, his tongue probed harder. Soon, she was panting and free-falling straight into ecstasy. He sat back, a troublemaking grin on his face and heat in his eyes. "You're so fucking amazing," he whispered.

She stared at the ceiling and took a few deep breaths, gathering her wits and her stamina. When she looked back at him, another wave of desire crashed into her. "I have a serious problem with this," she said, smiling.

The crinkles around his eyes deepened. "What?"

"You're wearing far too many clothes."

Jake laughed. "Did I mention you're fucking perfect?" he asked, hauling her up and tossing her over his shoulder. His palm smacked lightly against her bottom before he carried her into his bedroom and tossed her onto his mattress. "Lie down, Herman. We've got work to do."

She leaned back on her elbows, enjoying the show as he stripped off his shirt. Then pants. Then boxers. Until nothing remained but his broad shoulders, flat stomach, and the trail of fine hair leading to his thick erection. "Work, work, work," she said. "Don't you ever take a day off?"

"From this?" He crawled over her and hooked one hand under her thigh. "From thinking about you naked? Fantasizing about you under me? On top of me? Nope. Not a single day off. I'm a workaholic."

She slipped a hand between them and stroked. The soft skin of his cock was a perfect contrast to the hardness of his length. Above her, he closed his eyes and let out a ragged moan. The sound sent her body into overdrive, and in seconds, she was ready to go again. "Condoms?" she asked.

He kept his eyes closed and fumbled through the bedside table. "Gods, Eliza. I can't even think when you're touching me."

She stopped touching him. Jake opened his eyes and grumbled.

"What's wrong?"

"I can't find them."

She pressed her free hand to his chest, wishing she could do something to take his disappointment and frustration away. And then—just as she was having an internal debate on the merits of giving him a surprise blow job—realization dawned. "How do you feel about peach cobbler?" she asked.

"What? It's okay, I guess."

She grinned—a wide, illicit thing that threatened to split her in half with all the happiness she felt. "Stay here. Don't move."

She jumped out of bed and ran back toward the living room, where she'd dumped her purse. Less than a minute later, she was back with the peach-cobbler-flavored condom in her hands. She waggled it at him.

"In that case, I fucking love peach cobbler," Jake said.

"I thought you might."

"Did I mention that you're perfect? Like, absolutely perfect?"

She rolled the condom over him, taking her time and relishing the way he twitched beneath her touch. "Once or twice." She straddled his waist and leaned down for a soft kiss.

He palmed her ass, pressing her opening to his tip. "Well, let me tell you again," he said as he slid inside her while their eyes locked. "You are fucking perfect, Eliza Herman."

"Oh gods," she whispered.

Every single centimeter of her skin aflame. Every nerve ending sparking. Every movement turning her world inside out.

Turning her into more.

Turning *them* into something more.

Minutes passed. Maybe hours. Perhaps even a lifetime. None of it mattered, because Jake—*her* Jake—was inside her and they were moving together. As one. Everything else had ceased to exist.

He rolled her nipples into furious points. First the right, then her left, murmuring her name the whole time. Everything spun. The heavy way he looked up at her—like she was the star of his wildest, sexiest dreams—sent Eliza even closer to the edge.

She rocked her hips harder and faster, pressing him deeper inside her, begging them both for release. "Jake. Jake." It was the only word her lips could utter.

He tugged her mouth down to meet his, and their eyes locked. With a final thrust of her hips, release washed over her. Slow, then fast. Faint, then intense. Her body shattered around him, all control surrendered to the feel of his body trembling and twitching beneath hers.

"Eliza?" he whispered.

She struggled to catch her breath, and sweat beaded her skin. "Yeah?"

"You're so fucking perfect," he repeated.

She splayed a hand across his chest. His soft patch of hair caught between her fingers. She sighed, soaking up the feel of being so entirely intertwined with him. "Hardly. But this? Us? Fucking perfect."

"Hmmm." Jake kissed the tip of her nose before breaking into a playful grin. "I think we can do even better."

"You do?" She couldn't fathom anything better. Ever.

"I do. With practice, of course."

She laughed. "Well, you are my mentor. So if you think we need to keep practicing—"

"Oh, we're definitely going to need *a lot* of practice. In fact, I have a new rule I'd like to propose."

"What's that?" she asked.

He sank a hand into the hair at the nape of her neck and pulled her close. "We do that every day, twice a day, for the foreseeable future."

Eliza dropped her lips to his. "Deal," she whispered.

⟶

An hour later, Eliza's eyelids were as heavy as lead, but she fought to keep them open. Some distant part of her still believed that in the morning, the spell would be broken. She'd wake up in Jake's bed, everything would be awkward, and then she'd need to go into hiding for at least three years before she could ever show her face in the Agora again.

Until then, she wanted to soak in every moment. The way Jake's shoulder felt against her cheek, the way their legs intertwined beneath the sheets, the way their breaths fell in time with each other. Soft and slow.

"Jake?" she whispered. "Are you still awake?"

His fingers traced her shoulder. "Depends."

She shifted her weight to one forearm and sat up just enough to see his face. His perfect, stubble-covered face. "Depends on what?"

"Whether you're planning to leave the second you hear me snoring."

"You snore?"

He slipped his fingers between hers and squeezed. "I guess you'll have to stay the night and find out."

Eliza stiffened, mental alarms cutting through her contentment. "I want to, but—"

"Stay," he whispered. "Please."

His voice softened something inside of her. Eliza slipped back down to the mattress and settled in beside him. It felt so good to be curled up against his chest, and if she were a person who really and truly believed in Love and romance, she could definitely stay the night like this, snuggled into his warmth, their fingers intertwined.

Her eyelids dropped a little farther, and her whole body teetered on the verge of sleep. "Do you ever feel guilty?" she murmured.

"Guilty about what?"

"I don't know." Half her brain had already gone to sleep, because this was not a conversation to have naked in someone's bed, status post multiple orgasms. "Never mind."

Jake squeezed her shoulder gently. "Come on, Herman. Guilty about what?"

She sighed. Both halves of her brain were solidly in the awake-and-full-of-regret camp now. "That we sell something that doesn't really exist?"

"What do you mean?"

"Love. Not just the puppy love, crushes, attraction stuff we do, but actual, real capital-L Love. At least half the people who pay us are looking for it, and we take their cases like it really exists."

Jake didn't respond. His chest rose and fell under her cheek, and for three long breaths, she assumed he'd drifted off to sleep.

Then finally: "How do *you* define capital-L Love?" he whispered.

She shrugged. "I guess the happily-ever-after stuff. A Prince Charming—but one that doesn't keep you locked in a tower or kiss you when you're unconscious or whatever. Instead, he's a best friend who never lets you down but whose clothes you also want to rip off. A person who feels like an extension of you, but better." With a start, she realized just how much her version of Prince Charming sounded like Jake. "And if he has a horse, that's a bonus. A big bonus," she added, scrambling away from the thought.

"For someone who doesn't believe in capital-L Love, you've really thought a lot about it."

Now it was Eliza's turn to fall silent. She *had* thought

a lot about it over the years, especially when she was younger. But over the last decade, she'd solidified her belief and tucked it into the wall she'd built around herself. Bringing it out now made her entire foundation wobble.

"What happened?" Jake whispered.

A week ago, she would have thrown out some glib answer about seeing "too much" as a Cupid. But tonight she'd left her heart wide open and vulnerable, and he'd found a way in. She couldn't shut that door now, even if she'd wanted to. "My parents," she said. "Well, specifically, my mom. Remember when I took the licensing exam the first time? When we were kids?"

"Yeah."

"After my epic failure, I drove home in a panic. I was so upset I missed the fact that there was a strange black car parked in front of the house. All I could think about was how to tell them how poorly I'd done. As soon as I stepped in, I saw them."

"Your parents?"

"My mom and some guy. I still don't know who he is." Like it was eleven minutes ago, instead of eleven years, the memories rushed over her and took her into their undertow. "He stepped out of my parents' bedroom and slipped into the bathroom. I froze. At first, I thought it was a burglar. But then my mom appeared, all smiles while she adjusted the hem of her shirt."

"Shit."

"Yeah. Not a burglar. I started to say something, but the guy came out of the bathroom, wrapped his arms around Mom's waist, and kissed her."

"I guess it wasn't a friendly peck on the cheek?"

"I saw someone's tongue, so no." That day, sweat

had beaded Eliza's upper lip and the betrayal had made her skin feel three sizes too small for her body.

"I'm sorry. That sucks."

"The worst part was I knew it would break my dad. I wanted to tell him. It felt like he had a right to know. But at the same time, it wasn't that long after his first heart attack, and…"

"So you never told him?" Jake asked.

"Nope. I ran out of the house and walked around the neighborhood for an hour. It was so hot that day that I thought I might pass out. But by the time I got home, I had a plan. One that was definitely not legal, considering my unlicensed status."

"You enchanted them?"

"Waited until the next morning when my parents were in the office and stuck my mom in the butt with a push pin. Probably did it harder than absolutely necessary, but…" She shrugged. "By that night, my parents were planning a romantic getaway, and I never saw the mystery man again."

By the time she finished, her breaths were ragged and her head pounded with the pressure of the memories. She'd never breathed a word of this to anyone. Not even her brother. Partially because she would have gotten into a world of trouble with the Department for intentionally performing an unlicensed enchantment, and partially because she couldn't bring herself to admit to anyone what she'd seen. But her parents were still married all these years later, and she'd never had to break her father's heart.

The only casualty was Eliza's own belief in Love. The kind that supposedly grew warmer and deeper with the years. The kind of Love that—if she didn't know better—the Johansens had seemed to have. Of course, maybe that was just their excitement over their annual enchantment talking. Maybe the other three hundred thirty-five and a half days of the year that they weren't enchanted, they despised each other. Or, even worse, were little more than strangers.

Jake pulled her in a little closer. "Eliza?"

"Yeah?" She pressed harder into his side, letting the feel of him next to her ease the pain.

He kissed her temple. "I'm sorry."

"It wasn't your fault," she muttered.

"I know, but I'm sorry I wasn't there for you back then."

"We'd grown apart by then. Don't worry about it." She ran a finger along the center of his chest, tracing a line to his belly button. Everything had suddenly gotten too deep and too real. Maybe if she slipped her finger a little lower, they could change the subject all together.

Jake's hand closed over hers before she could find out. He raised her hand to his lips and kissed each of her knuckles. "I still think you're pretty fucking perfect. And if you'll give me a chance, Eliza, I want to prove to you that capital-L Love is real."

She was too tangled up in her memories and emotions to say anything for a long while. Terror and happiness and longing swelled up inside of her. Her fingers tingled and blood rushed by her ears. "Let's just see how tonight goes, okay?" she finally asked.

Jake pressed another soft kiss to her temple. "You got it."

Chapter 17

> "Cupids may be liable for common law alienation of affection where a spouse may show that (1) a marriage entailed genuine love between two spouses, (2) the spousal love was destroyed, and (3) the Cupid's malicious enchantment caused or contributed to cause the loss of affection."
>
> —*Alexander v. Federline* (Cal. 2005.)

ELIZA CREPT THROUGH THE FRONT DOOR OF HERMAN & Herman like a cartoon cat burglar. All she needed was a striped shirt and a sack with a dollar sign on it. Instead, she had swollen lips, a flush in her cheeks, and out-of-control sex hair. All of which she felt mighty smug about, but none of which she wanted to explain to her parents.

Apparently, she didn't need to explain anything because—despite her parents standing in her dad's office, well within earshot of the front door—they were too busy bickering to notice her.

"I told you it was a horrible idea," her mother said. "A million times, I said—"

"Can you please stop with the know-it-all act for thirty seconds?"

Eliza peered around the door. Her mother's nostrils had flared wide enough for anyone to see her rage from fifty paces. *Uh-oh, Dad. Abort ship.*

"Maybe if you treated me as your equal in this business, I wouldn't have to remind you when I'm right." Her mom nearly spat the words.

Eliza sighed. She wanted to sit behind the receptionist's desk, put on her headphones, and relive last night again and again, but it seemed she needed to play peacemaker. Otherwise, her father wasn't *just* going to break the no-stress rule; he'd tie it in a knot and toss it into the ocean.

"Hi, guys," she said.

"Eliza!" her dad called out. He gave his wife a furious glance before stepping toward the front door. "You're early."

She hung her jacket on the back of her chair. "I have some news I wanted to share."

Her mother's jaw went slack. "Good news or bad news?"

If she hadn't been glowing with the aftereffects of a three-orgasm night, Eliza might have gotten angry. Instead, she pulled out her license and slapped it on the desk. "I passed my exam. Fully licensed Cupid at your service."

Her dad whooped and wrapped his arms around her in a bear hug. "I knew you could do it!"

"Dad." Eliza laughed as he spun her. "Put me down. No heavy lifting, remember?"

"I didn't know you'd scheduled the exam, Eliza," her mom said. "Congratulations."

"I didn't tell anyone in case... Well, you know."

Her mother nodded. "Mmm."

"We would have been proud of you even if you'd failed, kiddo," her dad said.

"I know, I know." She slipped into the desk and powered up the computer. All this attention was making her squirm. "So what's going on today?"

"You have a voicemail," her mother said. "Came in yesterday afternoon." Judging by her tone, she expected Eliza to listen to it immediately.

"Anything else?"

"I'm going to take your father to his appointment today," her mother said. "We have a few things to discuss. Then I'm going to pick your brother up from the airport. Why don't you stay here in case someone comes in?"

Eliza looked at her dad, who gave her one of his patented can-you-believe-this-woman eye rolls. "Okay. See you guys later."

Her father gave her a quick kiss on top of the head, grumbled something about needing to change his shoes, and headed to the door. Her mother started to follow but turned back around and stopped in front of Eliza.

"Honey?" she asked.

"Yeah, Mom?"

Her mom let out a long sigh.

Here we go, Eliza thought. *A game of twenty-one questions all designed to nag me about being a responsible Cupid.*

"I'm really proud of you," her mom said. "You worked hard for this."

Her mother was proud of her? Proud enough to speak the words aloud? Eliza's mom-shaped baggage grew a smidge lighter, and she blinked back a few happy tears. "Thanks."

Her mother looked just as shocked by her own confession. But in the span of a breath, she was back to being all business, all the time. "Make sure you return the call before the end of the business day. The money-back—"

"Money-back guarantee. I know, Mom. I've got it. I promise."

⇒——————→

As it turned out, she didn't have it.

At least, she didn't understand half of the garbled voicemail. Eliza replayed it twice, and it made less sense each time. Between the static and the sound of a mariachi band in the background, Eliza knew only three things for certain: (1) the caller was kindly Mitch Johansen, whom she'd last seen on his anniversary, (2) he was *very* unhappy, and (3) he expected her at his house before close of business today, or he'd be "making a detailed report to the Department of Affection, Seduction, and Shellfish."

Fuuuuuuuuuck. On the list of things she wanted to do today, dealing with an unhappy customer was at the bottom, slightly below dealing with her parents and just above gouging her eyes out with a hot fire poker. But she could *not* have a complaint filed against her today, not on her first day as a fully licensed Cupid.

Eliza stared at the phone and then the front door. She'd promised her mom she'd stay at the shop while they were gone. But a threat of a complaint with the Department *and* taking a hit on their money-back guarantee seemed like as good a reason as any to break that promise.

Twenty minutes later, she sat outside the Johansens' house. The last time she'd been there, it had looked warm and inviting, even from the porch. A person could tell it was inhabited by sweet grandparents who kept a bowl of candy in their living room, just in case the grandkids stopped by. Now, if Eliza didn't know better, she would have guessed an old, crotchety man lived inside. The kind who yelled at kids to get off his lawn and turned his lights off on Halloween.

Maybe it was the way the plants on the front porch had drooped and browned since she'd last been here, but probably it was just her nerves.

You have this under control, she thought as she raised her fist to knock on the front door. *You passed the test. You're as qualified as any other Cupid out there.* Sort of. Mostly.

The door swung open before she could knock. "Finally," Mitch said.

"Hi!" Eliza did her best impression of someone who was bright-eyed and bushy-tailed. "I apologize. I was out yesterday, but I came as soon as I got your message."

The elderly man pulled her inside the house with an unexpected level of strength. The next thing Eliza knew, her butt hit the floral couch. It took two breaths to gather her wits, but when she did, she found herself sitting beside a sniffling, puffy-eyed Lily Johansen.

"Lily, are you okay?" Eliza reached out to her, but the woman pulled away.

"We want our money back," Mr. Johansen said. "And I want you to make this right, or I'm filing a complaint."

Eliza grasped for a single thread of calm in this mess. Why was Lily Johansen crying? Why was her husband glaring at Lily like she were Medusa incarnate? What in the worlds was happening? "Mitch, please. I'm not sure what's going on, but I'm happy to help—"

"Of course you don't know what's going on," he

spat out. "I told my wife we should have insisted on someone more experienced. Where's that man who was with you anyway?"

She cleared her throat. "I got my license yesterday, so I don't need to be supervised any longer."

"Ha! Don't need to be supervised." He paced, leaving footprints in the freshly vacuumed carpet. "We've been using your parents' firm for a long time, but after this—"

"Mitch," his wife said. "Please, sit down. You're making it worse."

Eliza turned to Lily again. Maybe it was wrong to turn her back on someone as angry as Mitch Johansen—Eliza had no desire to star in the next season of *The Winged One Confesses*—but she obviously wasn't getting anywhere with him. "Lily, what's going on?"

She blew her nose, then looked up at Eliza with tear-soaked cheeks. "It didn't work."

"The enchantment?" Eliza asked. "But when I left here, you were—well, happy." And why were they just calling now, the day after the moon cycle ended? She bit back that question, not wanting to invite Mr. Johansen to get even angrier with her.

"It worked for a little while. Then it…" Lily shook her head. "Petered out."

"For God's sake, Lilian. Really?" Mitch asked.

Before Eliza could make heads or tails of his outburst, the front door slammed shut behind him. She took a deep breath and replayed the woman's words: the enchantment had stopped working. That was completely normal, and she'd gone over what to expect with them that day. "Lily—"

The elderly woman wiped her nose and sat up a little straighter. "Please, call me Mrs. Johansen."

"Mrs. Johansen, you said you've used Cupids before, right?"

She nodded.

"So you're aware that the casts only last a moon cycle. And yours ended last night." She didn't need a calendar to calculate that one, considering what she'd been doing last night when Jake's had worn off.

"No." Lily shredded a tissue between her fingers. "It worked for a little while. A day, maybe. After that, I think we both were faking it for a few more days. He spent most of his time down in the cruise ship casino, and I stayed on the sundeck. Then"—she lowered her voice, even though the two of them were alone in the house—"Mitch's bojangle stopped working. Soon we couldn't even sit in the same room for more than ten minutes without a fight."

Eliza's thoughts spun at a hundred miles an hour, trying to keep up. "I'm sorry, Mrs. Johansen, when you say *bojangle*—"

Lily gave a solemn shake of her head. "Nothing. It's like he's dead down there. Maybe it's me. Maybe I—"

"It's not your fault." No matter who or what was at fault—likely Eliza, if her not-so-ancient history was any indication—she couldn't allow Lily to think she'd brought this on herself.

"We've had problems in the past, in the bedroom and out. You don't get through this many years of marriage without a few rough patches." Lily stared into the distance and hugged herself. "But nothing like this. All we do is argue, day and night."

"I'm so sorry," Eliza said. Sorry didn't begin to cut it. Sure, she was sorry, but she was also confused, unsettled, and a little bit afraid. She'd had a lot of mishaps in the last few decades, but nothing quite like this. Still, Eliza did her best to shake it off.

She wasn't a kid anymore, and she couldn't run away. She had to fix this. These were people's lives. People who'd been loyal to her family for years. People who'd trusted her to help them. People who seemed to have found actual capital-L Love.

Until Eliza came along.

"Is there a reason you didn't call immediately?" she asked. "I would have been more than happy to help you weeks ago. Again, I'm so sorry you've been suffering through this."

"The cruise. We just got home yesterday." Lily began to tear up again. "We spent the first day trying to have fun, but by the third day, we were pretending not to know each other. By the fifth, Mitch spent all his time at the casino and left me alone in the room. I just don't understand."

"I don't either," Eliza admitted.

Gods, how had she managed to bungle this so badly? Being stranded in the middle of the ocean with someone she hated sounded like a vacation from the Underworld. The only thing worse would be getting stuck with someone she hated on one of those cruises where everyone on the ship—

"And then we got food poisoning." Lily let out a little wail. "If I didn't know better, I'd think you had something to do with that too."

"I didn't. I swear. Can you think of anything the two of you might have done differently this time?" Eliza asked. "Maybe you're anemic, or one of you is on a new medication?"

Lily shook her head.

"Have either of you had a blood transfusion or any kind of organ transplant?"

"No. I don't know what was different this time."

Bile burned Eliza's throat. She knew exactly what was different this time: the Johansens had worked with a five-foot, five-inch disaster in Keds.

"Please just fix it, or Mitch is going to make your family pay for our divorce," Lily said.

Her words left Eliza's nerves frayed and sparking. She couldn't handle being responsible for yet another ruined relationship. Plus, her mother would lose her mind if she had to give the Johansens their money back *and* pay for their divorce lawyers.

Eliza stood and wiped her sweaty palms on her pants "I promise you I will fix this. But I'd really like to do some research first, just to make sure I'm doing everything right."

Lily responded by blowing her nose on her sleeve.

"I'll be in touch soon," Eliza said. "In the meantime, here's my cell phone number. Please call me if anything changes."

The woman took the card but didn't meet Eliza's gaze. "Okay."

"Will you be okay for a day or two?"

"If Mitch is back by then."

Eliza refused to think about the possibility that Mitch Johansen would go out for the proverbial cigarettes and never come home. "He will be."

Lily looked up at her with the smallest flicker of hope in her eyes. "You promise?"

Eliza swallowed back the lump of fear in her throat and gathered her resolve. If she'd managed to get her license after decades of disasters, she could do this. It was probably a common side effect with an easy fix. She'd ask Jake or do some internet research, and the whole thing would be fixed by this time tomorrow. "I promise."

And then she said a prayer that she wouldn't have to break Lily's heart a second time.

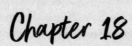

Chapter 18

> "The novice Cupid should be alert to any subtle signs of unusual behavior changes resulting from the heightened emotional state associated with enchantments."
>
> — *The Total Beginner's Guide to Enchantments*

ELIZA SANK INTO JAKE'S COUCH—THE SCENE OF THE first of last night's glorious crimes—and let the brown leather swallow her. Every Cupid textbook and treatise Jake owned littered the floor around her, having been consumed and then cast aside in her frantic search for answers. The clock on his wall read eight thirty, but her body insisted it was already two in the morning. Her mind might have been running at the speed of light, but her eyes were heavy with exhaustion.

"It must have something to do with me. I know it." She rehashed the details of the Johansen disaster for the third time since she'd shown up at Jake's apartment, completely unannounced. "I don't know what to do. He was so *angry*. Maybe if I can separate them for a few days—give everything time to reset and enchant them again? But what if that makes it worse? What if every time I enchant someone, I make it worse?"

Jake slid a cool glass of wine into her hand. "Eliza,

breathe. We've been at this for hours. There's nothing in any of these books that suggests you did this. Maybe they were on the verge of splitting up anyway."

"I just don't understand. Before, they were so...perfect together." An imaginary weight landed square on her chest. Apparently, her old friend Failure had come back to pay her a visit, and he'd brought his BFFs, Shame and Disappointment, for the ride.

"Look at me," he said.

She did. The concern in his eyes made Failure, Shame, and Disappointment disappear in a single heartbeat. "You really don't think I'm the problem?" she whispered.

His lips grazed her temple. "I really don't think you're the problem."

With Jake's warmth, the scent of lingering shaving cream, and his late-afternoon scruff tickling her skin, she almost believed him.

"If I can't figure this out, I'm going to lose my license. I'll have to go back to temping." She took a giant swig of wine. Moscato—sweet and fruity, and not to Jake's taste. He'd bought it for her.

"I know you're upset, but I really think you're getting ahead of yourself. You enchanted me, and I'm no worse for the wear."

"What if I'm a relationship killer?"

"You aren't a relationship killer, Eliza. I don't understand what's going on with the Johansens, but I do know that isn't it."

"Are you sure?"

"I am. And we're going to figure it out. Together."

"Thank you." She pulled him down beside her and

nuzzled into his side. *Gods, why did that feel so good? Why did* he *feel so good?* "Maybe I just need to relax a little. Let the answer come to me."

"That is a brilliant idea. You ever get stuck on a problem, and then later, when you stop thinking about it, maybe in the shower"—he traced her collarbone with one featherlight finger—"it comes to you?"

"Mm-hmm." Her brain fogged over with a surge of hormones—the touching-more, needing-more, wanting-more kind—and she only half knew what she was saying.

"I humbly suggest we take that approach here."

She grinned. "Do you?"

"We could sit here all night and rehash what the Johansens told you." His finger slid from her collarbone to the V of her shirt, sinking just low enough to send a rush of tingles to her breasts. "Or we could give our brains a break and see what happens."

The more they talked, the more they touched, the more sense this approach made. And the less apocalyptic the Johansens' problems seemed. She swung a leg over his hip and straddled his waist. "What *exactly* were you thinking we could do to give our brains a break?"

He ground his hips just a little, but the way he pressed up against her left no questions about the thoughts flickering through his mind. Jake sank his right hand into the back of her hair. His fingers splayed against her scalp, warm and gently tugging. "We have a few options," he said. "Option one: We have a replay of last night. I strip you naked, lay you on this couch, and taste every part of you. From here"—his left thumb brushed her temple—"to here." It skimmed her throat. "And here." He traced a line from her neck to her nipple, teasing through the fabric of her shirt. "Then here. *Lots* of time here." His thumb slipped down the seam of her leggings, lingering as heat flooded through her. He tightened his grip on her hair. "Hours even."

Eliza rose up, giving his hand room to caress the space between her thighs. "I choose that option. Option one, please."

Jake's low chuckle reverberated through her chest. "You don't want to hear about option two?"

She grinned. "I'm listening."

"Option two is bending you over the kitchen table and fucking you until you come around my cock. Then, I'll flip you over and do it again while I stare at your gorgeous face."

Eliza pushed harder against his hand. "Option two definitely has its benefits," she murmured. She leaned her head down until her body arched over his, and she caught his bottom lip with her teeth. Everything about this—everything about *him*—shined with perfection. The washboard abs. The hard line of his jaw. The thick bulge in his pants. The total confidence he exuded when he described exactly what he intended to do to her.

"Don't forget about option three," he whispered.

Eliza sank her mouth into his, sweeping and teasing his tongue with hers. With a flick of her wrist, she undid his pants and slipped her hand inside. She slid a finger along the underside of his throbbing erection and enjoyed every bit of the shudder that ran through Jake's body.

"My, how many options are there?" she asked when they finally broke apart.

His eyes locked on hers. "Infinite."

Gods, Eliza was coming undone. Slowly but surely,

with every word from Jake's lips, he was unraveling her. When he was done, she'd be woven into something entirely new or left as a useless heap on the floor. Either way, there was no stopping it now.

"Option three," she said. "Definitely option three."

"I haven't told you what it involves."

The sheer force of the happiness inside her nearly knocked Eliza to the floor. Jake was right. She wasn't a relationship killer. She'd enchanted him, and look what had happened. "Doesn't matter," she said. "I know it'll be amazing."

"Good choice." Jake pulled her shirt over her head, undid her bra with one hand, and palmed her breasts. Her nipples became tight, little buds under his touch. "Because option three is actually option one followed by option two."

⟫⟫————————→

The salty, smoky scent of bacon drifted into Eliza's dreams, slowly pulling her from sleep. She sat up in Jake's bed, drawing the down comforter up to her chest. Unruly hair escaped the knot at the base of her neck, and a thin line of dried drool stretched across her cheek. She rubbed at it with one hand while taking in the reality of what she'd done.

She'd stayed the night. Again.

She, Eliza Herman, had—after a night of stunning sex—settled into the nook between Jake's chest and arm and fallen asleep. Now she sat alone in his room, wearing nothing but one of his T-shirts, while he cooked her breakfast downstairs.

Once was an aberration. Twice? That was the kind of thing people in Love did.

Shit.

"You're awake." Jake stood in the doorway, shirtless with a pair of plaid pajama pants hanging low on his waist. It was like something out of a damn magazine. *Playgirl* meets the Sears catalog.

She pulled the covers closer to her chin. If only she'd gotten her lazy butt out of bed and into the bathroom, she would have had five minutes to pull herself together. Instead, she sat between his soft sheets wondering where her morning breath fell on a scale of pleasant mint to sewage fire. "You sound disappointed," she said.

Jake stepped into the room and crawled into bed beside her. His hand slid under the covers and up her T-shirt, running a line from her belly button to the tops of her thighs and back again. "Only because I was hoping to wake you up myself."

"Really? Because I could pretend—"

The roar of her stomach cut off her words.

Jake grinned. "After last night, you need sustenance."

After last night, she needed a lot more than sustenance. She needed more of Jake. All of him. And that scared the holy Hades out of her. "You're probably right," she said. "Give me a few minutes to find my clothes?"

In the span of a breath, Jake straddled her thighs. "Eliza Herman, that is the dumbest idea you've ever had."

"Are you sure? Because, once, I tried white-water rafting."

"You did?"

She nodded. "In college, during my face-all-my-fears phase. I accidentally enchanted the guide, and he got so distracted that our raft ended up stranded at the edge of some falls. Zero out of five stars, do not recommend."

Jake peeled back the comforter and took her in. The plain white shirt she wore had bunched along her thighs, and the thin cotton didn't leave much to the imagination. "You putting on actual clothes—instead of wearing my shirt—would be worse. One could even call it a tragedy."

Her insides melted into a warm puddle of gooey goodness. When he looked at her like that—talked to her like that—she felt less like a crusty blob and more like a sex goddess. *Look out, Aphrodite.*

"Besides," Jake said, "once you've had something to eat, I fully intend to bring you back up here to explore option number four. It involves you, on top of me, wearing this." He thumbed the hem of the shirt.

"Hmmm. That sounds promising." Eliza sat up and pulled him close. "Although I've come up with some options of my own that I wanted to run by you."

Jake gave her a naughty grin. Hopefully, he hadn't left anything on the stove, because if Eliza had any say in the matter, they weren't coming down anytime soon.

Bzzzzzzzzzzzzzzzzzzzzzzzzzzzzzzzzzzzzzzzzzzzzzzzzzzzzzz.
Bzzzzzzzzzzzzzzzzzzzzzzzzzzzz.

Eliza's phone shimmied as it vibrated on the nightstand, and her pulse kicked into high gear. What if it was one of the Johansens? What if they'd decided she was out of time to fix this? She grabbed the phone just before it vibrated onto the floor.

"Hello?"

"Elllllllliza." Sobs punctuated the woman's voice, followed by a loud hiccup. "Elllllizzzzza Herman?"

"This is Eliza."

"He's gonnnnne."

Eliza's heart rate ticked up to the speed of sound, and she feared she might experience a sonic boom in her chest. Someone had to be hurt or dying.

What's wrong? Jake mouthed as he climbed off her.

She shrugged. "I'm sorry. Who is this?" she said into the phone.

"Yooooooooooooolanda. He's gonnnnne."

Oh. *Oh.* "Hi, Yolanda." Eliza went into 911 operator mode. "Can you take a deep breath for me?"

A sharp, shaky inhale came through the other end of the line.

"That's great," Eliza said. "Now, who's gone?"

"Charleston." She sniffed. "My baby, he's gonnnnne."

"Your pig?" Not that she didn't feel for the woman, but why in the worlds had Yolanda decided to call her about this? At eight in the morning, no less. And how did the woman get her cell phone number in the first place?

"Pignapped. Eddie took him, that monster, and he told me all about what he paid you to do, with the groceries." More sobs filled the line.

Eliza groaned. "Where is Eddie now?"

"I don't know. If I knew, I wouldn't be calling you. I'd be out there getting my baby back."

Suddenly the smell of bacon wafting from the kitchen made Eliza feel very guilty. "Give me twenty minutes, and I'll be right over, okay?"

"If he hurts Charleston, I'm going to sue your family for everything they're worth. He's a prize-winning pig, you know. Three-time Northern California Swine of the Year."

Wow. Yolanda had turned the corner of desperation

and rage at full speed. Eliza took a deep breath. "I understand you're upset. I'll be there—"

Click.

She looked at the phone, then up at Jake, then back at the phone.

"What's wrong?" he asked.

"I'm not sure yet, but I'm going to need a rain check on option four."

Eliza crammed the last bit of toast into her mouth—Jake had packed them breakfast to go—and slammed the car door behind her. The morning breeze cut through her light jacket and yesterday's leggings, and she fought the urge to hunch against the cold. She needed to stand up straight and exude confidence.

"You're here!" The front door swung open before Eliza could press the bell, and an arm yanked them both inside the house.

Yolanda stood in the entryway, looking *a lot* the worse for wear. Strands of hair poked out in all directions, and puffy eyelids nearly hid her green eyes.

This was more than just a pignapping.

"Look what he sent me. My poor baby!" Yolanda shoved a phone under Eliza's face.

A photo of Charleston stared back at her. Except the "poor baby" didn't look so poor at all. He sat in a plastic kiddie pool that brimmed over with bubbles and ladies in bikinis. The damn pig even wore sunglasses.

The text beneath the photo read: **Boyz will be boyz.**

Eliza had had her doubts about Eddie from the

beginning, and his "boyz will be boyz" comment raised all her feminist feathers, but she couldn't understand what was happening here. "So, Charleston is fine?"

"He's not fine! Do you think Eddie bothered to fill that pool with dye- and fragrance-free soap? No. My baby is going to get hives. He has very sensitive skin." Yolanda's voice grew shriller with each syllable. "And do you know how many infections you can catch in a communal pool?"

Charleston looked perfectly fine to Eliza, but she wasn't about to chime in with her two cents while Yolanda continued her rant.

"Charleston gets very nervous around new people. He's probably miserable and anxious, and when he gets anxious, he gets diarrhea."

Eliza looked at the photo again. The pig did *not* look anxious. If anything, he seemed to be enjoying his swine equivalent of spring break. "Yolanda—"

"Don't *Yolanda* me. Do something! Eddie's *left* me. And he's taken my baby."

Jake's hand clasped her shoulder. "Yolanda, can you tell us a little more about what happened? Were you and Eddie getting along before this?"

She shuffled into the living room and flopped onto a nearby recliner. "For about two or three days after we met, things were perfect. Then he started getting jealous of Charleston. Saying I cared about Charleston more than I cared about him. Saying I babied Charleston too much. I tried to tell him there was room enough in my heart for both of them, but he wouldn't listen. Then I came home from work yesterday and Charleston was gone! Eddie left me a note saying what he'd done with *you*"—she glared at Eliza—"and then he started sending me these." Eliza's stomach grew heavy with fear. This sounded suspiciously like the Johansens' problem.

"Look!" Yolanda held out her phone. On it were a half dozen photos of Charleston. Charleston wearing bunny ears. Charleston in the front seat of a convertible with his whiskers in the breeze. Charleston and Eddie playing a game on a tablet…

"He seems okay to me," Jake said.

"He has strict screen-time rules!" Yolanda screeched. "I should have listened to my family. You're an abomination." She looked at Eliza with a half-hearted shrug. "No offense."

"Well—" Eliza started.

"I've been so alone for years. Then Charleston came along, and—" She pounded a hand on the arm of the chair. "And I wasn't alone anymore. Then Eddie came into our lives, and I thought I'd finally done it. I'd made my little family."

Eliza's heart softened. "Have you tried to call Eddie back?"

"Of course I tried to call him. I want my baby back! I even want *him* back."

"Eddie?"

"Of course, Eddie! Who else could I mean? He betrayed me, but I still love him. I can't just turn off my feelings, you know. I'm not a monster."

"Okay, okay." Eliza stood beside Yolanda and rubbed small circles on her back. "What did he say?"

"He won't answer. He just keeps sending the photos."

Eliza looked at Jake. His expression said it all: this was the first time he'd actually considered that Eliza might be the relationship killer she'd claimed to be. "Why don't you forward those photos to Eliza's phone?" he suggested. "We'll see if we can piece together a time-line and figure out where they are."

Yolanda's fingers flew over her screen. "There."

Within seconds, Eliza's phone vibrated in her pocket. "Thank you. Are you going to be okay when we leave?"

Yolanda answered with another sob.

"Do you have someone you can call to sit with you? Maybe a family member or a friend?"

Yolanda shook her head so violently her face red-dened. "I can't tell anyone about this. I can't."

Right. The abomination thing. "I'll call and check back in on you soon, okay? Do you have something to occupy yourself in the meantime? Maybe just surf Facebook for a little while or something? Anything to keep your mind off things."

Yolanda looked up, gripping her phone in one hand. "That's it!"

"What's it?" Had Eliza unlocked the secret to Charleston's whereabouts by suggesting the biggest time waster of all: social media?

"Eddie was always playing this stupid game on his phone. Maybe if I just download it, friend him on the game, and try to start a round, he'll fall back in love with me and bring Charleston home."

Eliza bit the inside of her cheek to keep her skepticism in check. "Or maybe you could scroll through Instagram for dinner inspiration? That's what I do sometimes."

A fire flickered in the Yolanda's eyes, and once again her fingers flew across the screen. "Too late. I already downloaded the game. This is going to work. I know it."

Eliza sighed. As long as Yolanda had something to keep herself occupied... "Call me if you need anything, okay?"

But circus-style music poured from the speakers, and Yolanda's attention had already been commandeered by whatever was happening on her phone. Eliza pried open the front door and was half-in, half-out of the house when Yolanda finally spoke again. "Don't forget what I said earlier." Her gaze didn't leave the screen. "If Charleston isn't back home soon, my first call is to my lawyer."

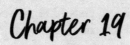

Chapter 19

Calif. CCR § **303.025.** No Cupid shall practice within this State without proof of insurance or other financial ability to respond to liability for malpractice and accidents arising out of the provision of love or affection services.

ELIZA TRIED EDDIE'S PHONE FOR THE SEVENTEEN-millionth time.

"Yo, you've reached Eddie. I'm probably out enjoying my life. Why don't you go out and enjoy yours? Don't leave a message. I won't call you back."

She hung up and tossed her phone onto the passenger seat. As she drove, Eliza caught a glimpse of the clock and panic seeped into her skin. She and Jake had spent all of the previous night driving around Gold Lea in search of a disgusting pig—oh, and Charleston.

They'd found nothing. And this morning, when Jake went to work delivering a few certified letters and packages for the Department, Eliza had set off again. So far, she'd found a half dozen old lottery tickets (losers, just like her), her old high school principal, Mrs. Broteck (who looked even older than Eliza felt), and enough Vic Van Love ads to wallpaper a prison (where she'd probably end up if she couldn't get this reverse enchantment under control). But still no Eddie or Charleston.

The phone buzzed beside her on the passenger seat. Eliza pulled over and glanced at the screen. Yolanda. Again. "Hello?" Eliza tried to sound as pleasant as June Cleaver.

"Where is he?" Yolanda's voice had dropped several octaves since yesterday. Instead of sounding like a panicked socialite, she sounded like an enraged seventy-five-year-old smoker who'd failed anger management.

"I'm out looking right now. I have some good leads." Complete and total lie. She could barely manage the duties of a Cupid, much less a private eye.

"Like what?"

"Uh, well." She grasped for a way to make her aimless search sound professional and organized. "I've driven by his house, and now I'm, um, looking for stores that have kiddie pools for sale. I figure this time of year, someone will probably remember a guy buying—"

"You don't have any leads, do you?"

Eliza stared at a smudge on her windshield. *Busted*. "No."

"Are you even trying? Because from here, it sounds like you aren't."

"I *am*." Eliza let a tiny bit of frustration creep into her voice. "But I'm not exactly qualified to investigate pignappings."

"*I'm not qualified to investigate pignappings*," Yolanda said in squeaky mimic of Eliza before lowering her voice again. "You don't seem qualified to do much, Eliza, and I think the authorities need to know."

Click.

Eliza's stomach dropped to Ron's floorboard. That didn't sound like an idle threat. Whatever had gotten into Yolanda over the last twelve or so hours had flipped a switch. A giant, angry, ready-to-do-life-ruining-damage switch.

With a shaky finger, Eliza scrolled through her contacts until she found the name she wanted. Just seeing the thumbnail photo beside Jake's name and number—him laughing at some dumb joke she'd made the day he'd saved her from Ron Weasley's tantrum—soothed her nerves. It would be fine. She'd call Jake, and he'd know exactly what to do.

"You've reached Jake. Please leave a message."

She hung up and sent a text instead.

Still no luck finding Charleston. Yolanda is PISSED.

Three little bubbles appeared at the bottom of the screen, then disappeared just as quickly. She waited, thinking the text must have been delayed as it flew through the airwaves to reach her.

She waited some more.

And a little more.

Nothing.

"Baaaaaaaabe…" The upbeat Sonny and Cher tune exploded from the speakers.

Eliza started at the blast of music, then hit the dash. "Ron. Just shut up for once. Please."

Shockingly, he did.

And then—thank the gods—the phone vibrated in her palm. But it was only a text from Yolanda that appeared on the screen. **Charleston needs his probiotics. Bring him home today. OR ELSE.**

And as if her words weren't ominous enough, Yolanda followed them with the longest string of knife emojis Eliza had ever seen.

Eliza stared at the message for a solid ten seconds before throwing her phone back onto the passenger seat. She pressed her head to the steering wheel and willed Jake to call her. But when her phone stayed silent, Eliza decided to try her brother. She hadn't seen him since he'd come home, because he'd stepped off the plane in the throes of conference crud (a.k.a. bronchitis). But it was high time that he helped her out of the mess he'd forced her into.

"Hi, you've reached Elijah…" his voicemail said.

"Hey. Call me. It's important," she said at the beep.

Asking her father for help was out of the question. He'd been prescribed another two weeks of no stress and cardiac rehab. Which meant Eliza had only one person left to consult: her mother.

The thought made her want to vomit.

"Oh well," Eliza muttered as she pulled onto the road. "If she doesn't know what to do, at least she'll have some warning about the lawsuits."

By the time she reached Herman & Herman, Eliza had nearly convinced herself this was a smart idea. Her mother had decades of experience as a Cupid. She'd served on the Northern California Cosmic Council, acted as liaison to the Department of Affection, Seduction, and Shellfish, and taught Public School Cupiding classes for years before Eliza and Elijah came along. If anyone would know what to do, it would be her.

A blue sedan sat in Eliza's usual parking spot, so she wedged herself in next to her mother's car—partially blocking her, but once she heard about Eliza's epic failures, her mother's blood pressure would probably be too high to drive safely anyhow.

Eliza pushed open the door. "Mom?"

The reception area sat empty and silent, but soft voices carried in from her mother's office. Eliza followed them, trying to clear her mind. Thinking too much about what she needed to say would only backfire. Best to spit it out first and think later.

"Mom? Are you busy? I really need to talk—" Eliza stopped short in the doorway. All at once, her blood turned to ice and pounded behind her eyes. She forced them closed, but when she opened them, nothing had changed.

Her mother sat at the desk in a rose print dress, her tan legs crossed. She had a mug of tea between her hands and a look of utter shock on her face. Beside her, a man about her mother's age cupped her father's favorite coffee mug and leaned toward Eliza's mother with a flirtatious grin, as if he hadn't even noticed Eliza standing there.

The exact way he'd acted thirteen years ago, when Eliza had walked into the house to find him leaving her mother's bedroom. Sure, he'd aged since then—more gray hair than black, some slackness in his jaw, a little more paunch around the middle—but there was no mistaking it. Her mother's paramour had returned.

Or he'd never left at all.

"Mom?"

"Eliza." Her mother stood ramrod straight as her cheeks turned a shade of primrose pink. "I didn't think you were coming in today."

"I wasn't."

Finally, the man unfurled himself and stood. He had to be at least six and a half feet tall, and his body held an incredible amount of muscle, considering he must have been pushing sixty by now.

"Hello, Eliza." He stuck out his hand. "I've heard so much about you."

Eliza didn't move. She was being rude, but she didn't care. "Interesting. I've heard nothing about you. Who are you, exactly?"

"Weston Presley. You're even prettier than your mother described. Join us for a cup of tea?"

Dry-heave city. She'd rather pour scalding tea onto her ladybits than sit here with these two. She couldn't believe her mother would do this. Again. It's not like her father had died; he'd gone off to cardiac rehab. He came home every night and slept in their marital bed.

"I was just leaving," Eliza said.

"Eliza, wait. I—" Her mother's voice followed her to the door, but Eliza slammed it closed. She wouldn't be caught dead asking her mother for help. Not now. Not ever.

She was officially on her own.

⟫⟫───────▶

"Please. If you'd both just sit down and listen to me—" Eliza's words were lost to the sound of a shattering plate. And then a bowl. Finally, a mug flew across the Johansens' kitchen and smashed against the wall.

"You never do the dishes, so why should I?" Mitch Johansen snarled. "Might as well eat off paper plates from now on."

"Why should *you* do the dishes?" Lily asked. "Maybe because I wash your crusty socks every Sunday. Explosive blister disorder, my foot. That's not even a real diagnosis, Mitch."

Eliza raised her voice even louder. "Maybe if we all just take a minute—"

"That's the problem with you, Lilian. You never believe me. Maybe if you'd taken off work just once to go with me to see Dr. Sphincter—"

"Dr. Sphinter. His name is Doctor Sphinter, and he's a chiropractor! He can't diagnose your foot disorder."

For one glorious moment, Eliza forgot all about the fight going on around her. What a shame that someone named Dr. Sphinter hadn't gone on to become a proctologist. But then a wooden spoon—*the* wooden spoon—clattered to the floor in front of her, and Eliza found herself back in the thick of it.

She'd walked into the Johansens' home feeling reasonably confident about her plan to reenchant them, but by now, after ten minutes of them yelling and breaking things, Eliza's confidence had gone down the drain, fled through the city sewer system, and run away to China. She was left with nothing but her bag of weapons and a newfound knowledge of the Johansens' chore schedule and medical concerns.

Eliza tiptoed into the living room, hid the Johansens' prized engagement spoon under the love seat before one of them could throw it out in a fit of rage, then slid back into the kitchen. Something had to give soon, and it was going to be either this fight or her sanity. Gathering her resolve, she hiked one leg up on a dining room chair, then the other. "Mr. and Mrs. Johansen—"

"Maybe if you'd *tried* to enjoy the cruise, instead of spending all your time at the casino, we wouldn't be in this mess," Lily said.

"Maybe if you'd *tried* to help me get the triple egg bonus, instead of spending all your time up on the deck ogling the lifeguards..." Mitch retorted.

"Maybe if you *tried* to stop being such a ninny..."

Ugh. Why hadn't Eliza learned to do one of those eardrum-piercing, fingers-in-the-mouth whistles she always saw on television? She stepped from the chair onto the kitchen table and promptly knocked her forehead on the light fixture. The whole thing rattled, and for a second Eliza saw stars.

Then her vision cleared, and she realized the stars were more pieces of plasticware flying around the room.

She reached into the messenger bag slung across her chest and plucked out her phone. With a few quick swipes, she pulled up a video of sirens—the fire-truck kind, not the mermaid kind—and hit Play.

The whirring and screeching of the sirens cut through the arguing, and the couple fell silent. They each stared up at her—standing on their kitchen table, while their light fixture rocked back and forth—as if they'd completely forgotten she was there.

Eliza turned off the siren video. "Listen up. I've got a plan, and I need you both to cooperate."

Lily stared at the floor, but Mitch crossed his arms and stared Eliza down. "Unless you can turn this woman into a bottle of scotch, I don't want anything to do with her."

"You don't even like scotch, you pretentious jerk!"

"Oh, *I'm* a jerk? You're—"

Eliza hit Play on the siren video again, and they quieted.

"Sit. Now." She hopped down and put two chairs together back to back. Maybe if they couldn't see each other, they'd stop fighting. Or at least stop throwing things.

It must have been Eliza's commanding, no-nonsense presence that did it. Or, more likely, the fact that the Johansens were members of AARP and running out of steam. But either way, they sat.

"I'm going to talk now, and you're going to listen." She didn't give them a chance to respond before she continued. "You love each other. Deep down inside, under all this"—she gestured to the mess on the floor— "you two really care about each other. You've had a bad reaction to your enchantment, and we're going to make it right, simply by starting it over again."

"No, ma'am." Mitch crossed his arms. "I'm done with this Cupid business."

Lily broke into sobs. "What's the point? We don't love each other anymore."

Eliza pulled a set of photos down from the refrigerator and handed one to each of them. Mitch held a picture of them with their grandkids, eating ice cream with sugar-soaked smiles. Lily held a picture of the two of them in front of a sign for Grand Canyon National Park, both laughing at something unseen in the distance.

Lily dabbed her eyes, and even Mitch sniffled.

"See?" Eliza said. "You love each other. This is just a rough patch, and it's going to be over soon. Here is what we're going to do—"

Ding dong. Ding dong. Ding dong.

The doorbell rang three times in quick succession, and Lily scurried from her chair. "That's probably my package. I put a rush delivery on it."

"Did you order one of those Mandroids? I swear, Lilian, if you made it look like my brother…"

The old woman disappeared without an answer. Once she'd gone, Mitch turned back into his kindly, distinguished self, like someone had flipped a switch. "Where are my manners? Can I get you something to drink, dear? I think we have some lemonade and peach iced tea."

Eliza blinked, trying to figure out where the surly old man with explosive blister disease had gone. "No, thank you. I'm fine. Mitch, are you sure I can't convince you to try one more enchantment? I really think—"

Lily returned empty-handed. "Just one of the neighbors. She wanted to make sure everything was okay."

"I hope you told her no. That this Cupid is holding us hostage," Mitch snarled.

I see we've completed the circle. "Mrs. Johansen," Eliza said. "Would you mind terribly if I had a moment alone with your husband?"

"Keep him. I certainly don't want him anymore."

The second she'd gone, Mitch's shoulders relaxed, his breath slowed, and everything about him said *fun grandpa*. "Did you say you wanted lemonade or tea? It's unsweetened, but we keep some Sweet'N Low around here somewhere…"

Hypothesis confirmed: When they were apart, Mitch returned to his sweet-old-man self. Together: nuclear warfare. If Eliza couldn't handle them in the same room together, she'd never convince them to gaze deeply into each other's eyes for an enchantment.

Her plans had slid right out from under her.

"Mr. Johansen, do you have any family you could stay with for a few days? Maybe one of your kids is around? I think giving you and Lily some time to cool off could really help things." Not to mention giving Eliza a few days to figure out what in the Underworld was going on.

"My kids all moved away."

"Oh." *Here Lies the Last of Eliza's Hope. Rest in Peace.*

"But I do have a cousin who lives across town, over in the retirement villas on Fifty-First Street."

"Really?" Her hope rose from its grave, crooked and slow like a zombie. "Can you call him and ask?"

"I guess. If you really think that's the best thing to do."

"I do."

Mitch pulled out his phone and ran his finger along the screen. "Hello? Is this the Gold Lea Retirement Villas?" He gave Eliza a thumbs-up. "I'm looking for my cousin, but he never hears his phone ring. Can you send someone down to get him? Yeah, sure. Apartment three-forty. Stu Vannerson."

Chapter 20

Calif. CCR § 820.198. Cupiding establishments shall maintain procedures that ensure all complaints involving possible failure of an enchantment shall be promptly evaluated, investigated, and where necessary, reported to the Department.

JAKE WAS REALLY TAKING HIS RUMPLED LOOK TO NEW heights. His button-down shirt had more wrinkles than a naked mole rat, a dried coffee stain looked like a patch on the knee of his jeans, and the cowlick on the back of his head could have made Alfalfa jealous. Yet Eliza still found him incredibly attractive. She'd nearly said *I'll take two orgasms to go* when they'd stopped by Starbucks in the Agora (yes, they really were *everywhere* these days), but she also found his frayed appearance and tired eyes worrisome.

"You sure you're okay?" she asked.

He nodded as he dumped a pile of books onto the nearest library table. "There's got to be something in here about this."

Eliza wished she felt as confident as he sounded. After leaving the Johansens' yesterday, she'd retreated to her apartment and done a million and one internet searches for anything that could help. She'd found the Cupid equivalent of WebMD—CyberAffection—and read up on all the possible side effects of enchantments. Hemorrhage? Yep. Insomnia? Of course. Loss of appetite? More common than not. Even the tiniest risk of cancer by exposure to the weapon cleaners got a nod. But actively *hating* the person you were supposed to be enamored with? Nothing. By the time Jake finally called her back and suggested they meet at the Agora to do some in-depth research this morning, she'd nearly given up.

And, of course, convinced herself she had thirteen kinds of cancer and a rare tropical brain parasite.

The gentle whir of a pneumatic tube filled the library, followed by a satisfactory thump. Mrs. Washmoore rose out of her tube and peered over those fire-engine-red glasses. "Well, well. I had assumed you two were going to the Pythian Game trials downstairs, just like everyone else."

"Hi, Aunt Rebecca. What books do you have on enchantment troubleshooting? I found these." Jake pointed to the stack of books he'd dropped in front of Eliza. "But we want to see everything you've got. Even the really old stuff."

The woman looked back and forth between the two of them with a disapproving stare. "Trouble in paradise, dears?"

Eliza looked at the carpet (boring), the stack of books (dusty), and the ceiling (intricately painted with portraits of Athena spread among olive trees and owls). Did Mrs. Washmoore know she and Jake were…whatever they were? *Dating* seemed too simple, but *a couple* felt way too complicated.

"Just doing some research," Jake said, his gaze pinned

on the table. Apparently, he felt as awkward about the whole situation as she did.

"Well, let me see what I can find. Any particular troubleshooting techniques you're looking for? It would certainly help to narrow it down. Your *kind* does have a lot of troubles to wade through."

On the table, Jake's phone began to vibrate. He scooped it up before Eliza could hand it to him. "I've got to take this—"

"No cell phones in the library, dear. No exceptions, not even for family."

He jogged toward the oversize wooden doors and pushed through. "This is Jake Sanders," he said, just before the door swung shut behind him.

"Now, then. Where were we? Oh yes. What type of troubles are you having, dear? I mean, I assume you're the one having the troubles. The Cupids in my family tend to have less trouble than most. An exception, really."

Gods, did she wish Jake hadn't left her alone. Should she give Mrs. Washmoore a few details or continue with Jake's vague story about research? Had he looked so uncomfortable a moment ago because they hadn't officially defined their relationship? Or had it been because he didn't want to tell his aunt exactly how bad Eliza was at her job?

"Between you and me"—Mrs. Washmoore pulled off her glasses and let them hang from the chain around her neck—"I've heard some rumors."

Eliza leaned in. "You have?"

"One can't work as many eons around here as I have and not pick up a few things. Of course, I don't say a word about what I hear."

Yeah right. But if other Cupids were having similar troubles, maybe Eliza wasn't the problem. Maybe she could talk with them, bring the issue to the regional Cosmic Council, and get everything straightened out. She'd get the Johansens back together, return Charleston to his daily probiotics schedule, and end up a hero in the process. "Are you hearing anything about problems with enchantments?" she asked.

"Such as?"

"Oh, I don't know. Side effects, non-matches, enchantments wearing off before the moon cycle ends?" Eliza mumbled that last part as quickly as possible, and for a second, she could have sworn the curls at the front of Mrs. Washmoore's head slithered. But the Fury put her glasses back on her nose and shuffled over to the librarian's desk.

"Oh my. No, nothing like that. I have to say that sounds like a very *unique* situation."

The coffee Eliza had downed soured in her stomach. She couldn't get any firmer confirmation than that. She was the problem, plain and simple. "Well, you know, if you hear anything…"

"Of course, dear. If you want, I'd be happy to do some research. I doubt we have anything here, but I might be able to request an interlibrary loan. The Southern California branch has a much greater selection. Probably because they're so close to Hollywood. You know how those Tinseltown types are; plastic surgery and enchantments are their main sources of entertainment."

"An interlibrary loan would be great," Eliza said.

"It may take a few days. These things often do."

In a few days, Herman & Herman would probably be

buried under a stack of lawsuits, but what did she have to lose? "That'll be fine. Thank you, Mrs. Washmoore."

Eliza pulled out one of the books Jake had left, expecting the librarian to disappear back into her tube.

"You know, dear…" Mrs. Washmoore lumbered over to Eliza's table and hovered over her shoulder, one hand lightly brushing her arm before falling away. "I think you should be careful. If the other Cupids get wind of your *side effects*, who knows that will happen? They aren't always a level-headed bunch."

Eliza's eyes widened. Her body temperature flashed between hot and cold. Had all the stress of the last month thrown her body into early menopause? For the gods' sake, she hadn't even hit thirty yet.

"Like Jake said, it's just a research project," she muttered.

"Well, don't let your little *research* project get in the way of his goals. My nephew has been wanting a spot on the Cosmic Council for as long as I can remember. Being connected with something untoward could ruin his chances. And I'd hate to see him fail because of a few out-of-control hormones."

Goose bumps sprang up along Eliza's arms, and confusion slid into the space between them. Why did she suddenly feel so poorly? Had she remembered to get her flu shot? "I would never want Jake to fail. At anything…"

Mrs. Washmoore looked at Eliza over the rim of her glasses. "Then we're in agreement."

"We are?" Eliza shook her head to clear it, but she only succeeded in flinging sweat across her face. "I mean, we are."

"Excellent. Just be sure to end things between the two of you before it's too late. Heartbreaks are such nasty inconveniences."

End things? "Mrs. Washmoore, I think there's been a misunderstanding—"

The librarian clamped a hand on Eliza's shoulder. She almost swore the smell of rotten eggs and garbage filled her nostrils, and the room seemed to burst into a million invisible flames. Then, as quickly as it had come on, the feeling was gone. Her body returned to normal, nonmenopausal temperatures. All she could smell were old books and Mrs. Washmoore's rose hip perfume. Her mind, however, was still whirling.

Eliza swallowed hard and watched the librarian shuffle back to her spot on top of the tube. "Wait. Please. What do you—"

"I'll call you when your books are ready."

Whoosh.

Eliza looked at the empty spot where the Fury had stood and then at the doors Jake had disappeared through. Had she just agreed to end things with Jake? And more importantly, was Mrs. Washmoore right? When all this came out, would his reputation be irreparably damaged? Was being with Eliza ruining his life?

"You sure you don't mind?" Jake asked.

"I'm sure." Eliza stared out at the minuscule Herman & Herman parking lot and tapped on the books on her lap. "I'm just going to read through these and see if anything rings a bell. Besides, my mother will probably stroke out if she doesn't have someone to answer the phones today."

"If you're sure. Because I can call in. This whole Department delivery thing is just a temp job for me. If I get fired—"

"Go. I'm fine. I promise." Eliza crossed her arms. "I'll call you if anything changes."

"Dinner tonight?"

"Let me see if my dad needs anything. I've been neglecting my daughterly chauffeur duties." She pushed open the car door and put one foot on the pavement, hoping Jake didn't see through her lie. Her dad had been cleared to drive himself back and forth to his various appointments days ago. "I'll see you later."

"Eliza…" His eyes narrowed until they crinkled around the edges.

It was adorable. And she hated him for it.

"What?" she demanded.

He laid a hand on her forearm. "Are you brushing me off? Is this because of that whole capital-L Love thing I said the other day, because—"

At the mere mention of their earlier conversation—at their heartfelt confessions and shared secrets—the despair and turmoil she'd been holding back since they left the Agora spilled from her lips.

"Not everything is about you, okay?" she said.

"That's not what I meant—"

"Just go. Please."

But as soon as he'd pulled out of the lot, Eliza regretted her words. She pushed her way into Herman & Herman and flopped down behind the desk. She'd call him later and apologize. Explain that she was stressed and tired and overwhelmed. In the meantime, what she really needed was a quiet afternoon of reading and thinking to get her head straight. Her mother was scheduled to be at appointments all afternoon. Whether they were with clients or her "friend" Weston Presley was to be determined. But either way, it would give Eliza some time to—

The bells over the front door sounded.

"Eliza—*ooof*. Come on, work with me. Eliza, are you here?" Helen's voice rounded the corner before she did.

Oh gods.

She looked up to find a puffy-eyed Helen and a dead-eyed ~~Jake~~ Jacque.

"Helen. Hi."

"I need your help. Jacque and I are having trouble again. I tried to call, but—"

Jacque's head began spinning slowly. "Error 89. Error 89." His mouth moved a smidge off base from the syllables.

"Oh no. Not this again. Why are you doing this to me, Jacque?" Helen rubbed her eyes. "Haven't I always been good to you?"

Eliza watched in horror as the robot's head spun like something out of *The Exorcist*. "Helen—"

"He started doing this yesterday when I put him on personal assistant mode. I switched him to virtual assistant to make it stop, but..." She held Jacque out toward Eliza. "Please help."

The rational part of her brain reminded Eliza that she could *not* enchant inanimate objects. But the other part of Eliza—the part that felt as frazzled and desperate as Helen looked, the part that worried her problems were keeping Jake from achieving everything he'd ever wanted—begged her to at least *try* to fix this. Even if it seemed completely unfixable.

"This way," Eliza yelled over the continual chant of "Error 89. Error 89." Somewhere in the noise, a phone rang, but she ignored it. Instead, Eliza hauled Jacque toward her brother's empty office and hoisted him onto the desk. The Mandroid weighed less than she would have guessed, given all his *capabilities*. "Does he have an off button?"

"I'll switch him to gaming assistant mode. That's all he's good for anymore." Helen stripped off Jacque's shirt and turned the knob. His head stopped whirring, and the silence—except for Helen's quiet sniffles—was sweet relief.

"Would you like a glass of water?" Eliza asked.

Helen gave a half nod, half sob. "Yes, please."

"I'll be right back." Eliza jogged out to the water cooler, filled a cup, and grabbed a fresh box of tissues from behind the receptionist's desk. If Helen's last visit was any indication, Eliza would probably need a few more, but this would be a start. She stepped toward the office and paused.

Music blared from the other side of the door, punctuated by an occasional sob from Helen. Eliza knew she'd heard it before. The melody made her think of cotton candy and summer nights. But she couldn't quite place it. "Helen—" she said as she pushed open the door.

Jacque lay shirtless across her brother's desk, his pants around his knees. The flap in his abdomen had been lifted, and beneath it, the touch screen was lit with all variety of white ovals. The music poured from his mouth. Helen sat between his legs like a kid with a pocket full of quarters at an arcade. She gripped his manhood (or was it Mandroidhood?) with one hand and used his testicles as buttons with the other.

"Just a minute." Helen sniffed. She jerked Jacque's penis up, down, and to the right, never letting her gaze fall from the screen in his chest. "I have to make it to a save point."

Eliza pressed the door closed with her back and tried not to keep her eyes from falling out of her head. A better person would turn away—this seemed like a weirdly intimate moment, after all—but then again, if Helen wanted her to fix Jacque, it wouldn't hurt to know *all* his functions. "His penis is a joystick?" Eliza asked. "I mean, a literal joystick. Not a euphemistic one."

"It's more responsive than the touch screen. Besides, this is the only joy he brings me anymore. Sometimes I want to rip it off, just to be done with it. But then I wouldn't be able to play *Egg Salad Saga* anymore."

"Oh."

Finally, the music rose to a crescendo, and the sound of coins clanking took its place. "Yes, highest score yet," Helen said, still gripping Jacque's penis.

Eliza couldn't help but notice that it stood at full attention. Maybe the Mandroid had conquered his old problem and found a new one. "Helen, what's going on?"

Jacque's mouth moved in answer, but it wasn't his stilted robot voice that came out.

> If your sex life's as squalid
> As month-old egg salad,
> Don't let Fates conspire

To thwart your desire.
Let Van Love write your love ballad.

"You have to listen to the ads to get more coins," Helen explained. She pulled the flap on Jacque's abdomen, and with that, his penis also deflated. Apparently he still had the erectile dysfunction issue. Or maybe it was more like erectile *malfunction*? Eliza shook the thoughts from her mind. She didn't have time for internal debate about the proper terminology for Jacque's penile malware. Instead, she needed the time and brain space to figure out what was happening. "Helen, how long have you been playing this game?"

She shrugged. "Probably since about eight thirty."

"You just downloaded it today?"

"Oh." Helen's chuckle held a hint of embarrassment. "No. I've been playing it for a while now. I had a free download code and decided to give it a shot."

"Where did you get the download code?"

"A friend of mine in a Mandroid forum gave it to me."

Eliza forced herself not to think too much about the contents of such a forum. But if she couldn't sleep tonight, she was definitely logging on to see what kind of stuff people posted. She was only (well, sort of) human after all. "Is that where you read about the Mandroids being invented by a Cupid?"

Helen nodded. "Man-A-Call. It's a company based in Tokyo. I know because I called their headquarters to complain. Three times. Not that it did me any good."

Tokyo… Her father's drug-induced ramblings about techno-Cupids…

Eliza leaned closer to Jacque, inspecting him for any

sign of, well, *anything* that would fit these puzzle pieces together. "Did you download the game before or after Jacque started having his problems?"

Helen tapped a finger on her chin. "Let's see. I had a dentist appointment on the thirty-first. Everything worked great then. I remember because..." She shook her head. "Anyway, I downloaded the game the next day." She counted silently on her fingers. "Three times a day for a while, then just once." Finally, she looked back up at Eliza. "He lost his mojo about two and a half weeks after I downloaded the game."

Eliza pressed her fingertips into the groove between her eyebrows. Yolanda had said Eddie played a game and was always trying to get her to join. They'd broken up before the end of the moon cycle. Helen downloaded this game, and Jacque had begun malfunctioning. Even Mitch Johansen had mentioned something about getting a *triple egg bonus* at the cruise ship casino. "What about those ads?"

"What about them? Like I said, you get more coins if you listen."

"Yeah, but is it always the same ad or different ones?"

"Mostly different ads for the same guy. Always with the limericks."

Vic. He'd said big changes were coming. Big *technological* changes that would make him a lot of money. Eliza's pulse picked up.

What if Vic somehow created a game that messed up people's hormones, a game that made people start falling in and out of love faster than normal? Relationships would disintegrate. Everyone would be looking for something new and better or, like Helen, they'd be desperate to get the old thing to work again. And who would they call? The Cupid whose advertisements they'd heard on repeat for weeks and months.

Holy Hades. This was huge.

Of course, Vic had taken out ad space on just about every medium available. Maybe it was nothing.

"How about we give Jacque a, uh, reboot, and see if that helps?" Eliza pressed her fingertips together in a miniature prayer. She never thought she'd be begging Eros for help fluffing a robot, but she needed to get Helen out of here so she could think.

"Thank you." Helen said. "I knew you'd help."

"I can't promise anything. Just like last time."

"I know. But I have faith in you." Helen looked up at her with admiration in her eyes. "You're the best Cupid in town, Eliza."

Eliza stifled a wry laugh. If only poor Helen knew. "You ready?"

"As ready as anyone can be in this type of situation."

That's saying a lot.

"Okay, where's his on-off button?" Eliza searched the area around his two—well, technically he had three, but one was much further south—knobs.

"Oh. It's right under his joystick." Helen lifted Jacque's testicles. A small black button sat where the sun surely didn't shine. "There."

Every time Eliza thought her life couldn't get weirder… "Why don't you go ahead and give it a push?"

"I've tried. I think he needs a Cupid's touch."

Eliza's face must have betrayed her horror, because Helen's chin began to quiver.

"Okay, okay. I'm going to push it." She braced herself.

Helen leaned over and stroked Jacque's face. "Come back to us, Jacque."

Eliza pressed the button, and—as a bonus, last-ditch effort—she grabbed her brother's stapler and knocked the Mandroid in the fluids reservoir.

Jacque's eyes blinked. His mouth moved. No error message to be heard.

"Okay, I'm going to switch him to one of his other modes," Eliza said. Outside, the bells over the door chimed. "Have a seat," she called out. "Someone will be with you in a moment."

Helen wrapped her long, slim fingers around Jacque's penis, as serious as someone about to perform brain surgery. "I'm ready."

Eliza turned the knob.

Nothing. Not even a switch. "Error 89. Error 89. Error 89."

"No," Helen whimpered.

"Shhhh." Eliza glanced at the door and patted her on the back. "I'm so sorry. I really don't know what else to do."

"Why did I spend so much money on this stupid thing? Just because I was lonely? Ha!" Helen raised her head and looked up at Eliza with sadness in her eyes. "I'm such a loser."

"You aren't," Eliza said. "We all make bad purchases from time to time. It's—"

"Please don't." Helen wiped her nose on her sleeve. "I'm a loser. A loser with no friends and a glorified iPad."

Quite frankly, Eliza would rather have had an iPad. "Helen, please—"

The office door swung wide open, and Eliza's mother stood on the other side, wide-eyed and openmouthed.

"Eliza, what are you… Good gods, is that Jake?" A hideous shade of green hiked up her mother's cheeks.

"His name is Jacque," Helen said. "Or it *was*. Thanks for trying, Eliza." She tossed Jacque over her shoulder and gave Eliza a sad smile before shuffling out of the office.

Her mother cleared her throat. "Care to explain?"

"I can't." At least, she couldn't explain yet.

But if techno-Cupids were real *and* they made Mandroids *and* those Mandroids could be enchanted, couldn't they also create a video game that reversed enchantments? And if anyone would use such a thing to cash in on other people's pain, it would be Vic Van Love.

She grabbed Elijah's phone and dialed, ignoring her mother's stare.

"You've reached Mitch Johansen. Please leave me a message, and I'll call you back soon."

"Hi, Mr. Johansen. This is Eliza Herman. Can you call me back when you have a moment?" She hung up to find her mother still in the doorway.

"Eliza, I'd really like to talk to you for a minute. Can we—"

"Maybe later, okay?" Eliza slipped out the office door. She didn't have time to deal with her mother right now. She had work to do…and a certain limerick-obsessed Cupid to interrogate.

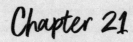

Chapter 21

> "When enchanting, Cupids should wear athletic shoes and lightweight, but not baggy, clothing that allows freedom of movement. Although togas are traditional, pants are recommended."
>
> **—Erosian Weaponry Fundamentals**

VIC VAN LOVE'S OFFICE LOOKED EXACTLY AS ELIZA would have expected. Outside, a ten-foot-tall Cupid who shot water from his bow towered over the parking lot. Inside, dark wood paneling met deep-red walls and plush carpeting. The man was a living, breathing stereotype. And if the size of his office was any indication, that stereotype was serving his bank account well.

Eliza approached the reception desk. She'd driven over here with fire in her veins, but now that she was on Vic's home turf, her nerves tempered the fire a little. She needed to be calm, quiet, cunning. She needed to lure him into a false sense of complacency and then strike when he least expected it. Or at least get him to admit to his *Egg Salad Saga* misdeeds while she taped the conversation on her phone.

"Welcome to Love Conquers All's Love Lounge," the slender redhead behind the desk said. "How can I help you?"

"I'm here to see Vic," Eliza said.

"Do you have an appointment?"

"No, but he'll want to see me."

"Hmm." The woman turned her gaze down to the computer screen. The name tag on her shirt caught the light. *Heather*. "Is this an emergency, or would you be able to come back tomorrow morning? I have a nine o'clock, a ten—"

"It's an emergency," Eliza insisted.

Heather looked up at her with narrowed eyes. She must have seen Eliza's take-no-prisoners expression and decided the emergency was both real and dire, because she offered Eliza a tablet and a tight smile. "Click on our app and fill out the paperwork. You're welcome to have a seat in the waiting area. Just hit Send when you're done, and the information will automatically upload to our system. I'll let Mr. Van Love know you're here. He's currently in a meeting though, so it might be a little while."

Eliza stared at the tablet in Heather's hands. She was tempted to bust through Vic's door, interrupt his meeting, and demand some answers. Let him be ashamed in front of a client. But she remembered her plan. Cool, calm, cunning. She took the tablet and flashed Heather a grateful smile. "Thank you so much."

"Feel free to enjoy the complimentary Wi-Fi while you wait. The password is 'Van Love conquers all.' One word, all lowercase."

Eliza picked an empty chair at the other end of the rectangular room. It put her far enough from Heather that she wouldn't be under the receptionist's concerned stare, but close enough to Vic's office that she might be able to hear any bits of conversation that leaked out from under the door.

Once she'd settled in, she looked at the tablet screen. At her parents' office, potential and returning clients provided their name, birth date, marital status, potential medical issues, and romantic histories the old-fashioned way: pen and paper. Yes, the pens walked off a lot, and sometimes reading the handwriting made it impossible to tell if the person had a history of influenza or infidelity, but it worked. More or less.

Vic, on the other hand, had taken the information sheet to a new level. Eliza opened the Love Conquers All app and was immediately assaulted by Vic's smug face telling her all about the types and costs of enchantments. Finally, the video ended and a message appeared: CLICK BELOW TO LET VAN LOVE CONQUER ALL.

Seamless, high-tech, and expensive. Exactly the type of thing someone with the skills and knowledge to build a relationship-destroying game would have in their office. Eliza sat up a little straighter, feeling all the more confident that she'd found the culprit.

Begrudgingly, she clicked to "let Van Love conquer all." A standard form took the place of the videos, and she began to fill in the information.

Name: Herman, Eliza
Birth date: February 14
Medical Conditions: None
Marital Status: Single
Returning Client: No
Have You Ever Employed a Cupid: No
Reason for Your Visit: My egg salad is squalid

Okay, maybe she wasn't going to be *totally* calm and cunning.

Eliza hit Send and watched her personal

information—and snarky comment—disappear into the nether regions of the internet. She ran a finger along the tablet screen, opening and closing apps at random. In her time as an IT help desk attendant, she hadn't gained many technical skills. But she had a tablet connected to Vic's network in her hands, and maybe, just maybe, she could find some proof of his involvement. She could get out of here and take her evidence to the authorities without ever seeing him face-to-face.

She glanced up at Heather. The model-worthy woman was deeply involved in whatever was happening on her computer. Eliza tapped the screen and opened up the settings. The tablet prompted her for a password, and she typed in *vanloveconquersall* before hitting Enter.

Nothing.

She tried two more of his annoying puns before the tablet told her to "contact an administrator for assistance." She clutched the tablet, waiting to see if she'd set off some kind of alarm. When Heather didn't look up, Eliza closed the app and pulled open the folder labeled Games.

Solitaire. Mah-jongg. *Minesweeper*. The usual old-school games she'd played on their family's computer. But then she saw the little white egg icon at the bottom of the folder. *Egg Salad Saga*. Eliza took a deep breath and hovered her finger over the egg.

If she tried it, she would find out—one way or the other—whether *Egg Salad Saga* could tear people apart.

But if it could, she might end up hating Jake.

Jake with his bright smile and kind eyes.

Jake with his "dumb ideas" and eager kisses.

Jake…who'd gotten her into this whole Cupid license bullshit in the first place.

Jake who'd had a hundred *dumb ideas*, literally—like a belief in Love.

Her finger inched closer to the egg, propelled by the force of the unexpected irritation spiraling inside her.

"I forgot to ask. Would you like something to drink? We have water, tea, soda, juice." Heather stood and walked to a wood-paneled mini-fridge a few feet from Eliza's chair. It had blended in with the walls so well that she hadn't even noticed it. She also hadn't noticed that Heather was *very* pregnant.

"No. I'm fine, thanks," Eliza said.

"Oh! Are you an Egghead too?"

"Excuse me?"

Heather pointed at the tablet and laughed. "*Egg Salad Saga*. I can't get enough. Sometimes I see those little eggs in my sleep."

Eliza closed the game. Vic had his own people playing this? It was one (horrible) thing to not care about strangers' lives, but it was another (really, *really* horrible) thing to ruin the lives of the people he worked with every day. "I've actually never played it before," she said.

"Really? Let me give you my referral code. If you use it, we both get five extra coins." She waddled back to her desk.

The door to Vic's office creaked open. "Heather, have you seen my extra set of pants?" Vic called out.

The venom in Heather's eyes would have put Medusa to shame, and Eliza nearly got whiplash from the sudden change in the woman's emotions.

"I told you, John," Heather said. "I'm not going to be your pants person anymore. And you have an emergency appointment waiting."

Vic's door slammed shut. A moment later, it opened again. "Send them in," he called.

Heather rolled her eyes. "Mr. Van Love will see you now."

If Eliza were a gambling woman—which she absolutely was not, especially after an enchantment disaster involving a roulette wheel and a blackjack dealer— she'd have bet that Heather's sudden flare of anger and annoyance was fueled by *Egg Salad*.

Well, that and the fact that Vic was a serious douchecanoe.

Eliza pulled her phone into her lap and toyed with the screen, trying to look more like a standard on-the-phone-all-the-time member of the public than a fellow Cupid pulling up the voice-recorder app on her phone. Then she stood and marched straight into Vic's office, phone in hand. "Hello, *John*," she said.

"Ah, look at that. Eliza Herman." Vic propped his shoes up on his desk, nonplussed. "Here for a little love emergency, are we?"

"Finally found some pants to wear, did we?" she asked, closing the door behind her. "What kind of meeting was that, by the way? The one that didn't require pants."

"Sorry, client confidentiality." He leaned back and laced his fingers behind his head. "What do you want? No, let me guess. You decided to take me up on my offer. Interesting. I couldn't take you on as a partner, at least not right away. We'd need to ease you into the brand. How do you feel about changing your name? I'm thinking Candy Valentine."

Eliza clenched her teeth so hard she could feel a muscle in her jaw twitch. "I'm thinking you're a monster."

"Now that's no way to talk to your future boss."

"I know what you're doing, Vic." So much for that whole calm and cunning thing. Furious and foolish was more like it. Her rage was on the verge of getting the best of her for the second—or was it third? Fourth?—time today. "I know why your business is booming, and I'm not going to sit here and take it."

Vic put his feet on the floor and leaned his elbows on the desk. "A sky-high advertising budget? Billboards? Service with a smile?" He gave her that smug smile that graced damn near every billboard on the interstate. "You should really smile more. Your resting bitch face can get a little intense sometimes."

"I'll take that under consideration." The red record button stared up at her as the seconds ticked by, each word chronicled for posterity. She was going to nail this bastard. Once and for all. And then take out a billboard of her own—featuring his mug shot. "You can hide behind your ads and your sleazeball getup, but I know the truth, Van Love. I know you've been screwing with people's hormones somehow. I guess if your couples break up in half the time, you can take in twice as many clients, huh? Who cares about real Love, right?"

The last words flew from her mouth without stopping to check with her brain. She didn't care about Love. She cared about the business her parents had built. She cared about all the work her brother had done to make it his own one day. She cared about the Johansens—the way they'd looked at each other that first day when they'd told her how they'd met and all their adventures since. She cared about…

Jake.

No. Just thinking his name lit a fuse inside her brain. It sizzled and crackled, threatening her with a massive explosion if she continued down this path.

"Just admit it, Vic," she snarled.

"Look, Eliza. I don't know what you're talking about. The only hormones going crazy around here are yours and Heather's. You're both bonkers, but at least she'll be normal again in two months or so."

Eliza sat up straighter. She definitely didn't expect his confession to come so easily. "Two months? That's how long *Egg Salad* lasts?"

"Two-month-old egg salad? Thank the gods you were born a Cupid and not a Demetrian." Vic shook his head. "Gold Lea would be the food-poisoning capital of the world."

She fixed her stare on his stupid, smug face. No way she was letting him get under her skin. "What happens in two months, Vic?" She spat his name, trying to rid the taste of it from her mouth.

"Do you really need me to paint you a picture?"

She glanced down at her phone. Still recording. "Yes. In detail."

"Okay, well, if you insist—"

"I do."

"Shall I start at the very beginning?"

"Please."

"When a man and a woman love each other very much"—he sounded like a preschool teacher reading a story at circle time, a thought that made Eliza want to hurl—"or, in Heather and I's case, when a man and a woman are lonely and drunk in the office after hours, they take off all their clothes—or in Heather and I's case—"

"Get to the point, Vic. How'd you do it, exactly?"

He looked at Eliza like she'd lost her mind. "On the receptionist's desk? And then on the floor behind the desk. And once on that chair where you're sitting. I'm not sure which time was *the one* where I knocked her up, but—"

Eliza jolted from her chair, barely keeping her phone from clattering to the floor. "*You're* the father of Heather's baby?"

His expression said it all. "Did you hit your head on the way over here or what?"

Every disgusting puzzle piece slid together in Eliza's mind. "And in two months…"

"Victor, Jr. or maybe Victoria, Jr.—we decided not to find out the sex—is making his or her way into the world. Hopefully with the knack."

"But Heather is… And you're…"

"Oh, don't look so shocked. *Some* people think I'm a catch."

Eliza pressed her lips together. Vic was a catch in the way catching an old boot on a fishing trip was a catch.

Muffled music sounded from somewhere inside his desk. He opened a drawer and pulled out a phone. Eliza caught a glimpse of the notification before he flipped it facedown. Vic Van Love had new eggs to boil in *Egg Salad Saga*.

"*You* play *Egg Salad Saga*?"

"Like you're so superior. I heard the music playing on the tablet out there," he said. He suddenly brightened. "Oh! Do you need a referral code, because—"

"Heather already offered me one."

"Of course she did." He sighed. "Are you going to

tell me what this hormone thing is all about? Because I've got another meeting to attend."

Eliza tapped her fingers on the desk. Vic knew the mother of his child played *Egg Salad Saga*. He also played it himself, and—believe it or not—the man looked genuinely clueless. Eliza knew he wasn't that great an actor. She'd seen his commercials.

Fabulous. Another dead end. One more failure for the Eliza Herman files. She ended the recording and sighed. "I'll see myself out."

"Great." Vic propped his feet up on the desk and swiped across his phone screen. That damn music started up again, and the first few notes made Eliza's stomach churn. She needed to get out of here.

"Oh, by the way," Vic said when she was halfway out the door, "thanks for your support. Even if you didn't mean to give it."

"What?"

"You know, the whole thing with the Cosmic Council. It's better that Jake doesn't run anyway. He's too young, too ambitious. He needs to let the world knock him around a little before he jumps headfirst into cosmic bureaucracy."

Eliza narrowed her eyes, unwilling to believe this jerkwad knew anything about Jake or his future plans. Especially things Eliza didn't know. "What are you talking about, Vic?"

"You mean you didn't know?" Vic gave her a look that said he knew she was clueless—and he was relishing every second of it. "After Jake enchanted you without your permission, he had to confess to the Department. Some of our people who work in the Department found out, reported it to the Council…"

The fuse relit, the fire in her louder and faster this time. "What do you mean, 'enchanted me without my permission'?"

He shrugged. "Some people get so uptight about scandals these days."

Eliza stared at Vic for a few seconds before slamming the door and marching out of his love lounge. She wasn't any closer to knowing who was behind *Egg Salad Saga*, but she'd learned something even more earth-shattering in the meantime.

Two things, actually.

One: She'd ruined Jake's future, exactly as Mrs. Washmoore had predicted.

Two: *If* Vic was telling the truth, she and Jake were just another enchantment. One he'd lied to her about.

Right now, she couldn't tell which she despised more. But an explosion was coming in three, two...

Chapter 22

"Love hurts."

—Apollo, customer complaint

ELIZA POUNDED HER FIST ON JAKE'S DOOR LIKE AN angry cop executing a search warrant. If she didn't know better, she'd think she had some Fury in her lineage, because the thoughts and images coursing through her—

The door swung open. Jake stood in front of her looking slightly less rumpled but even more enticing than she'd remembered. Boyish grin, forearms to die for, a mouth that knew exactly how to please.

A soul that fit perfectly with her own.

Or at least she'd thought it had.

"We need to talk." She pushed past him and into the living room. For one horrible moment, she sat on his sofa. Then she remembered all the ways they'd defiled that particular piece of furniture and opted to pace around the room.

"I was just about to call you," he said. "I put in a call to a buddy of mine from the Corps. He works at the Cosmic Center for Affection Research in Athens. I explained what's been happening—"

"Jake."

"Look, I know you wanted to keep this a secret for now, but he's trustworthy. I swear. He said the CCAR

has been doing underground research on how to reverse
enchantments for years now. I guess you're not the only
Cupid who has trouble—I mean *had* trouble—keeping
their enchantment levels in check. Anyway, it has something to do with concentrating Discordian powers. He
said the last round of the research was really promising.
Almost too promising. They had to scale it back after a
few people really lost it. He said if someone had gotten
ahold of that research—"

"Jake." She stopped pacing and stared at his face. It was
so beautiful and hopeful, and she resented it oh so much.
"Are you running for the Cosmic Council this term?"

"What?"

"The Cosmic Council. The deadline was yesterday.
Are? You? Running?"

"I… Well, I thought about it, and…" He ran a hand
over the top of his head. His tell. Vic had been right.

"Decided it was too risky to run with a scandal following you?" She crossed her arms, as much to close
herself off as to hold herself together.

"Eliza—"

"That's it, isn't it? It would ruin your chances
now that everyone, and I mean *everyone*, knows you
enchanted your mentee without her permission?"

Jake closed his eyes. His dark eyelashes fluttered the
smallest bit, and Eliza had to force away the memory
of how he'd looked when he was sleeping. Content.
Peaceful. Exquisite. Little did she know he was about
to blow her life to smithereens. "That is part of it, yes."

Until that very moment, Eliza hadn't realized she'd
been hoarding a tiny sliver of hope. That minuscule
piece of her had wanted him to deny all of it, pull her

to his chest, and reassure her that everything she'd ever felt for him had been real. Now that part of her was dead and gone.

How could he have done this to her? Lied for so long?

She may have enchanted him first, but that was an accident. And he knew about it.

"How did it happen? Did you stick me with a lancet when I wasn't looking? A paper cut?" Pain spiraled out of her, so fierce and intense she couldn't see straight.

"Eliza, please."

"Did you do it before or after I enchanted you? Am I still enchanted?" Hot, salty tears poured down her face and gathered at the edge of her lip. "Did I actually enchant you, or was that just part of your lie too?"

"You *did* enchant me," he whispered.

"Tell me then, am I still enchanted? When is it going to end? When am I going to stop feeling like this?"

Jake's face hardened. His fingers closed around the back of the couch and squeezed. "Do you feel enchanted right now, Eliza?"

"I don't know what I feel. Everything is so mixed up." She rubbed her eyes, and her fingers came back smudged with mascara. Oh well. She didn't care whether he found her attractive anymore. She wanted him to see exactly how much pain he'd caused her. "How could you do this?"

"I didn't."

"You didn't?" She took up pacing again. "But Vic said—"

"Let me guess. Vic said that I enchanted you in secret. Agent Oliver found out, and I had to withdraw from the election."

Eliza sniffed. "More or less."

"Well, good. At least someone bought the lie." Jake let out a heavy sigh. "I really didn't think Oliver believed it."

Confusion swirled in Eliza's stomach, still tinged with nausea but also relief. It was like stepping off a roller coaster after eating too much cotton candy. "Bought what?"

"Can you sit down, please? You're making me nervous." She sat, despite her better judgment.

"That day that Agent Oliver saw us, uh—"

"Groping on the hood of your car?"

"I was going to say 'saw us kissing,' but yes." Jake's shoulders relaxed a little. "After I dropped you off, I went to his office."

"You told *me* not to contact him!" Indignation reared its ugly head once again, and she crossed her arms.

"I know, I know. I'm sorry. But on the way home, I started to panic, thinking about you getting your permit revoked. I drove over there, just to see if he'd seen anything. Long story short, he'd seen a lot. So I lied. I told him I'd enchanted you in secret, and that he shouldn't hold the kiss against you. I even offered to step away as your mentor if that would help."

The tips of her fingers ran cold. He'd lied. To a government official. For her. "You did?"

Jake nodded. "He filed an incident report but let me stay on as long as I promised to not let anything happen again. And…"

"And what?"

"And I couldn't run for the Cosmic Council after that. Because if I ran, that would get people digging into my background. They'd find the report, and I'd be thrown out of the race. Oliver would be in trouble too."

"Why would he be in trouble?" Eliza asked.

"Because technically, he's my boss. Intentional enchantment without consent is a serious violation. He probably should have fired me."

Eliza dropped her hands to her lap and stared at them. She couldn't bring herself to look Jake in the eye. "That's not what I expected."

The couch cushions shifted as Jake sat down beside her. "Really, he let me off pretty easily, and look—it worked. You have your license, right?"

She did. But Jake had had to give up the one thing he really wanted—a spot on the Cosmic Council—in order for her to get it. And for what? All of her enchantments had gone so far off the rails that she didn't even know if she wanted a license anymore.

Once again, she'd ruined someone's life with her "gift." And this one hurt way worse than any of the others. Not to mention she hadn't asked for this. Any of it. *How dare he?* She hadn't wanted to be a licensed Cupid. Or his excuse for not following his dreams. "You shouldn't have done that," she whispered.

"You're right. I should have told you."

"No. I mean you shouldn't have done it at all." Her chest burned as she swallowed back her angry sobs. She wasn't going to break down. Not here. Not now. If she did, Jake would try to comfort her, and being in his arms would only make the pain that much deeper. "We shouldn't be doing *this* at all."

Jake hooked his index finger under her chin and forced her to meet his gaze. "What are you saying, Eliza?"

She jerked away. "I'm saying this is a mistake. We're a mistake. You gave up a seat on the Cosmic Council *for me*. You're ruining your life *for me*."

"I'm not—"

"And what's going to happen six months from now when you realize how much you gave up? We probably won't even be together then. And you'll be left with, what? A lot of resentment and a job as a deliveryman for the Department? I don't think so." The words poured out of her, faster and faster, until she wasn't even sure what she was saying. "This was all a huge mistake. I'm quitting the Cupid business, and we need to break up."

"Eliza, just listen to me."

"No." If she listened, she'd cave. And if she caved, Jake's entire career would be over. She had to stay strong, get out of here, and set things right with the Department. Maybe it was too late for Jake to run in this election, but if she could straighten things out with Agent Oliver, maybe Jake would have a chance down the road.

Eliza pushed herself off the couch with shaking arms and grabbed her things. "I have to go. I'm sorry, Jake. Thank you for everything."

"Wait, please."

She didn't look him in the eye as she pried open the front door. "Tell your friend at CCAR to look into *Egg Salad Saga*, okay? If anyone got into their research, that's who."

"Eliza, please."

She stepped outside and slammed the door shut behind her.

"Goodbye, Jake," she whispered to no one at all.

———————➤

Eliza woke up in her apartment with puffy eyes and a voicemail on her cell phone.

"*Hi, this is Mitch Johansen returning your call from yesterday. Look, I appreciate your hard work, but I think it's time to let this whole thing go. I've been staying with my cousin Stu. He's been keeping me busy with activities at the Villas. Bingo, water aerobics, technology classes, the works. We're even taking a field trip to the zoo in a few hours. Anyway, I've got a feeling that Lily and I weren't meant to be. I might even try my hand at meeting a few ladies at the zoo today. I know it probably seems sudden, but who knows how much time I have left? You can let Lily know, right? I just can't talk to her these days.*"

Apparently, Eliza had gone from matchmaker to divorce negotiator in the span of a few days. Poor Lily. Eliza pulled her covers up over her head and sank further into the dark. Maybe she could sleep for the next six months and wake up when all of this had passed.

Her phone buzzed.

She closed her eyes.

It buzzed again.

Her head throbbed.

One more buzz, and curiosity got the better of her. She peered out from under the blankets and grabbed her phone. Jake's tiny photo was on her screen, his words beside it.

Eliza, we need to talk.
I'm sorry.

Her heart twisted with longing, then suddenly tightened like a fist in her chest. "Ugh. Leave. Me. Alone." She pitched the phone to the bottom of the bed. Or rather, she tried. Instead, it bounced off the mattress, hit the corner of her bedpost, and the screen shattered, rendering it completely unusable.

"At least I won't have to deal with that anymore," she muttered. But her body and mind wouldn't let her sleep. All she did was vacillate between thoughts of Jake's stupid face and poor, sweet Lily Johansen spending her last years alone and heartbroken. "Gods damn it."

She tossed off the covers and headed for the shower. Mitch Johansen would be at the zoo looking to move on today, and Eliza needed to stop him.

At 10:01 a.m., Eliza pushed through the turnstiles of the Gold Lea Zoo. At 10:02 a.m., the rain started. The sky turned gray, and families flocked toward the parking lot.

Fitting.

She'd been to the zoo dozens of times growing up, usually on days like this. At least, all the times she'd gone after her eighth birthday. Most families went to the zoo on sunny days, watching the animals with delighted squeals as the kids ate ice cream and the parents tried to subtly impart educational information. But because of Eliza's inability to function in crowds without creating mass chaos, her family stuck to the gray, gloomy days. Fewer people on the premises meant fewer chances for disaster.

Even as a grumpy, emo teenager, she'd enjoyed coming here alone. Some days, she'd go straight to the ape house and watch the gorillas watching her. She'd sit on the bench outside their enclosure for hours while Zeus ripped open the skies with lightning and thunder.

The wet pebblestone beneath her feet brought Eliza straight back to her teenage years. For the sake of tradition, she bought a lemonade at the first snack stand in her path and then continued on, searching for any sign of an elderly tour group.

Please don't tell me they've left.

But the farther she walked, the less familiar things became. Exhibits had moved and changed since Eliza's last visit, and soon enough, she found herself standing in a downpour in front of the children's petting zoo.

She scanned the area, searching for a map or a hapless zoo employee who could point her in the right direction. But, of course, no one else in their right mind wandered the zoo on a day like this. With a sigh, she pushed open the door to the petting zoo and stepped inside. Someone in there could show her the way, and at least it would be dry—

Oh gods. It was *packed* with children. Gobs of them. They ranged from unbalanced toddlers to upper-elementary-school kids, and they swarmed the place with their sticky hands and happy squeals. Even a few parents got in on the excitement, clapping their hands and taking photos of their offspring with armadillos and goats.

A teenage zoo employee manned a podium a few feet from the door. She stood with her back hunched over her phone and the collar of her yellow polo shirt flipped up around the left side of her neck.

Eliza tiptoed her way through the throng. Even though most of these kids were toddlers, it couldn't hurt to be careful. Besides, there were enough moms and dads hanging around that Eliza was *sure* she could cause a marital disaster if she bumped into the wrong person. "Excuse me?" she called over the din.

The employee didn't look up from her phone. Light from the screen illuminated her pointy features, and as she got closer, Eliza recognized the music blaring from the device: the telltale sound of *Egg Salad Saga*.

"Hello?" Eliza tried again.

"Six dollars." The girl—her name tag read Rachel—held out one hand, but her gaze never left the phone screen.

"Actually, I..." Eliza struggled to be heard over the children—who'd seemed to grow even louder and squealier—and the music coming from the phone.

"Cash or card?" The girl swiped at her screen so quick her finger was almost a blur. This girl was an *Egg Salad* ninja or something.

"I'm looking for a map."

"Six dollars."

"For a map?"

"No, for admission. Cash or card?" Rachel said.

Talking to a brick wall would get Eliza further than this. "Can you put down the phone, please? It's really for your own good."

Gods, twenty-nine years old, and Eliza was already acting like a grandma. Next, she'd be complaining about school taxes and eating Werther's Originals from the bottom of her purse.

Come to think of it, she already did the Werther's thing.

"What was that?" Rachel's eyes flicked up for a millisecond before they darted back down to the game. The irritating music slowed, and a strange cracking sound—like thirteen eggshells breaking at once—came from the phone. "Damn it. I can't get past this level."

Eliza stretched her hand over the phone screen. Yes,

it was rude and invasive, but she'd come to the end of her very frayed rope. "Where are the maps?"

The girl's expression changed from annoyance to shock so quickly Eliza wondered if she'd sprouted horns and a tail. But there was no time to check for new appendages, because the children's squeals grew louder and more chaotic.

Eliza turned. Dozens of tiny feet pounded in her direction, but the children weren't the only ones making that horrible noise. The biggest squeal came from the rotund, pink pig tearing her way. A very familiar pig. One who'd appeared in quite a few of her text messages over the last few days.

"Charleston?" Eliza bent down as the pig pressed its snout into her leg. "What…? How…?" Her emotions were overloading. Confusion, disbelief, relief—they were almost as loud as the kids running over to pet Charleston's hairy back.

"Not again." Rachel set down her phone (*hallelujah!*) and came around to the front of the podium. "Everybody, get back, please. Give me some space. Come on, Porky. You've got to stay in your pen."

"Wait." Eliza bent down to hug Charleston around the neck. He nuzzled into her ear, letting out happy little snorts. "Where did you get this pig?"

"He's new. Having a little trouble adjusting to life in the petting zoo, huh, Porky? It's better than being bacon, trust me." She reached for the pig.

Eliza's heart beat at the speed of light. She clung to Charleston, and believe it or not, he snugged up against her. It was like he remembered her. Oh schnikes. The last time Eliza had seen Charleston—

No. She'd had a lot of weird Cupid mishaps in her life, but she had not enchanted a pig.

Probably.

"This is my friend's pig." She hugged Charleston closer. He let out a contented snort into her neck. "She's been looking for him everywhere."

Rachel shrugged. The movement was so typically teenage that Eliza almost felt sorry for the girl. Back then, Eliza had probably tried to seem just as indifferent to the world.

"I can call a manager if you want, ma'am, but I doubt this is your friend's pig." Rachel reached for the collar hanging around Charleston's neck. Plain red, not a bedazzlement in sight. Yolanda would have a hypertensive crisis. "We make sure to confirm ownership of all animals."

"Please call the manager."

"Great." Rachel sighed. Obviously she found it anything but. "Let me take Porky back to his pen. Then I'll call someone."

Eliza sat at the edge of the pen, while Charleston ignored the children to lie in a pile of hay near her feet. By the time the manager showed up, the rain had let up and most of the families had fled the petting zoo.

"Someone is having an issue with Porky?"

Eliza turned. She'd know that voice anywhere. He'd made her childhood a torment of teasing and rumors, and then he'd had the nerve to show up at her licensing exam with the intent to trick her. To be fair, the Department had made him trick her. But Jonathan Ellis could have helped an old lady cross the street, discovered time travel, and cured cancer, and Eliza would still hold on to her childhood grudge.

"Actually, I'm having trouble with *Charleston Samuel Durst the Third*."

"Eliza?" He blinked a few times, and she couldn't help but think of Yolanda's Mandroid. Eliza even liked Jacque better than Jonathan Ellis.

"Yes. And this pig belongs to my friend Yolanda."

"According to the paperwork we got from the Humane Society, he belongs to the Gold Lea Zoo."

"Okay, but this pig was pignapped. Taken from his home and his *very* upset mother." Eliza reached down and petted Charleston's hairy back. "Please do the right thing. Just this once."

He crossed his arms. "Do you have some kind of proof of ownership? Registration papers? Photos? Anything?"

"Yes!" She reached for her phone. No one would be able to deny it was the same pig once they saw the photos Yolanda had forwarded... "Shit. I have photos, but my phone is broken."

Jonathan shrugged. "I'm sure you can understand my dilemma here. If I let everyone who claimed to own one of our animals just walk out of here with them—"

"How many people really claim to own one of your petting zoo animals?"

Jonathan raised his eyebrows at her. "You'd be surprised."

"Allow me to rephrase. How many people *over the age of ten* claim to own one of your petting zoo animals?"

"Look, let's say I believe you. But if you have no proof, I'm not sure I can help you."

Eliza's head throbbed with the fire of a thousand suns. Yolanda's phone number was trapped in her shattered phone. She didn't want to drive to Yolanda's house, sit in an enclosed space with her, and come back to the zoo to track down Jonathan, but she would if she had to. Especially since Charleston looked so darn cute snuggled into his hay fort. "You're not sure you can help me, or you *can't* help me?"

Jonathan nodded toward a door labeled Manager. "Why don't we go have a chat? I wanted to talk to you after the licensing exam that day, but you ran out of there so fast."

"If we go have a chat, will you give me the damn pig?"

"I'd be willing to discuss it," Jonathan said as he held open the door to his office.

Office, as it turned out, was too generous a term. The space was a storage closet that had been only semiconverted into an office. On one side sat Jonathan's desk and computer. On the other, a chair sat in front of a row of industrial shelves that held boxes labeled with terms like *raccoon tails* and *skunk glands*.

Eliza sat and pushed her chair as far from the skunk glands as possible. "What do you want for the pig? I'm not exactly swimming in cash here. I could maybe do fifty bucks."

"I don't want money."

Ah. He wanted a favor. She'd opened this Pandora's box before and found herself fondling a sex robot. Twice. "I don't do enchantments anymore, if that's what you're after."

"Yeah right."

"I mean it. I quit the Cupid business." It was the first time she'd said it aloud since her fight with Jake, and the words grated her already-raw emotions. Maybe if she said it enough times, she'd callus and stop hurting so much.

Or maybe she'd just rip herself wide open.

"So, you took that test for the hell of it?" Jonathan said. "Seemed like a fun way to pass the afternoon?"

"No, I... It's a long story. But it doesn't matter." She sat back in the chair and crossed her arms. "I'm retired now."

"Look, I really need your help." Jonathan fiddled with a box on the end of the shelf. Its label read *opossum milk*. His voice softened. "I'm sorry about all the crap I did to you when we were kids. I was dumb and embarrassed and insecure. I know I should have apologized before now—before I needed something from you—but I could never get up the guts."

Eliza needed a minute or three to process what he'd just said. Had Jonathan Ellis really just apologized? *And was she actually thinking about forgiving him?*

"Thank you," she managed, once she'd gotten her shock under control. "Now, what can I help you with?"

"Here's the deal. When I applied for this job, I sort of billed myself as the zoo reproduction whisperer. The zoos have these strict, planned reproduction programs, and over the past few years, the Gold Lea Zoo has had a lot of problems getting its residents to reproduce."

"By residents, you mean..."

"The animals. Do you know how much it costs to ship in lion sperm from across the country?"

"Can't say I've ever priced that one out."

"Well, let me tell you—it's a lot. When they hired me, I promised I could get the animals to do it on their own, without all the shipping and handling fees."

Eliza did not want to know what exactly the *handling* fee on lion sperm covered. "And?"

"And I've managed to make it work with most of our animals. But—"

"Wait, you have?"

He nodded and stood up a little straighter. "You'd be surprised what a little privacy, good food, and Marvin Gaye can do."

"Marvin Gaye? Seems a little on the nose."

Jonathan shrugged. "The heart wants what the heart wants. I've had good luck with most of our animal pairs, except the sea lions. No matter what I do, they just aren't interested in getting their groove on."

"So what? They're sea lions. It's not like they're an endangered species."

"Actually, three species of sea lion are endangered."

Embarrassment warmed the tips of Eliza's ears. "I didn't realize. So, you're working on repopulating them? That's actually—"

"Of course, our sea lions aren't the endangered ones. But they are very *special* sea lions."

She sighed. For all this trouble, Eliza was going to need these sea lions to knit her a sweater and make her breakfast. "And you want me to enchant them?"

"Exactly." He clapped his hands together. "You enchant the sea lions, and I'll give you Porky."

"Charleston."

"What?"

"The pig… Never mind. It doesn't matter. I know you never got this through your skull when we were kids, but I can't enchant animals." She was choosing to ignore the way Charleston seemed to like her so much.

That was probably just a side effect of missing all his probiotics.

"I know, I know. But I did some research online, and I have an idea. If you try it, I'll give you the damn pig, even if my idea doesn't work. Scout's honor."

Eliza really should have stayed under the covers this morning. She sighed. "Okay. Take me to these special sea lions."

Chapter 23

"The ignorant sheeple associate Cupids with love, but I ask you this: If these Cupidistas promote love, then how come America's divorce rates have risen steadily since the Cupid Disclosure? Answer: Chemtrails."

—the *Cupid Cabal*

ELIZA STARED DOWN AT HER BROWN FLIPPERS, BROWN jumpsuit, and brown arm paddles. Thank the gods, no zoo patrons seemed to be hovering nearby. They were all watching the sea lions swim in a sunken tank a dozen or so yards away. "Someone better have Charleston waiting and ready to go as soon as this is over," Eliza said.

"You got it." Jonathan handed her the mask. The whiskers and long snout looked sea lion adjacent, but the creature could have just as easily been a giant, terrifying beaver.

"And I want another lemonade. A large."

"I don't really have any sway over the concession stands."

She shrugged and slipped on the mask. "Worth a shot."

"The website said all animal species have their own versions of Cupids. So you can enchant humans, but somewhere out in the ocean there's a dolphin Cupid that enchants them, and in the jungles there's an elephant Cupid, and for sea lions there's a sea lion Cupid. That's where you come in." He pointed to her costume. "We fool their hormones into believing you're a sea lion Cupid."

"What was this website again?"

"The *Cupid Cabal*. Some of the best information and news about enchantments I've ever come across. You should really give it a read. There's a lot going on in the world that we don't even know about. Did you know that the real Eminem was a Cupid, but the Illuminati killed him and replaced him with a clone? That's why none of his recent albums have been as good as *The Marshall Mathers LP*."

"None of that is true," Eliza said through the mouth of the mask.

"You really think *Revival* can hold a candle to *The Marshall Mathers LP*?"

Oh boy. Eliza did *not* have the time, energy, or interest to argue about this particular internet conspiracy. "You know what? You're probably right. Let's go ahead and get started."

"Technically, this is a little early in the year for sea lion mating," Jonathan explained. "But we've warmed the water temperature and given them enough artificial light to make it seem closer to summer. All you have to do is hop in there, do your thing, and get out. Shouldn't be a problem."

Funny how he'd failed to mention the lack of oxygen and giant sea beasts. "What's my weapon? How about one of these flippers? That seems like it would work without much trouble."

"That's part of your sea lion body, Eliza. You can't

use your body. *The Cupid Cabal* said you need to use a weapon. They also suggested—"

Here we go. "Okay, okay. No flipper. What would you like me to use?"

He held up a giant fish. "You don't need blood, right? You're special or whatever."

"Or whatever," she muttered. "Let's get this over with."

"Let's make some sea lion love." Jonathan took a step toward the exhibit and motioned for her to join him. She followed him along the edge of the exhibit, where a tank of salt water rose up to Eliza's chest and sank down under her feet, giving patrons a great view of the sea lions' activities above and below the water. Then Jonathan led her up a roped-off staircase labeled Employees Only and stood on a smooth cement ledge that hung over the water.

Eliza drew in a deep breath and adjusted her whiskers. How in the world had her life come to this? "Ready."

"Lions! Lions!" Jonathan called out. He blew a small whistle hanging from his neck.

The sea lions waddled out from the shallow end of the tank. In the water, they'd looked like beautiful, graceful beings. On land, they looked like several hundred pounds of human-eating monster. Both animals lumbered to their posts—identical platforms near Jonathan.

"Go on," he whispered. "They have to see you're one of them."

And that's how Eliza found herself standing between the sea lions on the middle platform, flapping her front flippers and making a range of poorly imitated sea lion barks. When Jonathan raised his right hand in a salute, Eliza and her sea lion compatriots raised their right fins to their heads. When Jonathan clapped, Eliza and the sea lions did too. When Jonathan threw each of them a ball to balance on their noses, Eliza ducked. The *actual* sea lions could have been members of the Harlem Globetrotters.

Jonathan stood near her platform and leaned in. "I think they're ready. Wait for my signal."

She barked in response. *Might as well go all in, right?*

"Lions! Nap time." Jonathan stepped into the shallow water and stretched his arms out wide. The sea lions waddled to the water and stretched out flat. Eliza followed suit, and Jonathan laid a dead gray fish on her stomach with a quick nod.

She didn't move a muscle, imitating the lions and also trying to keep from being eaten by them. Jonathan had promised they wouldn't move until given the cue, but she had a fish and they didn't. Their basic senses of fairness had to be offended.

"Good morning, lions!" Jonathan called out.

The two actual sea lions sprang up, facing each other. Eliza grabbed her fish by the tail and swung. She made contact with the first sea lion, then the second. And then she dropped her fish and got the hell away from there.

The last thing she needed today was two angry sea lions coming after her. She just hoped they weren't *Egg Salad Saga* fans. Hades, at this rate, they'd probably try to sue her too. Just like everyone else.

"Give me my pig," she said to Jonathan, ripping off the mask.

"Good God, look at them go," he whispered.

Eliza turned in time to see the lions swimming side by side into the bottom of the tank. If she didn't know better, she'd think they were holding fins. And if she *really* didn't know better, she'd think that was Mitch Johansen standing at the edge of the tank, hovering glumly but a little too closely near a petite elderly woman. "Excuse me," Eliza said, slipping the mask back on.

Time to take this show on the road.

She waddled over to the crowd of retirees and let out her loudest sea lion bark.

Mitch didn't even flinch. The poor man looked like a coma patient that someone had taken out on a walk.

Eliza wrapped her fins around him. "Would you like a photo with Scarlett the Sea Lion, the zoo's newest mascot?" she asked.

"Let me find my phone." Slow as antique molasses, Mitch pulled out his phone. "Wait," he said, arm outstretched. "Is there a fee for this?"

"No charge for you, sir."

"Good." Mitch handed his phone to Stu.

"Say Cheez-Its," Stu said.

"Cheez-Its," Mitch muttered.

Eliza barked. Because…well, why not? And by the time Mitch had his phone back, the other woman had moved on to the next exhibit.

"Crisis averted," Eliza said when the men had slipped away to visit the penguins.

"It's really too bad that we don't have an actual zoo mascot," Jonathan said. "I'd hire you in a heartbeat."

She pulled the mask off her face and gulped in the cool air. "Don't mess with me, Jonathan. I'm unemployed, and I *will* take you up on that."

Eliza paused. What was happening? Were they becoming *friends*? Or at least not sworn enemies?

He grinned. "If we ever get the funding, you'll be the first person I call."

"Thanks." Apparently, she was qualified for something after all. "Now where's my pig?"

>>>>>————————>

Eliza stood on Yolanda's porch and patted the top of Charleston's head. She'd changed out of her aquatic costume, but not until she'd gotten back to her car before realizing she was still wearing it. She'd stuffed the whole thing into her trunk and decided to drop it back at the zoo later. Right now, she had a pig to deliver.

Charleston pushed against her leg, seemingly unaware of all the trouble he'd caused. "Ready to go home, big guy?"

He snorted in response.

Eliza reached for the doorbell, but before she could press it, the door flung open.

"Charleston!" Yolanda swooped down and nuzzled the pig's face. "My baby. You're home!"

Eliza cleared her throat. Moment of truth. Would Yolanda forgive her for Eddie and the pignapping, or would she slam the door after promising death and destruction? "Hi, Yolanda. I found him at the zoo. They'd adopted him from the Humane Society as part of the petting zoo."

"Petting zoo?" She hugged the pig's neck a little tighter. "All those tiny, grubby hands trying to touch you. I'm so sorry, baby. Mommy is never going to let that happen again."

"He was originally found at the Fig Leaf out on Highway Five."

"The strip club? He took my baby to a *strip club*?"

"I guess Charleston is all grown up now," Eliza said.

Yolanda finally raised her head, giving Eliza a stern look. "He hasn't even hit puberty yet."

Well then. Eliza pulled a piece of paper from her pocket and held it out to Yolanda. "They found him with a note taped to his back. They sent it along with him."

"I'm sure it's from Eddie. I don't care what it says. Keep it."

"Are you sure?"

Yolanda glared at the paper for a few seconds before standing and snatching it from Eliza's hand. "No."

"I can go if you'd like…" Eliza said.

Yolanda ignored her and opened the note. "'I'm not scared of what we have,'" she read. "'I'm just not ready to commit.'"

Uh-huh. Sure. Just like he wasn't scared of blood.

"I guess you aren't interested in getting back together with him?" Eliza asked.

"You know, I don't know why, but I woke up this morning and realized I wasn't interested in him anymore. I deleted all his texts—except the pictures of Charleston, of course. I deleted his number. I even deleted that stupid game so he couldn't contact me there."

"Sounds like a good idea." Eliza gave her an encouraging nod. "Are we okay now, Yolanda? I'd be happy to offer you a free enchantment from Herman & Herman. I'm stepping away from the business for a while, but my brother—"

"No, thank you." She bent down and snuggled the

pig a little closer. He let out a contented grunt and gave Yolanda a snouty kiss on the cheek. "I've got everything I need right here."

If only Eliza could say the same.

➤➤➤➤➤➤➤➤➤➤➤➤➤➤

She'd barely made it back under her pillow fort when someone pounded on her front door. Eliza slid further into the darkness, wishing a plague of locusts on whoever had the audacity to stop by unannounced. *But maybe it's Jake?* Her heart leapt at the thought before hardening into cold steel in her chest. Jake was the last person she needed to see right now. *I'm not home. I'm not home. I'm not—*

"Eliza, I know you're in there. I saw your car in the parking lot." Her mother's voice was loud enough to disturb the entire complex. "I need to talk to you. Open up."

Eliza crawled out of bed, shoved her still-damp hair into a ponytail, and wandered toward the living room. "What is it? I'm not working today." *Or ever again.* She pulled the door to find both of her parents *and* Weston Presley. Elijah shuffled in behind them.

What the...

Her mother pushed past her and settled in at the kitchen table. Her father, Elijah, and Weston followed.

"Well, jeez, come on in," Eliza grumbled.

"Honey," her mother continued, ignoring her sarcasm, "this is our friend Weston Presley."

"We've met," Eliza said. "Multiple times."

Weston raised an eyebrow but didn't say anything.

"Weston is an Athenian," her mother said. "He's following up one of his investigations, and he'd like to ask you a few questions."

Exhaustion, both physical and emotional, permeated every inch of Eliza's being. The last thing she wanted was to talk to this guy. "Can we do this another time?"

"Uh-oh." Elijah shook his head.

"What?" Eliza snapped.

"Let's see. Sweatpants. A messy hair…thing. Empty bags of M&M's everywhere."

The tips of Eliza's ears burned. "So?"

"You slept with Jake, didn't you?" Elijah asked. "And then things went down the toilet, right?"

Her father, gods bless him, interrupted. "Why don't we let your mom ask the questions right now? You two can catch up later."

Eliza forced down all the emotions clogging her throat. "Mom. Dad. Please. Can you come back later? Maybe in a few hours. I'm really not feeling well." She faked a cough. "Maybe I've got Elijah's bronchitis."

Her mother's face screwed up in annoyance. "If you would listen to me just once—"

Just once? Maybe if her mother didn't use that condescending tone *just once*, she and Eliza could be in the same room together. Maybe if her mother had believed in her abilities *just once*, Eliza wouldn't have become such an epic fuckup of a Cupid. "Why? So you can remind me of what a failure I am? Or so you can keep pretending you aren't screwing this guy behind Dad's back?"

"Eliza!" Her father's voice boomed deeper than she'd ever heard it.

"I'm sorry, Dad. I didn't want you to find out this

way. I didn't want you to find out at all. But when I was a teenager—"

"She saw me kiss Beverly," Weston finished. He turned to Eliza. "Your mother and I dated for a few years back in college. We graduated, wanted different things in life, and went our separate ways. But about thirteen years ago, I took a job here in town and looked her up. She'd always been the one that got away. She and your father were separated at the time—"

"Wait. What? No, they weren't." Eliza looked to her brother for confirmation.

He shrugged.

"Eliza..." Her mother's expression shifted from discomfort to pity. It only fueled Eliza's rage.

"Well, you weren't," Eliza argued. "You've always lived together."

"It doesn't matter," Weston said. "I came bursting into town, ready to win her back. Hearing she and your father had separated was like winning the jackpot and getting the Fates on my side at the same time. But she wouldn't have me. Said she was still in love with your father and wanted to fight for their relationship."

Eliza stared at the table. She was nearly thirty years old. She hadn't lived with her parents in ages. Why did this hurt so badly?

"So I guess that day I saw the two of you coming out of her bedroom, you'd had a friendly *chat* about how much she loved my father."

"No. She was searching for an old necklace I'd given her. It was my grandmother's."

"You kissed her."

"I did," Weston said. "I shouldn't have, but I did. It

was a last-ditch effort to get her to change her mind. I've since apologized to both your mother and your father."

Every nerve ending in her body felt frayed. This couldn't be true.

Could it?

She pressed her fingers to her brow and tried to clear her brain. Most of her teenage memories were clouded by mishaps and embarrassment about her Cupiding skills. Being picked on in school, not living up to her parents' hopes and dreams, spectacularly failing both her driver's test and Cupid test within the same week. (Surprisingly, the highway patrolman did not take kindly to having his foot run over mid-parallel-park even after the injury resulted in a lasting relationship between himself and the postman.)

But when she peered beyond those memories, others came into focus. The week she and Elijah had suddenly been shipped off to their maternal grandmother's house in Wyoming, followed by the week they spent in San Diego at their paternal grandmother's house. The extended business trip her father went on just before the Weston debacle. The way everyone—not just hormonal, emo teen Eliza—had been quiet and tense.

Maybe she'd been so obsessed with her own problems that she hadn't bothered to notice the storm raging around her. Maybe Weston's story had grains of truth in it after all.

"Why did you separate?" Her voice came out as a whisper.

"Your mother and I had a rough patch when you were a teenager," her father said. "Trying to keep a marriage happy while getting the business off the ground and raising two teenagers was almost more than we—more than *I*—could handle."

"Tim," her mother said. "Please…"

He looked at his wife with fierce tenderness in his eyes. "If we want Eliza to be honest with us, we need to be honest too," he said before turning back to his children. "I made some mistakes. I got caught up in a woman I met at the Agora. These days, people call it an emotional affair, but back then we didn't have a term for it, at least not that I knew of. All I knew was that I was unhappy, and I wanted a quick fix. I asked your mother for a trial separation. It was stupid and lazy, and it took me a while to realize that. But once I did, your mother was strong enough to forgive me."

Tears streamed silently down her mother's cheeks, but she stared at her husband with pride etched into her features. "We worked harder to fix things than we'd ever worked before," her mother said. "And once we got back together, something just…clicked."

"Me," Eliza whispered.

"What?" her mom asked.

"Me. After I saw you that day with Weston, I came up with a plan. I enchanted you both. I never told anyone. Not even Elijah."

Her parents fell silent as they looked at each other. For two aching heartbeats, Eliza was certain they'd get angry or, worse, decide their reconciliation had been a big, fat, enchantment-based lie.

But then they laughed.

Her father's deep belly laugh intermingled with her mother's lighter, melodic one—the sounds of Eliza's early childhood, before she'd woken up on her eighth birthday with "the knack." Back when they'd spend weekends at the beach house, Eliza curled up with a book and Elijah running around in the sand.

"Eliza, do you have any idea how many times you've enchanted us over the years?" her dad asked. "Once, you dropped a spoon on my hand while we were doing dishes, and your mother and I hardly left the bed for a week. Another time, you brought home a Scholastic book order form and gave your mother a massive paper cut. She was insatiable that month. We tried so many—"

Eliza's ears were going to bleed if she didn't put a stop to this. "Dad, stop! Too much!"

"Torturing your children is still illegal, Dad," Elijah added. "Even if they're adults."

Her mother blushed and put a hand over Eliza's. "What your father means is that it's only an enchantment, Eliza. Those exciting moments come and go throughout the years, but real Love…that takes work and patience. And it's worth *everything*."

For once, Eliza listened to her mother. Really and truly listened. "And you two really Love each other." She realized the truth of it as she said the words. Another truth pricked at the back of her skull, but she ignored it the best way she knew how.

By talking about how badly she'd screwed up her enchantments.

"What did you want to ask me?" she asked.

"It's about your car, honey," her mother said.

"Ron Weasley? Did something happen to him?"

Weston cleared his throat. "Eliza, have you ever wondered how your, um… How Ron has managed to stay running after all these years?"

She shrugged. Was this guy investigating automotive maintenance techniques or what? "Regular oil changes?" Even that was a stretch. Ron had hit a thousand miles past due for a change…two thousand miles ago.

"What about that thing you did, honey?" her father asked. "That day he was acting up on the way to my appointment?"

"The jiggle, jiggle, tap?" She turned to Weston. "He has a wire or something loose, so when he starts acting up, I jiggle some things around under the hood until he starts working again."

Weston whipped out a tiny notebook and started scribbling. "Have you ever enchanted other inanimate objects? Or is your car an anomaly?"

"What?" She looked from Weston to her parents and then her brother. Each of them studied her intently, as if she were about to explain the meaning of life. Or at least a surefire way to win the lottery.

It was official. The stress of this whole financial deficiency thing had broken them.

She turned to Weston. "Do you have a badge or credentials or something?" If this guy was a charlatan taking advantage of her family in their time of need, she was going to call the police so fast—

He handed her a leather case with both a badge and a credential. And, much to Eliza's surprise, Weston Presley appeared to be exactly who he claimed to be.

"Eliza," her mother said, "I'm sure you've heard the rumors about techno-Cupids? Cupids who can enchant objects and use technology in their enchantments?"

Eliza's stomach dropped. "Yes."

"Well, it's not just some rumor in the *Cupid Cabal*."

Her father splayed his fingers out on the table as if searching for something—anything—to hang on to. "Last year, when I was in Tokyo—"

Her mind flashed back to that day in the hospital. Her father's pale face. The beeping machines. His drug-induced ramblings. *The time I went to Tokyo.* "You really went to Tokyo?"

He nodded. "Last year, when we told you we were heading to the annual Cupid Accreditation Conference in Dallas, your brother and I visited Tokyo. We were looking for new ways to expand the business—"

"Techno-Cupids are real, Eliza," Elijah interjected. He looked like a kid who'd been given free rein in a taffy shop. "The current theory is that their powers are evolving with the increase in dependency on smart technology. Basically, technology is getting so *smart* that whatever gene causes the knack is mutating to allow machines to be enchanted."

Even though she'd spent the last few days chasing a seemingly crazy theory about techno-Cupids and *Egg Salad Saga*, she'd spent decades being taught—by some of the people sitting across from her at this very moment—that Cupids had many limitations. Among them, the ability to enchant humans and *only* humans.

"You're serious?" she asked.

Her parents nodded in unison.

"So, you've never enchanted another inanimate object?" Weston asked. "Or maybe a nonhuman animal? We've heard—"

"No, I've never..." Her voice faded as memories rushed by. Charleston the pig. Jacque the Mandroid. Hilda and Freddy the sea lions.

"You have, haven't you?" Elijah said before turning to their parents. "She has."

The world stopped spinning. Had she really... Was she really... "I, um, I think I have."

Her apartment burst into a flurry of activity and questions. When had she first enchanted Ron? Were there any unwanted side effects? How sure was she about the pig? How long did Jacque manage to function? Did the sea lions actually mate?

"I'm sorry," Eliza repeated time and again. "I really don't know. I didn't realize this was even possible. I mean, I suspected techno-Cupids were real, but...not that *I* was one."

Her mother gave her a quizzical look. "But you suspected that *someone else* was?"

That was the only opening Eliza needed. She launched into the saga of, well, *Egg Salad Saga*: the enchantments falling apart, her clients playing the game nonstop, Vic Van Love and his stupid advertisements...

By the time she'd unloaded the full story, Eliza was out of breath and running on pure adrenaline. Finally, she was going to get to the bottom of this. With her family's help, she could get the Johansens back together, end all these lawsuit threats, and ride happily into the sunset.

Maybe she could even make things right with J—

Anger popped and fizzled in her brain. *Nope. Not happening.* She pushed all thoughts of a certain dark-eyed Cupid from her mind and looked expectantly at her family.

They looked back at her like she'd taken a page from the playbook of Lyssa—the spirit of rage, frenzy, and rabies.

"What?" she asked, deflating.

"Liza," her father said. "Techno-Cupids *enchant* things. They don't make people hate."

"But—" she started.

"Honey, I can't imagine how stressed out you must be right now," her mother said. "This is a lot of new information to process. For all of us. And you're so new to purposeful enchantments. There are bound to be some bumps along the way for a newly licensed Cupid."

"You don't believe me?" Eliza asked.

But they didn't have to answer. She knew they didn't. Pressure built in her chest, squeezing and squeezing until she expected to shatter. Her family wasn't going to help her. There would be no riding off into the sunset. There would only be Eliza, her techno-Cupid abilities, and her pile of failures.

"You'd rather believe this is *my* fault." Her temples pounded and fireworks went off at the edges of her vision. "You can believe that techno-Cupids are real. You can believe poor, clumsy Eliza screwed up all her cases. But you can't believe that someone is reversing enchantments."

Her father reached for her hand, but Eliza pulled it away. "Your mother hasn't had any problems with her enchantments," he said softly.

Weston cleared his throat.

"What?" Eliza practically bared her teeth at the poor man.

But without acknowledging her anger, he put his notebook away and gave Eliza a small smile. "I should go. But I appreciate your candor, Eliza. Especially after everything that happened all those years ago."

The mere mention of the Weston Presley incident was enough to tamp down her anger and replace it with tears stinging the corners of her eyes. She swallowed back a knot in her throat. "Sure."

"I'm sorry I wasn't able to be of more help with your *situation* with the Department," Weston said to her parents. "In my opinion, they're being completely unreasonable, but for all the Cosmic Council's sway over the Descendants, we don't matter at all to the State of California."

"What do you mean?" Eliza asked.

"We can talk about it later," her father said.

At the same time, her mother said, "The Department called this morning to say there have been some complaints about our services, so they decided to accelerate our fees. They're due tomorrow by eight in the morning."

Eliza's stomach dropped for the sixteenth time that day. "What kind of complaints?"

"It doesn't matter." Her father reached across the table and patted her hand. "We're going to fight it. In the meantime, while the lawyers work it out, we're going to shut down for a little while."

But it did matter. Those complaints had to be about her. *No. No, no, no, no. NO.*

She'd failed. She'd failed her parents, her brother, all the couples she'd enchanted. Herself.

Weston stood and offered Eliza his hand. "I'm afraid I'll have some more questions for you in the future, if you're willing to answer them."

She nodded, still dumbstruck. It was as if the universe had decided to drop not one, not two, but three giant sacks of quicksand on her head. By the time she managed to dig out of the first, another came and threatened to pull her under.

"In the meantime," Weston continued, "you get some rest, Eliza. I'll see about updating your information in the Descendants' Scroll. I've been adding a small, inconspicuous note to the entries for Cupids with your abilities. The world isn't quite ready for techno-Cupids yet, so I've been saying simply 'advanced' under the abilities portion. We haven't found every one of them yet, but I think we're getting close."

Lightning struck as surely as if Zeus himself had thrown the bolt down at her, blasting the mental quicksand into the abyss.

The Scroll. At the library. Under lock and key—and Mrs. Washmoore's watchful eye.

Whoever was behind the *Egg Salad Saga* scheme *had* to be a techno-Cupid. Or maybe a techno-Cupid working in connection with someone else? Say…a Fury? If she could just get to the library and somehow see the register—maybe she'd get Mrs. Washmoore drunk at Dionysus and convince her to show it to Eliza, or maybe Eliza would just play the old oops-I'm-a-klutz card and "accidentally" knock the Fury over and steal the key from her lanyard—she'd be a lot closer to figuring out who was behind all this. And once she found out who was behind *Egg Salad Saga*—and got those complaints redacted—she could figure out how to fix all the lives she'd ruined.

Her parents'. Her brother's. The Johansens'. Maybe even Helen's.

Everyone's except her own.

Because despite the way her world had been totally

upended in the last hour, she couldn't let go of that small, hard kernel in her chest. The one that made her feel ready to explode at the thought of Jake. The one that made her feel disgusted at her own stupidity. She'd started to believe in capital-L Love, like a capital-L Loser.

There was no coming back from that. Especially not by eight o'clock tomorrow morning.

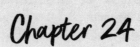

Chapter 24

Calif. CCR § 579.107. A person may only lawfully utilize those love charms, potions, and substances defined in the Schedule of Controlled Aphrodisiacs pursuant to a valid prescription and supervision of a licensed Cupid.

ELIZA MARCHED TOWARD THE AGORA AS IF TODAY was just another day in her very calm and very normal life.

"Hello, Eliza," Mrs. Washmoore said. "Back again?"

"I wanted to see about that interlibrary loan you told me about." She slipped her ID through the groove in the plexiglass.

The woman didn't touch it. "I'm sorry. Nothing has come in yet."

"That's okay." Eliza pushed the ID a little farther into the booth.

"Didn't you check out some library books the other day?"

"I did. All interesting reads so far." Eliza pushed the ID as far as she could manage without getting her fingers stuck. She really didn't have time for this. She needed to get into the library and get her grubby little hands on the register.

"And you didn't bring them with you today? Maybe you should go home and come back. The late fees are very strict these days. All automated, and I really have no discretion in the matter."

"I've got a couple of weeks left." Eliza bit the inside of her cheek to keep her impatience from showing and caught a faint whiff of rotten eggs and garbage again. *I really need to find a new deodorant.* "I think it'll be fine."

With a tight smile, Mrs. Washmoore picked up Eliza's ID and ran it through the scanner.

Finally. Eliza took a step forward, ready to burst into the Agora as soon as Mrs. Washmoore opened the doors.

Instead, the light on the scanner glowed red and the building stayed closed. "I'm sorry, dear," Mrs. Washmoore said. "There must be a problem." She didn't look sorry. In fact, she looked downright giddy.

Eliza tapped her fingers against the counter. "Can you try again, please?"

"Of course." Mrs. Washmoore ran the ID again.

Red.

She tried a third time. And a fourth. Red lights every time.

"Maybe you're putting it in upside down?" Eliza asked, nerves in a jumble. "Can you try—"

The woman's curls rattled. "I know how to do my job, Ms. Herman. Despite what the Erosians seem to believe."

Oh, shit. Fury on the edge. "I'm sorry. That's not what I meant. Would it be okay if you just let me in? I can sign on a piece of paper or something? Leave my license with you? It's not like I'm a stranger."

"I'm not allowed to override the system. Maybe you should come back tomorrow."

"Mrs. Washmoore, I really, *really* can't wait until

tomorrow. Is there someone you can talk to? The IT department?"

Mrs. Washmoore's blue eyes turned cold as she narrowed them, and for a second, Eliza swore she was about to unleash the fury of her inner Fury. A gross overreaction considering how polite Eliza had been, but maybe the woman was just having a bad day. Maybe someone had switched her to decaf. But then Mrs. Washmoore's expression calmed, bringing her back to the wrinkle-faced woman Eliza had grown to know over the past few weeks.

"Let me see what I can do." She disappeared into the tube with a whoosh.

Eliza forced her shoulders to relax and took a deep breath. It was going to be fine. Mrs. Washmoore would return with some cute, geeky Hermesian who'd have the whole situation figured out in five minutes flat. And five minutes wasn't going to make or break Eliza's plans. She could even use that time to brainstorm how to get back on Mrs. Washmoore's good side. After all, if the Fury was going to let Eliza take a peek at the Scroll so she could take note of the advanced Cupids and finally track down the maker of *Egg Salad Saga*, they were going to need to be BFFs—at least temporarily. *Relax. Stay calm. Pull it in. Relax. Stay calm. Pull it in. Relax—*

"I'm very sorry, but there's nothing we can do today, Eliza." Mrs. Washmoore's voice came from an overhead intercom. "Please come back tomorrow and try again."

"But I—" The blinking light above the intercom went dark. "Hello? Mrs. Washmoore?"

Nothing.

Eliza stared at the hole where the woman usually

appeared, hoping against hope that Mrs. Washmoore would reappear at her post.

No dice.

"Gods damn it." Eliza took a quick step away from the building. There *had* to be another way in. And she *had* to find it soon. Sooner than soon. She needed to be in the library yesterday. She power walked around the side of the building, scoping it out for breaches in security. Could she slide through an open window? Climb through the air ducts the way people did in the movies?

"*Wooooooooooo!*"

A fifteen-passenger van barreled through the parking lot. She gave the driver, a Satyr thinly disguised as a delivery driver, the stink eye. Getting run over by an unmarked van would be the cherry on this shit sundae.

Two more vans passed in quick succession, and she caught a glint of a gold dolphin logo on the vehicle's back door. Thursday. Eliza would bet her last dollar—which, coincidentally, was in her back pocket right now—that those vans were full of sea nymphs being shipped into Dionysus for Nereid Night.

Eliza jogged around the side of the building, where a pudgy man with a clipboard pointed toward the Agora's service entrance. "Bring 'em around this way. Careful now. That tank's sloshing out the rear end." Another group of men and women, too muscled to be fully human, carried long, rectangular tanks on their shoulders. Only a few feet of water filled the inside, but that was enough for the nymphs perched on the backs of sea turtles. Ten or so yards away, a group of twentysomething guys moved along a patch of grass. To the untrained eye, they looked like a group of bearded hipsters in ball caps playing Ultimate Frisbee. But every Descendant that passed could see them for what they were: a group of Satyrs using ball caps to hide their goatlike ears and Ultimate Frisbee as an excuse to graze while waiting for Nereid Night.

Eliza tucked herself behind a nearby car and watched as she pretended to rifle in her purse for a set of keys. If she could make it past the goat-men, the Kratosians, and the Nereids, she might be able to make it inside.

"Tommy, I told you," a familiar, melodic voice said. "He clashes with this outfit. You promised you'd help me out."

"I tried, but all the dolphins were booked tonight." Muscle Man—a.k.a. Tommy—shrugged his gargantuan shoulders.

Quinn sloshed with the movement and adjusted her purple shell top. "Listen, my tips are so much better when I look put together, and I have another student loan payment due next week. There's really nothing you can do?"

Eliza recognized the sweet, lilting tone Quinn was using. She'd heard it many times during their sorority sister days, and it never failed to get Quinn exactly what she wanted.

"Okay, okay." Tommy lowered the tank back into the van. "Let me go find Ben. Maybe he has an idea."

"Thanks, Tommy. You're the best."

Why hadn't Eliza been born a Nereid? Sure, there were cons, but getting whatever you wanted whenever you wanted it seemed like a pretty good deal.

Wisps of an idea took shape in her mind, solidifying with each passing second.

No, she hadn't been born a sea *nymph*. But she had recently experienced life as a sea *lion*…

Eliza forced herself to walk calmly and casually around to the main parking lot. As soon as she was out of sight, she burst into a run. She made it to Ron, panting and wheezing, and jammed her key into the trunk.

It wouldn't budge.

Eliza took a deep breath. If she was really a techno-Cupid, this would be the moment of truth.

"Come on, Ron." She tapped her key lightly against the bumper. "We've been through so much together. All those bad jobs, all those bad haircuts, even a few bad kisses. Just give me this one thing, and I promise you can retire."

Nothing.

She smacked her wallet against the taillight. "I promise to feed you premium gas from now on."

Nada.

She kicked one of the tires with as much force as she could muster before leaning close to the keyhole. "I'll never make you go through the car wash again," she whispered.

The trunk popped open with a groan.

Her sigh of relief was so deep that it vibrated in her toes. There it was—her sea lion costume. The bodysuit, the fins and flippers, the mask with its horrible whiskers. It was no dolphin, but it was dark brown—and it wouldn't clash with Quinn's top.

A few minutes later, Eliza waddled through the parking lot as inconspicuously as possible—which was about as inconspicuous as obscene graffiti on the wall of the Louvre. But by the grace of the Fates, she didn't pass a single soul on her way back to the vans.

The closer she got to the open door of the van, the

tighter her stomach knotted. Quinn had to say yes. A
Delta Iota Kappa never turned her back on a sister.
Partly because the sorority was full of Descendants and
no one wanted to turn their back on a Fury, but also
because they looked out for one another.

"Quinn," Eliza whispered when she reached the van.
"Quinn."

Her friend looked her straight in the eye. Not the sea
lion's eyes, but the place where a thin piece of mesh let
Eliza see out of its mouth. "I told you, Leroy, I'm *not*
interested. Please stop showing up here. I'm working."

"No!" Eliza waved her fins and shoved the mask up
onto her forehead. "It's me."

"Eliza?"

"Can you sneak me in with you? Please?" She hop-
climbed into the back of the van. Or rather, she tried.
It took her three failed attempts, two strings of curse
words, and one pep talk from Quinn before she waddled
into the vehicle. "I promise it's for a good reason, but
it's a really long story and—"

"Get in the tank."

"Really?"

"A Delta Iota Kappa never turns her back on a sister."
Quinn heaved Eliza into the water.

She slipped and slid against the slick glass at the
bottom of the tank, and through the mesh of her mask,
she could have sworn the turtle gave her a look that said,
I know, right?

"Stop squirming," Quinn whispered.

Eliza obeyed and took up her now-practiced sea
lion position with her legs stretched behind her and her
weight balanced on her palms. Quinn draped herself

across Eliza's back and rested her forearms on the edge of the tank.

"Sorry, Quinn," Tommy said without looking at Eliza. Instead, his eyes stayed firmly glued to the curve of Quinn's shell top. "I asked around, but—"

"Kyle found something." Her voice adopted that melodic quality again. "Can you put Delores in another tank though?"

Tommy reached into the tank, and his biceps bulged perilously close to Eliza's front flippers. There was no way he wouldn't see her. No way he wouldn't realize Quinn sat atop a human dressed as a sea lion. No way he—

"Oh, Tommy," Quinn said, smooth as the finest silk. "I meant to ask, how did your powerlifting competition go last weekend?"

The man was entranced. "Had a great squat and bench press, but I didn't hit my goal on the dead lift," he said with eyes locked on Quinn's. His fingers grasped the edge of the turtle's shell.

"Oh no." Quinn stuck out her lip in a perfect pout. "You'll get 'em next time."

"Thanks, Quinn." Tommy had gone full puppy-dog-eyed with gratitude. And the turtle looked almost as grateful when Tommy plucked it from the tank and laid it in the back of the van. "Let's roll," Tommy said when he returned.

Suddenly, the tank was in the air, and they were on the move. Salt water sloshed over the sides, stinging Eliza's eyes and nose. Her elbow cracked against the glass, and pain shot up her arm.

Quinn must have heard the *clunk*, because she whispered, "Hold still."

Eliza tightened every muscle she could in an attempt to follow Quinn's directions. Her abs, her biceps, her calves, even her butt cheeks. If only she'd gone to more of those yoga classes she'd signed up for last summer.

"Well, well, well. Quinn Patel," a male voice said.

The tank came to a halt. The water did not. It rose into Eliza's mask and into her mouth. The resulting cough that escaped sounded almost like a sea lion. She threw in two more barks for good measure, until Quinn jabbed a heel into her side.

"Sorry, new lion. You know how they get excited." Quinn shifted toward the bouncer, all charm.

"I do," he said. "I really do."

Eliza wanted to gag at the leery pitch in his voice. Was it possible to undress someone with your tone? If so, this dude was totally doing it to Quinn.

"You can put her in tank seven," the bouncer said to Tommy. "I get off in an hour. I'll have someone check on you then, Quinn."

"Sounds great."

The next thing Eliza knew, she was fin-over-teakettle, flopping around in more than ten feet of water. Quinn grabbed her by the arm and swam them both to the rear corner of the tank, where she pressed Eliza up onto a rock.

"Are you okay? Bark if you are."

Eliza blinked and sputtered, but finally she let out a raspy bark.

"Thank the gods. I don't think anyone saw. They were too busy watching Penelope do shots off a shark's back."

Eliza whipped her head around. She wouldn't mind seeing that—

"Eliza, what's going on?"

Focus, Herman.

Eliza told Quinn about *Egg Salad Saga* and the techno-Cupids as briefly as she could—leaving out her own status as one. She already half expected Quinn to demand that Eliza see a doctor, or at least an Asclepian. Or preferably a doctor who happened to be Asclepian.

"I just have to get my hands on the Scroll," Eliza said. "But Mrs. Washmoore won't let me into the building."

And then she waited, searching her friend's face for any clue of how her story had landed. Finally, Quinn spoke.

"Techo-Cupids are real? For real, for real?" Her face lit up like a hundred suns.

Eliza let out a half sigh, half laugh as relief worked through her. "For real, for real."

"Whoa," Quinn whispered. "And you're going to take one of them on? What about Mrs. Washmoore? You don't think that old bat is a part of this, do you?"

"I don't know. Maybe?" Eliza ran her hand along the edge of the boulder. "I guess I'll find out soon."

"Then you better get out of here and go save Cupid-kind." Quinn gave her an encouraging smile. "See that ladder over there?"

Eliza squinted through the wet mesh. Finally, she saw the ladder nestled between the corner of the tank and the boulder. She barked.

"You can just say yes."

Eliza barked again.

Quinn rolled her eyes. "You're freakishly good at that. Anyway, I'm going to cause a distraction. It's dead in here this early, so it shouldn't be a problem. Once I do, you climb up and over."

Eliza squeezed her friend's hand. "Thank you."

Quinn floated to the far side of the tank and pulled herself up. "Who wants to kiss a Nereid? It's good luck!" Her singsong voice rang out across the bar, and soon there was a line of Descendants stretching from Quinn's tank. Eliza could swear half of them hadn't even been in the place a moment ago.

It didn't take long before the first sounds of a scuffle rang out. Shuffling feet and a few dude-bro Descendants muttering variations of "Move out of the way." Quinn threw a wink over her shoulder at Eliza and mouthed, *Go*.

Eliza went. She swam across the tank as fast as her fins could take her, praying no one looked too closely at the oddly shaped sea lion dog-paddling in the background. Her hand caught the edge of the ladder, and she pulled herself up. Her masked head poked above the waterline, and she fully expected someone to notice that the sea lion had grown feet and was getting the heck out of here. A real Little Mermaid–type situation—except she was running toward a library instead of a hot prince. *Potato, po-tah-to*.

But no one paid her any mind at all. All three Nereids were now running impromptu kissing booths, and even the bartender had abandoned her post to get in line. Eliza could have lumbered out of the tank belting songs from *The Minotaur*, and no one would have given her a second look.

Instead, she tiptoed the rest of the way up the ladder, got to the top, and froze. Her tail was not cooperating at all. The fabric was too tight along the thigh to let her get a leg over the edge of the tank, which left her with two choices: belly flop over the side of the tank like an actual sea lion or rip the tail in half.

My sea lion days are over.

"One, two, three." She yanked on "three," and the fabric of her tail ripped straight up the middle. That gave her just enough leeway to haul one leg over the side of the tank and then the other. Halfway down the other side of the ladder, her tail snagged on a rung, and fueled by the knowledge that she was *actually getting away with this*, Eliza tugged. The tail gave a satisfying *riiiiiiiiip* before setting her free.

When her feet finally found solid ground, she ducked into a nearby dark corner, ditched her mask, and wrung the water from her hair. But it was only when she glanced down at the tatters of the costume that she truly felt the breeze on her lady bits.

Chapter 25

> "Reiterating the importance of appropriate attire: proper legwear cannot be stressed enough. Contrary to popular depictions of Cupids, diapers are highly discouraged."
>
> **—Erosian Weaponry Fundamentals**

NOT ONLY HAD ELIZA'S TAIL RIPPED, BUT IT HAD ALSO taken a good chunk of her bodysuit with it. In fact, the bottom half had been reduced to a strip of elastic with a hunk of floppy black fabric attached to the front. Thank the gods she'd left her underwear on.

Even if Quinn managed to distract every Descendant in the Northern California area, someone would notice the pants-less Cupid sprinting toward the library. *Don't panic. Do* not *panic.* She scanned the room for anything that she could wrap around her bottom half. A discarded T-shirt, a curtain, a starched white tablecloth…

Eliza snatched the tablecloth from the booth, secured it around her waist and between her legs as best she could, and slipped into the nearest hall, then up the stairs. At every echoed creak and shuffle, she held her breath and prepared her story: she'd gotten carried away at Nereid Night and jumped into a tank before getting thrown out of the bar. She was just on her way back to the car. No big deal. Probably happened every Thursday.

Maybe the gods were looking out for her after all, or maybe they were just too busy laughing to send anyone to stop her. In any event, Eliza only ran into one person on her way to the library—a Maenad wearing a mink stole and a dress made to look like ivy.

"Oh, hi," Eliza said, diving into her story without being asked. "Great dress. Mine isn't so great. It's been a really long night. See, I was at Dion—"

The Maenad held up her hand, nearly blinding Eliza with her diamond-flecked nails. "Honey, if a Cupid doesn't end up wearing a diaper on Nereid Night, it wasn't Nereid Night. You know what I mean?"

She did not. "Right, absolutely."

"You have a good night," the Maenad said before continuing her jaunt down the hall.

"You too," Eliza called over her shoulder. Once the woman had gone, she sprinted the rest of the way to the library and poked her head into the open doorway. Silence. She was utterly alone. Now all she had to do was find the Descendants' Scroll and—

"Eliza?"

Hearing that voice sent her emotions into a tailspin. *Turn around,* she told herself. *(Don't you dare turn around.) It'll be fine. (It's going to be a disaster.) Jake's here because he cares about you. (If he cared about you, he wouldn't have lied to you.)*

In the end, she turned. But she only let herself look at his feet. Something told her that anything more might rip her heart straight down the middle. "Hi, Jake."

"What are you— Is that a tablecloth?"

She glanced at the tablecloth bundled around her lower half, then stood up straight and proud. *Gods, he is gorgeous*. No, this wasn't how she wanted to run into her ex-whatever, but she was going to rock it anyway. "It might be."

"Hey…" He took a step closer, eyebrows furrowed with concern. "Are you okay?"

Her heart cried out in agony, begging her to throw herself against him, tell him everything that had happened to her in the last few days, and plead for his help.

But part of her—a part that seemed to burn brighter with every second that she stood in his presence—wanted him gone. Far away. Far enough that he couldn't look at her with those stupid gold-flecked eyes and try to convince her that he was anything but a lying liar who lies.

"Jake?"

"Yeah?" he said, taking a step forward.

She took a deep breath, unsure which version of her would win out. "Leave," she finally said.

"What? Eliza?" He took another step closer. She took one back. "What's going on?" he asked. "This isn't *you*."

She adjusted her tablecloth and stared him dead in the eyes. Unseen spiders crawled beneath her skin, shooting hot poison into her veins. Every painful bite pushed her closer to rage. "You barely know me anymore, Jake. You haven't in years. This *is* me. Take it or leave it. But preferably leave it."

Holy Hades. She shook out her arms, trying to find herself beneath the layers of hurt and anger. Where had that come from? And why did she feel like she was starring in a Greek-inspired version of *Dr. Jekyll and Mr. Hyde*?

"Eliza, please—" Jake reached for her.

She whipped her arm away. Apparently, Mr. Hyde was here to stay. "Don't you dare," she snarled.

Jake gave her space but didn't leave. "Something is wrong with you. I'm worried—"

"I don't need a babysitter anymore, Jake. I'm *fine*." Luckily, the room seemed to be empty, because she certainly wasn't using a library-appropriate voice. "In fact, I'm better than fine, so you're welcome to leave now."

He crossed his arms. "You're wearing a tablecloth, dripping wet, in the middle of the library on a Thursday night, and you want me to believe you're *better than fine*?"

Ugh. Why wouldn't he leave her in peace? The clock was ticking. She turned toward the row of glass cases where the official Descendants' Scroll lay in its place of glory—right next to a display titled "Ares through the Ages."

Eliza took a step closer to the Scroll, and icy panic shot through her veins. The key. Mrs. Washmoore had the key, and she didn't—*couldn't*—know Eliza had made it into the library.

Time for plan B. Jake—the old librarian's perfect, can-do-no-wrong nephew—was here, desperate to talk to Eliza. Maybe she had a use for him after all. She whipped around, ready to coldly manipulate him into doing her bidding.

Except…

Standing face-to-face with him, Eliza couldn't help but notice the genuine concern in his eyes. She couldn't forget the way he'd made her feel all those times he'd believed in her more than she'd believed in herself. And she couldn't look away from his sure, protective stance—ready to whisk her away from whatever was causing her so much pain.

If only he knew *he* was the source of that pain.

She forced back the acidic anger that burned her throat with memories of the good times. Eating French toast. Laughing at their childhood escapades. Kissing in the moonlight. And the more she tapped into those memories, the weaker the rage became. But the more she felt like...*herself*. "Jake?"

He waited as if observing a wild animal.

"I've figured out what's causing the enchantments to go wrong," she said, tamping down a tiny flare of fury. "And I need your help."

Once she'd crossed that hurdle, the rest came pouring out. Her meeting with Weston Presley. How she'd been enchanting Ron Weasley for years. That the stuff with the Mandroid wasn't simply a coincidence. *Egg Salad Saga*. The Descendants' Scroll.

What she needed him to do.

"I swear I wouldn't ask if there was another way, but I'm running out of time and you're the only one she would even *consider* letting into the case. If you can just get the key from her, I'll do the rest."

Jake looked down at her, his expression cloudy and unreadable.

"Please," she whispered.

He stepped into her personal space, and she braced herself, expecting another flicker of anger to ignite inside her. But instead all she found were sorrow and desperation.

"You're sure?" he asked.

Eliza nodded. "I don't know what's wrong with me, why I'm so mixed up inside about you and me, but I've never been more sure about anything than this. I need that key, Jake. Please."

He hooked a finger under her chin and forced her gaze up to meet hers.

Eliza's throat constricted and sweat broke out along her hairline. Everything was too bright but also too dark, and a vein in her neck throbbed uncontrollably. She jerked her face away. "Don't."

Jake's hand fell back to his side. "Please tell me what I can do to fix this. If you—"

"What you can do is get the key. Please."

He blew out a heavy breath. "Stay here. I'll be back in ten with the key. I swear. And then we're going to figure this thing out. Together."

And then he disappeared into the main hall of the Agora, leaving Eliza alone with her tumbling feelings.

"Well, this *is* quite the turn of events, isn't it?" A familiar voice snaked through the stacks, followed by an all-too-familiar face steeped half in shadow.

Eliza started before she let out a sigh of relief. "Agent Oliver? I didn't realize you were, um…" She didn't know how to put the whole internal is-he-a-Descendant debate into words without being offensive. But his presence at the Agora settled it once and for all.

"Just say it." He stepped into the light, and what Eliza saw made every muscle in her body tense. *Run. Run*, they all seemed to say.

"Here," she sputtered. "I didn't realize you were in the library."

One half of the agent's usually bland face had contorted with discord. No. Not just discord, but capital-D Discord. The kind that could turn someone's entire world inside out and upside down without so much as an explanation why. His right eye bulged, bloodshot and angry while the rest of his right side sank into mere skin on bone. Just glancing at it made Eliza's entire being feel empty and hollow.

Not only was Agent Oliver a Descendant; he was a Descendant of Eris, the goddess of discord. And Eliza was in terrible danger.

"You're Discordian?" she muttered.

"Part. On my mother's side."

Eliza took a backward step toward the door. Her heart beat at a million miles an hour, and she just wanted out of there. Away from the contorted half of his face that made all the hope and light drain from her body. "I didn't, uh, realize."

"That's because I'm three-quarters Wingless. I can only sow discord when intense emotions are present. I'm essentially useless. Or I was until you came around." His face snapped back into shape, and Eliza breathed for the first time in what felt like minutes. Back to the same old Agent Oliver—mildly bored and moderately annoyed at all times. And just as quickly, Eliza went back to feeling like herself—moderately confused and markedly anxious about what in the worlds was happening.

Where is Jake? She glanced at the clock. Of course, if Oliver was here *and* a Descendant, maybe she could explain the *Egg Salad Saga* debacle. "Actually, I'm glad you're here," she said. "I wanted to talk to you about—"

"The Descendants' Scroll?" He smirked. "And how I caught you red-handed trying to steal it in order to expose *all* the Descendants to the rest of the world?"

"What?" She jerked backward. Why would he think that? She would never—

He held up his phone, and with a few swipes of his

finger, Eliza's voice played through its speakers. *If you can just get the key from her, I'll do the rest.*

"That's not what it sounds like! I swear."

"Funny. It sounds to me like you—a newly minted *techno-Cupid*—decided to take all of us public. Perhaps because you were angry that the Council wouldn't let you charge for your techno-powers?" He lowered his voice to a dull monotone, as if offering someone condolences at a funeral. "Pity how Cupids always let power go to their silly little heads."

"No. That's awful."

He ignored her and continued. "Or maybe because you got in a fight with that boyfriend of yours. Love really does make people act irrationally. Hmmmm." He tapped a finger on his chin. "I'm not sure yet, but I'll think of something."

Oliver had overheard her entire conversation with Jake. He knew she was a techno-Cupid, and he knew about the enchantments gone awry. "You. You're behind *Egg Salad Saga*."

He smirked. "It's my best work to date."

"But…how?"

Oliver stared at the ceiling as he paced. "Let's just say that a certain company wanted to sell their enchanted *personal assistants* in Northern California, and they were willing to do anything to make that happen. Anything."

"So the Mandroid company—"

"Created *Egg Salad Saga* at my behest. Once we cracked the code, it was easy. Too easy, really."

Eliza's mind became a funnel cloud, spinning and spinning until her thoughts became as blinding and terrifying as a tornado. "Why are you doing this?" she demanded. "Why are you trying to frame me?"

"'Frame' is such a boring word, don't you think?" His face switched back to the mask of discord. "I prefer something more exciting, with more syllables. Something like 'ultimatum.'"

Eliza backed away, desperate to put as much space between them as possible. If he wasn't so close to the door, she'd try to make a break for it. "Agent Oliver, I don't know what you think is happening, but—"

"I'll tell *you* what's happening, Eliza. *You* are a Cupid. Cupids are the scum of the Descendants."

She opened her mouth to protest, but he stopped her with the bulge of that bloodshot eye.

"And now you—the worst of them all—are getting even *more* powerful? Going to make not just humans but also robots and other animals miserable with every flick of your wrist? No, thank you."

His words swam in front of her, crashing into her face and making it hard to breathe. "But—"

"Exactly." Oliver pressed the tips of his fingers together. "*But* it doesn't have to be that way. Because you, Eliza Herman, have a choice."

Something about his expression said there wasn't much choice involved at all.

"Option one," he continued, "help me keep sowing discord among enchantments. It would be a match made in the heavens. With your unheard-of level of enchantment power, my inner Discordian slithers out whenever I need it. Not like all those times I had to come in behind that Van Love character. Ruining his enchantments was far more work."

On any other day, she would have been ecstatic to hear about Vic's shortcomings. Today, Oliver's words just made her feel nauseated. "Why?" she whispered.

"Why? *Why?*" Oliver cackled. He'd truly gone off the deep end. "Oh, Cupids, how do I hate thee? Let us count the ways." He held up an index finger. "There was the time all the other kids in my PSC class made fun of me for being a Wingless. Then there was senior prom, where the Cupid in my class decided to make my girlfriend fall for him. They left me standing alone at the punch bowl all night. And then there was college, when I got turned down for the Love University scholarship because of my *Winglessness*. Meanwhile, the asshole they gave the money to went on to start his own little family business. You may have heard of it. Herman & Herman?"

"My father?"

Oliver was too lost in airing his grievances to respond. "And then there was the kicker. I gave up trying to find a way to fit in with the other Descendants. Quit trying to find a way to make my mark on the world. I signed up for the California Civil Service exam and moved on with my nice, *normal* life. No more Descendants. I became a *normal* guy who blended in with all the other *normal* people. After twenty years with the Department of Natural Resources as an everyday bureaucrat, I'd nearly forgotten about Cupids altogether."

He paused and gave her a pointed look.

Blood whooshed by her ears, making her dizzy and drowning out almost all sound. "And then?"

"And then they transferred me to the godsforsaken Department of Affection, Seduction, and Shellfish. I'm still ten years out from retirement, and I can't get away from you. No one even acknowledges that I'm a Descendant. But I've got nowhere else to go. Nothing to do except wrangle you heartbreak chasers into complying with a few measly regulations."

Eliza glanced over her shoulders at the long bay of windows. Where was Jake? "That's horrible," she tried. "I'm really sorry they transferred you like that."

Maybe all he needed was some sympathy. Well, sympathy and a straitjacket, but she only had one of those options to offer at the moment.

"It's gotten better." He gave her a smug smile. "Once I figured out the plan."

"Plan?"

"Interfere with enchantments. Create an army of unhappy customers right here in Gold Lea. Get all the Cupids to shut down or leave town completely. And it worked. I unraveled enchantments here and there until the only holdouts were Herman & Herman and Van Love. But once I got *Egg Salad Saga* up and running, even they were starting to fold. I knew that as soon as I got rid of them both, my office would shut its doors. No more Cupids to regulate, no more desk to sit at every day. Early-out retirement. An RV to take me away from Gold Lea once and for all. Finally!" He laughed. "I had a use for my abilities. And it was almost *fun* to use them. Until you came along."

A new white-hot rage grew within her. This one far different from the one she'd felt every time she'd looked at Jake. This one felt justified. Necessary. Laser sharp. "You've been interfering with my family's enchantments?"

"For years. Your mother is especially interesting to follow. Her enchantments always have a certain bitterness to them. Sowing discord after her is like eating the darkest chocolate—you only need the smallest bit to feel satisfied. Yours, however, are so sweet that every day feels like the day after Halloween—I end up overdoing it but can't get enough."

"But I—" A new thought struck her. "Is this why I feel this way? So angry all the time?"

He laughed and rubbed his palms together. "Oh, that would be perfect. I forgot you'd been enchanted. Have you been playing *Egg Salad Saga*?"

"No." And she hadn't been enchanted either, but she wasn't about to tell Oliver that.

His face fell. "Then no. You must just be a bitch."

"Hey—"

"You've been a pain in my ass from day one. At first, I thought I could give you just enough room to screw things up for yourself. I wouldn't even need to depend on *Egg Salad Saga*, because you would mess everything up yourself. Then you figured out the most basic level of competence and threw me for a loop. But that's when the fun *really* started."

Now she really was going to be sick. She'd pictured a million scenarios where her incompetence resulted in something horrifying, but never one where being good at her job meant disaster. "What do you mean?"

He stepped close enough for her to see blue veins beneath his pale, tissue-like skin. "I feed off of others' emotions. Your enchantments are freakishly powerful. Which, in turn, makes my discord freakishly powerful."

"And?"

"Ah, yes. You never had any appreciation for preamble."

Eliza pretended to make eye contact while taking in the library in her periphery. If she could make it past the receptionist's desk, she might be able to dodge Oliver enough to sprint through the doors. "Get to the point, Oliver," she said, shuffling slightly toward the desk.

"The point is, I've realized I don't have to limit myself to taking out Cupids in the Gold Lea area. Of course, one silly video game isn't going to stay popular forever. And the Mandroid company doesn't need any more favors from me. But with the help of a certain powerful techno-Cupid, I can build an empire. Sow discord anywhere. Why wait for retirement to see the world when I could do it now? With you. Picture it: digital clocks that cause divorces, air conditioners that spur the darkest arguments, cars that drive relationships straight to crazy town."

"No." The words flew from her. "No way, Oliver."

"That's where the ultimatum part of this comes in. I guess I'll have to tell everyone how you died trying to get your grubby little techno-Cupid hands on the Scroll. How a Cupid was ready to reveal *all* of the Descendants to the world." He picked up a chair and slammed it into the nearest display case. Glass shattered, and blue lights flashed along the ceiling. The library doors slammed shut of their own accord, and a deep voice came from overhead.

"*The Agora has been locked down. This is not a test. I repeat, this is not a test. All Descendants should shelter in place until further notice. This is not a test. I repeat...*" The voice droned on and on, and Eliza could hear the shuffle of panicked feet outside the library doors.

So much for leaving the library. But maybe this meant help was on the way.

Oliver reached into the shattered display case—"Ares through the Ages"—and grabbed the tall bronze urn that had once been Ares's prison.

"No!" Eliza ducked just in time for the urn to fly by her head.

And—*Whoooooosh. Thunk.*—then to crack old Mrs. Washmoore straight in the forehead.

She'd come up through her pneumatic tubes at exactly the wrong time. Presumably to see who had set off the library's alarm system. But now she lay beside her desk, still breathing but out cold.

Help was definitely not on the way.

And Oliver was approaching with a spear in his hands.

Which left Eliza only one choice: run.

Around the shards of glass, over Mrs. Washmoore's unconscious form, through the stacks, and around the study carrels she ran. She zigged and zagged as fast and as far as she could from Agent Oliver and his pilfered ancient spear.

Maybe there was no way out of here, but someone had to come looking for Mrs. Washmoore eventually. And until then, she'd have to find a place to—

There.

Along the expansive bay of windows, the creators of the Agora had built long, cushioned benches for lounging. And under the bench on the end, a minuscule alcove beckoned, small enough to hide a terrified Cupid.

Eliza dove for it, scrambling through the space on her belly and worming her way into the nook until she could pull her knees up to her chest.

Somewhere in the distance, Oliver panted and cursed

and alternately called out, "Elllliza. Come out, come out. Ellliza."

She held her breath, willing her heart rate to slow from the speed of light. How was this happening? How had she not seen this coming? How would she make it out of here alive?

Footsteps echoed off the floor near her hiding spot. She pulled herself into a tight ball and waited.

And waited.

And waited.

Until finally the steps passed her and moved toward the end of the library. As they did, Oliver's taunts grew angrier and angrier, and his threats grew more and more explicit. But still, she let out the breath she'd been holding. He'd passed her by. He'd—

Riiiiiiiiiiiiiiiiiiiiiiiiiiiiiiiiiiiiing.

Riiiiiiiiiiiiiiiiiiiiiiiiiiiiiiiiiiiiing.

No. No, no, no, NO. Eliza fumbled in her pocket for her phone. With the shattered screen, she couldn't tell who was calling, but it didn't matter. They'd have to be her final hope.

"Eliza?" Jake's voice shook. "Are you there? What's going on? I came outside and—"

Pale, stubby fingers reached into the alcove and swiped the phone from her hands. Oliver leaned in close enough for Eliza to see each vein in his bulging, bloodshot eye. "Well, well, well. Look what I found."

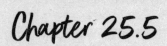
> **Calif. CCR § 412.331. (12)** A Cupid may use an enchantment in self-defense only with a reasonable belief that they or another is in imminent danger of serious bodily harm or death.

"HELLO? HELLO? ELIZA?" I'M PRACTICALLY SHOUTing now, and when the voice on the other end finally speaks directly into the phone, it's familiar. But not because it's Eliza.

"No, I'm sorry. Who is this?" the male voice asks.

"Jake. Who is this?" I stare out at the exodus of Descendants pouring from the doors. No one is being allowed in, but it seems everyone is coming out. Except the one person I'm searching for.

"Oh. Mr. Sanders. Hello, this is Trevor Oliver. I came across this phone on the floor of the library. I wasn't sure who it belonged to, so I was going to drop it off in the lost and found."

Eliza was right. He *is* a Descendant. I have a hundred questions to ask, but only the most important comes out.

"Where's Eliza? Is she with you?" My adrenaline kicks through the roof. If she's not in the library, and she's not out here with everyone else...

Oliver clears his throat, and a cacophony of

indecipherable noises follows. Then it quiets, and all I hear over line is the alarm raging inside the Agora.

"Hello? Oliver? What's going on in there?"

"Oh, it's nothing. Probably just someone bumped an alarm. You know how sloppy everyone gets on Nereid Night."

Sloppy or not, I've never, in all my years of picking up shifts at Dionysus, seen anyone set off chaos like this, no matter the day of the week. "Have you seen Eliza at all?" I ask.

"You know, now that you mention it, I did see her a few minutes before the alarms started. She mentioned wanting to get a drink at the bar before the specials ended." He laughs. "Well, I guess now we know who was clumsy enough to set off the alarm, don't we? Some things never change."

There's an edge to his voice, small enough that I don't realize it at first. But sharp enough that it cuts deep. This isn't the voice of Agent Oliver, the bored bean-counter from the Department. This is the voice of Trevor Oliver, a Descendant with something to hide.

And I know what that something is. Or at least part of it. Eliza wouldn't go to Nereid Night on her own. Not tonight. And especially not wearing a tablecloth.

"Wait," I say. "Oliver? Where's Eliza? Oliver!"

Click.

I redial with shaking hands, but the call goes straight to voicemail.

Something is wrong. Very wrong. And Oliver just cut off my last lifeline to Eliza.

"Fuck," I mutter, pushing my way through the throng of people. But just as quickly as I progress toward the doors, the herd pushes me back. Within minutes, I'm sweaty, bruised, and further from entering the Agora than I'd been before.

I pace the parking lot. My skin is too tight for my body, and everything inside me is screaming in protest. I need to be inside that building. Now.

And then I see it. Bright orange reflected in library's row of mirrored windows.

Ron Weasley. American classic. Eliza's pride and joy—and, if what she told me a few minutes ago is true, her strangest suitor to date. Also known as my last hope.

I sprint to the car. My mind is spinning at eighty miles an hour, but it keeps focusing in on one thing and one thing alone: those library windows.

"Ron," I say, prying open the door to the gas tank and pulling out Eliza's spare key. "We're going on an adventure."

But the damn thing obviously doesn't love me the way it loves Eliza. Because when I throw myself into the driver's seat and turn the key, nothing happens. Not even a tiny groan.

"Come on." My knee bounces with anxiety, but I force myself to give the car a steady pat on the dash. "Start up for me, okay?"

I turn the key again.

Nothing.

"Ron. Look, I know we've had our differences." *Gods, am I really doing this?* "But maybe this time we can put those aside, okay?"

I give him a little gas this time as I turn the key.

Silence.

The crowd outside the Agora is expanding, and it

spills into the parking lot. If I don't get this show on the road, Ron and I won't be going anywhere—at least not without running over a dozen unsuspecting Descendants.

"Look." I lean in close to the horn until my breath creates condensation on the steering wheel, and I grip the worn leather with all my might. "Eliza's in trouble. Big trouble. And if you don't start this time, I don't know what's going to happen to her. So you better get your shit together and turn over, okay?"

I give him a flick for good measure, take a solid breath, and turn the key.

"I'll stand by yooooooooooou."

The music blares from the speakers, and a half second later, Ron roars to life.

"That's it, Ron." I shift into Drive and let my foot hover over the gas. "Time to save our girl."

The music grows louder in response, and I know that's my cue.

Ron's done his part, and now I have to do mine.

I lay on the horn, my foot slams the gas, and the next thing I know we're flying toward the library windows.

One way or the other, we're coming in.

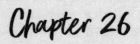

Chapter 26

"Love is a battlefield."

—Ancient Erosian proverb

THE WORLD EXPLODED.

Shards of broken window flew in every direction, exposing the inside of the Agora to the outside world and leaving Eliza in horrified awe. Cool air streamed through the hole in the library wall, whipping up dust and loose pages of library books.

And Ron Weasley—her weird, beautiful, piece-of-crap car—sat squarely in the middle of it all. Like a knight in shining (orange) armor, come to rescue her from the castle. If the castle were the library and the wicked queen were Agent Oliver, who happened to be pinned between Ron's bumper and the wall.

But when Ron's passenger door swung open, Eliza realized how wrong she'd been. Ron—for all his amazingness—was just the horse her knight had ridden in on.

On the floor, pieces of glass caught the light, sending a hundred rainbows across the room. Overhead, a breeze stirred. Crisp air brushed her skin, bringing with it thoughts of soft sweaters and bonfires on the beach. She was overcome with the scent of fresh peaches and clean sheets.

All of her favorite things. Including the person standing in front of her—the one she suddenly knew she could never live without.

"Jake!" she called out. "Over here!" She tried to stand, but the weight of the chains Oliver had wrapped around her held her to the floor. "Next to the classics shelf."

He'd come back. For her. Through a wall, ignoring the alarm system, and risking expulsion from the Agora forever, Jake had come back for her. And in the span of three heartbeats, he was kneeling in front of her and working the links away from her skin.

Jake—who was still risking everything for her.

An hour ago, that would have sent Eliza into the depths of self-loathing. Irritation and sadness would have balled up inside of her until she lashed out in a fit of rage. But now, looking at him, it was as if a deep, thick fog had lifted from inside her. Suddenly, her head and her heart were clear.

"Almost got it." He glanced up at her as his fingers worked frantically at the chains.

In that brief look, Eliza saw herself the way Jake must. She wasn't an epic failure of a Cupid. She was Eliza Herman, the strongest Cupid—no, *techno*-Cupid—in all of California. Probably in all of North America. She was kind and caring, and she could sing a mean rendition of any song on disc three of *Pow! That's What I Call Love Songs*.

And she saw Jake for who he really was. For the man he'd become since they'd been friends running barefoot all those years ago. He wasn't a liar or someone who didn't trust Eliza to make her own decisions. He was a skilled, savvy Cupid who knew exactly how to navigate his way through the world. He was smart and funny, and he bought her Dunkaroos for her birthday.

He was her best friend.

The keeper of her secrets and her heart.

Her stomach did backflips every time he grinned at her.

Even the *thought* of kissing him raised her body temperature three degrees.

Love—capital-L, happily-ever-after—was real. And she had it in spades.

"Are you okay? Did he hurt you?" Jake threw a glance over his shoulder at Oliver, who was still struggling to get out from behind Ron.

"No. I'm okay." She was bruised and battered, but everything would heal with time.

Jake tore at the chains until she could wiggle free of their weight. "Gods. I was so scared," he said, wrapping his arms around her.

Eliza buried her face in his chest. Scared didn't begin to describe the terror she'd felt when she'd been forced, at spearpoint, under the chains that had once imprisoned Ares. "Thank you," she murmured.

"What happened?" Jake pulled her back to look into her face.

"It was Oliver." She rushed through the answer. "He *is* a Descendant. And he's been interfering with all my enchantments, sowing discord. But, that's not important right now. I mean, it is. But Jake, I L—" She froze. Where was Oliver?

Whooooosh.

They both turned in time to see the top of Oliver's head disappear into one of Mrs. Washmoore's pneumatic tubes.

"Let's go!" Running on adrenaline and fear, Eliza sprinted to the receptionist's desk. "Come on." They couldn't let Oliver get away. He still had that recording and his sinister plans to end all Cupids and—if the empty case was any indication—now he had the Descendants' Scroll to boot.

"*Code Phaethon. Code Phaethon.*" The monotone, disembodied voice returned to the speakers. "*All Descendants must evacuate the Agora or return to the bunker level. Destruction will begin in five…*"

All at once, Eliza was back in PSC class, preparing for her ceremonial first trip to the Agora. She'd had to learn all the codes back then—including Code Phaethon—and she could almost hear her teacher's voice in the warnings over the intercom. "*All Descendants must evacuate the Agora or return to the bunker level…*"

The Scroll had been stolen, and now the Agora would self-destruct. Bit by bit, the walls and ceiling would crack and crumble, crushing everything in their path. Because if the thief made those names public, there couldn't be any physical evidence left to confirm the presence of Descendants. Instead, there would only be an old, fallen building and a raving lunatic with a sheet of paper. And of course, Dionysus—the Agora's very own bunker.

Eliza glanced down at Mrs. Washmoore, who was still splayed unconscious on the floor. The lanyard where she usually kept her ID had disappeared, but now and then a stray snake slithered out from her hair. At least the librarian was still alive.

Jake gasped and shook the woman's shoulders. "Aunt Rebecca?"

She gave a faint moan, but her eyes didn't open.

"She came in when the alarms started," Eliza said. "He knocked her out with the urn." She whipped her head back and forth between the tubes and Jake. But before she could say more, a horrible *craaaaaaaaaaaack* came from above them.

A chunk of plaster—shaped like Pegasus's head—crashed in front of them and crumbled to dust. And then another hunk—a six-foot-wide lyre—fell from the ceiling.

Eliza wrapped her arms around Jake's waist and gave a good, long squeeze. Far longer than she should have, considering that the library was crumbling around them. But she needed this moment—this reminder of what she was fighting for—before she plunged into the depths of the Agora in pursuit of a madman.

"You take her and get outside," she finally said, nodding to the broken windows. "I'm going after Oliver." She stepped into the small circle on the floor without giving Jake time to respond.

"Eliza. No. What are you doing?" He pulled her to him before the pneumatic tube could suck her under. "He's a psychopath. You don't want to run *toward* him. You need to get out of here."

"You don't understand." The minutes since Oliver had disappeared seemed to tick by at the speed of sound. Each one put him closer and closer to his goal. And if he got away, Eliza's life—and maybe Jake's too—would be over. The thought spurred her forward.

She reached up and brushed her fingers across his cheek. "Jake?" Her voice was so weighed down with emotion, it caught in her chest. "I Love you. So much. I always have, even when I was too young or stupid or

hurt to know it. And I'm always going to Love you. Real
Love. The capital-L kind."

"Eliza—"

"I have to go."

"Please—"

"Let me save you this time."

"If you—"

She waved him off and stepped back into the circle.
This was it—her turn to be the knight in shining armor—
and he wasn't going to stop her.

Except…

Nothing happened. She did a frantic search for a
button, a switch, a knob—anything that would suck her
into the tube and put her closer to Oliver. But she didn't
move an inch.

"How does this work?" she screeched. Mrs.
Washmoore had made it look so easy, zipping back and
forth from place to place in milliseconds. "Isn't there an
owner's manual or something?"

Without a word, Jake hefted Mrs. Washmoore over
one shoulder. "Scoot over."

She scooted but kept her feet firmly planted within
the bounds of the ring.

He moved to the center of the circular space and used
his free hand to wrap Eliza's arms around his waist.
"Hold on. Tight. And by the way, I Love you too." He
grinned and then stomped his left foot twice, so fast Eliza
may not have noticed if she hadn't been pressed to him.

They flew.

The three of them moved through the bowels of the
Agora faster than Eliza would have ever dreamed possible. Were they going east or west? Up or down? Was

that Mrs. Washmoore's foot pressed against her rib cage or her own?

"Jake—"

They turned a corner between floors, and Eliza's stomach dropped so low it disappeared. The rush of it swallowed her words. Down, they were definitely going down.

Eliza gave up all pretense of bravery and clung to Jake in abject terror as they moved faster and faster. How fast could the body travel before it blew apart into a million pieces? How fast could she travel before she threw up her lunch in a million pieces?

The oxygen vanished from her lungs. Icy sweat dotted her forehead, and her hair clung to her face, obscuring her sight. If pneumatic tubes were the travel of the future, Eliza was never leaving Gold Lea again.

Suddenly, they hurled to a stop, and Jake and Mrs. Washmoore collapsed into a heap in the darkness.

"Shit." Jake's voice came from somewhere beneath his aunt. "Oh gods. Eliza, please. Pull her off me."

Eliza, who'd had the fortune of landing on her butt a few feet away from the pile, planted her unsteady feet on the floor. Still woozy, she fumbled in the dark until she found Mrs. Washmoore's side. Eliza pushed, and the woman's unconscious body rolled off Jake with a thud.

"Are you okay?" Eliza asked.

He groaned. "Where are we?"

Eliza splayed her hands on the lush carpet. The faint smell of seaweed filled her nostrils. And down the hallway, a dull purple glow faded in and out in time with a deep bass beat. "Dionysus," she said. "We're outside of Dionysus? You brought me to the bunker. Jake, I told you—"

"I brought you Oliver."

"He's in there?" Eliza pointed to the Dionysus entryway.

Jake pulled himself to his feet, wincing as he moved. "Two quick stomps take you back to the drop-off point of the person ahead of you. Aunt Rebecca let me use the tubes after hours. Easier to get back and forth from the Dionysus to the dumpster at night."

As Eliza's eyes adjusted to the darkness, she could see the way he held his arm at an odd angle. "Are you okay?" But she knew the answer. That arm was broken, maybe worse.

"I'm fine." He grimaced.

But the look on his face revealed the truth he was hiding—from himself as much as Eliza. Jake was in pain. *A lot* of pain.

And that knowledge made her insides burn with a rage so bright, it put her anger over the last few days to shame.

Oliver had hurt Jake. And now the bastard was going to pay.

"Help me with Aunt Rebecca," Jake said. He grabbed one of Mrs. Washmoore's armpits with his good arm and motioned for Eliza to do the same. She tucked her anger into one of the deepest, darkest pockets of her soul and took the woman's other armpit.

What had looked like a faint purple glow in the hall became a fluorescent maze of purple and blue light once they pried open the reinforced door of the bar. Smoke machines created puffs of glowing, green fog around them, giving everything the appearance of a nymph-infested swamp.

Music drummed loud enough to drown out the alarms, and a hundred or more bodies moved in time to the beat. The entire place was a sweaty, swarming mass of arms and legs and sea creatures. Apparently, Nereid Night was still going strong.

And Eliza immediately wanted out.

Instead, she and Jake made their way toward a row of tables near the dance floor. Together, they lowered Mrs. Washmoore into the closest booth, next to a group of partying Monopods. Once Eliza was satisfied the Fury would be safe among the single-footed, she scanned the room.

Immediately, a pale, half-dull, half-bulging face caught her eye across the dance floor. "Jake—"

"Here she is! This is the one I was telling you about!" The Maenad from earlier—she'd shed her mink stole, but there was no mistaking the ivy dress and diamond nails—grabbed Eliza's elbow and pulled her into the crowd.

"She *is* adorable!" another Maenad cooed, bopping to the music. She'd twisted her long hair up around the top of her head to look like bull horns. "It's so great that you're embracing your heritage." She pointed to Eliza's tablecloth.

"Uh, thanks but—"

"Oh my gods." A third Maenad twirled circles around them. Just watching her made Eliza dizzy. "You should let us give you a makeover."

Eliza wasn't about to take on a supporting role in a raving-ones version of *Clueless*, but saying that would be beyond impolite. "Maybe another time," she shouted over the music. "I really need to get going."

"Just one more song." The first Maenad grabbed Eliza and spun her further onto the dance floor.

"I really can't." But the more she tried to pull away from the trio, the deeper into their swirling circle she ended up. In vain, she held her arms against her chest to protect herself from their crazed dancing as she tried to dodge and weave her way through the mess. "Excuse me, I'm just going to squeeze through here... Or, okay, maybe here. No? Well..."

"Eliza!" Jake's voice broke through her panic, and in seconds, he was there, prying her from the dance floor with his good arm.

"Oh! Look at him," the bull-horned Maenad purred. "What if we—"

"Go, Jake. Go!" Eliza shouted.

They pushed through the mass of bodies as fast as they could manage, but by the time they reached the edge of the crowd, Oliver had vanished.

No. No. Where is he? Where?

She quelled her growing panic. It wasn't over yet. She hadn't come this far—held at spearpoint, trapped under the weight of magical chains, and shot through a series of tubes—to give up now. Oliver *had* to be here somewhere.

Eliza scanned the room.

Shirtless (exceptionally hairy) Satyrs swimming in Nereid tanks? *Check.*

A tree nymph playing a conch shell? *Double check.*

A group of Dactyls passing around a little of Glaucus's "magical herb"? *Check, check, and check.*

Stocky, balding man with a bulging eye and an ax to grind?

Nope.

"He couldn't have gone back out the front from here," Jake said. "We would have seen him."

Eliza nodded. Jake was right. And that meant Oliver was either somewhere in here among the writhing bodies, or he'd slipped behind the bar and snuck out the back.

If she were an angry half-Discordian, where would she go?

"Out the back?" Jake asked.

"Out the back."

Several sweaty minutes later, they'd inched their way along the perimeter of the dance floor, ducked behind the bar—where the bartender had long since jumped ship to make out with a Siren in the corner—and slipped into the kitchen.

Compared to the constant *thump, thump, thump* of the bar, the space was gloriously silent. Well, almost.

"*Code Phaethon. This is not a test. I repeat, this is not a test.*"

Jake glanced around the empty kitchen. "All the kitchen staff must have evacuated."

Eliza didn't know if that made her feel better or worse. The only people left in the entire building were her, Jake, Oliver, an unconscious Mrs. Washmoore, and a lot of really smashed Descendants. At least she wouldn't have to explain why she was trespassing in an Employees Only zone…

Something swayed in her periphery, and Eliza whipped around. "Jake?" she whispered.

"Yeah?"

They froze in silence until, along the far wall, a metal prep table rattled ever so slightly.

"There!" Eliza pointed as Oliver tumbled out from his hiding spot, overturning tables and littering the floor with stainless-steel cookware.

For a brief moment, he stared straight at Eliza as he ran, the Scroll still tucked beneath one arm. She sprinted after him, knowing—without glancing back—that Jake would be right behind her.

They weaved through rows of sinks piled high with pots, along a line of refrigerators that seemed to stretch forever, and finally down a dim corridor far from the Dionysus kitchen. Eliza's breath came in ragged spurts, and by the time they'd run into the complete darkness, every muscle in her body begged her to stop. But she only ran faster, with Jake beside her, spurred on by the sound of Oliver's footsteps ahead.

She pushed through her pain.

They were gaining on him.

She forced her legs forward.

They were going to catch him.

"*Ooof.*" Eliza slammed into something solid, and searing pain exploded from her kneecap. She fumbled in the dark for the offending weapon, and her fingers closed in on something round and soft and covered in thick hair. "What the—"

She let go just as the lights flipped on.

A head—the very head she'd been holding—rolled across the floor.

Luckily for everyone involved, it belonged to a practice dummy.

Through the dark depths of the Dionysus kitchen, Oliver had led them to the weaponry practice range.

"Some people really don't know when to give up,

do they?" Oliver's voice echoed through the empty gymnasium. He stood on top of the weaponry rentals desk with one hand tucked into the gap between the buttons of his shirt, like a Discordian version of Napoleon. "They fail their Cupid exam, and years later, they come back for more. They get hit with a dozen extra rules, and they keep showing up every day just to humiliate themselves. All their enchantments backfire, and they try to fix them anyway."

"You're the one that should give up, Oliver," Jake said. "It's two on one, and the entire Agora is surrounded."

"More like one and a half versus one." Oliver nodded to Jake's swollen, hanging arm. "And let's face it, we've both seen her in action. She's not exactly a threat."

"Excuse me?" she sneered.

The agent smirked. "Do you *really* think you would have passed your exam if I hadn't taken matters into my own hands? If I hadn't let you out of demonstrating a certain set of weaponry skills?"

Rage bubbled up Eliza's throat. The Cupiding exam. She hadn't had to shoot the bow and arrow, not because she'd been the victim of a happy coincidence. Because Oliver had needed her to pass. That was the only way she'd become his puppet.

He'd used her. He'd taken advantage of her need to make her family proud. Of her need to make herself proud. And now he was rubbing her face in it.

"Fuck you, Trevor-no-comma-Oliver." She stepped forward.

"*Mmmhhhmmmhmhmp.*" The muffled sound came from behind the rental desk.

"Who's back there?" Jake demanded.

"I didn't hear anything." Oliver stared at Jake as though he'd lost his mind.

Eliza crept forward.

A leg poked out from under the desk. "*Hmmmmppp!*" Eliza froze.

"Who's back there, Oliver?" Jake repeated, moving to the right and drawing the agent's stare farther from Eliza.

Oliver's face split into a wide grin. "No one for long." He pulled his hand free. In it, he held a gleaming sai.

Eliza dove. Before she could think, before she could breathe, she was on top of Oliver's hostage: the weapons rental clerk. He thrashed beneath her, held in place by a thin, golden net—one of the weapons that had been on display in the Ares through the Ages case.

"Hold still," she whispered, tugging at the freakishly strong—and scorching hot—material. "What are you even doing down here? There's a Code Phaethon, gods damn it."

"I came back for my phone," he whimpered.

But she didn't get anything more from him, because with every one of her movements, he cried out in pain as another massive stream of red and silver Love Luster flew from his body. It rained down on her, clogging her throat and obscuring her vision.

Which gave Oliver just enough time to yank her upright by the ponytail.

"You make it so easy, Eliza." He cackled, forcing her to the other side of the desk. The sai's point pressed against her rib cage, and she didn't dare move.

"Let her go!" Jake's voice boomed. "Now."

"Hmmmm." Oliver pursed his lips in mock concentration, and that one bulging eye rolled around in his head. Seconds passed, then eternities, until he spoke again. "Nope."

The sai bit into her skin. A trickle of warm blood seeped into her shirt.

"You had a choice," Oliver whispered. "We could have walked out of here together without a single bit of blood being shed. Now, look what you made me do."

There was no mistaking the vile promise in his words. He intended to kill them all. Her. The poor rental clerk. Jake.

Except she wasn't going down with a fight.

And neither was Jake. "No!" His shout rang through the gym as he charged over the desk. The weight of his body knocked all three of them to the floor. As if in slow motion, the sai spun from Oliver's hands and slipped under a shelf.

Eliza pressed a blistered hand to her bleeding side and scrambled to her feet. The cut was shallow—thank the gods—but it burned like the deepest depths of Tartarus.

"Eliza, move!"

She jumped to her left. At that moment, a chunk of marble statue—a hand holding an anvil—crashed into the very place she'd been standing.

Another hand—this one firmly attached to its owner—grabbed her by the shoulder and shoved. Her back slammed into the edge of the desk, and instant tears blurred her vision. She swung blindly at her opponent, throwing fists and elbows and knees but only meeting air.

Another hit. This time to her bleeding side.

Her lungs seized. Her ears rang. She doubled over. Vomit climbed her throat. And she braced herself for the final blow.

But it didn't come.

"Run!" Jake's voice came from somewhere far away. "Eliza. Run!"

She forced her vision to clear and stood. Less than ten feet away, he struggled and winced as Oliver twisted his broken arm behind his back.

"Go, Eliza. Now." Jake's face turned a desperate shade of purple. "Please!"

The walls shook, and the floor began to buckle.

The enchantment was over. His mentorship obligations were over. Even their short-lived relationship was over. And despite all that, Jake was sacrificing himself so she could get away.

Eliza looked at the doorway. She could make a break for it—run bleeding down the dark hallway until she found someone sober enough to help her. Maybe, just maybe, she'd make it back in time to save him.

Or—she glanced at the case of rental weapons and the shaking, terrified, lovelorn clerk hovered beside it—she could settle this right here, right now. Once and for all.

She narrowed her eyes and stood up straight. Pain shot through her rib cage, but she ignored it and turned to the clerk. Eliza was *not* going to leave here without the Love of her life. "I'll take the bow and arrow, please."

The clerk's eyes widened. Burns covered his body where the net had touched his skin, but he scrambled to his feet anyway. "Yes...yes, ma'am."

Oliver's laugh sent shards of ice down her spine. He loosened his grip on Jake ever so slightly and took a step toward Eliza. "The arrow? Next you're going to tell me—"

Jake jerked his head back, cracking Oliver in the jaw.

The agent's roar lit up the room as he let go of Jake. At that moment, the bow and arrow hit Eliza's blistered, outstretched palm.

Now or never.

Every muscle in her body contracted in searing, blinding pain, but she forced her way through it. This pain would be nothing compared to the devastation of losing Jake. Her best friend. Her confidant. Her *everything*.

With shaking hands, Eliza nocked the arrow and aimed for the spot between Oliver's eyes. Blood soaked her shirt, and pain spots appeared in the corners of her vision. She pulled in a ragged breath, squared her stance, and—just as Jake had told her all those times—loosened her grip.

If she hit her target, she'd save the best thing in her life. And if she failed, she could only hope she'd meet Jake again one day in the Underworld—where they'd reminisce about how her final act had been to stand in the library, wearing a freakin' tablecloth diaper, while fighting for them both.

Three…Two…

She let the arrow fly.

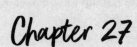

Chapter 27

Calif. CCR § 287.120. Employers of one or more licensed, actively practicing Cupids must carry a policy of Cupids' compensation insurance for personal injury or death of an employee by accident or occupational disease arising out of and in the course of the Cupid's employment.

THE UNDERWORLD BURNED BRIGHTER THAN ELIZA had imagined. It also smelled like Pine-Sol, and apparently her organs made noise, because all she could hear was a steady *beep, beep, beep* that perfectly matched the rhythm of her heart.

A woman stood over her in a white coat. A green stethoscope hung around her neck. "Eliza? Can you hear me? You're in the hospital. I'm Doctor Branderson," she said.

"No, you're not. You're Persephone."

The woman chuckled. "Do you remember me? We met about six or seven weeks ago when you brought your father in."

Eliza rubbed her eyes. Sure enough, the beeping was a heart monitor, the bright lights were the fluorescent bulbs overhead, and the Pine-Sol smell was— well, probably Pine-Sol. "How did I get here? What day is it?"

"You've been out for a few hours, but everything is fine. You're a very lucky lady."

"Lucky?" Her memory was foggy and grayed out in places, but she knew *lucky* wasn't a word anyone would use to describe her.

"Don't worry. Amnesia is common and usually only temporary in these scenarios. You took a big fall while out camping. A few cuts and bruises, burned your hand in the campfire, one broken rib. Nothing permanent."

This doctor wasn't just off her rocker; she was off the entire porch. Eliza did *not* camp. The sheer number of calamities that awaited her in the great outdoors was simply too much to handle. "My parents?"

"I'll get them." The doctor disappeared behind a white curtain, and soon enough, her parents and Elijah stepped into the room.

"Eliza!" Her father wrapped his arms around her. Her mother and Elijah followed.

"What happened?" she asked when they'd gotten their fill of hugs. Why couldn't she remember how she'd ended up here? And where was Jake? She needed Jake. She couldn't shake the feeling that she needed to tell him something important.

"You were so brave, honey," her mom said. "We're so proud of you."

Elijah nodded. "You're a legend."

"Why?"

"You don't remember?" her mother asked. "The library? Agent Oliver?"

The memories crashed over her. The Scroll. The bow. Jake yelling at her to run. It was like she'd been sliced open with the sai all over again. "Where's Jake? Is he okay?"

Her dad laid a hand on her forearm. "Honey, you have to stay calm. The doctor said—"

"Where is he?"

The curtain beside her bed flew open. There, making a hospital gown look like something straight from the pages of *GQ*, lay Jake. He rubbed his eyes with one hand, groggy with sleep. His other arm was in a cast. "You didn't think I was going to let you off that easily, did you, Herman?" he murmured.

She sat straight up and tried to push her way out of the bed, but the tubes and wires that connected her to a host of machines held her back.

"Hold on, Liza. You don't want to rip out your IV." Her dad guided her gently back to the bed. "Dr. Branderson said you could get up and move around in a little while. They have to switch out some of the equipment first."

She'd been thrown back right where she'd started: desperate to touch Jake but unable to leave the safe zone.

"I'll come to you." Jake pushed the curtain aside the rest of the way and struggled to his feet, smiling at Eliza the entire time. Halfway across the room, his smile fell and he swiped his good hand behind his back. "Uh, nobody look at my ass."

"No promises," Eliza said.

Her family groaned.

But she didn't care, because soon Jake had wheeled his IV pole over and sat on the edge of her bed. His position gave her the perfect view of his broad back and just a hint of the top of the aforementioned ass.

Her heart monitor beeped a little faster. "Why did the doctor say I'd been camping?"

"The Department has asked us to keep things quiet for now. The Cosmic Council agrees," her mother said.

"They aren't going to be able to keep it quiet for long," Elijah said. "Now that Charlie Jenkins put it up online."

"Charlie Jenkins?" Eliza asked.

"The weapons rental clerk," her mother replied. "Apparently, he recorded portions of your heroics and posted them to social media. The Council is working on taking the posts down now. He's sent you some get-well flowers." She gestured to the window where five floral arrangements soaked up the early-morning sun.

"Which ones?"

Elijah smirked. "All of them. You really got him good." He pulled out his phone, swiped a few times across the screen, then held it out to her. "Watch."

Eliza pressed Play on the video. The shaky footage showed a bloodied, battered Eliza with the bow and arrow aimed at Oliver. Her arm trembled as she yanked it back and let the arrow go with a battle cry that could have rivaled any Amazon. She collapsed at the same moment the arrow pierced Oliver in the gut. Across the room, he fell to the floor in a heap of shouts and blood and Love Luster.

On the screen, Jake shoved the Scroll into his pocket and scooped Eliza up with his good arm. Then he was sprinting to the upper levels of the Agora with Charlie Jenkins at his heels. Who, of course, narrated the entire encounter.

"We're headed to the library," Charlie panted. "Everything is falling down around us. I don't know if we're going to make it out of here. Please make sure

my mom sees this. And make sure someone feeds—
Ooof." Thunk.

The screen went black.

"What happened? Is he okay?" Eliza asked.

"He's fine. He tripped over something and dropped
his phone." Jake shrugged.

"But the Agora?" Her rib cage tightened with anxiety.
Obviously, they'd made it out, but what about everyone
else? Was there anything left of the building?

Her father gave Jake a proud nod. "Jake returned the
Scroll before the building entirely collapsed. It's very
damaged but salvageable."

"And Oliver? Is he…" She couldn't bring herself to
say it.

"He's alive and in for a long stay at the Tartus
Correctional Facility," her father said. "He admitted
everything. That he'd slowly picked off all the Cupid
businesses in town. That he used his position with the
Department to further his goals. That he bribed a techno-
Cupid company to create that anti-enchantment game.
That he sowed discord in all your enchantments."

She glanced at Jake. He nodded in confirmation.
"You saved us all, Eliza."

Holy Hades. She'd done it. *They'd* done it. Together.

"Liza." Her father's voice was solemn and somber.
"More than anything, we're so happy that you're okay.
If we'd lost you…" His voice cracked and faded as tears
shone in his eyes.

"If we'd lost you, *we'd* be lost," her mother finished,
brushing a strand of Eliza's hair from her forehead. "But
we are so very proud of you. I know I don't tell you—
any of you—enough, but I am so amazed every single

day by how kind and brave and intelligent my children are. *Both* of my children."

Eliza felt the sting of tears gathering in her own eyes. "Mom, you don't have to—"

Her mother held up a hand. "I've been so focused on the business for all these years because I wanted to build Herman & Herman into something worthy of you both. I wanted to leave you two something special. And in the process, I lost sight of telling you, and showing you, how special you are. I'm sorry for that. And I'm sorry for not believing you about *Egg Salad Saga*. We should have listened to you, Eliza."

The tears spilled onto Eliza's cheeks. *She's proud of me. And she's sorry.* Those were exactly the words Eliza needed to hear. And her mother was exactly the person she needed to hear them from. Eliza wrapped her arms around her mother's waist and pulled her in close. She smelled like comfort and flowers and *home*. How long had it been since Eliza had stopped to embrace her mother? *Too long.*

"I'm sorry too, Mom. About everything. And I'm sorry I couldn't help you save Herman & Herman from the deficiency."

"Oh, honey." Her mother kissed her forehead. "The Department waived the deficiency in gratitude for your actions."

Her father chuffed. "I think they just don't want us to sue."

"Either way, Herman & Herman is going to be just fine." Her mom patted Eliza's knee as she stood. "Because of *you*. Come on, you two," she said. "Let's leave Eliza and Jake to get some rest."

"Wait." Eliza pulled her mother's hand. "What about my clients? All the ones Oliver interfered with?" She thought of poor Lily and Mitch. Yolanda and her crazed, mixed-up feelings about Eddie. Even Helen and Jacque.

"The techno-Cupids involved have shut down *Egg Salad Saga* and instituted a nationwide recall. Soon, everyone who played it will be back to normal. All that's left is to reverse the discord Oliver sowed with your clients. It can be done with reenchantment, if the same weapon is used a second time. We've made calls." Her father pulled out his phone. "Yolanda Durst declined reenchantment, so we didn't contact Mr. Pearson. We left a message for Helen Rothchild, and"—he clucked his tongue—"the Johansens were interested, but they haven't been able to find the weapon. Mrs. Johansen said it was—"

"A wooden spoon! It's under their love seat in the living room."

Her parents looked at each other, then at Elijah. "Let's go," her mom said. "I'll call Lily and let her know we found it."

"Wait." Eliza tugged her mother's hand one last time. She took in the lines on her father's face, the gray hairs along her mother's part, the patchy beard growing along her brother's jaw. It had been a rough few weeks. They all looked a little worse for wear, and if Eliza had to guess, they all *felt* a lot worse for it. But somehow, some way, her family was stronger than ever. And she'd never felt more like she belonged to them. "I love you guys."

"We love you too," her parents said.

Even Elijah chimed in with a *ditto*.

When they'd gone, Jake laid a soft kiss on her forehead. "I told you the world needs you."

Eliza rested her head on his uninjured shoulder. She wasn't so sure the world needed her, but she did know one thing for certain: she needed him. "Jake, earlier, at your apartment… I mean, after Vic said those things…"

Gods, why was this so hard. It was like *that* version of her—the angry, terrorizing version that had felt so many conflicting things—had been a bad dream.

"About that," he said. "Hold on."

She watched as he hobbled over to his bed and grabbed his phone from the tray. "What are you doing?"

"There's someone who made me promise to have you call her as soon as you woke up. And trust me, she is not someone you want to cross."

Two minutes later, Eliza was on the phone with Mrs. Washmoore. "I should never have done it," the Fury said for the third time. "It's not an excuse, but Jake is the rising star in our family. I didn't want to see him throw it all away. So I intensified your anger a little, hoping it would lead the two of you to break up. And that day at the library, I knew he was there and moping about your breakup, so I pretended your card wouldn't work. I hope you'll forgive me."

Eliza took a long moment to let the confession sink in. Mrs. Washmoore had hit her with a good old-fashioned Fury charm: the whammy. Instead of physically torturing Eliza, she'd taken the mental route. Mrs. Washmoore had used her powers to fan the flames of Eliza's deepest fears and insecurities until she was a rageful, irrational mess.

And she'd almost lost the love of her life because of it.

But at the end of the day, Eliza was far too exhausted

to hold a grudge. Plus, maybe all that anger had come in handy when she'd had to face down Oliver. "Thank you for letting me know."

"Of course. Now that I know what happened, I see how wrong I was about you. Jake is lucky to have such a lovely Cupid by his side."

Eliza stole a glance at Jake. She intended to be by his side for as long as he'd let her.

"And maybe when you're feeling up to it, you can come by the library and I can show you more about interlibrary loans," Mrs. Washmoore said. "I think you'll really enjoy some of the collections from the Northeast."

"That would be nice," Eliza said. "Thank you."

"Certainly. And once the whammy wears off, I hope you and Jake will come over for dinner."

"Wait. When it wears off?" She looked at Jake again, and a steady stream of emotions flooded her chest. None of them were anything like anger.

"Yes, probably in about three or four more days. Maybe five if you're close to your cycle."

"I don't understand. I haven't been angry at Jake since yesterday afternoon."

Silence filled the line. Jake looked at her quizzically.

"Well, mane of Medusa," Mrs. Washmoore said. "I guess I shouldn't be surprised."

What? What is it? Jake mouthed.

Eliza shrugged, then switched the phone to speaker. "Mrs. Washmoore—"

"Aunt Rebecca?" Jake added.

On the other end, Mrs. Washmoore cleared her throat. "A Fury's fire turns most things it touches to ash. But a fire can also burn away impurities and leave you with solid gold. You two, my dears, seem to be made of the strong stuff."

Eliza said goodbye and hung up the phone. She didn't need Mrs. Washmoore to tell her Jake was something special—that *they* were something special. She felt it every time he looked at her. Every time he made her laugh. Every time he lit up the darkest, most wounded parts of her and made all her faults seem worthy of celebration.

"Get over here and kiss me," she said.

And thank the gods, he did. His lips caught hers, soft but urgent. Warm but relaxed. It was new and exciting... but also like coming home. "I love you," she whispered. "Capital-L Love you."

"That's very interesting. Because I also capital-L Love you." His warm breath grazed her ear, and goose bumps spread along her body. "But before you say anything else, you should know one thing."

"What's that?" she asked. His mock seriousness made her laugh. Gods, she loved how he made her laugh.

"Ron Weasley died for good. Your car, not the character. Spoiler alert, I guess."

"No!" Her poor, not-so-trusty Mustang.

"He made the ultimate sacrifice for you, Eliza," Jake said solemnly.

"You don't exactly look heartbroken about it," Eliza said.

Jake kissed her forehead. "That shade of orange was *atrocious*."

"Don't speak ill of the dead."

"What? He was my biggest rival."

Eliza gave him a gentle, playful shove. "Well, from

the looks of it, you won't be driving for a while, so maybe I'll just borrow your car until I can find a way to get Ron fixed."

"Hmmm. I'm not sure he's fixable, but I was thinking neither of us would be driving for a while."

"Why is that?"

"Because we're both going to need a *long* recovery period. With lots of bed rest."

Eliza grinned. "Interesting."

"But we can talk about that later," he said. "We have something else to discuss at the moment."

"We do?"

The head of the hospital bed slid back. "Such as this." His lips found her jaw. "And this." They caressed her neck. "And this." He captured her mouth again. "It's going to be a very long discussion."

"Sounds like it," she murmured.

"Years of discussion."

"Decades."

Jake smiled down at her. "Lifetimes."

Epilogue

Calif. CCR § 430.04. A rebuttable presumption of love shall be established by the simultaneous presence of at least three of the following: (A) romantic gestures, (B) sleeplessness, (C) impaired rational thought, and/or (D) emotional instability.

"'HAPPY BIRTHDAY TO YOU. HAPPY BIRTHDAY TO YOU. Happy birthday, Elijah and Eliza.'" Her father drummed his hands on the table. "'Happy birthday tooooo youuuuuu.'"

Thirty candles flickered on the cake, and her brother gave her a pointed look. "I can't believe we're still doing this."

"You're never too old to celebrate your birthday," their mother said. "Now blow out the candles before the wax messes up my beautiful buttercream."

"Go ahead," Eliza said.

Elijah looked at her like she'd lost her mind. "Seriously?"

She glanced to her left. Jake's gaze caught hers, and she grinned. "I'm good. I think you need it more this year, Elijah." In fact, aside from the whole nearly-killed-by-an-A.S.S.-agent thing, this had been the best year of Eliza's life.

"Oh gods. Someone alert the authorities. My sister

is happy on her birthday. We have a potential body-snatcher situation here."

"Just blow," she said, "before Mom loses it."

Elijah leaned forward and extinguished the candles with one hearty breath.

Immediately, they all relit.

Jake squeezed Eliza's hand. A swarm of butterflies flapped their wings in her stomach, sending her into a lovely, twirling tizzy. He planted the smallest kiss on her cheek. That touch was enough to heat her body in *lots* of exciting places. "Happy birthday," he whispered.

"No making out at the table, please," Elijah said. "It's bad enough that I have to know you're boning my sister. I don't want to see it too."

A flush crept up Jake's neck, but all Eliza did was laugh. "Please. Like you didn't 'bone' half of my friends in high school."

"You only had three friends in high school." Elijah leaned back in his chair.

"Yeah, and you slept with two of them," she said.

"Better than half then." He high-fived himself.

"Okay, that's enough." Their mother took the cake away to the counter and began pulling out the candles. "Go outside. Your presents are in the backyard. I'll be there with the cake in a minute."

"The backyard?" Eliza asked.

"This is it, Liza," her brother deadpanned, "the year we finally get our ponies."

"Just go," her dad said. "We'll be there in a minute."

With a shrug, Eliza tugged Jake's hand and slipped out the back door.

"Surprise!"

The chorus of voices caught her completely off guard. But they were voices that made her heart happy.

The Johansens stood with their arms wrapped around each other. Elijah had been able to reenchant them with the wooden spoon, breaking the discord and sending them straight back into marital bliss.

Helen and Jonathan Ellis sat nearby. Following a successful sea lion pregnancy, Jonathan received a promotion. When he stopped by the office to tell Eliza all about it, Helen happened to be on her way out. Unenchanted sparks flew—followed shortly thereafter by a little requested Love Luster—and the two of them had been inseparable since.

Then there were Yolanda, Agent Smith, and the mutual light of their now-married lives, Charleston Samuel Durst the Third. With Oliver gone, Agent Smith had been promoted to agent-in-charge of the entire Northern California region. She'd administered Eliza's new (legitimate) licensing exam—which, of course, she'd passed with flying colors. The next day, Agent Smith stopped by Herman & Herman to hand-deliver her new license. With a new and improved photo, *thankyouverymuch*.

"Can we speak in private?" the agent had asked.

Eliza had escorted the woman into her office—*her very own office*—and taken a seat behind the desk. Seeing a Department uniform still sent shocks of anxiety through her, but she'd breathed through it and forced a smile. "What can I do for you, Agent Smith?"

"Ms. Herman, this is quite unorthodox, but…" The agent shifted in her seat uncomfortably.

Eliza felt a pang of empathy for the woman. Love was

hard and weird and usually uncomfortable. She pulled out a new client folder. "Is there someone in particular you're interested in?" she asked.

Agent Smith looked up, her expression brightening. "A woman I went to college with. We were friends then, but we lost touch. A few years ago, I ran into her at my vet's office. She was more beautiful than I'd remembered, and we hit it off like no time had passed. We've been in touch off and on since then, and I can't get her out of my mind. No matter how hard I try. Everything about her is so vibrant. You should see how adorable she is when she talks about her pet pig. It's like something out of a movie."

"Pig?" Eliza asked.

She nodded. "That pig is the luckiest bastard alive. If Yolanda Durst looked at me like she looked at him, I'd never want another thing in my life."

Nearly six months post-enchantment, they were still going strong.

Even Mrs. Washmoore was there, with a present in one hand and—*holy Hades*—Old Man Vannerson holding the other.

"Is that…" Eliza whispered.

"They met in a Pat Benatar fan club or something," Jake said.

"Enchantment? Non-enchantment? Is it serious or just a friends-with-benefits situation?"

Jake shuddered. "I've tried not to ask too many questions."

Too bad for him. The librarian-bouncer-Fury had become like a surrogate great-aunt to Eliza, and she couldn't wait to hear all about their Love story. "Well, as soon as this party is over, I'm hunting down Aunt Rebecca and asking *all* the questions."

Jake laughed and wrapped his arms around her waist. "Happy birthday, Eliza."

"Best one yet." She rose up on her tiptoes and kissed him. Short enough for public consumption, but long enough to tell him how much she appreciated him—and what she wanted to do later to show it.

When they broke apart, he stepped back and ran a hand over the top of his head. "There's your present. From me, I mean."

She followed his gaze to the cedar tree where she'd had her first disastrous love-casting experience twenty-two years ago. Another donkey piñata hung from the branches.

"It was the only one I could find that wasn't Valentine's Day themed," he whispered.

"A piñata? Really? Did my brother put you up to this?"

Elijah put a baseball bat in her hand and gave her a shove toward the tree. "It's time to face your fears, Sis."

"You knew about this?"

Her brother crossed his arms. "Innocent until proven guilty."

Eliza paused beneath the piñata. After all these years, the thought of taking a swing still made her a little queasy. But as she looked around the yard at all the smiling faces, she knew: if ever there was a time to face her fears, this was it.

"What, no blindfold?" she joked. "No one's going to spin me around until I puke?"

"Baby steps, Herman." Jake took the bat in one hand, wrapped his free arm around her waist, and pulled her in

for another kiss. The birthday crowd broke out in hoots
and whistles behind them. She wanted to stay in that kiss
forever, until they were old and wrinkled and covered in
liver spots. But eventually Jake pulled away.

"What was that for?" she asked.

"Luck." He put the bat in her hands and stepped away.

Eliza raised it over her shoulder like she was about
to swing for a home run. Or, at least, how she *thought*
she might swing for a home run if she'd ever played
baseball.

Bat at the ready, she took one last look at the crowd.
Her parents had joined and watched with their arms
wrapped around each other. Elijah stood beside them,
smirking, and Jake hung off to the side looking both
proud and deeply terrified.

Her brother cupped his hands around his mouth.
"Swing already. I've got places to be."

"Like where?"

"Your friend Quinn promised me a birthday drink."

Oh gods.

She swung.

The bat cracked the donkey wide open, and a single
item fell from its insides.

A box.

A very small silver box.

A size-of-a-ring-box box.

Eliza's pulse took off at a wild sprint. This wasn't…
It couldn't be…

Then Jake was in front of her, on his knees.

And it *was*.

"Eliza, I Love you." His voice shook a little. "You
have terrible taste in cars, you never check your email,

and you don't squeeze the toothpaste from the bottom of the tube—"

She laughed with tears in her eyes. Big, fat happy ones. "This is the worst proposal ever."

"—And you never let me finish what I'm saying without making a smart-ass remark." His shoulders relaxed a bit, and he gave her a full, wide grin. "But I still Love you. Capital-L Love you. I'm going to Love you tomorrow, and I'm going to Love you ten years from now."

"I capital-L Love you too," she whispered.

"Will you marry me?"

"Absolutely, I will." She dropped to her knees—desperate to be in his arms—and dropped the bat in the process.

It struck the back of his calf, and the crowd gasped.

Jake's eyes clouded, and their next kiss was too long and too deep and perfectly rough. His ragged breath trailed along her jaw when he finally came up for air. "Did you do that on purpose?"

She batted her eyelashes and gave him her best *who me?* look before bursting into laughter. "No. Sorry, I'm still just a klutz."

"Damn. Well, I'm going to make you pay for this when we get home, Herman," he whispered.

"Promise?"

He kissed her again, slow and teasing. "Promise."

Acknowledgments

I'm not going to write acknowledgments this time.

I can't do it. There are too many people to thank and too few words to express my gratitude. Besides, who reads these things?

Other authors, looking to see if their friends mentioned them. That's who.

So if I wrote this, I'd have to thank people like Debbie Burns, Angela Evans, Marie Meyer, Meredith Tate, and Annika Sharma. I'd have to tell everyone how they write some of the best books I've ever read, how they're always there to celebrate or to cry with me, and how they've become some of my favorite friends in the world.

You know who else reads acknowledgments? Publishing people.

Then I'd have to thank my genius editor, Mary Altman. I'd need to tell everyone how lucky I am to work with someone who has truly brilliant ideas *and* politely tells me to dial it down when I discuss Mandroid anatomy in too much detail.

Of course, then I'd be on the hook to thank everyone else at Sourcebooks—including Laura Costello, the assistant editor extraordinaire who's also helping me inch closer to my dream of being BFFs with Amy Poehler.

Whew.

Wait.

If I thanked them, I'd *definitely* have to thank my agent, Jessica Watterson, who is the true behind-the-scenes hero of this book. Plus, then I'd have to mention that she's not just an agent. Over the years, she's become my friend too.

See? This is already way too long and inadequate, and I haven't even mentioned my husband. He also reads these, and I really don't want to get divorced. Not only that, but he's responsible for the funniest parts of this book, and I would never finish anything without him.

Plus, there's my lovely sister-in-law, Katie, who let me write *a lot* of weird things about Mandroids while sitting alone in her house.

After all that, I'd still have to talk about Kyle. I'd have to explain that my hilarious, kind, ridiculous friend passed away while I was writing this book. I'd have to tell everyone how I once witnessed him literally jiggle, jiggle, tap his car back to life (and then he refused to explain how he'd done it, except, of course, to say he'd given it the jiggle, jiggle, tap). I'd have to say something about how Kyle enchanted us all with his quiet observations, quirky sense of humor, and unending love for WWE. And he would have been *so* embarrassed to be mentioned in the final pages of a "kissing book."

Good thing I'm not writing acknowledgments this time.

About the Author

Amanda Heger is a writer, attorney, and bookworm. She lives in Maryland with her unruly rescue dogs and a husband who encourages her delusions of grandeur. She strongly believes Amy Poehler is her soul mate, and one of her life goals is to adopt a pig and name it Ron Swineson.

RESCUE ME

In this fresh, poignant series about rescue animals,
every heart has a forever home

By Debbie Burns, award-winning debut author

A New Leash on Love

When Craig Williams arrived at the local
no-kill animal shelter for help, he didn't
expect a fiery young woman to blaze into
his life. But the more time he spends with
Megan, the more he realizes it's not just
animals she's adept at saving…

Sit, Stay, Love

For devoted no-kill shelter worker Kelsey
Sutton, rehabbing a group of rescue dogs
is a welcome challenge. Working with a
sexy ex-military dog handler who needs
some TLC himself? That's a whole
different story…

My Forever Home

There's no denying Tess Grasso has a way
with animals, but when she helps Mason
Redding give a free-spirited stray a second
chance, this husky might teach them a few
things about faith, love, and forgiveness.

"Sexy and fun…"

—RT Book Reviews for *A New Leash on Love*,
Top Pick, 4½ Stars

For more info about Sourcebooks's books
and authors, visit:

sourcebooks.com

HOOKED ON A PHOENIX

Locked in a bank vault together...
They might redefine the meaning of "safe" sex

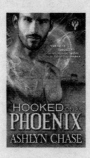

Misty Carlisle works as a bank teller in Boston's financial district. She's had more rotten luck in her life than most, except when her childhood crush shows up to cash his paycheck. Then her heart races and her mouth goes dry.

Gabe Fierro is a firefighter—and a phoenix. Like his brothers, his biggest challenge is finding a woman open-minded enough to accept a shape-shifter into her life. When his boyhood friend asks him to watch over his little sister, Misty, he reluctantly agrees. But when the bank where she works gets held up, Gabe does everything he can to protect her. The two of them end up locked in the bank's vault... where things get steamier than either of them ever imagined.

"Shapeshifting done right! This fast-paced romance is a must-read."

—RT Book Reviews, 4 Stars

For more info about Sourcebooks's books
and authors, visit:

sourcebooks.com

DATING THE UNDEAD

V-Date: The Undead Dating Service
It's Bridget Jones…with vampires

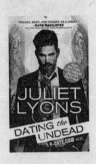

Silver Harris is done with men. But when she shares a toe-curling kiss with a sexy Irish vampire on New Year's Eve, she decides maybe it's human men she's done with… Logan Byrne can't get that kiss out of his head. So when his boss assigns him to spy on V-Date members, Logan isn't sure he can go through with his mission—not if it means betraying Silver.

In the tight-knit London community of centuries-old vampires, history and grudges run deep, and dating the undead can be risky business.

"Snarky, sexy, and steamy as a sauna."

—Katie MacAlister, *New York Times* bestselling author of the Dragon Fall series

For more info about Sourcebooks's books and authors, visit:

sourcebooks.com